MITCHELL

The Devil Always Answers

The Devil Always Answers

MITCHELL

First Edition

NOAI
(For better or worse)

The music touched the spirit planes, low and high.
Their voices filled the clear night sky.
A majestic voice joined from above.
One of infinite gentle love.
With tears like torrents flowing forth,
She held her breath and flew true north,
Without fear of what lay in wait,
She flew into the burning gate.

CHAPTER 1.

THE LAST TOUCH.

Before he knew it, Phil was downstairs looking for Dave or Janet so he could pay the bill. With his hunger for conversation and company satisfied, he was ready to move onto the next village. He heard pounding coming down the stairs as Dave appeared cursing his teenage daughter under his breath and his heart sank, it was going to be fleeting farewell. She was demanding to stay overnight at her friend's trailer, and there were going to be boys.

Putting visions of his daughter, Chelsea, out of his mind, Dave got back to playing the good host. Phil accepted the invite. He was always receptive to small talk especially when it was about himself. He nattered on about his trip and his next stop and it wasn't long before the subject returned to the ancient shoe.

"Phil," said Dave, "this shoe business is really interesting. According to legend, the Devil, for whatever reason, the Devil's prerogative I guess, decided to reap pain and torture upon the folks of a tiny upstate hamlet. Imagine Phil, being the object of the Devil's wrath. Anyway I digress. A little too self-absorbed or engrossed in himself, the Devil accepted a bet with this chap, AND LOST. He ended up trapped in one of his own shoes.

It's only a legend Phil, but you never know. There's a museum with a little-known exhibit telling you all about it if you're interested in that kind of thing. So, the chap after capturing the Devil also revealed that…" The two jumped, as the loud bang of a slamming door shook the house and them alike. It signaled the end, of the story of the Devil's captor, of the shoe, and of attention to Phil. From the second floor they heard a torrent of insults pour out of Chelsea's mouth and the door slamming again.

It was time to get going. The proprietor was so distracted that Phil could have left without paying, but of course, he didn't, he wasn't that kind of person. He secretly wished that he could be, but that just wasn't Phil. He paid by credit card but he could see that he was only an afterthought in his host's preoccupied mind, so much so, that Phil almost left before Dave remembered something. He quickly disappeared returning seconds later with it in his hand. With little ceremony, he handed Phil a sealed brown envelope and told him to open it only after he'd left town.

"I know how superstitious you are. Don't want to tempt the Dev..."

Before they could both laugh, the house shook again at the hands of the daughter. Thanking Dave, Phil placed the mysterious envelope into the car's glove compartment and instantly forgot about it as more shouting pierced the air. After a quick weak handshake and a couple of indifferent platitudes his distracted host almost forgot his name. It was patently obvious that Phil's departure was overdue.

Phil wisely chose not to wait for Janet to say goodbye as he could still hear her and the daughter arguing upstairs. She obviously had her hands full and had probably forgotten about him too. So he walked around the car to the driver's side, got behind the steering wheel, and drove off with a brief, stiff wave.

It was the last time he would see Dave or Janet alive.

Dave was so engrossed with his daughter that he entirely forgot about the shoe, which sat on the windowsill where Phil had left it earlier in the morning. Phil had deliberated whether he should or shouldn't place it back in the china cabinet. He dared himself to do it, to open the cabinet door and put the shoe back where it belonged without permission, but he wasn't that brave. He'd also thought about handing it over to Dave in person, but that would have meant he would have to find and interrupt him, a little too risky. Phil did what he'd done all his life, nothing.

The windowsill seemed an appropriate place, it was a spot that the host would easily find it and so that's where he'd left it. It wasn't an apathetic deed, just halfhearted and uncourageous, it was Phil's way. His fears had cost him in the past, missed opportunities, one after another. And they would again in his future; because he didn't know what the secret the shoe concealed. He was the last to handle it, it was his touch. He was the one who would be held responsible.

Left alone and exposed instead of the safety of the china cabinet, the shoe started to succumb to the sun's relentless hot dry rays. With every passing hour the shoe came closer to submission. By the time evening reached the township of Hecate, the shoe's uppers had shrunk, the stitching was failing, and more than a suggestion of a crack was creeping around the toe. Evening turned to night, and Dave, Janet and Chelsea all went to bed.

As Dave's mind churned over the stressful day, a thought suddenly sprang into his mind, "John Abbott. That's who captured the Devil."

No one went to bed happy that night, they would never have gone at all if they knew it was their last.

CHAPTER 2.

HOPE IN THE VILLAGE CALLED CLEARSTREAM.

Even by early settler standards, ClearStream was a little jewel. Nestled in the Appalachian Mountains, its architectural roots lay in Philadelphia's glorious structures, although others claimed the quaint villages of the English Cotswold's were its inspiration. Whatever the influence, these pioneers had expressed their heritage in their vision for this parish, a gem in the colonized new world.

ClearStream was a blend of natural beauty and human creativity, co-existing in delicate, tender harmony, where gray stone houses and thin sidewalks jostled for space with the equally confining roads. Front doors of shining royal colors, a skyline of protruding chimneys and wheat thatch or dark teal slate roofs made for a postcard perfect picture. Gardens were kept weed-less, God forbid. Low ceilings, dark wooden beams and wide fireplaces made the pubs welcoming and cozy.

Narrow quaint humped backed bridges spanned a spring born stream and connected the town's two halves. Trout laden, crystal-clear water nourished the healthy, strong and handsome townsfolk. The water was the cause, or so they said.

From the bottom of the village you could look upstream and see a shining, silver staircase of waterfalls nine steps deep. At each shallow pond, sleuth gates fed tiny little streams that rolled down the gutters of multiple roads, keeping it clean and unbearably pretty.

ClearStream people were proud of their town, a little too proud. In time, outsiders began to view the town's folk as haughty, snobbish, and unwelcoming. Some went as far as saying they were spiteful. One went much further. Was it their cleanliness, healthiness and purity, was that *his* motive?

ClearStream was once the classic rural, romantic and picturesque hamlet. That is how it was. But not anymore. Not since *his* visit. And *he* was there only a year.

Repulsive, crusty scabs of sulfur appeared in blotches on the stone buildings. The town square and churches suffered the most. The mortar between the stones leeched bloody, yellow and green pus. The once beautiful, sparkling, trickling gutters were now ribbons of slimy algae. Their source, where the village got its name, became a slow-moving, steaming, putrid river.

There were indications of healing and hope in the town square. The evil looking vents in the marketplace floor no longer smoldered. The deep crevasses had stopped oozing blood, and people now dared to look down them without fear of seeing Hell. And there were signs of life too.

People moved freely for the first time in almost a year, all heading in one direction, to the marketplace. It steadily filled with the poor, ragged people, happy to be alive. With a light drizzle falling, they shuffled forward with determination on their faces, but also with a look of hope and joy, a strange and seldom sight of late.

As they trod towards an erected stage in front of the town hall, they took care to step over the narrow, deep crevices. Even though they couldn't see Hell, it didn't mean they couldn't reach it. Before long, the entire village population of ClearStream had assembled.

The stage was made of oily, dark planks worn smooth and slippery with age.

And blood.

It was just high enough for the back of the crowd to see the men sitting in a crescent. The village scribe, Mr. Roy, sat on the end. All his fingers were missing. A telling sign.

As if to honor the occasion, the drizzle stopped and the sky lightened. For a moment the sun tried to come out, but was too exhausted to manage it so dark the year had been. A hunched and battered looking man ascended the stage via the steps at the side. He proceeded slowly but deliberately to the front and center where he looked out across the crowd. The man demanded attention. He was dressed in a red coat with tails, a black triangular tutor hat, a white frilly blouse and black knee-high boots. In his left hand, he awkwardly began to swing a brass bell as he cried.

"Oyez. Oyez. Oyez." The bell clanged rather than chimed.

Upon hearing the cry, the crowd stopped talking and moved closer. In the strong, clear voice that got him the job, the town crier began his introduction.

"Thank you for coming, thank you." He let the last of the murmuring end.

"I know that all of you, the Mayor and I included, have been through the most terrible of times, and it is only by the strangest of happenstance that I now make this address. As you all know, my name is Allan Hughes, and I have been the town crier for almost fifteen years. Like everyone here, I have lived in this village all my life, so you all know the man I will present to you shortly. A man I have known since childhood, a good man, a man who always stood by his word, so now, I give you, the Honorable Christian Manning, our mayor."

The mayor climbed the steps at the side of the stage, careful not to slip due to his painful limp. His body was a weak and twisted shell and any movement required careful consideration. His right arm was missing, a permanent blood-soaked bandage, black in color, covered the stump.

But he wasn't the only one. It was a commonplace affliction shared with many in the crowd. His face showed that he had experienced misery and pain first-hand, but also told of a strong-willed man, he had to be, he was still alive.

He lifted his head and with sorrow in his eyes, looked at the crowd, causing them to hush. They had heard his screams from the torments and torture. He had suffered with them. These were his qualifications to stand before them as their mayor. So, what he had to say to them, he had earned, he had every right to address them. In a weak voice the mayor began.

"Thank you, Allan Hughes, ClearStream Town Crier." he paused and took a breath. "Many of you may remember that Allan was actually, like me, right-handed. Our arms were taken from us by the man who has dominated our thoughts and lives for the past year."

"I look at everyone. Not a man amongst you has not suffered." He paused again to scan the crowd, which sadly confirmed the truth in his words.

Mutilation and pain were etched into every soul. It was even true for the head of a small family of strangers clustered together at the front. He had noticed this family of out-of-towners from backstage, and had made special note of it, because strangers didn't come to ClearStream. With their backs to the crowd, no one had seen their faces. "Good job." he thought.

"Everyone has become very suspicious lately, and these strangers would come under intense scrutiny if they were noticed. I'll keep an eye on those folks." the mayor noted to himself, before beginning again.

"A year ago, I would have found it impossible to believe that a creature so evil and merciless existed. That is because, until that time, I had never met the Devil.

When a stranger came into my office wanting to present an offer to the village, I was suspicious. I didn't know who *he* was at that time, but a little voice, deep down, told me to beware, to deny *his* request, but I ignored it. And for that I am eternally sorry." Not a word came from the crowd. If he had not borne such appalling treatment at his behest, it would have been very different. With the silent endorsement, the mayor forged ahead.

"And so that dreadful Demon stood here before us, and on this very stage, pronounced *his* bargain." Christian laced his last words with sarcasm.

"I remember it well, as I sat to his right, like his 'right hand man'.
He promised wealth.
He promised health.
He promised fertility."
People of the town knew that it was true. They too had all fallen for the Devil's smooth words and silver tongue.

Instead, *he* took our pride, our joy, our health, our loved ones, our innocence and our daughters' virginity.

Instead, *he* gave pain, fear, torture, torment and hell.

I will not dwell further, we are all trying to forget, but of course, it is impossible. I do not believe that even in my death I will. The Devil was cruel. We were nothing more than playthings for *him* and those of us that have survived will be scarred forever.

We have suffered at *his* hand. All of you have lost loved ones. All of you have lost limbs.

We were not on Earth, but in Hell. But now the person, who brought Hell to Earth, is now gone, or I should say, captured. I feel safe enough to say *his* name aloud.

The Devil.

The Devil did this to us." Christian Manning lifted Allan Hughes' stump in the air. Many in the crowd were quietly sniffing as they were recalled their own terrible ordeals.

"Soon I'll be introducing you to a man, the man who captured the Devil, Mr. John Abbott."

A murmur rippled through the crowd. Nobody knew of that name. An uneasy moment swept over them in case it was a hoax. The mayor quickly continued to quell their feelings of apprehension,

"In a moment I will ask John Abbott to address you, but first, let me tell you of how he came to be in our employ.

I had been sneaking into the south corner of Denise Hill's wheat field. In that field, left barren and wasted, was a secret place where I would pray. When I heard a voice reply to my prayers, I thought I was imagining it. A trick of the mind, or worse again, *his* mind. When I heard it again, I thought that God was replying to my prayers. Again, I heard the hushed whisper, but it came from John Abbott.

He was crouched in a ditch, and lord knows how he got there unseen, or how he knew that I'd be there that day? But he was there, and so was I." The mayor stopped as the crowd whispered of fate and destiny before resuming.

"John Abbott told me that he had heard of the dark times that had engulfed us and that he thought that he could help. And even though we were desperate and at our end, he asked no price, other than that of the hand of my daughter." A muted silence followed. They all knew that the mayor's daughter had tragically 'passed away' the previous week. Mayor Manning recalled his lovely daughter's memory and fought back the tears before resuming loudly.

"As if the Devil knew, *he* savagely raped and killed my daughter, the very day I was to see John Abbott, to tell him that she had agreed to the price. Now I could not pay him. I told him so. And John told me, yes, he told me, that he would attempt to do it anyway, because I had been honest with him."

The mayor struggled to talk as he choked up with tears. He swallowed, took a breath, and spoke quickly as he was scared that he might not be able to finish.

"So now I ask of you all to give him the greatest round of applause that anyone has ever received. I present to you, Mr. John Abbott, Devil Catcher."

There was cheering, whistling, clapping and stomping. After the applause died down, a small, mouse-like man appeared next to the mayor as if by magic. His eyes were bright and his movement's quick. He walked to the front of the stage without hesitating, and he appeared to have no fear of addressing the audience. The crowd hushed as they saw him.

He was so small and frail; how could he trap the Devil? It was plain for all to see why he desired the mayor's daughter in marriage as payment. Renewed cheering erupted; they had taken the man to their heart; he was one of them. The spontaneous applause died down and he prepared to thank the throng.

John Abbott began. "Honored, honored. Thank you so very much, thank you, thank you." Then he took a deep breath and in a high and appropriate voice, continued the address.

"You have all suffered unimaginably, evilly." he looked over the crowd. "When I heard of your plight, I was so overwhelmed that I just had to do something, and I believed I could.

I hid for a week in a field of wheat before I finally made contact with your mayor.

We whispered in secret, mindful of prying ears, and I told him that I thought I could help. He was of course skeptical, but also desperate, and after he had thought about my offer, he returned to the field the following day and accepted it. He knew the price was high, but he had discussed it with his daughter, and both were willingly and nobly prepared to pay." John Abbott paused to let the crowd appreciate the sacrifice that the mayor's daughter was willing to make on behalf of the village.

"Except of course, the Devil took her. But to honor her passing and commitment to your village, and out of respect for your fine Mayor, I said that I would still attempt the deed. That day, you're brave, grieving Mayor escorted me to the Devil's residence, the Town Hall behind us."

John Abbott went on to tell the crowd how he snared the Devil. His tone was flat and matter of fact. He didn't want to give the impression that he was bragging or being arrogant. And he had other reasons for his dispassionate and emotionless delivery. For he knew the Devil was a prisoner in *his* prison, and he didn't want to give the perception of gloating, not for the audience, but for the benefit of the Devil. Just in case *he* could still perceive, or even worse, influence events from *his* cell: it was a wise precaution.

John Abbott continued in his unwavering monotone, elaborating how the Devil was paranoid and envious. They were the reasons for *his* sadism, *his* lying and deceit; *he* distrusted and envied everything and everyone. *He* saw scheming and conspiracy everywhere and with a raging jealously of God, *he* waged *his* evil and sadistic war upon humans. Though they were mortal emotions - *he* was greater than human, so everything worked on *his* scale, an eternal mortal scale.

John planned to take advantage and use the Devil's own exaggerated delusions against *him*, using himself as bait. He described himself as a small and modest man, who would provide the Devil with passing amusement and entertainment, if only for a short while. He hoped that the Devil would be unable to refuse the temptation to parade *his* prowess, and he was right. The Devil granted his wish for an audience *his* curiosity was so heightened.

He explained that because of the nature of *his* being the Devil experienced the feelings of mortals - mind, spirit and soul, and the feelings from another plane, beyond our own.

The dimension of Entanglement.

Feelings on this complex, expansive and exclusive level, could mutate. Paranoia and jealousy contorted all thought. So off balance was the Devil's psyche that any experience was distorted, and all emotions became amplified and exaggerated into malevolent actions. Subsequently, frustration became rage: not tempered with any understanding or calmness. Impatience became recklessness, as pride overruled satisfaction. A warped perspective and compromised objectivity made *him* susceptible to all the failings that people experienced; greatly magnified. *He* was a wildly swinging seesaw; the trick was, to tip *him* in the right direction.

John Abbott told how he hoped that the Devil's inquisitiveness would persist past the initial introductions. *His* mind and dimensions worked beyond our comprehension, and *he* could swiftly resolve the unexplainable. John's only hope was *his* over confidence.

The Devil, secure in *his* belief of absolute superiority, let *his* guard falter and heard the proposal, the wager. It only took a second of thought for the Devil to respond. *He* sat before John, *his* supremacy assured, *his* confidence extreme, *his* arrogance excessive.

When *he* heard the stakes, "My Soul if I'm wrong: the town if I'm right." *his* laughter shook the town. John Abbott saw members of the crowd nod as they remembered how they shuddered when they heard the howl, and how they secretly thanked God, that they weren't in *his* presence.

The Devil agreed without hesitating because he felt there wasn't a chance of losing. Relishing the contest, *he* willingly removed *his* shoes upon John's request, and handed them to him.

John never removed his eyes from the Devil's stare, which hurt and stung, and not before long he saw a litany of emotions race through them. At first, there was joy and excitement, which swiftly evaporated to anger and loathing. But John didn't endure *his* stinging eyes for these. He had to convince the Devil, make him believe that this was real; make him question his hasty commitment to the wager. He awaited confusion and reservation, a fertile bed for a seed of doubt. John needed to be ready because if they passed, the Devil's emotions would proceed to boredom. Then the Devil would discount the wager and enslave the doomed John Abbott forever. He only had one chance. He prepared himself for the moment.

The Devil's emotions ebbed and flowed, their intensity caused John's eyes to burn and he dearly wanted to close them, but he knew he couldn't. He had to watch. John could see every passing thought feverishly mount until rage finally turned to anxiety and consternation. John had to seize the moment; this was that instance; now.

The Devil's doubt and paranoia raced through his mind. "Why else would a small man seek out this challenge and risk his soul if he didn't have some power, some trick. Was he another of God's prophets - only this time cleverly disguised? Instead of spewing *her* propaganda and falsehood's concerning my mental state, *she* sends an angel, intent on perpetrating an evil deception upon me, possibly to humiliate, or chastise, or even to cure me. Have I been rash?"

In *his* mind, John Abbott's unaccompanied presence could only mean one thing, he *was* dangerous.

Now was the time to sow that seed, turn irrational apprehension into reality, tip the scales, and let Entanglement do the rest. He had staked everything upon this gamble. Belief *can* become one's reality.

John returned one of *his* shoes back to the Devil, and as *he* accepted it, John spoke.

"You know, you can get stuck in shoes, don't you?"

Terror exploded in the Devil's eyes. It was true. This small innocent man was indeed an agent of *her* scheming mind, and he had fallen for it.

He was gone.

The Devil was imprisoned.

In his own lonely shoe.

The Devil's own paranoia became truth.

From his trouser pocket, John pulled out a white lens cleaning cloth of soft fleece. He placed it over his hands, delved into his jacket, and produced a man's high heeled sleek black leather and suede right shoe. It was crafted no doubt by a master shoemaker, as it radiated sophistication and wealth. He brought it out slowly and carefully, cradling it in the middle of the white cloth with both hands. He slowly raised his hands up in front of his face until the shoe was high above his head.

"I give you, the Shoe."

John stood still before the crowd, who became silent and deflated. They expected to hear a story of gallantry in battle, of valor and swordplay, not one of subtle psychology. How could this possibly be true? He trapped the Devil, in one of his own shoes? Was it that simple? Stunned, the crowd searched their memories for signs of weakness in the Devil's armor.

At first, none could think of any. All they remembered was how *he* instilled deep-rooted fear and cowardliness into everyone's hearts. Mass and public torture does that, and they recalled how *he* flaunted *his* absolute contempt and disdain.

But in the latter months, *he* had forgotten 'appointments', to the relief of those lucky souls. *He* had become blasé and dis-interested in some of *his* sessions. They recalled only last week when a tiny dab of mud splashed onto *his* trousers and stained *his* normally impeccable appearance. Yes, heads in the crowd started to nod, as individuals realized within the Devil's complacency there was the potential for exploitation - *his* guard was indeed down, *he* could be fallible.

Nevertheless, it would take a mad man to take *him* on. They began to appreciate John's bravery, armed with nothing more than his own wit and intelligence. Foolhardy; most would say. They looked at the stage with renewed gratitude and, for the first time, awe. To their dismay, they saw that John had already started to wrap the shoe in the lens cloth ready to put it back into his coat. John Abbott had finished his address and was exiting the stage.

As he reached the steps that descended to the market place floor, he turned and said, "Thank you, I will leave today, and I take the shoe with me, for should the shoe open at the toe, then the Devil will once again roam free. And be warned, *he* will never put himself in jeopardy again."

The crowd needed to display their gratitude for the man, and as *luck* would have it, they got the chance. As John Abbott descended the steps the young, small, girl of the Whittle family, Dottie, ran to the bottom of the stage stairs. She grabbed his small hand in hers and they left together. The crowd cheered and whistled. So, John Abbott got his reward after all. It was a happy finale for the day and the village, or so they thought, because the day wasn't over.

CHAPTER 3.

ENOUGH STRANGERS
FOR ONE DAY.

Arm and arm with his future bride, John and Dottie had taken only a couple of steps before the family of outsiders approached them. They hardly had time to make their introductions before the ClearStream folk surrounded them. They were ready to protect John Abbott with violence. John high-pitched voice and cries for tolerance and patience went unheard because of the noise of the mob.

"Quiet!" boomed Allan Hughes from the stage and he swung his bell. "All of you stand back." With disgruntled muttering, the protectors in the crowd moved away a short distance.

"The mayor has just alerted me that strangers are amongst us and are there, in front of John Abbott." Allan instantly regretted his words, as the crowd thought they were given permission to attack.

"Get back, all of you. Back." clamored Allan Hughes, accompanied by more frenzied bell clanging. "More. Thank you." Allan Hughes bell's last clank left an echo in their heads.

"Let us show these people from abroad, that even though we have suffered immeasurably and unjustly, to those that share our suffering, we are still fair and decent people. The strangers did not look out of place in ClearStream. They too, carried injuries.

Turning his attention to the family, he spoke sternly. "Now speak, but be warned, our generosity is thin."

In the brief silence that followed, the head of the family made his discourse. "My name is Richard, my wife, Clair and our son, Henry. We have traveled far, and as you can see, it was not easy." He drew the crowd's attention to his missing hand, all that remained was a red tinged stump. The wounds on the people of ClearStream festered black, but they knew the mark.

"We have our own blight in our village. The Red Witch Boleyn attacks our commune and inflicts us thus." Despite his injury, he lifted Henry into the air to show that for one of his eyes only a red hole remained. The people of ClearStream feeling ashamed of how they had reacted against these strangers started to clutch their own wounds. Their common bond. A boy called Collie Collins reached up to one of his own eyes, knowing he would only find a black hole.

Richard continued, "We are on a pilgrimage, and because we knew of your predicament, we deliberately avoided here and gave ClearStream a wide berth, I'm sorry to say. But upon our returning journey we heard of the John Abbott miracle, and have made this detour to ask for his assistance in the eradication of our own tormentor."

Richard turned towards John. He got down onto both knees. "I have no money, save this to get my family home, the two-horse carriage. It's yours. Will you, can you, help us? The carriage is yours."

A hush descended on the crowd; a crow's call echoed over the square. Time seemed to stand still. John Abbott bent down to his bags and pulled out the left shoe of the Devil's pair. He looked into Richard's eyes. "Keep your carriage." and gave him the shoe.

The crowd cheered. Dottie jumped into John's arms and kissed him passionately. It was the happiest moment the town had ever seen. After the raucous died down, *John Abbott explained that a shoe, when placed in a wall of your house, would trap a trespassing witch.* Without exception, everyone went home and put a shoe into at least one wall of their house that night.

The children of ClearStream left, seeking lives not maligned with Devil filled dreams, and they talked. The tradition spread across the North Eastern United States where, to this date, shoes can be found in the walls of old houses. When uncovered, normally during renovations, another old shoe sometimes replaces it, and the original, burnt. But it's not always the case. Occasionally, people keep them, to their peril.

CHAPTER 4.

Days in the Sun.

John and his newly wed, Dottie, settled in a small village a long way from ClearStream. John hoped his achievement would pass into folklore, and John Abbott would be a forgotten man. He especially hoped that this would be true for the Devil. But he didn't delude himself. He knew he was a marked man.

Nevertheless, the couple started to enjoy life. John and Dottie set up shop as candle makers. He considered himself very fortunate to have found Dottie. The business held its ground and the couple started a family. Happily, a son became the newest member of the Abbott family. They called him John, and feeling blessed, John and Dottie strove to provide him with all that life could offer.

John the First was small, and so it was understandable that John the Second was too, but the resemblance to each other was eerie. If it wasn't for both looking their ages, they would have been mistaken as twins.

When John II turned *twenty one*, the sign on the front of the shop was replaced to read 'John Abbott and Son.' Dottie cried she was so proud. She was even prouder when he took a wife, and a grandson swiftly followed who was named, John Abbott the IIIrd.

For the first time since they had left ClearStream, John was concerned. One day, when they were alone, they discussed the forbidden subject. They had never told their son about his father's past, and when questioned about how they met, or how his mother got those deep and savage scars across her body, they lied.

They explained that John met Dottie at an agricultural fair. They fell in love at first sight. Dottie's father had saved her from a thrashing machine when she was very young, and that was how she acquired the scars. Her father didn't approve of John. So they eloped.

John had reservations with the naming of his grandson and he wanted to air them with his wife. "Dottie, I'm a little concerned about the name of our grandchild, now I don't want anyone to be alarmed, but…"

"He's only done it because he admires you so much John, you should be honored." Dottie replied sweetly.

"I know that Dottie and believe me, I am." he said with tears of pride welling in his eyes. "Maybe I'm just getting old and scared, I'm sorry to bring it up, forgive me, but tomorrow, I'm taking you know what to the museum in the city. It's a week's travel, but it'll be safe there, it's just too much responsibility."

"John, you are so kind and loving, how can I not forgive you?" and she kissed him on the forehead and they went to bed.

The following day, he packed his bags and set forth for the State Capital, the only place that John Abbott believed could safely contain the Shoe.

He entered the museum by the public entrance like anyone else. He was surprised how big it was, he'd never been in a building of this size before, and it was intimidating. He gave his name at the large visitor's desk to the nonchalant attendant and asked for the curator. His high-pitched voice screeched in the big hall. Surprisingly, only a few minutes passed before an orderly returned with him and John asked the curator if he would be interested in a donation.

"Depends on what it is now, doesn't it?" He was a big man, especially compared to John.

"May I show it to you in private?" John was afraid he would be dismissed out of hand if he couldn't emphasize the significance of the Shoe in person.

"This way." He gruffly showed the way down a dark corridor that led to a room marked private. When the curator opened the door, a musty smell filled John's lungs. In this room used for analyzing artifacts and specimens, John was hopeful that the curator would take him seriously. Feeling foolish, "I'm not asking for any money. Just a place, a safe place for this Shoe" He retrieved it from his packsack and placed it on the table in the middle of the room. "To be stored, and err, looked after."

The curator carefully examined the shoe. He leaned on the table with both elbows and made sure the shoe remained in the middle. His caution surprised John who watched as the curator studied it thoroughly. The Shoe had lost none of its haunting beauty, but curiously, the curator seemed more interested in the toe's stitching. Suddenly he commanded John to tell the story, and to leave nothing out. John dreaded this, but he knew it was inevitable. If the museum was going to take possession of the shoe, then the curator needed to know why.

He waited for John's response. John wasn't confident that the curator was going to buy it so fantastic was his tale, but he had little choice. He freely told the whole thing from beginning to end without pausing. And at the end he didn't know whether the curator would laugh or cry, because it sounded, even to him, too bizarre to be true.

"So, the Devil is trapped in his own shoe because he believes he can be?" the curator asked, seeming to be doubtful.

"Because." said John, "it is no longer belief, it is fact, actually. The Devil's conviction in this matter has surpassed faith and has become reality. *The Devil can now be trapped in Shoes.*"

Putting the shoe down in the center, the furthest from any dangerous edge, the curator looked John Abbott in the eye, and warmly extended his hand.

"Thank you, Mr. Abbott, Thank you. I am Allan Hughes, the town crier's bastard son. My crippled leg was twisted by *him*, my eye also taken." He took John's small hand and shook it firmly.

"When my orderly told me who was at reception, I came as quickly as I could. By the way, sorry I gave you such a hard time, I just had to be perfectly sure, and, as you can see, I am.

What are your recommendations Mr. Abbott? How should I handle such a thing? For I have every reason to be very wary of your possession."

"Mr.?? I didn't catch your name. Sorry." said John, stunned at the turnaround of events.

"Allan Hughes. I was born Collie Collins."

"You took your father's name? Mr. Hughes."

"I hated him for not acknowledging me. But he didn't tell

me until his last breath, that the Devil vowed to kill all his living relatives. As I was a bastard, he saved my life. I call myself by his name in honor of his steadfastness. Even so, I suffer…"

Allan Hughes, even with one eye and a lame leg, considered himself a lucky man. First, he was alive. Second, he managed to get an education, paid for by his father and in addition, he had the opportunity to use these scholarly skills. And somehow, he managed to snag himself a beautiful wife called Olivia. His only regret was that he was never able to be a father. Having a son was all he wanted to make his life complete. His wounds from his youth were the obvious culprit, he was sure the Devil knew who he was; the target of his torture was no coincidence.

He became the curator after his predecessor passed away, amid a project that he and Allan were working on. The board happily offered him the position as he was impressive, hardworking, and talented. That was fifteen years ago, and today, he thanked his lucky stars again. Had John Abbott shown his artifact to the previous curator, who had no patience for non-ancient, non-European or non-Egyptian artifacts, or for small high-pitched people, he would have been shown the door. And should he have entertained John Abbott; he would never have believed his story. But who, other than Allan Hughes, would have on that count? Now the Shoe could be and must be given the appropriate respect it demanded.

"Recommendations?" John carefully thought for a moment. "Well, the Shoe is the means with which he is confined. However, if you locked the Shoe away, for instance, in a safe, then that will become the new method of detention nullifying the shoe. And the Devil will become free. In other words, if the Devil perceived the application of additional incarceration, then the Shoe will cease to be the primary means of imprisonment, and he would escape. A locked glass display cabinet would be fine. It will stop other people from stealing it without the intent of further confinement.

Also of course, care of the Shoe is paramount. Make sure it gets its fair share of dubbin and love. Eventually the Shoe will age, and the stitches will break. But it's possible to postpone the inevitable, almost indefinitely." said John now completely at ease.

"Come with me John, we'll pick out the fixtures together." said Allan friendlily. They spent the rest of the day designing an exhibit.

Allan invited John to stay the night and he was delighted to accept. They exchanged many stories, but they avoided all to do with the Shoe, the Devil and ClearStream.

"So how many children do you have John?" asked Olivia.

"Just one, John the IInd." replied John the Ist.

"We had him in the first year of marriage. We were so happy. He looks just like me, talks like me too." His voice squeaker than normal for fun made Olivia laughed. Allan was taking mental notes, he was grievously injured by the Devil in ClearStream and his guard had never truly come down. It's common, that sons look like their fathers, yet he detected something strange in the fact that John mentioned it so affirmatively.

"We tried for another, but with the shop and John to look after it never happened. And we were so happy with John, that it never concerned us. Now John has had his first child, named John again, John Abbott the IIIrd. Not my idea." He stressed this, and Allan could see that he spoke the truth. But it confirmed Allan's initial wariness and suspicions. But suspicious of what?

Allan was very astute, possessed a very good memory; sometimes too good. He'd certainly liked to forget the torture and mutilation he endured in his youth, and now this disturbing feeling.

As John prepared to leave the following morning, Allan took him aside and gave him a 'finder's fee' along with his heartfelt thanks.

"John, I will always remember you. The day that you trapped the Devil you gave me one of the happiest of my life. I couldn't pay you then, but I can now. Mr. John Abbott: Devil Catcher. On behalf of the Museum, for services rendered to humanity, I present this plaque, as a small token of our appreciation." He pressed a small wooden plaque into John's hands, that John knew he had spent the night carving.

John struggled to contain his tears and his composure, and bidding his farewell, they shook hands and vowed to write. And in those days, they did.

CHAPTER 5.

ERA ENDED.

In a blink of an eye, and not a moment too soon, John Abbott the IIIrd turned *twenty one*. Granddad John's health was not particularly robust, and his prognosis wasn't good. However, he kept his spirits up, and enjoyed his wife and family to the fullest. The money from the Museum had paid off debts, put them on sound financial ground, and had provided their grandson a university education. When he was home, son and grandson were both by John's side whenever possible. This made Dottie laugh and she used to joke.

Which one of you is John? Oh, that's right you're all Johns. OK, which one of you is the one I married? 'Cause there's a whole lot of washing up to be done out there in that kitchen."

They would all snigger and deny their names.

"God, you're all so alike." she'd mutter loudly.

But John continued to deteriorate. Far too soon, he took a turn for the worst and became perilously close to death. He lay in his wife's arms, gasping for breath, fighting for the last seconds of his life. His family clustered around, and he emotionally bid them farewell. Everyone cried. With tears pooling in the corner of his eyes he quietly asked everyone to leave, except Dottie. Even more tears flowed as they all saw the beauty; he was going to share his dying seconds alone with his love of his life.

"Are they gone Dottie?" he asked weakly.

"Yes, John, it's just me and you now." she gently replied while caressing his forehead.

"Good. This is the end, Dottie. I love you and always have." he spoke a little quicker. "Thank you, Dottie. Thank you for coming with me, for leaving ClearStream. And thank you for bearing us our son. It is his son, John the IIIrd, which I leave in your charge. I love you Dottie, but please promise me this. If John has a son, don't let them name him 'John'. He can name him anything, there's free will. I hope again in this. Please don't let him name him 'John'. Please ..." With this wish, John Abbott the I[st], 'Devil Catcher', gracefully passed on, as Dottie cried her heart out.

Like good sons, John II and III took control. They organized the funeral arrangements, and dutifully sent word to Allan Hughes bearing the sad news. The funeral was Tuesday, a week from the day.

~~~

Dottie and sons, wearing their Sunday best, mounted the front of the funeral cart with the small coffin in the back. They left the funeral home, and slowly made their way to the cemetery almost an hour later. With muffled sobs, they approached the gates that guarded the cemetery. Normally a deserted area, today they were surprised to see scores of horses tied up to the cemetery railings. They entered between the two large stone mounts that supported the big wrought iron gates. A solemn, magnificent sight greeted them.

More than two hundred strangers, dressed in black, lined both sides of the cemetery driveway. They were grouped together as families; as couples or just lonely souls. Each group contained at least one person with some form of dismemberment, always someone older.

"Mum, what is this?" whispered John the IInd as the horse and cart plodded up the drive.

"Sssh." hushed Dottie, as they passed the first groups, Jeff White and family and Charles Barber on the left and right respectfully. A member of each party clutched a small panel that identified all their members. Allan Hughes, a thoughtful man, realized that she probably wouldn't know or be able to recognize most of the mourners.

She didn't know the first two groups, she was young when she left ClearStream, but she knew there were going to be people she did know, like her father, if he was still alive. Dottie understood what was happening and who was responsible. She wept uncontrollably with thanks and pride. A man called Mitchell Webb stood on the left. Peter Deverell on a back of a cart, legless, opposite him on the right. Malcolm Barry Stevens, wife and children, all grown up, as was to be expected. Derrick Robson, the village doctor, a busy man back then, one-half of
~~~

his face burnt beyond recognition. A person called Fergie. Alex Wiphler, a kid around the corner from her. And so on.

Every group they passed left their post and joined the procession behind the trudging hearse. Steadily it grew, until the whole village solemnly followed the coffin. Shortly after the last group joined, they arrived at the open grave, which everyone fanned around and encircled. Dottie was overwhelmed. Sadly her father was not there. She had not seen her him since that last day in ClearStream, and therefore, had not known of his death. As if she needed another reason to cry.

The clouds were low and the sky was dull. A slight wind lifted several brown dried leaves off the ground and blew them around the feet of the congregation. It was a suitably grave gray day. A respectful hush consumed them.

Breaking the silence Allan Hughes began the proceedings.

"It is normal for a man of God, a man of the cloth, to perform a funeral." he waited, breathed, and regained control of his emotions.

"But I dismissed him." The statement rang out across the wind, his voice was the same as his father's, strong, powerful and resonating.

"How, I ask you, could his qualifications surpass ours?"

"I am Allan Hughes, son of town crier of the same name, illegitimate son of Bev Collins. You might have known me as Collie Collins. I asked you all to attend this funeral." Announcing yourself as a bastard would have caused a collective gasp in the era, but this was a different audience, and it wasn't quite news. The ordeal with the Devil surpassed any petty taboos of the time.

"The funeral of Mr. John Abbott." Another solemn pause. "Please, could the young men here lower the coffin off the cart, and place it over the grave. Thank you."

A couple of minutes passed as two strong sons respectfully lowered the modest casket onto the planks and ties. When they finished, they retired back to their parents' sides.

Allan waited a few more seconds to let the throng settle. He spoke slowly and clearly.

"We are a chosen few. We have been victims and prisoners to a super natural force of evil, who tortured and tormented us with wicked delight and malice. Some, I for one, had given up hope of rescue, from God. *The Devil had come to ClearStream for reasons only known to him,* and he gave no indication of ever leaving. There was only one-way out, and that, of course, was death. From out of nowhere, when we were without hope, when we had lost our faith, John Abbott came to our salvation.

With unimaginable bravery and resourcefulness, John Abbott freed us from his tyranny. It was good over evil. He performed a super human feat: without aid from others and without consideration for his life."

Allan raised his voice, "A dark angel defeated, by a mortal man, by John Abbott." And as the overcast sky drew darker, he asked, "Who amongst you cannot thank this man? I answer for you. None. Your presence here is a testament to your gratitude, and I know that this journey, across hundreds of miles, has exacted a huge toll upon you. I fear that some of you may not make the journey home."

"He saved us." a weak and stuttering voice from a wheel chair interrupted Allan.

"Yes, he did." blurted out another voice.

"Aye." said another. And another. And another.

All the old and wounded souls said their piece, and as quickly and as spontaneously as it started, it ended.

Allan waited again before continuing, "Thank you. It is true. He did save us. Those of us, who suffered first hand, are here to pay homage to John Abbott. Many suffered and are not. Honorable Christian Manning, our mayor, bequeathed his daughter to John Abbott before her premature death. My father, town crier Allan Hughes is another, and there were many more. Now is the time to remember them. Please place them in your thoughts."

He bowed his head, and everyone followed, including John Abbott II and III, both completely dumfounded.

"Thank you." said Allan. He proceeded reverently as if he was on a pulpit.

"Thank you, John Abbott. You came into our village to save us. And you did. You saved us from the Devil, you saved us from pain and death. You saved our lives. "

He turned towards Dottie and so did everyone else. "We are happy Dottie that you chose John as your husband. We are happy that you have borne a son, the image of John, and that he too has born a son, John Abbott the III.rd."

He gave a glance and a nod, and the coffin descended into the grave.

There was no music, no hymns, no ashes to ashes, no dust to dust. The dark overcast sky said it all. The plain box lay still at the bottom of the grave. The only sound was that of the sighing wind. Allan stood at the head of the grave with the mound of dirt behind him. He turned and taking the spade, shoved it into the loose soil. Turning back with the shovel full of earth, he was just about to throw it into the grave, when he saw something fly and land on top of the coffin. Stopping in mid motion, he stared into the dark hole.

"What was that?" he thought.

It was a shoe.

Peter Deverell, the man without legs, had thrown a shoe into the grave. He must have saved it all those years just for this purpose. Allan Hughes, moved to tears, stood and leaned on the spade, took one of his own shoes off, and threw it in too. And so it was. Everyone filed by the grave, removed a shoe and reverently dropped it in. Then they quietly shook hands with Dottie and her children and disappeared into obscurity.

Allan Hughes waited until the end and then, accompanied by his wife and the Abbotts, slowly shoveled in the remaining pile.

The granite head stone read:

John Abbot
The Devil Catcher

Underneath the simple words was his date of birth and death.

Whilst John Abbott the III.rd lamented the passing of his grandfather, he cast his eye over the crowd with unexpected pleasure.

A small thin girl unashamedly gazed his way. As the funeral finished, the girl's parents came over and introduced themselves to Dottie. She knew them by name only, recalling their introduction at the grave. The two families exchanged pleasantries. John the IIIrd now arm in arm with the girl, the small group sauntered to the graveyard entrance engaged in polite conversation.

Her parents departed as a couple and the girl, Irene, stayed behind, with John. There was initial concern from her family, and then John the IInd walked over to his son and unexpectedly, shook his hand, which shocked them.

John the IInd had thought that his father was someone very remarkable indeed; and that his mother had some secrets of her own. Obviously, they had lived different and special lives before he was born.

So why shouldn't Irene choose his son as her husband at a funeral? John the IInd had quickly put his reservations about their age difference aside. She was only seventeen and he was twenty one. Time would even that out quickly. And they'd only just met? So, what? Let them have their day. She was from a good family and his son needed a bride.

When Dottie saw her son give his wholehearted approval to his, she had little choice and added her blessing. Irene's parents were last to concede, but the tide had turned against them. They saw how much love Dottie had for her late husband. They saw that John the IInd was the image of his father. They noticed the devotion the family extended to each other.

John Abbott the Third wed Irene shortly after meeting, very much in love. Dottie was very happy with Irene, who reminded her of herself, in looks and personality. And of-course John the IIIrd might as well have been John the Ist, they were so much alike.

As her wedding gift, Dottie had told them that she would answer all their questions about the family. It was the only means to abate the constant harassment she endured from John the IInd who sought the truth about his parents. The family, with John the IInd especially attentive, finally found out about his father and mother.

She asked for no interruptions and no questions. She described in detail the village in all its charm before *he* arrived, and the decimation *he* inflicted upon it and more importantly, them. She left nothing out. Her clear blue eyes shed tear upon silent tear in recalling those times. She spoke of not one loving moment, not one moment of joy, not one moment without fear in that bleak time. She had no reason to be ashamed, embarrassed or coy anymore. The story was long past telling. She showed them the scars on her body and told of the rapes and burns, she, and every other maiden, endured. The story sapped her life's blood with every word. But she continued, until she described the day a bird was heard calling, and a smile went unpunished. When his omnipresence didn't crash down upon you like a hammer on the kneecap.

"*His* oppression never rested and reached every corner. And still, somehow, your father defeated *him*." She looked deeply into their eyes. "Your grandfather, John the IIIrd, and your father, John the IInd and my husband, JOHN ABBOTT THE Ist.

"He ended the tyranny. He was only a man. Now he's gone, I wish I could die too." She cried in front of her silent children. John was gone, John the IIIrd would be moving out soon, and she would be alone.

John the IInd had great anticipation for this day of revelation. The answer to all the questions, revealed. His concealed anger at her deception and conspiracy of silence, misplaced. Now abashed of those feelings, he cried in her arms, relieved. He understood why she, they, had kept a strict silence. Any thought of the graphic and horrifying torture was too much to bear. No wonder the town's folk all turned up at his funeral. No wonder Allan Hughes dismissed the clergyman. No wonder his father never spoke about it.

"Where is that Shoe?" he accidentally said aloud.

"The Shoe, my son, is in a safe place now. Let me tell you that story, as it is still part of the same." And Dottie continued to recount John I's trip to the museum. She told of how he made the acquaintance of Allan Hughes, and where the money came from for John the IIIrd's education. She left nothing out, and John the IInd was beginning to realize why. But it was too late for him to stop her. She had revealed all and was preparing for death.

The young families understood what society would have thought of them, if they had been public with their history. They would be regarded as sorcerers. Since people were put to death for less, the secret became the heirloom of the Abbott family. The John Abbott lineage continued with the birth of John the IIIrd's first, and as it turned out, only child.

John the IIIrd returned home with his wife Irene for the Christening. They had chosen a name for their beautiful son but wanted Dottie's approval first. It was only ten months since they were married, since Dottie had told them of their heritage. Now she was very frail and weak, and when she greeted them at the door, she smiled one of her last smiles. In front of her on the porch, was John the IInd, John the IIIrd and the latest addition.

"John Abbott the IVth?" Dottie said shakily, but happily.

"Grandma, is that OK? We want to honor our grandfather, so is it OK? How did you know?" John the IIIrd carefully placed the baby into Dottie's loving arms. She peered into the angel's little face and smiled.

"John Abbott the IVth is going to be identical to his father. All of John's heirs are going to be identical to him. There is one child per generation, always a boy. Somehow, the parents are always going to find a way to call him John. Now I know why John was so concerned. He saw the pattern with the birth of our grandson. That's why he took the shoe to the museum. He was hoping to break the pattern."

"But it didn't work John dear; number four is alive and well." She spoke to the sky. "I understand John. I understand what you did and why. I now see the story, the whole picture from beginning to its end. But you knew that too John. Even from his prison cell, he can still influence the world. I see now. I see what you saw. I see why you were scared. Even if I could honor your request; *he* is greater than us, it's not me that denies your request; it's *him*."

She looked back to John and Irene, "Yes; please do. It's a beautiful name. Welcome to the world, John Abbott the IVth." In the process of handing him back to Irene, she died.

The Abbott family mourned for the second time within a year, and for the second and last time, Allan Hughes made the long journey. He had gladly accepted to the surprise of John Abbott the IInd, as the journey was long and expensive. The entire family was extremely pleased when he accepted the invitation.

"He is a great friend and a true gentleman." they all pronounced.

This was true. Allan Hughes was a great friend of the family, but not necessarily a true gentleman. With his glaring injuries, he had to rely on his sharp intelligence and cunning to get him through life. He had the looks and matching voice of a navy admiral destined to take command and he had used those gifts to their fullest. He had taken his Devil given injuries and used them to his advantage, not to enlist sympathy, but to instill respect, loyalty, fear. The museum's board had big plans for Allan Hughes from the moment they met him.

Under his shrewd leadership the museum had brokered several high profile acquisitions that had put the museum on the map. But if you crossed him, beware. His injuries endured in his youth left him physically mutilated. He was emotionally and mentally hardened and vengeful should he ever be, or perceived to have been, wronged. However, he was loyal defender of those he trusted, liked or respected. A very short list. John Abbott, of-course, had a lifetime membership. But Allan Hughes could also read people, situations and the times. He could detect lies and deception and would use this knowledge to outmaneuver his opponents in negotiations. He was a shark and a fox.

Allan was honored that John the IInd would request his presence. "Another example of the fine man John Abbott the I[st] was, to bring up such a noble son." Allan Hughes judged men well and his staff was understandably loyal to him. However, Allan also had an ulterior motive for performing Dottie Abbott's ceremony. He was interested in her lineage. Ever suspicious, Allan Hughes did not believe in chance or coincidence. He was a man of science and logic and had seen many strange things in his position at the museum. He understood breeding and strains, mutations and freaks, twins and cloning, but what he saw in the Abbott lineage defied explanation. This trip would confirm or dispel his suspicions and determine his subsequent actions.

He expected nothing less than the warm, respectful, and solemn reception he received at the Abbott household. It was a cauldron of mixed emotions of joy and sadness, the birth and death, laughing and crying. The Abbotts were touched with Allan's attentiveness. He spent time with the family, asking many questions about how they were as children, their looks, personalities and desire for additional children. The unsuspecting clan didn't realize that interrogations were taking place. Allan Hughes casually couched his questions with finesse. He conveyed the appropriate respectfulness when he heard them reiterate Dottie's last words, and the notes he took seemed to be for her eulogy.

Indeed, his speech was eloquent, and the small throng cried as he recanted how the small young girl, brutalized but not defeated, chose her own destiny. She defied the Devil's will by living life to the fullest and bearing her courageous husband, John Abbott, a fine lineage and inheritance. Allan feared that the family's success wasn't in defiance of *him* at all; in fact, all his senses shrieked the opposite. He sensed that he was witnessing some grand design, one that he wasn't privy too.

"And who was that handsome young man standing alone on the fringe?" His senses went on red alert. Accepting thanks for his shining eulogy, the small crowd of grievers left until only the lone man remained. If he hadn't approached John the IInd and him, Allan would have made it his business to make an introduction. He held out his right hand.

"My name is Richard. My father was Henry and he was son of Richard. My Grandfather accepted a shoe, from John Abbott to capture a witch, The Boleyn Red Witch. Unfortunately, I only heard of John Abbott's passing many months after his funeral. I would have liked to attend it. But at least I have attended Dottie Abbott's funeral. It's all I can do. Our family is so indebted to them. Many people in Boleyn are. The village, Boleyn now bares the evil Witch's name, not something one should foster, I believe.

Did you know John Abbott and Dottie gave the shoe to my granddad without payment, in fact, they even turned down a horse and carriage as consideration."

Allan Hughes was most impressed that he had made the journey to honor a woman on behalf of his grandparents and father, if of course, he was whom he said he was. He appeared educated, fair minded, respectful. "Let's see him handle the acid test." Allan reached back into his archives and retrieved a memory, his common bond with Richards's father, Henry.

"How is your father? I never met him, although he and I suffered similar fates."

"Your eyes." said Richard, passing Allan's authentication trap.

"And he, and my mother, passed away several years ago, God bless their souls." Richard said without realizing that he'd just had a narrow escape.

With Allan's approving nod, everyone returned to the Abbott residence, where Allan relentlessly interrogated Richard about his family and his beliefs. He had seen in the Abbott family: truth and honesty. He now saw it in this man, this Richard. His questioning had only one purpose. The son he never had. He Passed.

In moments of weakness, he couldn't help himself but to envy John Abbott's propagation, but now, those days were over. His happiness now complete, or so he thought, but life still had more in store for this crusty old captain.

With the funeral over it was time for Allan to leave. The last farewell almost brought him to tears. When Allan left the house, they all lined the small path to his waiting carriage, in appreciation and love. As each said goodbye, they took his hand and shook it, imparting their knowledge that this was their final farewell, and handed him a simple carved wooden plaque that had all their names including John the IVth.

He climbed into the carriage and quickly instructed the driver to go, so that they wouldn't see him cry. Richard did however, and told his new mother, Olivia.

His first day back at the museum saw a busy Allan, aided by Richard, instructing his staff on a series of new tasks, most of which didn't make any sense. But he knew what he wanted, and their trust in him was unquestioning.

Despite the emotions of the last few days, Allan Hughes had unfortunately confirmed his worst suspicions. "The Devil, although safe and sound imprisoned in his Shoe, was definitely alive and scheming. He had plans for the Abbott family - that was clear."

Sometimes he thought he got it, only to find some flaw with his analysis. The designs of the ticking time bomb caged in the Shoe, only emphasized the need for stringent precautions.

Therefore, cabinet designers were hired and intricate lockless glass cabinets were constructed, designed to highlight the Shoe and related items, especially the "Abbott" plaques. The cabinets required no lock and key and the glass tops gave the illusion that one could reach in and take anything. They conformed and exceeded John Abbott's specifications. Small, beautiful engraved, brass plaques itemized each artifact with an allotment number, in the range of 600 to 699.

A scroll of plain calligraphy told the entire story up to the death of Dottie. The language used was somber and plain just like that of the tone John Abbott used in his address to the ClearStream assembly. The cabinet was also going to contain another shoe, as a comparison. Allan said it would highlight the beauty and intricacy of the Devil's Shoe. The handsome set occupied the main entrance, one of five showpieces in a semi-circle, the highest traffic area for the museum.

The Devil's Shoe lay hidden in plain sight. Appropriately, the Shoe's item number was 666.

The Devil's Jail exhibit was the most bypassed cabinet in the museum. The showcase was now an unobserved cabinet, since anyone stopping to inspect it was actually on the way to the washroom. Allan was happy indeed, because unknown to everyone, he had switched the Devil's Shoe with the ordinary comparison one, item 614.

Allan Hughes retired a satisfied man.

He had outsmarted everyone.

CHAPTER 6.

VERY BRAVE PHIL.

Phil was vacationing alone as usual, alone and lonely. By avoiding freeways, and instead, driving from town to town Phil desperately tried to fill the emptiness. He would strike up meaningless conversations with waitresses much younger than himself, or anyone offering some friendliness. It always ended in the same way though, polite rejection. He had given up trying to compete in life, in trying to find a wife or even just a girlfriend and had resigned himself to the role of the humble, self-depreciating, middle-aged man.

He wasn't ugly. He was just average in height, build, average everything. If he had put any effort into himself, he could rise above this but his self-esteem, relentlessly crushed since his childhood prevented him from knowing this. He needed self-help courses, but so profound was his inferiority complex, that he couldn't consider taking that step. The cause of his low self-worth was his elder brother, Bill.

Bill was the alpha male personified, big, brash and loud. Bill never missed an opportunity to put Phil down. He even chose Phil's name. In his childhood, Phil was left to the ruthless devices of elder brother for long periods thus childhood seemed to last a lifetime. Phil was nothing other than Bill's sidekick and punching bag. Things hadn't changed much even now that they were older.

Bill married a catch. The position of chief editor of his father-in-law's newspaper business quickly followed. In a humiliating act, Bill offered Phil a reporter job at the newspaper. Phil didn't really have a choice to refuse, he couldn't get a job anywhere else, and at least this job involved travel. The salary was poor, some of it was on commission, and there wasn't much commission for the stories that Phil put together. Nevertheless, it was a steady job, with built in job security. Phil knew he was there to stay. His brother would never give up the sport of bullying him.

This year was no exception to any other. Phil was still alone, with no thought to escape his brother's repression. Phil didn't know this. He was running the program that been implanted in his head. Instead of trying to date or build his own circle of friends, Phil delegated these duties to his brother. It became impossible to accept this responsibility as his own, he had attempted it earlier in life, and Bill made damn sure that he wouldn't do it again. Consequently Phil depended solely on his brother for all means: his social circle, which was measly; his financial deals, which were botched; his career, which he was minion; his life, which he endured.

Brainwashed to be unimportant and subservient, he was nothing more than a lonely middle-aged man, doing lonely middle-aged things. Now driving across the state, he looked for a place to stay where he could meet people, talk, and feel socially acceptable. Phil always avoided the big hotel chains. He preferred small townships with bed and breakfasts. He always arrived at these places early so that he could talk to the proprietors and fill his void.

Today he drove across the state heading for a little town called Hecate, seeking a bed-and-breakfast with a vacancy.

Dave and Janet ran "Two Be or Not Two Be". They were extremely friendly in that B&B's host fashion, and freely told story after story of local life and gossip. They competed against each other to tell their little boasts. Phil got right into it. Another glass of wine accompanied with lots of laughter. They were especially proud of their B&B's name, after the famous line from Shakespeare, jesting whether it was Hamlet or Macbeth.

Dave stopped Phil before he went to bed. He had something to show Phil and he pointed to it, tucked away at the back of the glass china cabinet. It was an old shoe, an antique.

"That's a strange piece of china Dave." said Phil jokingly.

"Hah ha, yes." retorted Dave, "I'll tell you that story in the morning."

CHAPTER 7.

Inn keepers' Stories.

In the morning, Dave and Janet served up a breakfast of bacon and eggs, pancakes and coffee. Phil the perfect polite guest thanked Dave and Janet for such a wonderful breakfast. The bacon was magnificent and created a whole conversation on its own. They had picked up where they left off the previous night, friendly and jolly.

As Janet cleared the breakfast table, Phil confessed that he'd been thinking about the object in the china cabinet and the yet untold accompanying story. Dave was all too happy to tell it.

Dave began. "Janet and I were thinking about expanding the dining room, but we couldn't think how. Then we had this great idea to create an archway through the wall, between the hallway and the dining room." Dave pointed to the archway. "We didn't get a contractor as it was only a small job, and we were certain it wasn't a supporting wall. We started to take away the plaster, and then we cut through the slats. Although it was dusty and dirty, it was an easy job really, and when the dust settled, we found a shoe, hidden inside of the wall. There, now it sits in the curio."

Dave walked over to the hutch, turned the key to the glass door, and pulled out the old shoe.

"Back in the 17th century Phil, people still believed in witches. Yes, spell casting, broomstick brandishing, witches. Mounted on their brooms and flying all over the countryside terrorizing people, and generally being a damn bloody nuisance I suppose. But they also believed that a shoe could trap a witch.

You see, people believed that witches could travel down the hollow seams of walls, but if they entered a shoe, the toe ensnared her. There wouldn't be enough room for them to turn around. The shoe would be the witch's prison forever. When they built this house back in the 17th century, someone put an old shoe into the inside of the wall, probably the owners.

It's been here all this time, and quite honestly, it's in pretty good nick considering its over 300 years old. It was a bit grimy, so I cleaned it up and polished it, put a bit of dubbin on it, and decided to keep it as a memento of this old house. Look at the style, fashion repeats itself, I think we wore shoes like this when we were young and doing disco." They both laughed, before Dave continued.

"You know what. Just to honor the wishes of the owners, I put an old runner of mine into this wall when we finished. I'm sure the manufacturer didn't anticipate that repurposing."

As Dave laughed, he handed the shoe to Phil who carefully examined it, front and back, uppers and lowers, heel and toe. Old stitches of cotton thread held several pieces of worn leather together in a patchwork shape of a shoe. The style boasted a raised heel, shaped like a piece of a roman column, and a big rust tainted buckle decorated the front.

"My God, I'm holding a real piece of history. It took a deliberate action of ordinary people, just like you and I Dave, to put this shoe in the wall. Not a king or queen, just a middle-class paranoid person, who believed in witches. My god how incredibly superstitious they were then. Thank God times have changed and that's all behind us."

"But you see Phil." retorted Dave, "they didn't just believe in witches, there were witch..."

At that moment, the front door flew open and a pretty teenage girl crashed into the hallway. "Dad, do you know where, OMG, I've just had a shiver go right down my spine, ooh. Anyway Dad, can I..."

As Dave became preoccupied with his daughter, Phil knew this was his cue to get ready to leave. Wondering what to do with the shoe; he put it down on the windowsill.

Phil knew exactly when his time was up. His brother had 'conditioned' him many times when he'd outlived his usefulness. Time to go.

As he packed a huge fight broke out. Chelsea was screaming at her parents, who were doing their best not to scream back because of Phil. It was embarrassing for everyone.

All she wanted was to attend a sleep over at a friend's trailer. "So what if boys are there? Janet was worried about one certain boy, James Drinkmore, who had a bad reputation. Chelsea had had a crush on JD along with all the other girls at school. James Drinkmore wasn't really that good looking, or tough, but he was 'kwel.'

Doors banging loudly, Phil had no doubt he had outstayed his welcome. The sooner he could get out of there the better. He was done and ready to go in minutes.

When Dave had taken Phil's credit card, he had slipped a mysterious sealed brown envelope into his hands. Phil put it away in the glove compartment of the car and out of his mind. As for the shoe, it stayed where Phil put it: on the windowsill.

The brown envelope and the shoe were casualties of forgetfulness and bigger events. The morning had swept by them all.

On the road, with the direction of travel well established, Phil couldn't help himself. He analyzed and graded everything that happened. "What did he do right? What did he do wrong?" He gave himself marks. The previous night he did really well, nine out of ten. But this morning, he was doing well until that daughter of theirs turned up, and shifted the focus of attention from him to her. Still, Phil gave himself an eight out of ten. "Not bad. No, it was a seven."

As he left the little town, he realized that he only had one more day of his holiday left, and he didn't feel like going onto another village. The more he thought about it, the more depressed he became.

"Screw the vacation. Go home, watch some TV, and check into work tomorrow."

He hit the highway, and downgraded the seven out of ten to a six, and then a four. He tried to keep these negative thoughts out of his head, he didn't want another zero, but the bad taste in his mouth was killing him. Zero it was.

CHAPTER 8.

LAZINESS WILL GET YOU EVERY TIME.

Phil's journey home was uneventful. He got home around 11 o'clock at night, after picking up some fast food down the road.

"It can wait." he thought to himself, as he left his baggage in the car, "I'll unpack tomorrow morning."

He lived on the third floor of an apartment building. He turned the key to get into his apartment and realized how stupid he was. He should have brought the baggage up after all. After cursing he closed the door and accepted it as another of his inadequacies. He admonished himself for beating himself up over such a trivial matter. "You're turning into a basket-case Phil." He went to the bathroom, cleaned himself up, and turned in. Phil climbed into his bed and instantly fell asleep.

~~~

The sun had been beating down all afternoon on Dave and Janet's B&B. It shone through a certain window and pressed its weight upon the solitary unprotected shoe. Old and tired, it was no match for the buoyant and formidable sun. By the end of the day, it was ready to give up.

Dave busily spent patching up the relationship between the stepmother, Janet, and his daughter who as a teenager, had become rather rebellious. When challenged by Janet's authority, or backed into a corner, she would use the 'not my real mother' card. It badly hurt Janet.

The fight that day was more vicious than normal. Lately, Chelsea and Janet had been at odds with each other constantly, so Dave tried to mediate and bring the family together. Emotionally exhausted, Dave and Janet had finally ordered Chelsea to bed that night,
~~~

and after even more tantrums, she had thankfully gone. With the earphones on full blast out of spite, her head hit the pillow and she fell into a peaceful sleep.

Dave and Janet, however, didn't get off so easily. Janet was distraught with the day's arguments and required a great deal of consoling. She vented for over an hour until she was finally tired enough to sleep.

Dave's mind also raced. "Yes, that damn Drinkmore boy…" Just as Dave was about to drop off, he remembered that he hadn't put the shoe back into the china cabinet.

"Bugger it, it can wait till morning."

CHAPTER 9.

A NEW LEASE.

The sun had dried and parched the old leather. With the contrast between the hot day, and the cold night air, it couldn't take much more punishment. The stitching between the toe and the sole gave way and the shoe's last defense was gone.

In a damp dark corner somewhere in the world of consciousness, a tiny malignant seed of loathing and malice flickered. From a hibernation so complete and stationary, it was impossible to detect life, emerged a raging torrent. It had dreamed and longed for this day or night. The sun had unwittingly granted her wish.

In the overcast night, not a soul bore witness to the wispy green smoke that squeezed out of that gap between upper and sole. The tiny smoke column looked like a genie coming out of a bottle. At first it was just a little whiff, but it kept coming, and accumulated above the shoe, in an ever-darkening puff of green smoke. Soon the volume of the cloud was the size of a small individual. It became more and more like a person. A faint beam of light from a passing car shone through the window, revealing the outline of an evil looking image. Slowly the appearance of a small woman consolidated and condensed. Her being was taking definition.

Facial features filled in, and a tall witch's hat began to develop. Light no longer had the strength to pass through the cloud. It wasn't long until a flapping black cape began to look as if it could keep out the cold. A wooden broomstick congealed underneath the dark shape, looked strong enough to hold the weight of what was now an almost fully formed witch. Creases in the clothing took form. And the ribbon of smoke, coming out of the shoe, became thinner and weaker, until finally there was no more.

A fully coalesced entity now existed in the space that the smoke once occupied. Perched on the broomstick, floating, the *witch* seemed like a wax manikin. Life was not a force within it. Then, a spark of green light, smaller than a pinhead, floated out of the toe. The shoe fell to the floor. The green wraith entered the floating entity. Immediately the manikin ignited into a highly charged being of lethal intent.

Every atom of that floating being wreaked evil. Her potency was intense. Unhurried and unafraid of another beam of light, she hung in midair and slowly turned her head. Life indeed was coursing through her body. A glance into those evil green eyes would leave little doubt about that. Even though there was no wind inside the house, the witch's scrawny hair protruding from under her hat fluttered and her cape flapped. With a mental thought, she brought the broom around and silently glided to the center of the room.

"Good," she thought, "ever obedient, ever faithful, my loyal broom. Always by my side."

With consummate ease, she dismounted, and her feet touched ground for the first time in centuries. She stood in the middle of the room with both feet astride, stretched her arms up, and let out a yawn, as if she had just woken up after a Sunday afternoon snooze. Feeling a range of motion that she hadn't felt for a long time, she just stood there, taking it all in. Inside the pointed black suede shoes, she crunched her toes, then she clenched her fists, and finally she rolled her head around her neck.

Not just life had returned; the feeling of life had too. It had been a long, long time.

Alive, she raised her hands to her face and felt her scrawny fingers massage her leathery skin. Her cheeks were shallow, and her chin and nose were pointed. A large mole clung to her cheekbone. As her fingers passed over to caress it, a broad smile appeared upon her mouth. Her smile exposed a wretched set of teeth; some were missing. A putrid smelling breath exuded and infiltrated the dining room like an open sewer. She stood in the middle of the room and whispered a solemn declaration.

"I am Hecate."

With every breath she felt stronger. With every movement she felt more alive. With every thought, revenge.

She heard the movement of a sleeping body upstairs in a bedroom. A dark light erupted in her green eyes, as a flood of excitement swept over her. Now in the shadowy room, all she could see were faint outlines of furniture illuminated by the window. With her right hand, she reached under her cloak, and retrieved a crystal ball. Holding it in the palm of her hand she whispered a small spell. It dribbled from her lips in the form of green wisp of smoke and floated through the air towards the ball, and when it touched it, it cast a pale greenish light. The light wasn't strong enough to see colors other than pale green, black and white.

She looked around the dining room. For the first time, she started to see the belongings of the family that lived here. The dining room and its chairs, a grandfather clock, paintings on the walls, a strange box with a glass front with a wire ending at a wall. She could see that this was just an ordinary family dwelling, and she could now feel that ordinary family sleeping above her.

This was so exciting that she began to have trouble focusing on the room, as the thought of innocent flesh kept intruding her mind. Impossible to contain her glee, she let a little cackle escape her dry and cracked lips. She was about to get back on her broom, when she saw a portrait of the family she now desired so badly. The frame was of the finest pewter, and the painting was the most incredibly accurate and lifelike painting she had ever seen.

"Maybe," she thought to herself, "these are wealthier people than I at first thought. A family that can commission a painting of themselves, from a painter of such talent, has to be wealthy."

She touched the photograph with her scrawny finger amazed to find that she couldn't feel the paint. Without warning, a rage from a depth that she had never felt before tore through her body like a forest fire. This rage born by her long imprisonment had boiled over.

In an instant, she was on her broomstick. She flew up the stairs at supersonic speed, with the crystal ball floating in front of the broom acting like a green fog lamp. She crashed through the bedroom door and saw Dave and Janet asleep. She leaped off the broom, onto the end of their bed, and stood above the startled couple.

With their sleep shattered, they both jumped up with shock. They sat straight up hardly awake, still believing they were dreaming. Wishing they were dreaming. Simultaneously, they clutched at the sheet in front of them for protection, drawing it close to their chins in an unconscious reaction. There actually was *a Witch standing on the end of their bed.*

Petrified Dave and Janet, so dumbfounded, couldn't say a word. Their bodies, their minds and their faces, were frozen. A vicious loop of paralyzing fear played through their minds like a broken record. They stared up at the grotesque face that filled their tunnel vision. As their minds choked under the onslaught of shock, they both attempted to plead for mercy, but their mouths betrayed them. Hecate didn't threaten them with anything other than her stare, but Hecate's stare was a weapon of a different league.

The longer she looked at them the more they were lost. Her lizard like green eyes drilled deep into their heads, as she stole and consumed their will and strength. Like children going back in time, Dave and Janet could now only feel horror and abandonment. In the back of their minds, they cried for their mothers. It had been a long time since Hecate had had so much pleasure and she held them there, in their lonely dark, cold places. She slowly reached her hands towards their necks. Their faces now were unrecognizable. Their skin stretched tight across their bones, their hair white and brittle and their breath shallow and painful. They looked and felt a hundred years old. As her clammy bony fingers wrapped around their necks, only their eyes moved as they began to bulge in their sockets. She lifted them both out of their bed, one in each hand. She remounted on her broom sidesaddle, their necks deliciously in the nook of her hands, and floated towards the bedroom wall being careful not to kill her prey outright.

Her stare never left their eyes.

She held them both against the bedroom wall, and then let go. They levitated. She tilted her head, and both Dave and Janet rotated in the same direction. She stopped them when they were exactly upside down. She spread her arms. Dave and Janet copied. Holding the inverted and incapacitated couple against the bedroom wall, she purred with anticipation of the deed she was preparing to do.

CHAPTER 10.

LOST AND WORSE.

Ashley and Jewels opened the door and let Chelsea into the trailer. The coolest party ever just stopped, leaving only one boy behind, the handsome James Drinkmore.

Without warning, the floor beneath their feet starts to move. The bright sun faded and the blue sky grayed. JD released Chelsea and with his arms wide open, he receded and faded away. JD had gone. Instantly knowing that it was a dream, Chelsea tried to recapture the feeling of JD's arms around her. She couldn't.

Her eyes began to focus on a greenish light coming from under her bedroom door, and she heard strange noises that seemed to be coming from her parent's room. As if sleep walking, she got out of bed. Shadows moved across the eerie light on the floor of her room as if to warn her not to go any farther. Still in a dream state, she opened her door and walked down the short corridor to her parents' bedroom. With every stride, she became more awake, more concerned, and more scared. The sight of her parents' broken door sunk in. But it was too late, she had taken one too many footsteps.

With her two hands braced against the remaining shards, Chelsea leaned forward and pushed her head through the opening into their chamber. She didn't know that she had doomed herself with this action. So horrific was the site that she froze in place. A scream choked her as it tried to escape from her throat. An intense pressure came upon her from all sides, and she tried to move by pushing herself back with her arms that suddenly felt like lead.

She saw a witch's profile, and that face that turned towards her.

Hecate felt Chelsea's presence long before she saw her head poking through the hole in the door. She turned her head deliberately towards Chelsea. The gaze between them connected. Her stare chilled her blood, stole her breath and stopped her heart. Mesmerized, Hecate commanded Chelsea. "Enter."

To the horror of her dangling parents, she did. As if entranced, Chelsea obeyed without resistance, and stood exposed and vulnerable in her nightgown. For Hecate, it was turning out to be a fantastic night. She had escaped the shoe and she was about to feast upon the souls of two good people and more.

Hecate's stare drilled deep into Chelsea's eyes. She saw Chelsea's mind attempt to retract, to recoil, to retreat. "Come closer."

Like an automaton, Chelsea approached. Hecate knew what she was going to do, and she knew the torture it would inflict upon the parents. It was the finale, before they died a horrible death.

"Good."

"Come closer, my dear, closer." and Chelsea did as she was told, the commands were too powerful.

"Stand in front of me my dear." And she did.

Dave and Janet hung upside down against the bedroom wall, with pain throbbing through their heads, as they watched their daughter obey the witch. Their minds centered on Chelsea and they started to slide down the face of the wall. Hecate noticed this immediately, but she wasn't dismayed in the slightest. She took the limp hands of Chelsea's in her own and raised them with the palms facing up. As she raised those hands upwards, her parents moved back up the wall.

"Do you see sweet child; do you see the power?"

To the horror of her parents, they saw, upon their daughter's face, the slightest tinge of pleasure.

At this betrayal, Dave burst through the wall of fear and screamed at Chelsea.

"Chelsea!"

Surprise stuck Hecate like a slap in the face. It was an incredible feat of strength on the part of Dave. Without warning she became limp and fell out of the spell. The enraged Hecate jerked Dave back to the rightful position. Then she pulled the hairpins out of Chelsea's hair, and threw them towards Dave. They flew like missiles and as they drew closer to their target: they turned into nails, piercing Dave's feet and hanging him from the wall. Dave let out a cry of pain, hanging upside down like a bat. He turned his head towards Janet, who was floating upside down next to him, their faces only feet apart. She saw in his face, pain and terror.

Then Hecate took Chelsea's chin roughly between her thumb and fingers and turned her face around to look straight into it.

"See what you made me do."

Chelsea's will crumbled with that wrinkled hand on her face. Then the witch said to her in a venomous tone, "And now, you do your mother, child."

Chelsea's wobbling legs could no longer bare her weight. Hecate moved her grip to Chelsea's neck. Gasping for air, her pegs had to start to work or she would suffocate. And in so doing, she began to breathe hard. As color began to come back to her face and replenish the strength in her limbs, Hecate loosened her grip until she was standing unassisted. She looked at her father hanging upside down from his heels, and saw the blood running down his shins. Then she looked at her stepmother and saw Janet mouth the words, "Do it."

The witch didn't miss a thing, she followed Chelsea's gaze to Janet's eyes, and she saw Janet was sliding down the wall again. With a sharp jerk of her head, Hecate snapped Janet back into position and then turned to Chelsea. With a screeching voice, she told her,

"Do what you're told you little bitch."

"But she's my mother." Chelsea whispered.

Janet crashed to the floor. The spell was wholly broken. It had been a long time since Chelsea had called her "Her Mother" with love in her voice. Now, in the deepest and darkest of all nights, she had and meant it. In the moment when the opportunity to inflict pain and degradation was presented, she had chosen to show her love.

Unfortunately, Janet had been upside down when she fell, and had banged her head on the floor. She lay in a crumpled heap at the bottom of a wall and struggled with waving arms and legs in a desperate effort to get upright, but she did. Fearlessly, Janet strong and unafraid looked straight at Hecate and lunged at her. Hecate stood her ground and Janet smashed into the witch with all her force. As she struck the witch, Chelsea crashed to the floor while the witch stood firm.

Although shocked that the witch remained standing, with blood and rage flowing, Janet thrashed at the witch with all her might. The witch stood motionless. Janet stepped back and paused, before slapping the witch across the face in a vicious blow. Chelsea let out a sharp cry of pain, causing Janet to turn and look at her.

Her cheek was glowing pink, and it dawned on her that the cries of pain had been coming from Chelsea. She had been hurting Chelsea with every strike.

Now she recalled Dave's voice screaming at her to stop during her frenzied attack. At the realization of what was happening, the defiance in her eyes turned to submission. Now a hint of a smile began to emerge from the witch's mouth. Payback time.

In resignation, Janet fell to her knees and buried her face in her hands. She looked up across to Chelsea lying on the floor and she went to reach for her. Before that hand had moved an inch, Hecate's hand grasped Janet's wrist and twisted it violently. Janet cried in pain, and then without warning, she rose into the air before crashing against the wall. She somersaulted in midair and slammed into the wall mirroring Dave.

Hecate threw her head back and let out a wild blood-curdling laugh, and then she performed a little jig, dancing up and down on the spot. She cackled and laughed with glee and danced in a circle with her arms flailing and feet clomping. Hecate stopped her dance in mid-step and looked down at the prostrate Chelsea.

Mesmerized by the performance, Chelsea had left it too late. A small opportunity to escape had passed her by.

Like a rag doll, Hecate's will picked Chelsea up off the floor and two hairpins appeared in her hands. Like daggers, she threw them like a magician at his assistant in a spinning wheel, and as they flew, just as before, the flying darts turned into nails before hammering into Janet's ankles. But it wasn't over yet. Two more pins appeared in Chelsea's hands and she threw them. This time the target was Dave's hands.

Hecate approached and bent down so her face was close to theirs.

She said in a mocking tone, "Goodbye, whoever you are."

Hecate reached out with her right hand, extended her index finger at Dave's heart and muttered something that couldn't be heard. Then she looked at Janet. It was her turn to die.

Chelsea's eyes protruded with horror as she stared straight at the witch. Hecate, exhausted, walked towards Chelsea - straight into her body and claimed it as her own.

"This is nice. Really nice." said Hecate, satisfied.

She could be her true hideous self, and she could be a sweet little darling. She felt herself. The smoothness was unprecedented, never had she felt skin so unblemished. She switched back to herself and twirled on her pointy leather shoes with aplomb.

Her escape from that cramped, cold smelly shoe, an imprisonment of a lifetime, of many lifetimes, had ended. She was going to make up for time lost for that there was no doubt, but now, she needed to find somewhere safe, secure and secret to sleep for the night.

Summoning her broom beneath her, she glided like a southern queen from the room and down the stairs. A thought opened the front door and she smelled the outside's welcoming freshness. About to taste freedom, a gust of wind drew her attention to the rippling pages of a book. She stopped the fluttering sheets with an outstretched hand and received the sharp pain of a paper cut in reward.

"OUCH"

She saw the name of the culprit. Alone on the offending page, was his name. She licked her wound and committed his name to indelible memory.

"phil?"

"PHIL!"

Like an armed cruise missile, she roared into the fresh cool midnight sky hardly caring. Hatred is explosive too.

CHAPTER 11.

WHAT A CHANCE.

Phil woke up to a morning that was no different from any other. He still had to go to work, and he was still alone. He got out of bed and performed his routine shower, shave, dress. He had returned home late at night very tired, yet was plagued with bad dreams he couldn't remember.

"Maybe this will be a new day, a new beginning?" he thought to himself, as he did every day. He dressed in black trousers and a checkered shirt, made his way into the living room and put his coffee on. He didn't read the newspaper; it was his job to make them. So, he turned on the TV to get the day's weather and sat down in front of it sipping gingerly.

Checking the time, he got up and put his mug upside down in the empty sink, turned the TV off and made his way out. He locked the door behind him, took the stairs and got into his car, and cursed, noticing that he hadn't put his luggage away from his holiday.

"Maybe this will be a new day, a new beginning? Well that's screwed right off the bat." Phil reflected as he drove off to work.

"The vacation's over, and I did nothing, as usual." Phil always had more than ample reasons for berating himself.

Fifteen minutes later, he parked his car in the newspaper's car park. With every step closer to the office, he became more and more depressed, wishing that he were somewhere else. He entered the building and made his way up to the executive floor. Phil took the stairs. He always said it was part of keeping fit, but the reality was he didn't want to be in close proximity with his coworkers.

Everyone stood together in that tiny elevator. He couldn't stand their eyes looking at the back of his head, their ears listening to him breathe; them knowing that he was the boss's brother. He knew they whispered about him in the corridors and that they sniggered behind his back. Take the stairs Phil. It's safer.

Once in the office, Phil was much more comfortable, He said 'Hi' to all his fellow reporters, knowing they hated him. But what could he do? Phi wasn't paranoid either. He settled down at his desk and started the day.

Phil liked to clean his desk before leaving on holidays. With a resigned sigh, he found his desk overflowing with garbage and it wasn't the first time either. The lack of respect was evident, but he pretended it didn't faze him at all. He piled up all the rubbish into a neat stack and put it to one side.

The root cause of his problems emanated from behind the door of the corner office not twenty feet away. The door to the corner office opened and a young good-looking editor assistant called Kelly closed the door behind her. Phil had seen her sniffing around the chief editor's office many times, his brother Bill's office.

The walls were translucent glass, not clear enough to see anything, but it looked like the two people in the office were extremely close. Phil wasn't surprised one bit, he knew his brother too well, and he shrugged off any feelings of disgust. Rumors had been swirling and that meant two things. Bill and Kelly were having an affair. And Bill, supremely in tune with the office background drone, would be aware of this and would be ending it shortly.

It wouldn't be long, Phil thought, before Bill will let the intern go. They all ended up the same: dumped and broken hearted. They all thought that Bill was leaving his wife for them. But no woman ever separated Bill from his wife, or more accurately, Bill from his wife's father's money and business. Her father awarded him the position, recognizing talent when he saw it, and Bill didn't let him down. Begrudgingly, Phil had to admit that Bill was a damned good chief editor and he warranted it.

A reporter was heading his way. He knocked on the door and entered in one motion.

Phil went about his business, half listening to the conversation between the reporter and Bill. He distinctly heard the word, Hecate. Phil didn't know what to do. He wanted to hear what they were talking about, but he couldn't just barge in. So Phil walked up to the office equipment cabinet just outside Bill's office and pretended to look for something. He listened intently, and his heart jumped when he heard the words "To Be or Not to Be."

"My God." he thought, "I was there yesterday. This could be something to do with me." He summoned his courage and pushed his head into Bill's office.

All reporters hate other reporters muscling in on their stories, and the reporter, Mike, was no exception. He looked at Phil and said sharply, "What the fuck do you want?"

Phil knew that his brother wouldn't stick up for him and that Bill would enjoy the sneer. Ignoring Mike's insult and tone, Phil said, "Did you say Hecate?"

"What's it to you?" Mike said completely annoyed.

Retaining his composure, Phil replied "I thought I heard you say Hecate and a Bed and Breakfast, called To Be or Not to Be. I was just there yesterday. Oh, I was just getting some office equipment, when I heard you say it outside the door."

Mike turned to Bill for confirmation that he was going to be the lead on this story. Bill who wasn't above tormenting his staff as well, looked at Mike, and Phil, indicating that Mike should fill him in on the details. Pissed, Mike got the message. He turned to Phil and told him what he knew.

"I've just had this phone call from the police in Hecate, and I know it's pretty sketchy at the moment, but there seems to have been a murder at the bed-and-breakfast called To Be or Not to Be and…"

Phil interrupted Mike. "It's true. I stayed in that bed-and-breakfast the night before last. I should do the story. I have inside knowledge."

A hush of the office outside meant that Bill's wife had entered the floor. For a moment, no one spoke, and all eyes focused on the office front door - Kelly's eyes especially. Seconds later, an older woman appeared at the entranceway. As she appeared, Bill picked up his jacket, swung it over his shoulder, and spoke in a commanding tone.

"Good work Mike. Phil, you and Kelly head down to Hecate and get the full story, and report back to me." and with that, he linked arms with his wife and headed to the elevator.

Phil was impressed by how smooth his brother was at manipulating people and situations. Not only did he put that snot Mike in his place, but he had disarmed Kelly's advances. The potential confrontation with his wife was averted, but it was also the exact right business decision.

Just because Mike had received the tip didn't make him the best person to do the report, Phil did have the inside story. Whereas Phil's reporting skills were average, Kelly's abrasive nature and good looks would complement Phil's awkwardness around people. Between them, they would be able to ask the right questions and put together a decent report. Crowned by sending Kelly out of the office, he could dump her from a distance.

"Smooth bastard." thought Phil.

Phil and Kelly exited the newspaper building. Phil took the elevator down for the first time in quite a while, an indication of how good he was feeling. Yes, he understood that the reason Bill awarded Phil his victory was Kelly, but he would take any win that came his way.

Kelly, on the other hand, was in a funk. She was used to getting her way; if she wanted something, she normally got it. Her father was a conduit of cash, especially after her parents split. It wasn't until he re-married and the money dried up that she had to do anything at all. However, her good looks opened doors, and she easily found good employment with a career path. Not that she needed a career, and she didn't need to sleep her way to the top either, she started there, with Bill.

But something was wrong.

When she had Bill to herself in his office, he was defensive and elusive. When presented with the chance to distance himself, he took it, preferring the company of his job, and then wife, rather than hers. She didn't understand what was going on. Didn't he love her? Those nights when they were in the office together 'working late', were they a lie? Sneaking off to hotel rooms, what was that all about? Running on autopilot, she followed Phil towards his car. It wasn't until she was about to get into the passenger seat that she snapped out of it. "We've got to go to my place so that I can pack." she said with bitterness in her voice. Phil on the other hand was almost skipping as he gibbered on about his recent trip. She hadn't heard a word.

Kelly got into the car, and Phil asked where she lived. It was a fifteen-minute drive away, and it took all that time for Phil to stop babbling.

Kelly was dazed at Bill's aloofness towards her. Phil parked the car at her place and started to walk with her towards the building.

She looked at him and said, "Where are you going?"

Taken back, Phil said "With you, to help you get your stuff."

"No. No. No." Come back in an hour's time, I'll be ready then."

Phil turned around and went back to the car with his shoulders slouched. He sat in the car and then decided to drive to a strip mall and grab some food. He didn't need to go back to his house as he hadn't unpacked from his previous trip. After an hour, he headed back to Kelly's place.

He must have sat there for another 30 minutes before Kelly finally appeared, pulling two suitcases behind her. She had changed into slacks. He thought; "She dresses up fancy for him, but for me, I get the boring workmanlike clothes, idiot, what do you expect, he's the boss."

They set off towards Hecate. Determined to improve Kelly's mood, Phil tried light conversation but after all attempts failed, he let her stew in her own self-pity.

He couldn't remember how far it was to Hecate, and after most of the day had gone, Phil thought to himself, "Was it really this far? "Always seems to be further when you're going someplace eh, Kelly."

Silence was his reply.

"Well, don't say I didn't try." he thought when she suddenly commanded,

"We should stop soon; it's getting dark and we can carry on tomorrow."

He agreed out of the willingness to please. Instead of pressing onto Hecate, they stopped at the first decent motel in a passing township. Getting separate rooms for the night, they both retired. Tomorrow, they would continue onward to the nearby Hecate to start their investigation and reporting in earnest.

CHAPTER 12.

A GOOD SUPPER.

Hecate soared around the night sky above the town bearing her name. The hundreds of years in solitary confinement hadn't changed a thing. She sat sidesaddle on her beloved means of transport, her broom. She flew effortlessly and gracefully through the crisp night air. The 'sacrifices' though had drained her, so she began to look for a place to stay and rest.

She gravitated to a small, run down church on the outskirts of town. She glided smoothly into the belfry and landed gently on a wooden landing next to the rusty old bells. Leaning her broomstick against the wall, she led down on the planks and fell instantly asleep. She didn't dream, after centuries of nothing else, a dark, blank, empty night was the ideal way to end the perfect day.

She slept until the following evening and woke up rested and hungry. Sitting up, she watched the last light of day slip away, giving forth to the night. Perfect. Ravenous, but not for the standard fare of mortals, not that she was immortal, just less mortal than most. Pondering what she could have for dinner, she searched through the memory of the teen she'd absorbed.

"There, go back a bit, there, a young man, James Drinkmore. Yes, this one looks good, shallow, self-absorbed and juicy". Without hesitating, she climbed onto her broomstick and followed the thoughts of Chelsea to the home of heartthrob James.

Assuming the form of Chelsea, she snuck round the house. She knew the bedroom window of James well from dreaming about entering it many times. The light was on so *Chelsea* threw a stone against the window. After a few stones the curtains, an American flag, were pulled aside, and a face appeared. Hastily, the window opened.

"James, its Chelsea."

"Chelsea! Give me a sec." The window was shut loudly, and the racket of a teenager struggling to find and change into clothes followed. Half-dressed, he crashed out into the yard, allowing the tattered screen door to smack shut.

JD ran over to the shadowy part of the garden where Chelsea was crouching behind an old rusty pickup. "Chelsea, Chelsea." he whispered in a hushed voice.

"Over here." she replied. He found her, grabbed her shoulders and looked her in the eyes. "What happened?"

"JD, take me somewhere, I've gotta talk to someone."

JD disappeared into the house and stormed back out with the keys to his truck. Fascinated by this loud horseless carriage, Hecate rode along in amazement, until JD slowed down.

"I'll tell you when we should stop JD." She put her hand on his leg, "Don't stop here. Find somewhere quiet, dark and isolated."

JD drove like a mad man.

Just outside the township's limits he turned down a lonely dark lane, pulled over, and parked in an even darker secluded graved-way.

Perfect he thought, with a smile on his face.

Perfect she thought, with a smile on her face.

Trying not to just grab her, JD looked over to Chelsea and said in a frenzied burst.

"Chelsea, what happened? The police are looking all over for you. Your parents, they're dead. People say it was some satanic ritual. Where have you been? Are you alright? God, you look great."

He had barely finished his last sentence before grabbing and kissing her; for some reason, she had never looked so hot. He let her go, and Chelsea just sat there saying nothing, seemingly oblivious to what he had done. He filled in the silence before it had a chance to get awkward.

"Chelsea, what happened?" compassionately this time. Chelsea started crying and sobbing.

"It was terrible JD terrible, I can't talk about it, just hold me."

He grabbed her again. Kissing her passionately, he groped at Chelsea's breasts and legs. Fumbling with her clothes and kissing feverishly, but beginning not to enjoy the feel of it; he decided to peek at Chelsea to see what she was thinking. The shock of what he saw should surely have killed him. Chelsea was gone. Hecate was in her place.

Her haggard face and wide-open evil and green eyes filled JD's vision. Instinctively, he leapt backwards and screamed, "What the fuck!"

As his arms and legs desperately tried to propel himself away from whoever; whatever, was sitting in front of him, the full appreciation of this horror, and what he had been doing with it, began to sink in.

"Argh," almost gagging, "What..."

Hecate, just continued to stare at him, but the gleam in her eye that was only a spark a second ago, was now a lighthouse beacon. "What's wrong my love?" She spoke seductively mimicking Chelsea.

"What...What... WHAT..." JDs back pressed up against the driver's door. "What. I'm getting out of here." Without losing his gaze upon the witch, with his fumbling hands behind his back, he found the door handle. But it wouldn't unlock. Turning now and desperately, with both hands, he yanked and heaved but it still wouldn't budge.

Hecate's screeching laughter forced JD to cover his ears.

Turning back to face her, he bravely yelled. "Who the fuck are you and what the fuck have you done with Chelsea?"

Hecate recognized his strength. JD wasn't as shallow as she'd expected, there was spine. And that was intolerable. There was only one remedy for such defiance. Pain.

"It's time to teach this little toad a lesson." Hecate always put thought into action. Quick as a cobra, she had JD by the neck and her boney hand squeezed.

She started to crush the life out of his body.

"Ah. Sleep, little baby boy. Good." His eyes glazed over and his head tipped back as he was passing out.

"Not too quickly now, Hecate dear." She loosened her grip slightly, as she didn't want to finish him off too swiftly. Where's the fun in that?

"OUCH!" cried Hecate.

JD head butted her in a sudden and vicious attack that took Hecate off guard. Faking his unconsciousness was the distraction he needed to launch his defense. It wasn't over by any means. With his back against the door, he kicked her with both feet knocking her further off balance. Then turning, JD pulled on the door handle, and shouldered the truck door open. Falling face forward onto the wet ground, he scrambled onto his feet and started to run. Anywhere, who cared, he was free.

Running along the dirt road, he distanced himself from the truck by a couple of hundred yards before he couldn't run any further. Buckled over and panting, he stopped and decided to risk a glance back. He looked over his shoulder. She wasn't driving the truck down the road as he expected.

"What the fuck?" He retraced what had just happened and he started to wonder if it even did. Still scared, he decided that he should be a little more cautious, so he crouched down against the hedge-side. Controlling his breathing and his heart, he started to creep back towards the truck.

"I wanna see who this bitch is." he thought, but he had only gone a few yards when he heard a noise behind him; and the hair on the back of his neck stood on end. He suddenly wished that he had just kept on running.

CHAPTER 13.

YOU DOING GOOD.

Hecate stood over the body lying on the ground. A drop of green blood fell to the ground from her face. She raised her hand to her nose and pinched it with her finger and thumb. "Ouch, little bastard." and gave the body a kick. Holding her breath and trying not to swallow, she gently moved the thumb and finger up and down, left and right. Wincing with the pain, a tiny little click announced that the nose was back home.

"Finally."

Immediately, the throbbing pain receded, and the bleeding ebbed.

"Ow.", but feeling much better, she looked down at the body and smirked. "So, this was the boy friend?" she said to herself. "Well, bit of a scrapper actually, gave you a bit of a run for your money Hecate." she continued. She picked him up and tossed him over the front of the broom. Then she flew back to the truck and dumped him in the back before sitting on the tailgate.

She pondered, "Now what." Needing inspiration, she went through the junk in the back of the cabin. "Ah."

Hecate pulled on the end of a set of jumper cables. Wondering what they were, or what their original purpose was, she took the cables up into the overhanging tree. She glided up to a strong looking bough, wrapped one end over it, and left the other end dangling. Then she tied a hangman's knot. She sailed back down to the ground and hauled JD up to the limp noose, and slid his head beautifully through it, like a thread through the eye of a needle. With muted squeaking from the stretching wires, she gently exchanged JD's weight from the broomstick to the cables until taught. JD's body twisted right and then left, gradually losing momentum with each passing twist, until he hung stationary, silently, forlorn.

"A job well done." thought Hecate cheerfully.

She floated on her broomstick admiring her work, feeling content. Pleased with her new lease on life, "Things looked pretty damn good."

She did a quick recap. The escape, the portrait, the two glorious crucifixions, the abduction and now this. "Making up for lost time." she thought to herself.

Then she recalled the paper cut.

And its owner.

The trigger.

"THAT PHIL! Breathe Hecate, Breathe."

The twinge of pain from her nose was nothing as she doubled over in agony from a different source. Holding her stomach with both hands, she warily dis-mounted and tried to hold her ground, luckily for her she wasn't in mid-flight. She clutched her abdomen. Flickering like an old light bulb, Chelsea and Hecate's images battled for dominance. It was a fight Hecate could not win. Chelsea's mortal coil was in the last throes. She had been inside Hecate for a day and was now surrendering to Death. In Death came release and Hecate's will was insignificant to that force, outmatched, Chelsea passed. Her body exited Hecate. She stood beautiful and serene for a moment, and then collapsed to the dirty muddy ground of which is our world.

"I hate that, (him)" gasped Hecate still holding her gut while trying to stand up.

The energy that had drained from her in that tiny act forced her to sit down, and in a detestable act, she sat on the warm corpse of Chelsea. Hecate had been feeding upon her spirit until she could survive no more and mercifully, she was taken from the world.

The realm of Death was inevitable and when he summoned the soul, it answered. Chelsea's pristine appearance at the transition of life to death was how she appeared in the hereafter. Chelsea's face was a picture of horror, fear and despair. But at least she was at peace, something that Hecate always resented.

She took a final scan of the landscape: JD swung from a tree and Chelsea lay clumped on the bare ground underneath him. She had her fill; she whipped skyward on her flying broomstick like a rocket and headed for the belfry: satisfied and happy.

CHAPTER 14.

SHOOT. NOT A GREAT START.

Phil didn't sleep much that night in the scrawny motel room. He had much to think about. There were many strange emotions running around in his head that he hadn't felt in many a year. Primarily, he was still excited by the way his brother had treated him. He knew that he'd only used him to get out of an awkward situation, but he still treated him with respect, relatively. Nevertheless, it felt so genuine. Phil replayed the conversation repeatedly in his head, listening for nuances of sarcasm and belittlement, but he couldn't find any.

"Has Bill had a change of heart? Is my brother now looking at me as more than just an errand boy?" a tantalizing, but erroneous thought, and Phil knew it. "No, it was just a matter of convenience and duty, he had to get rid of Kelly and couldn't trust that asshole Mike to do it, whereas he knows I will, God I suck. Whatever, I'm still out here reporting, and probably on the biggest story of my career. Who cares if it's under false pretenses?"

Phil didn't care if he merited the task or not, he was enjoying it and was going to 'take it' as it was. An unusual thing for Phil to do. Extracting every morsel, he continued to play the tape through his mind's eye, savoring every moment. Then there was the underlying reason for everything, the murder. And his return to the scene of the crime. This was also a very exciting prospect. Tomorrow he, "And a very attractive young woman." would be returning to the bed and breakfast that he knew so well. He didn't care that his stay was only one night long, and that the proprietors befriended him out of obligation. He knew them personally, and this gave him a massive insight and advantage for the report. This could be the one story that he had looked for his whole life, a story that could elevate him as a reporter, rather than his brother's brother.

Suddenly the naysayers in his head wrestled the positive thoughts away from him, telling him that his fellow reporters will know of the circumstances surrounding his visit here, and they will demand the most compelling piece of reporting ever told. Then a strange and unfamiliar feeling gained a foothold in that brain, positive thoughts. He managed, most un-Phil like, to concentrate on these good feelings, for one of the few times in his life.

Using the momentum of this achievement, Phil turned his thinking towards tomorrow, and his visit to the B&B. He constructed a list of things he would ask the neighbors, things he would observe; questions he would ask the police. More importantly, how he would insert himself into the story, without making it too obvious that he was on an ego trip. Any thoughts he had about Kelly, however, he pushed to the very back of his mind. He didn't want to go there, and he didn't want to give any reason for his brother to backtrack on this sudden, seemingly newfound respect for him. He rolled over in bed and smiled, before falling asleep a satisfied man.

Phil and Kelly hadn't bothered to ask for a wake-up call. Upon rousing Phil reached for his watch and saw it was around seven o'clock.

"Should he phone Kelly to wake her up?" He dialed her room number and waited. After the fourth ring, Kelly answered the phone. Sounding irritated and groggy, she spat her words at Phil.

"It's seven o'clock Phil. Seven."

"Sorry Kelly, I didn't know what time you woke up. You did notice that today we've got quite a bit to do."

"Click."

"Okay, Okay, I'll meet you at the car at eight." Phil responded to himself. He patted himself on the back for not taking this to heart.

He got out of bed, had a shower. A half an hour later, he was set to go, so he went outside and walked around the motel car park. Taking some deep breaths and stretching his legs, he looked up at the sky; it looked like it was going to be an overcast day. He popped into the motel front desk and asked the clerk if she knew anything about any murders in the district. She hadn't; a good sign for a reporter, so Phil tried to impress her with his knowledge. She conveniently found an excuse to go to the back room, leaving him alone in the scruffy reception area.

"Two rejections in one hour, the day's not shaping up to be such a good one." thought Phil. Focusing on anything positive, was difficult for Phil; so, he convinced himself that this was good preparation for probing the police. This was just the practice run he needed for more pointed and persistent questioning. He headed towards the car, this time he didn't expect to see Kelly there. She surfaced at 8:45.

"I think once we get to Hecate, we should go directly to the B&B and check it out before we do anything else, what do you think Kelly?" said Phil attempting to be friendly.

"I think we should get a coffee first before we start thinking about thinking." retorted Kelly bitterly.

After a coffee at the closest franchise, they resumed their trip upstate. No matter what Phil said to Kelly, in the form of friendly banter or otherwise, she shot it down with monosyllable replies. It progressed to the point where Phil gave in, and just drove. They finally arrived at Hecate, but by now neither was in a good mood. Kelly was still smarting from the cruelty of her lover, and Phil was just sulking.

Once in Hecate, they went directly to the B&B. He told her that this was exactly what it looked like, the way he'd left it, what Dave and Janet were like. They stood in front of the police tape and Kelly was just about to duck underneath it, when she heard Phil start up the car. She heard his annoyingly whiny voice telling *her all people*, to get into the car.

"Police Station."

She stood there mentally debating the request, *which was the right thing to do*, or whether to just go ahead and climb over the tape just to screw with him.

Just as her hand was on the tape, a police car turned round a street corner and headed straight towards them. Phil hopped out of his car and approached the police car that had stopped. The officer would have had some interesting questions for Kelly, as to "why she was halfway under the police tape." if he'd hadn't done it.

The officer was not a pleasant man, so Phil didn't ask him what had happened at the house, only where the police station actually was.

They found the police station buzzing but the front desk was vacant, so they both stood by the counter and waited.

"We should go and get someone." said Kelly impatiently.

"You can't do that." resisted Phil, "just wait, there'll be someone here soon."

Phil was a person who always followed procedures and processes, he avoided risk. So, he waited, and worst still, made Kelly wait. It seemed an impossibly long time and Kelly lost her patience with the police, and Phil. She blasted out loud that Phil had actually known the couple. Just as she predicted, it got their attention. Phil suddenly became a person of interest.

The police led the timid Phil away and they wouldn't allow Kelly to accompany him. Several hours of questioning followed, while Kelly, forced to wait, became bitter and frustrated.

Almost from the beginning of the interview, the detective had the evidence of Phil's innocence from his receipts. With his drive back from Hecate at the end of his vacation, he had to fill up twice, and he had the fast food receipt from around the corner of his apartment.

Luckily, for Phil, it provided solid proof that he wasn't their man; yet, they continued to interrogate him. So even though the police had hard evidence of Phil's innocence, they just thought to give him a hard time anyway.

The police wanted a witness to testify that he was in the office the following day. This confirmation was supplied by a bitter Mike, who was sorely tempted to lie. Bill wouldn't provide the alibi; his secretary claimed he was out of the office, although Phil heard him laughing in the background. Phil moved as if to get out of his chair, but the detective had a different idea, and shoved him back down.

He was beginning to think that he was in real trouble now, still detained. Just then, the door opened, and an officer stepped in and whispered something into the interviewing detective's ear. Phil strained to hear, only caught a smidgen.

"JD, Che… missing."

The detective put his hands on the table's edge and pushed his chair back. He turned back to Phil and said in a matter-of-fact voice, "You can go."

Outside the interrogation room, officers were hustling, making phone calls, and looking very diligent. The Hecate police station was small like Hecate, and so the confines of the station magnified the increased activity. Phil joined Kelly at the bench by the front desk where she had been sitting. She grabbed Phil's arm above the elbow roughly, and said, "What's going on?"

"I don't know. They frigging questioned me, like for hours in there; they thought I'd done the murders."

"Yes, like as if you could do anything like that." Kelly replied.

Officers were leaving the building and getting into their patrol cars, and so Phil and Kelly decided to follow them. Phil had a radio receiver that picked up police frequencies in the back seat. He asked Kelly to see if she could pick up the police's communications.

Kelly was furious from sitting and waiting on a hard bench, and ignored, by the men in the office, who were all too busy and immersed in their work to bother to get her a coffee.

This gave her plenty of time to think about things like Bill and her. He hadn't called yet, and they had been apart for almost two days.

"He ships me off on this pokey little mission with his loser brother, for what? To get me out of town? Was that it? The way he went off with his wife like that, back in the office. I thought he was going to leave her. What did all those things he said mean? Were they lies? Was this whole thing just a sordid affair?"

"Get the fucking radio yourself you asshole." she yelled at the top of her voice, taking her rage out on innocent Phil. "You stupid idiot. You left me there with all those policemen making passes and gawking at me all that time."

The sudden onslaught stopped Phil in his tracks. There wasn't anything he could have done about how long she waited or the way she was treated. All he wanted was for her to get the radio, and perhaps tune to a police channel. Instead, for no apparent reason, he was the target of her attack.

"What?" He stuttered.

"You heard me asshole." Kelly shot back.

"What?"

"Are you deaf? You want me to get the radio? I have to get the police's attention just to talk to you. Then, what do you do? You go off with the boys and leave me out of it. After I'd done all the work to get them, even to look at you. And really, why would anyone ever look at you. You're pathetic. No wonder your brother thinks you're a wimp."

"I was being interrogated for murder thank you very much. I..." Phil attempted to stem Kelly's tirade.

"Phil, for god's sake, just standup and be a man. You think your brother would have taken that kind of treatment. No, he'd just go in there and demand to see the boss, and he'd find out exactly what's going on."

"Hey look, that's not fair." said Phil.

"Hey look, that's not fair." mimicked Kelly in Phil's tone. "Just admit it Phil. You're just a big fat failure. Be a man like your brother."

Phil bowed his head. He knew she was right: about everything. But what could he do? Bill was his older brother and had had to live in his shadow to live at all. Bill had made sure of that, as far back as Phil could remember. Shielded by their parents' complacency towards bullying, Bill never let Phil say anything. He would immediately jump in to draw attention to him, and away from Phil. The parents focused on Bill and forgot Phil. His whole life had been a never-ending struggle against his brother, his parents' favorite child.

Phil stood up to Bill, just the once. He was the youngest in Bill's gang. One day they were running about in the woods playing and climbing trees. Bill was the only one who wanted to play a certain game. No one said otherwise; they were all too timid, until Phil said, "No, let's play something else."

"What did you say kid?" Bill had quickly turned and aggressively advanced on his younger brother.

Phil had thought, "Now's the time to make a stand." So bravely, Phil repeated, "Let's play something else."

Bill walked up to Phil and pushed him over. He knelt down hard on Phil's chest. As Phil gasped for air, Bill pinched Phil's nose and put his other hand over his mouth. Phil buckled and wrenched, but with no air and the weight of Bill on his chest, he couldn't fight. With tears streaming down his face and with pleading eyes for mercy, Bill taunted him, and did not let go.

Phil woke up, dirty, bleeding and broken. He had learned his lesson and now he wasn't much more than Bill's slave.

Phil, looking straight ahead, said nothing in response to Kelly's accusations. Kelly sat stiffly realizing that she had gone way too far. They sat silently for what seemed like ages. Eventually, making sure that he avoided eye contact with her, Phil started to turn towards the backseat.

"Get out of my way." Kelly said irritably turning to get the radio. Her way of saying sorry. Kelly fidgeted in her seat as she twisted round to retrieve it. Phil tried quelling his feelings of anger and humiliation and debated whether to accept her apology.

In silent acquiescence, his way, he accepted the nonverbal sorry, but he was smarting badly inside. Acrimoniously, Phil and Kelly acknowledged each other's silent apologies and got back to the business of reporting.

They drove to the location that the police had descended upon and parked out of the way. After the police left they waited a quarter of an hour, not exchanging a word, until Phil broke the stiff silence by starting the car. He drove the short distance to the house and pulled into the driveway. Kelly was surprised at his boldness.

They both got out of the car and slammed the doors. They saw one of the cheap, lace curtains in the front window pull to one side before it fell back to its original position. Kelly almost pushed Phil out of the way as they climbed up the stairs to the house.

"What the fuck do you want?" A poorly dressed middle-aged woman answered to door. She had a cigarette in her left hand and closed her threadbare housecoat with her right. She took an immediate dislike to Kelly, with her designer slacks, polo neck cashmere sweater and matching shoes.

Kelly recognized her mistrust and took a step backward to allow Phil to finish the introductions. Confident that he would screw up and confirm her insults, "He was her class anyway."

"Hello, my name is Phil..."

"You ain't the police. They just left. Bastards."

"No kidding." said Phil. "A couple of hours ago they were ready to charge me with murder."

"So, what are you, reporters?"

"Yes." said Phil.

"Didn't take long. Vultures."

"No kidding." replied Phil for the second time in so many sentences.

The woman paused and looked at the odd couple curiously. Then let out a burst of laughter. "Well, get on with it." And let them in.

"But wipe your feet. I'm Deloris."

She turned around and led the way into the house. Phil and Kelly both entered and did what they were told, although Kelly didn't think it was necessary.

They entered the living room where they sat down, her in an old armchair and the two of them on an old, non-matching sofa.

Phil had struck up a rapport with her in their introductions, and he, venting a little, told her his story to do with his encounter with their mutual enemy, the police.

Further building on his bond he refrained from asking any questions.

"Pretty smart." thought Kelly resenting that, "after telling her so much about himself, she'll start to talk soon." and she did.

She described her son as a good boy, who wouldn't hurt a fly, and his past issues with the police? They were all false and erroneous accusations. Phil took casual notes; he had to do substantial paraphrasing when she talked about the authorities. He also let her see what he was writing so that she wouldn't get suspicious. Kelly stayed silent, begrudgingly becoming impressed with Phil's reporting skill.

Deloris had a head of steam and continued to regale her story. "The reason the police were here (this time) was really serious. *Murder.* That's not my son. Sure, he was in a couple of fights at school, and I'm not saying that his old man didn't knock him around a bit (and me), before I threw him out. But he ain't no murderer. They come in here, and tell me that him and that Chelsea slut, killed her parents and run off together. Bull-shit."

"So, Chelsea is missing?" chimed Phil in surprise.

"Hey, don't you start, I thought you were on my side." she responded defensively.

"No, no, I'm not suggesting that he has done anything. It's just the police haven't told us anything, so I'd assumed that she was dead too." replied Phil, just as sensitively.

"You know what assume stands for kiddo. Make an *ass*, out of *u*, and *me*." Deloris cackled.

Phil laughed, and Kelly thought, "God, like we've never heard that before." as she stove to conceal her growing resentment towards the slick interview.

"He was in his bed that night and I told them so. But no, they go off on their dumb ideas. Where's my son I tell them, he's not run off, he's a missing person. Where's his truck they ask me? How the hell should I know, it's not like I have all that GPS computer stuff to tell, they've got that, they should find him for me, not the other way around. He wasn't even dating that girl, I think, there's a few girls you know, can't remember 'em all." she said proudly, "I tell you, you find that truck, you find my boy. He loved that truck."

"Tell me about the truck, would you please Madam." Phil asked.

"Madam? Haven't been called that in a while."

"Deloris, what kind of truck was it? Do you know the license plate number?" Phil gently asked, and Deloris described the truck down to the rust and hitch. Soon Phil had a photograph of JD posing in front of the truck and a shot of Rye as they left. Kelly had been quiet for the whole interview.

Afterwards, when they were safely on the road, driving towards the local chicken diner Deloris had recommended, Kelly remarked with disdain, "Trailer trash."

"Sure, you're right, but she's still a good person." thought Phil, "Christ Kelly, her son's missing, and the police aren't searching for him as a missing person, but because they want to question him for murder. She must be beside herself with worry."

The truth was though, that Deloris didn't worry as long as JD didn't cost her anything. "It was time he moved out anyway." she had said to the closed door after seeing Phil and Kelly out.

"I know she's down to earth, but, well…" said Phil running out of steam.

Kelly looked at Phil and said, "You want to fuck her."

"No." he exclaimed, not lying, his brain hadn't caught up to his feelings yet.

"No." spoken in a slightly higher pitched voice. "I just feel sorry for her. No. OK. Where do we stand, where we're going to eat?"

"Bitch." he thought to himself.

"You're a terrible liar Phil." thought Kelly, taking mercy on him and not drilling him more about Deloris.

"Well, we're not going to that diner she recommended that's for sure. We're going to a real restaurant." Phil resisted the temptation to say that Kelly was a snob. It would have been suicide. So, he shut up, and headed for the best hotel and restaurant in town, it was after all, on expenses. And as he was actually doing two jobs for Bill, so "Yea. Why not?"

Over dinner in the hotel's lounge, Kelly went over their notes concerning the story. In fact, if it wasn't for the interview with Deloris and the knowledge that Phil brought to the table, they didn't really have anything at all.

"What have we got?" asked Kelly in the most pleasant voice since the trip started.

"Let's see, the personal knowledge of the B&B before their deaths, and the interview with JD's mother." replied Phil.

"Ok Phil, you hero." she said sarcastically.

"Fuck, you and Bill were made for each other." thought Phil.

"What haven't we got? Besides her in your bed." said Kelly, mocking him.

Phil ignored it, "We don't know anything about the murders, and that's what we're here for."

"Right, you haven't got the guts to go back there and ask her out." said Kelly still goading Phil.

"Whatever. The police haven't been any help, and they certainly don't want to either, we're on our own."

"When I was in the police station, **waiting for you**, I asked a whole bunch of questions, and not one of them would even give me the time of day." continued Kelly. She hadn't told Phil this as she didn't want to look like she had tried and failed.

They talked about Deloris and the police to fill in the time, and besides a jab or two from Kelly, it was the best they had got on the whole trip.

"You know what, after dinner, we should go back to the crime scene and take a look around, you know, inside."

"Yep." said Phil, but he was dreaming about Deloris and wasn't listening.

CHAPTER 15.

AN INCH.

Phil was lying on the bed watching TV when a knock on his hotel door interrupted his favorite show.

"Hello Kelly" Phil said, shocked by this surprise visit, and for a split second he thought of wonderful things. He was, after all, on a roll.

"Ready?" inquired Kelly.

"Ready?" responded Phil.

"Yea, ready, for the visit to the B&B."

"Tonight?" Phil had no idea what Kelly was talking about.

"Yea, tonight, don't you remember? We're going to go to the B&B and go over the place. Remember?" Kelly was getting annoyed.

"We are?"

"Yes, oh for God's sake." She pushed by him into the room. "I said that we should go to the B&B tonight after dinner and you did say OK, OK, remember now?"

"Shit." thought Phil, "I don't remember agreeing to that. I better say *yes*, otherwise there will be hell to pay, and just as we were getting on so well, I better get my ass in gear."

"Yea, OK, I forgot, sorry, I turned on the TV and…" he said. It wasn't a good save. He turned the TV off and put his jacket on.

Crime scene tape surrounded the house.

To Phil's alarm, Kelly ducked under the tape with brazen bravado. She looked back at him still behind the tape. She beckoned him impatiently.

His mind raced. "Shit, she did that on purpose, and now I'm caught between a rock and a hard place." He reluctantly willed himself under the impenetrable barrier, "No wonder my brother thinks I'm a wimp, I had to summon up all the courage I have just to go underneath the police tape, and I'm even following a girl. Shame on me."

"Kelly, wait, I know the way." declared Phil reclaiming some pride.

"OK, come on then, we don't want to hang around here outside where everyone can see us." she replied in a hushed and urgent tone. Leading the way through the front door and into the foyer, they shut the front door quickly behind them. Darkness engulfed them like a net. They waited for their eyes to adjust to the dark.

"Even though we haven't technically broken anything, we've certainly entered now, and I don't think a judge would make too much of a distinction if we got caught." Phil thought to himself.

"Where's that key ring flashlight, and why's Phil shaking?" thought Kelly.

Using the flashlight's brightness, she scanned the entrance of the B&B. Phil motioned to Kelly that he wanted the carry it.

"Not a chance, I brought it, it's mine, get your own flashlight buddy." thought Kelly and didn't give it to him.

"OK." said Phil, 'What do we do next?'

"The breakfast room is to the right." They advanced a couple of steps and peered into the breakfast enclave. They both turned to the right and the flashlight's wide beam gently bathed the room. There was nothing out of the ordinary there, just the normal B&B furniture and fittings that Phil remembered from a few days ago - including the china cabinet.

As Kelly was about to move the flashlight beam away from the room, Phil's eye caught sight of something lying on the floor under the windowsill. There it was. *The old shoe that he had held in his own hands a couple of days earlier, only now the toe of the shoe was splayed open. The upper and the sole had separated, threads, broken and frayed.* Kelly saw what Phil was looking at, and not to be out done by him, she moved towards it with the intent to pick it up.

"Stop" blurted out Phil. He realized what Kelly was going to do. Her hand was only an inch from the shoe.

"It's evidence." Phil said in a much quieter voice.

"OK, ok, don't have to yell at me. God." Kelly said bitterly, but she also realized that she had actually obeyed the fool.

"Sorry Kelly, oh, and thank you for bringing the flashlight."

"Yea, OK, thanks." she said unwillingly.

They scanned the entire ground floor and without noticing anything of consequence, they returned to the hallway, to the bottom of the stairs. At first, neither of them could identify a new and weird feeling.

Phil said in a whisper, "I'm feeling a little scared, I mean," he paused "I mean, a little apprehensive."

Kelly thought, "Baby, I'm not going to admit it." Without realizing it she uttered, "Me too."

In single file, they ascended the stairs, and grew more nervous with every step they took. The stairs, old planks, shifted under every footstep. Phil had focused on the noise Kelly was causing as she tiptoed. Phil thought to himself, "The strange thing about old wooden stairs is, the less noise you want to make, the more creaking and squeaking the staircase makes. There's actually no way up an old wooden stair case if you want to keep quiet."

"Will you stop making all that noise, Phil, God, you're like an elephant."

"Me?"

The stairs turned ninety-degrees for the top two remaining two steps.

"Hey, that's the room I stayed in." said Phil, pointing to a closed door directly in front of them.

"And that's the bathroom door."

"Who cares?" replied Kelly grumpily.

The master bedroom door. The dim light attempted to illuminate it from the landing.

They saw the hole and the sight of the shattered opening caused a surge of trepidation and dismay. They advanced slowly towards it. As the flashlight's white beam faltered, an eerie green light crept into their minds.

Phil and Kelly poked their heads through the broken door, just as Chelsea had done. Their eyes witnessed the scene, their brains wished they hadn't. The police had left plenty for the imagination. They had drawn the outline of the two proprietors upon the wall in thick white chalk.

The outline traced two dead people. Two crucified people. Inverted. It was a satanic posture.

Pools of caked blood had collected under each outline. Holes in the wall indicated the presence of nails.

Without saying a word, both of them gaped at the dry pool of black blood. Phil and Kelly stood still for ages. A gentle wind blew causing a lace curtain to flutter over the window. Foreboding enveloped the room and the trespassers' hearts. Their imaginations spun wild. It was easy *to see* the bodies hung there. It felt horrifying and terrifying. Right to the bone. A feeling of being watched. A feeling that a torturous and agonizing death was stalking you. *It was real, tangible, all-encompassing fear.*

Panic erupted. They bolted. They fell over each other as they fought to pry their heads out of the hole. Turning around, they fled down the stairs. Crashing through the front door, Phil remembered to slam it shut for some reason. They raced to the car, not caring if they were seen or not. They were.

CHAPTER 16.

NIGHT TRESPASSERS.

Hecate, the witch slept contentedly and dreamed of the crucifixions. She dreamed of last night's murder of JD, the expression of the girl called Chelsea, the head butt that floored her, and the revenge that ensued. The dream was paused as she woke wide-awake. Something was afoot. Her green eyes instantly focused. She was high up among the clouds.

She circled round and round in the night sky, trying to identify the source of her feeling of trespass. Slowly she gained her bearings and followed the scent. It led back to the B&B, the home of the imprisoning shoe. Lowering her altitude she gazed upon the house and watched. She felt fear and intrusion emanating from the house. She watched and waited. Suddenly two people burst through the door and climbed into another horseless carriage. She made a mental note, she couldn't see their faces, but she remembered their essence, their true identities. She didn't need to see their faces to know who they were.

CHAPTER 17.

SKY CHASE.

Somehow Phil and Kelly got into the car. Without a second thought, Phil started the car and zoomed away from the B&B. A few blocks later Phil's fear had not diminished. Nor had Kelly's. The drive back to the hotel seemed to last forever.

It wasn't silence. It wasn't a hum. It was just a strange feeling that seemed to affect sound, light, the senses. The sound of the tires on the road, the small engine, the streetlights, even the air seemed to be pressing against them. He drove faster and faster without complaint. Gratefully, they finally arrived at the hotel.

With extreme effort, Phil slowed the car down. He steered towards the back of the hotel to park the car. They looked at the short journey from car to hotel door, it seemed long and perilous. They waited to accompany each other to the back door, and the safety of the lobby. They hadn't exchanged a word. It seemed to be uncommonly dark, foggy, muffled and confined. The pillars supporting the upper level appeared to be closer together than they could remember, casting longer, deeper, darker shadows.

Kelly was so scared she thought about linking arms with Phil. If not for Kelly, Phil would have run. Their fear felt urgent, worse than the return drive from the B&B. And they didn't know the reason.

Phil and Kelly plunged into the light of the lobby via the car park back door. They had no idea that that door may have saved their lives. They felt a damn sight safer now that they were inside even though only a pane of glass separated them from the outside.

As relief lifted they attempted to walk casually into the main lobby area; hiding that they had been scared witless by the dark. They endeavored to walk nonchalantly past the reception desk, towards the elevator. Phil pressed the third floor button.

His hand shook. "No comment, eh?" He thought, "You were scared too."

When the elevator got to their floor, they impatiently waited for the doors to open,

"Ladies first." Phil said, beckoning Kelly to exit.

"What an idiot, thought Kelly." She jumped at the chance to get out of there and head for her room. "Screw you Phil, wish Bill was here, then I'd be rushing to my room for a different reason, and we wouldn't have separate rooms either."

As Phil headed for his, he thought of Deloris, "Wish sh…"

CHAPTER 18.

WILLING HERSELF.

The night was dark, as heavy low clouds obscured moon and stars alike. It was perfect. Hecate followed the horseless carriage from the cover of clouds without concern of being seen. Skillfully riding the broom, she skimmed the underneath of the clouds yet struggled to keep up. The incredible machine with its amazing bright eyes challenged her broomstick riding skills.

"These strange machines' really go fast." she thought to herself. She was becoming tired from the short sprint and was just about to give up following, when it slowed down and pulled into a large building. She lost sight of the carriage as it disappeared underneath the upper level of the horseless carriage stables.

"There they are." she excitedly exclaimed to herself. She was ready for anything. She descended at lightning speed. The wind tore at her cape and hat. But no matter how hard she tried; it was obvious that she was too far away to get down before the two would escape into the building.

Hecate cursed vehemently after that long sprint; she missed her prey. "Damn. Toads. Bastards. I'll get them one night: the buggers." She steered out of her rapid descent and climbed back to cloud level.

Floating like a buoy in a harbor, Hecate bobbed on the soft moist breeze. Nestled under the clouds, her mind pondered the question. Who were those people? She hadn't seen their faces, although not a necessity for recognition, it would help her in deciphering who they were.

"Oh well, something to think about tomorrow, it's been an interesting night, think I'll just relax and enjoy the ride home." She turned her darling broomstick around and headed off to the belfry at a slower pace.

She just couldn't get them out of her mind.

"Wondering who they are again aren't you Hecate?" she mused wickedly to herself. "Like to find that out?"

With a flash of inspiration. "The B&B, let's go back and check out what they were doing. Oh, you're so clever Hecate." she purred.

The broomstick was putting some miles on tonight as she swung it round and plotted the new course. The return trip was taken at a much slower pace even though she was eager to go back. The chase had taken quite a bit out of her.

"Maybe it was a good job that couple did escape. Maybe I would have been too tired to handle them."

Not a chance.

She surveyed the landscape below and started to meditate on the new world, really seeing it for the first time. The world her reincarnation had bestowed upon her. Her vantage point included scores of horseless carriages with big white eyes and intense red tails. Of course, she had seen those many times since her rebirth, she had actually been in one but had never really contemplated them.

She saw wide, long, smooth stone roads, illuminated by lights hanging from branchless trees. People were healthy, clean, fed, clothed, happy and unafraid (she noted that especially) and strolled relaxed and carefree. What an incredible world. Music that she could never have imagined pulsated out of boxes. People talked into tiny oblong, hand held devices, some even had moving pictures. The world was full of countless amazing contraptions and facilities. She had used a toilet and washed in a public washroom. She liked this new world and the power of it.

"And you know what, Hecate?" she said to herself.

"They even named the town after you." She looked around and took it all in.

All these distractions shortened her journey, and before she knew it, she descended towards the B&B. For a place that was supposed to be secure and off limits, tonight the B&B was having more visitors than peak season. Swooping in like a landing bird, she set foot silently on the verandah, "Beautiful." she cooed. She'd gone from a bird in flight to a burglar on the prowl.

Stealthily, she pushed the front door open a tiny amount, and slid through the gap like a snake. The door closed behind her. Her crystal ball of green light lit the place. She made her way past the umbrella stand and console to her left. The living room was unchanged since she last saw it, right down to the photograph she examined with the touch of her finger.

"They tricked me, making me think that they were rich. They deserved to die."

Thinking back to the intruders, she wondered what reason, "*Why did they visit this place in the middle of the night.*"

"What were they looking for, Hecate?"

There was something on the console in the entranceway so she wandered over to it and picked it up. It was the visitor's book and this time she was much more careful being wary of its savage pages. Using her crystal ball for light she flicked through the book to the last page; she would get her revenge on that entry. She would rip the page out and burn it.

But what she found wasn't a source of elation.

She looked at the date - *it was the 21ˢᵗ century.*

She stood mortified. She knew that her imprisonment was long, not just from the feel of captivity, but also from the progress of technology.

"*But for this long, for years, for decades. Centuries. Oh my God. It's been all this time.*"

She stood quietly in the dark and let her breathing return to normal. She closed her eyes and tried to choke back her emotions. *For hundreds of years she had dwelled in that prison: wasted time, trapped and confined, waiting and hoping, a living death.*

Hecate was never a pretty woman - she was ugly, old and evil. However, she never felt, acted or thought of herself as old. Tears welled up in her eyes, eyes that hadn't shed a tear for eons. A brutal and savage rape of an eleven-year-old child named Hecate, was the last time tears had sprung forth. Her father was not the best of men.

Those tears had caused her to will and summon the Dark One that terrible night.

She'd overheard priests whisper to each other that God works in mysterious ways, so don't expect him to answer, not like The Devil, he always answers.

If God won't answer her prayers, then The Devil might.

He did.

She signed the contract. She had committed her soul.

She had acquired powers. She extracted revenge.

Vengeance was in her blood. She felt its fire again. Somebody was going to pay. Dave and Janet, Chelsea and JD were incidental. Someone was going to suffer for the years lost. *The man who owned the shoe.*

Wiping her moist cheek dry, her eyes focused on the floor and there it was. Her captor. The Shoe. She reached for it. And stopped.

There was a smell, an essence on it.

She bent down and absorbed its taste.

It was he.

The man in the book.

It was he.

The man whose essence had just escaped her.

Phil.

His was the last touch.

Maybe even the first touch?

Maybe even the only touch?

Maybe he was the one who placed the shoe in the wall?

Maybe he was the captor?

She had just lost him to that building.

Now she knew why the intruders had come back, to find the shoe and destroy it.

Conceal from her that he was the one.

"But he hadn't found it, Hecate, no. Luck is on my side, it was right there. And he didn't find it. I should go back, right now and kill him."

She turned towards the door and began her quest to exact her revenge, but she stopped. She took another look at the visitor's book and checked the date again.

"Who wrote this date anyway?" Hecate said aloud.

"Phil? Phil. PHIL! HIM? AGAIN?"

It was Phil's signature.

Forgetting her past skirmish with the book she went to grab the page and rip it out.

Putting the last paper cut to shame, this one was more than vicious.

Like a wolf, Hecate let out a huge blood-curdling cry. It shook the sky and earth. Inaudible to human ears but not to their souls. The town of Hecate shivered. For miles around dogs howled and cats whined. The hair on peoples' necks and arms stood on end. Even burglar alarms went off.

The first cut wasn't the deepest and she might have disregarded Phil for his trespass in time, but now?

Four strikes?

Four strikes.

It was personal.

What kind of witch would she be to let that pass?

She wasn't that kind.

Like a bullet, she soared to the highest her broomstick had ever taken her. If she could, she would have fallen from the sky like a giant meteorite, and delivered upon his soul a crushing blow. But she couldn't. He was lost in that building's labyrinth of rooms. She had no idea where he was.

Her rage poured and spewed; her green eyes concealed nothing. Only one emotion existed for Hecate. Hatred. It burned in her eyes like a green sun.

His hand delivered the dagger to her heart.

Not Twice.

Not Thrice.

4wrice.

She would plan. She would scheme.

She would conjure. She would find.

She would smite.

She circled, spiraled above the wispy clouds, her hands cold and frosting with the altitude, and looked down upon the world. She was within reaching distance of the moon, but she couldn't touch it. She was exhausted. She drifted back to Earth like a feather to the ground with a receding rage, and her anger, tempered. She headed for the belfry, emotionally spent and drained. Taking a vow does that.

CHAPTER 19.

EVEN PHIL CAN LUST.

Sometimes Phil felt that he was a jaded man, that the Gods had it in for him, or that he was doomed for some reason. Things never worked out for him; negative karma always found him. Phil didn't know how right he was.

He had been the last person to touch Hecate's shoe. Out of the hundreds of people that had handled it, he was the last. If Chelsea hadn't distracted Dave, then he would have put Hecate's shoe back into the china cabinet.

Phil had placed it on the windowsill because he was too lazy and scared to interrupt the proprietor. So, the sun and night conspired against Phil: the rays sawed through the failing thread and the night's crisp air pried the toe open.

The night Hecate secured her escape, Dave had been too tired to head down stairs and put the shoe back into the china cabinet. If he had, his essence would have been restored.

Tonight, Phil had stopped Kelly from touching the shoe as it lay on the ground before her. She had been only an inch away from it. If only he had let her pick it up, her essence would have been the one. Phil's last touch endured. Phil, the ill-fated.

Thank God he didn't know. If he had, he most surely would have committed suicide and put himself out of his misery. His life had been meaningless and jaded, so why would it change? He would have been right, one of the few times.

So, upon entering their respective rooms, Phil and Kelly bolted and chained their doors. Both turned on every light and searched their rooms, armed with gritted teeth and determination. Only after the rooms were deemed *clear,* did they collapse on their beds and start to feel genuinely safe.

Exhausted, physically and emotionally, the sortie to the B&B had done them in. Unknowingly Phil and Kelly were performing the same actions, feeling the same things, and recouping in the same manner. They hit the mini-bars. As they opened their first bottles, a flash of cold fear ripped through their beings shredding their fragile belief of safety to pieces.

Phil was watching TV and had finished his third mini-bar bottle. He was considering drinking more, Drinkmore, Deloris. The mindless chatter of some gossiping talk show faded to nothing as his eyes closed, and he fell asleep.

She danced for him, teased him, advanced upon him; she was an exotic dancer, and he was the proud Sheik. Sitting on his throne of soft silk cushions, her lace headscarves and perfume enticed him. She drew closer and closer to him, moving and swaying sexily, her hips inches from his face. Her rich rosy lips, her sensuous breath filled his lungs, he reached for her, teasingly, she pulled away, and invited him to chase with her eyes and assets. She turned around and around, Phil's hands and arms were manly and strong. He grabbed her, he pulled her close, and he turned her to face him. She was a witch.

Phil sat up in shock with his eyes wide open.

"Oh my God." It was a dream. Shaking, he got up, and looked in the mirror. His face had a look of terror.

"What's going on?" he muttered, "The B&B, the drive home, the walk to the hotel, especially that. What was that all about? I was scared shitless."

His hands were clammy and moist and he wiped them on his pants. He was still dressed. He turned the TV off, and was determined to do the same for himself. He got into the clean pressed sheets of the freshly made bed and tried to put the day's events out of his mind.

It was impossible. Tormented thoughts plagued him.

He went over the police interrogation and then Kelly's tirade. He dared visit the image of Deloris Drinkmore giving her interview, and then, the evening.

"This was where things started to get a little spooky. We entered a crime scene and became more than scared. That was to be expected. We risked being caught by the police and spending the night in jail, and probably worse. That's what caused us to be so scared" he rationalized.

"That was it, and not the sight of the slaughter, I mean murder, which caused us so much anxiety." However, he couldn't shake the feeling that their fear was disproportionately high.

"Group hysteria. Hah. That was it, and that explains the rest of the night, the drive home, and the gauntlet march from car to lobby. The bad dream." Satisfied with his analysis he finally managed to drop off.

In the adjacent room it was a different story. Kelly was less concerned with the day's events than with the lack of attention from Bill. She repeatedly ran over the last time they had been together in the office, looking for some previous overlooked act of affection. She couldn't find one. Then there was the lack of phone calls.

"Explained by this repressive and clinging wife, but surely there would have been some time when he would be away from her? He's the boss. He would have to be in the office without her for at least some of the work day. Why hadn't he called then? Phil. That's it. He doesn't want to talk to or listen to that brother of his. Fuck, he can screw my life up even when he's not trying."

Having uncovered the root cause, Kelly's mind stopped churning and she fell asleep.

CHAPTER 20.

REPEAT VISIT REQUIRED.

Phil woke up earlier than normal having had a good night's rest. He had a shower and spruced himself up a bit, getting all those little tufts of beard he normally missed.

He got started on his preliminary report. Bill would call today, to check up on the progress of the story. He got his scratchpad out, went over his notes and compiled a decent synopsis of the events. The only thing missing was a dramatic ending. Overall, the report was adequate and solid.

He called Kelly's room. "What did she expect, Bill, at this time of the morning?"

With this low note, they arranged to meet for breakfast at nine. Phil bought the morning's newspaper to have something to read while he waited. She was forty minutes late. Kelly looked pissed off though she tried not to show it.

The silence was broken by Phil's cell. It *was* Bill. He asked for Kelly. She smiled and snatched the phone out of Phil's clutching hand. After ten minutes a smiling Kelly returned the phone to Phil who was ready for Bill's questions with his notes at hand. He'd learned in the past that if he was to avoid a complete dressing down, that he had better be prepared. After receiving a mild tongue lashing, Bill told them stay an extra day to see if there were any new developments. He'll call tomorrow.

Kelly was elated that Bill called and had nicely promised her all kinds of things. She was disappointed that she had to spend another day with Phil in this god-forsaken place. Phil didn't mind staying another day, and Bill had told him the real reason was to keep Kelly at bay.

"If she was so smart, how come she didn't see it?"

Making small talk, Phil suggested, "Maybe we should pass by the police station to see if JD has been found?"

"Oh Yea, trying to find a reason to see Deloris again? Eh Phil?" she joked merrily.

As they had no leads, they decided to do just that. Kelly ribbed Phil the whole way there. "Amazing what a bit of attention from Bill can do." he thought.

Just a single block from the station, a stream of police cars with sirens blaring sped past them in the opposite direction. In a small town, this was worth following, investigating. Phil turned the car around and almost hit a parked car.

"Phil, you almost hit that car, come on, they're getting away." Kelly goaded. It was almost impossible to lose them even when they were out of sight. "You just follow the sirens." They left the city limits and headed down a country lane, and then turned into a gravel laneway.

The last police car of the posse stopped at and blocked the entrance. Phil and Kelly arrived seconds later and parked beside it. With the sirens off, it was surprisingly quiet. The police car lights flashing gave a ghostly effect to the whole scene.

From the side of the road they attempted to proceed on foot. As they marched forward, the officer in the car in front of them quickly got out, and with an outstretched hand halted their progress before they could interfere with the crime scene.

"Woah, there guys." Phil stopped dead in his tracks. Kelly ignored him and kept on going.

"Hey, OK, Ma'am, stop right there." The officer moved to intercept Kelly. She turned and walked straight towards him not in the least perturbed by authority.

"So, what's going on?" she demanded in an equally commanding tone.

"Stand back Ma'am." Another officer appeared with police crime scene tape and both of them started to tape off the entrance to the gravel laneway.

Kelly wasn't put off in the least. "Hey, hey, what's going on? Hey come on, we're reporters." The two officers both zeroed in on Kelly who was now leaning against the tape and stretching it.

"OK, Ma'am, you need to step back from the tape, Ma'am" the original officer told her in an annoyed voice.

"OK, OK, I'm sorry officer. Sorry, got a little excited there you know. Sorry, look standing back." She took a step back as he'd requested.

"Look, look. Gap, gap." It was funny, and the two cops couldn't help themselves and laughed.

While the cops were hitting on Kelly, Phil pretended to be preoccupied with his cell. Phil's whole life had been spent not being noticed, it was natural. He moved closer to the tape. With his head bent down, he watched the police lower a body from a tree; it looked like he was hanged.

"Oh my god." He recognized JD from the picture Deloris had given him. "It's JD for sure. Well this is a new development. Someone had hung JD. I could hardly recognize him. His face looks really weathered and battered.

Two policemen delicately clasped JD's torso, as another cut the jumper cables with the 'jaws of life' sheet metal cutters. They stood on the back of a rusty old pickup truck parked almost exactly under the swinging corpse, JD's pickup. The officers showed a great deal of respect, something that surprised Phil. Solemnly, they placed JD onto one of the black body bags spread out on the ground.

"Two body bags, where's the other body and who is it?" wondered Phil. "There, by the trunk of the tree."

At the roots, a car blanket traced the raised outline of a second body. Finished with JD, the two officers moved over to the other corpse, and while Kelly and the two officers were flirting, the world learnt its identity.

"Chelsea." whispered Phil to himself.

The body of the young girl wearing a nightgown lay exposed to the morning sun. Phil had seen Chelsea in life. Rebellious, self-centered and trying, but full of life and fight. The Chelsea, in the body bag, was not the same person. Her face, that of a sixty-year-old, her body wracked and withered, she looked like life and soul had long gone before death found her.

"Thank God," thought Phil with compassion, "that her parents aren't around to have to identify the body." The body bag was zipped from foot to head and as the zip brought the two sides together, it closed around her face.

Phil felt a deep loss for Chelsea, for JD, for youth lost and for potentials unfulfilled. He remembered this line for his report, and he wasn't being cold-hearted or disrespectful.

He tuned in to Kelly and the cops. "The crafty vixen," he thought, "listen to her, she's getting the scoop out of them and they don't even know it."

Phil didn't take much time to put it all together. "JD had gone over to Chelsea's house. The parents weren't going to let her go out. Chelsea had lost it and had stabbed one of them. The other parent fought back and tried to disarm her. JD defended her and suddenly, both parents were dead. They tried to stage the scene as a satanic murder. Chelsea and JD went into hiding. She started to have remorse and wanted to turn herself in. JD didn't want to. He feared an adult trial. No, he didn't want to confess at all. Staging the crime scene like that, they would be crucified, by the press, the cops, the public. Chelsea and JD quarreled. They fought. It went too far; he didn't mean to kill her. Now, filled with remorse, his life in ruins, he takes his own."

"Yep, it's going to be a field day. And I'm in the middle of it, the biggest story of my career." beamed Phil. All compassion gone, all remorse and sorrow to the wind. He just saw a big paycheck. He imagined an American tragedy. What were the signs that this was going to happen? Why didn't the school system recognize them? What's our city doing to help our adolescents in distress? How can we avoid tragedies of this nature?

"Big story eh Phil, and it's ours." Kelly had finished charming the force, and was now standing next to Phil, and smiling widely. She had worked the scene and had sneakily obtained the official line, and they were off to the races.

"Now to be fair, Kelly it's my story." said Phil. "I'm the..."

Kelly exploded. "What the fuck are you talking about, your story. Look buster, if you think for one second that this is your story; then you've got another thing coming. We're in this together, God forbid; I didn't spend three days in your miserable company for fuck all. Bill sent *us* here together, to get the story, and that's what we've done. You fucking great blow hard." She stormed off down the gravel lane, in dress shoes.

Phil was in shock.

"It's my story." he told himself weakly. "I was the one at the B&B before the murder. I was the one who slept there. It was me who knew the proprietors Dave and Janet, and Chelsea, sort of. I was the one questioned for their murders, me. It's my story. Mine."

"Now you're in trouble buddy." laughed one of the officers.

"Yep." said the other "Nothing for you tonight." followed by louder, course laughter and comments.

Phil hardly heard them, but he was embarrassed enough to quickly get into his car and close the door. He was wondering what to do. First, get away from those hyenas and then stop and think. He started up the car and reversed back up the laneway. In the rearview mirror he could see Kelly stumbling.

"I have to catch up and talk reason to her." So, Phil turned the car around and then tentatively crept up to Kelly. He wound the passenger window down and shouted across the void.

"Get in, let me explain."

Flustered, he tried again, "Kelly, get in, let me explain, please."

She looked at him silently and raised her middle finger.

"Come on Kelly, get in."

She ignored him and with determination she ploughed on ahead.

Phil stopped the car and watched her walk away. He was lost.

Just sitting and thinking, Phil sat in his car contemplating his next move. She had turned the corner and had disappeared out of sight, that was about five minutes ago. A calculation Phil was relying on. Hopefully time would cool her temper.

"If she knows I can't see her, she'll slow down as she'll be scared of getting too far out of range." It was a long walk to town, so he figured that she would be tired and would accept his offer of a lift, and then they could talk it out.

"It's still my story." he affirmed to himself. He put the car back in gear and drove around the corner. She was gone.

CHAPTER 21.

SOMETHING OF A BAD DAY.

Phil ground to a halt. If he thought he was lost before, no words could describe how he felt now. How had he missed her? Was she hiding in the bushes? Phil had no idea about women. He put the car into reverse and backed around the corner. He did a full three sixty. Spraying gravel, he launched the car forward and looked forward, backwards, and side to side. Now he'd driven further than she could possibly have walked.

"Something's happened to her." He didn't like the conclusion that jumped into his mind. With the freaky things that they had seen felt and experienced recently, anything was possible.

Murder and abduction crossed his mind. "What should I do? Am I wrong about the whole thing? Is the murderer still out there?

Should he report Kelly as a missing person? Where had she gone? What's happened to her? Think. Phil. What should I do?"

In a daze, he parked in a strip mall attempting to weigh his options, but his mind kept going around in circles. He gave in and got a coffee. A little fresher, but still with no plan, Phil went back to the car and just started driving. Around a corner he saw a police car parked diagonally across the road. He was at Deloris's house. Phil pulled over and with one foot in the car and the other on the road he leaned on the open door, and watched a sobbing Deloris being led towards an open police car door. Was the policeman was supporting her or arresting her? She continued to wail and scream.

When she looked in Phil's direction, she recognized him and cried out. "Phil. Phil, Phil, please." Phil's heart went out to her and he started to move towards her.

"Hold it right there lover boy." the officer yelled.

"Hell, the police are so rude." Phil thought.

"They're taking me to the morgue Phil."

She climbed into the cramped back seat as it was occupied with someone. Then the police vehicle sped off towards the hospital. Having no choice, Phil tailed the cruiser still worried about Kelly.

By the time Phil had paid for parking and had found a spot, all signs of Deloris and the police had gone. In the hospital, a busy nurse toiled behind a small reception desk, and ignored Phil.

"Where's the morgue?" asked Phil, a third time.

She finally replied. "Who are you, sir?"

Flustered, Phil was about to answer, when he saw a board of signs right above the nurse's head. "Mortuary." The sign pointed left.

"Moron" Phil thought to himself as he turned and went down the left-hand corridor.

"Sir." she called after him in a loud voice.

"You ignore me, I'll ignore you." Pushing through double doors, he strode down the corridor passing a couple of gurneys. He followed the signs, went down a stairwell and into the morgue.

"Deloris." said Phil swiftly followed by, "Kelly! You're here."

He looked at their faces and he knew that they'd been talking.

Kelly had stormed off from Phil and had seen a police car on the road in front of her. She tapped on the window, and in a bold move, told the driver that the officers Baker and Bowyer, the two cops she had been flirting with, had said she could get a lift to the police station.

"That would be you, yeah?" She had asked through the now open cruiser window.

"Get in." the officer said in a commanding voice and off he drove.

Kelly had struck up a buoyant conversation with the man when a crackling radio interrupted them with its request.

"Officer Evans: proceed to the residence of a Deloris Drinkmore and escort her to the morgue, she's required for the identification of a body."

"Listen Kelly." They were on first name basis. "I can't take you back to the station as I have to..."

"Forgive me for eavesdropping Officer Evans, but I happen to know Deloris, and maybe she would like some company to the morgue. I mean, it's not a place anyone would want to go to alone, and since she kicked out that asshole husband of hers, she's got no one to lean on."

As she seemed to know Deloris quite well and as it seemed to be actually quite a good idea, Officer Evans agreed to the proposition and headed off to Deloris' house.

Phil looked at Kelly and then at Deloris. They were tight. Not knowing what to say, and completely lost on how Kelly was here, he couldn't help himself.

"Kelly, how did you get here? I mean, I looked all over for…"

"What do you care, Phil, eh, you selfish bastard. You think it's your story eh, Phil? Kelly here, don't count for nothing. She ain't done nothing eh? It's all you, eh? You answer me, Phil?" said Deloris with words that stung.

Phil began to defend himself, but before he could even get one word out, Deloris continued. "And Kelly, not only done all that work with the police, but then she came here with me and comforted me. When I saw poor JD's body there. And you; where were you? Can't even get here on time to… to…" She broke down crying. Kelly took her into her arms and held her, she looked over to Phil and smiled wickedly, yeah, she knew this was breaking Phil's heart.

"Let him keep his God damn story.

Phil stood alone and said nothing. He was of the opinion that whatever he said or did, would just make things worse. If he tried to give comfort to Deloris; if he said he was sorry to Kelly, the result would be a tirade. As normal, Phil chose his default defense tactic; he said nothing. Deloris sobbed and sobbed, and Kelly hung onto her, extracting every ounce of torment from Phil that she could.

Slowly, the crying subsided, and Kelly released Deloris from her grip. Deloris saw that Phil and Kelly had to talk, so she shuffled away from them and sat down on a bench next to the wall.

"I thought he was a nice guy?" she thought to herself, as she watched Phil slowly approach Kelly.

"Kelly." Phil started, "I'm sorry, it's our story, ours. Sorry."

"Yeah, too right it is." and she stormed off again, leaving Phil and Deloris alone. Phil finally had enough courage to go over to the bench and sit down beside her. Eventually Deloris said. "I'm going."

Phil sighed, "She didn't even ask if I could drive her home. What was that?" Just as she rounded the corner of the corridor, she gave Phil a long glance over her shoulder.

"Should I follow her?" He asked himself. Phil didn't understand women at all.

Kelly had taken a taxi back to the hotel and had her suitcase packed. This was the end of the trip - of the double murder of Hecate report. She was going home no matter what. She had had enough of Phil, enough of gawking policemen. She picked up her cell and dialed Bill back at HQ. He didn't pick up.

Phil had never been on such a strenuous, emotionally draining reporting assignment. He drove to the police station where the mood was upbeat and cheery. Despite the tragic deaths of four people, the good news was that the police had their man and they'd closed the case. He asked the sergeant if he could use a small nook to write his report. After describing a brief outline revolving around a slightly embellished role of the local police, they gave Phil a plush desk and he sat down to work.

Phil's mental notes from the morning poured out of his pen like water out of a tap. He invited the sergeant in for proofing, by the look on the man's face Phil had hit the target and a hearty slap on the back confirmed it. He titled it, "*Police Close Gruesome Homicides in Record Time. A story by The Investigative Reporting Team. Phil and Kelly: reporting from the brave town of Hecate.*" His two-hundred-word limit ended up being six hundred words. It just couldn't be précised and keep its identity.

"Let Bill do whatever with it, I'm tired, and the story is the story." Phil sounded quite bitter; he was bushed.

"The fax machine is over there, be my guest." said the sergeant. When the last beep of the fax machine sounded, Phil looked around the police station, recalling his interrogation and all the events that followed, and left as quickly as possible. It was a job well done despite all the histrionics and tantrums. Indeed, it was sweet, even though there had been times when he had been scared out of his pants.

He sighed. "Back to the hotel to hear the music." A resigned Phil headed home.

~~~

Bill had been in the office all day, working hard on various stories, and doing his best to fill a paper that was sadly lacking. There were no stories on the boil. On days like this, the editor went to the well, retrieved one from the sad story shelf, and pumped it up as if the entire world depended on it. His job was to sell papers any way he could. Bill was a damn good editor, but today, it just didn't happen, until his door opened and the secretary dropped Phil's fax right in front of him.

"It's from *The Investigative Reporting Team.*" she announced.

He picked it up. "Spicy." he said and devoured the six hundred words in seconds.

"Damn. Jackpot." Bill was at odds with himself. He certainly didn't want his little snot nosed brother to score, but he needed this bad today. Suddenly a wicked thought went through his mind.

"I could give all the credit to Kelly. Bad idea. Might give her the wrong idea, besides people already know this is Phil's story." Oh well, chalk one up for the kid. Shit, the kid saved my ass."

"Hey, do we have a couple of pictures of Phil and Kelly on file. Dig them up, put them together like a real estate couple and indent them inside the story. Print the story as is, page 3. New Column, *The Investigative Reporting Team.* Roll them."

Happy with the way the day had turned out, begrudgingly thanking his brother, he pressed the flashing light for line one on the four-line phone. Expecting to have his wife on the other end he was surprised to hear a man's voice.

"Hello is there a Bill…" a person's voice said.

"Chief Inspe…" said Bill instantly recognizing the distant voice. He knew all the big wigs.

"Got me first time as always Bill, how you doing?" said an authoritative tone.

"Business is good, stories not as glamorous as when you were… you know. Cleaning house. How's it going?"
~~~

"No complaints, got anything boiling?"

"No, just had a good one though, by my loser brother no less." said Bill.

"Still riding his sorry ass then I see."

"Yeah. Still." said an unrepentant Bill.

"Well send the lackey over to Boleyn, 'cos we've got a doozy. Crucifixion, but you didn't hear it from me." The call ended abruptly.

"Sounds like a job for *The Investigative Reporting Team*" Bill laughed. He punched line two and called them.

~~~

Phil had reluctantly arrived at the hotel, worried to see her.

He couldn't delay it anymore. He knocked on Kelly's door and waited for the argument. She didn't answer, so he knocked again. He was actually relieved that she hadn't answered and was about to give up when his cell rang. He answered it expecting Kelly.

"Bill, hi." said Phil in a tired voice.

Kelly's door flew open and she reached out and grabbed Phil's cell. "Give me that." She slammed the door shut in his face.

Phil wearily sat down on the floor with his back leaning against her door with head in hands.

He could hear Kelly laughing for what seemed like hours. Then without warning, the door opened causing Phil to fall into her room.

"Get out, and he wants to talk to you." She threw the phone at him as he struggled on all fours to crawl away. He felt the door against his feet as she impatiently shoved him into the hall.

He picked up the phone and said "Bill?"

"Yeah, Phil, its Bill, who did you think it'll be?" he said nastily.

"Yeah, OK, what's up?" said Phil, ignoring the gibe.

"OK, I've talked to Kelly and she's right on board, there's been another *Crucifixion* or so I've been led to believe. It's a couple of states over from where you are, and I want *The Investigating Reporting Team* to *investigate and report*, he said in a whiny voice. Kelly has all the details. By the way, why couldn't you come up with *The Investigating Reporting team?* I bet she's doing everything." The phone went dead.

~~~

"Just my lousy luck." thought Deloris, "I always fall for the jerks, thought this one was different. I thought I'd got lucky. "Jez', he didn't follow, how much more obvious does a woman have to get? Shit." she sat down in front of the TV and cried. When JD was home, he stayed in his bedroom and watched TV, or did other things with friends, girls. It had left Deloris with the rest of the house for her devices, or vices. But the house seemed so empty now even though not much had changed, she really needed some company. Phil should have been it, but Phil was too non-worldly to get her advance. "She hit the liquor cabinet; a kitchen cupboard.

"God damn, I'm out."

~~~

Phil laid down on his bed and fell into a fitful sleep. Before he dozed off, his one consolation for the night was that she had told Bill that '*The Investigating Reporting Team*' was her idea. "Finally: a bit of ammunition." When he woke up, the sun had already been down for a couple of hours and a growl in his stomach told him he was hungry. A strange feeling, called self-esteem, flirted with him for a moment. He put his jacket on and left the hotel.

He bought a takeout at a Lebanese dive and ate it in his car,

"How was she doing? I wonder if she needs a shoulder to cry on? I'll pass by her house just to see how she is." He gathered courage while driving there; he imagined how he could waltz up to the front door and sweep Deloris off her feet, but when he pulled up in front of her place for real, it was a different matter.

"Just do it." And gritting his teeth, he did.

He walked up to her front door and knocked. He waited, knocked again. His hands were damp and clammy, his shoulders hunched over, "I'm so pathetic." Fear was beginning to take control. "How can I be this nervous about knocking on a pretty woman's door? Please don't be in. Go. Phil, get out while she's not answering." He turned and was about to run back to the sanctuary of his car, before he reached into his pants and retrieved his wallet. He pulled out a card that had his cell number on it and pushed it under the door. Then fled like a little boy running from the school bully.
~~~

"My God, I'll be glad when I'm out of this town; I used to be a normal guy, now I'm a blithering wreck. Scared shitless yesterday by an empty house, oh, and in the hotel car park, and now, the same here, just knocking on Deloris's door. Better go in case she comes back."

The rain, predicted for the evening, had started to come down, just as Phil started the car. In his rush to get out of there, he'd forgotten to turn his lights and windshield wipers on. He flicked the switches, just in time to see a figure dodge out of his way, an arm waving, as if trying to attract his attention.

"I think I just got the finger. Yeah, that was it. Was it a woman?"

If the lights had been on a fraction earlier, he would have recognized Deloris walking on the sidewalk returning from the liquor store. A bottle in one hand and the other outstretched, waving at Phil's leaving car.

Deloris swore. "Shit, I can't believe it, and now it's raining hard." She didn't have an umbrella, so she ran as best she could for the last fifty yards to her house. Closing the door behind her, she flicked the light switch but it didn't come on. She was just about to swear, when a knock at the door interrupted her.

"Phil. He did see me." She quickly turned and opened the door without looking through the window.

Her scream pierced the night. The open door didn't reveal the man that would keep her warm and comforted. The bottle fell to the floor, and Hecate stepped over it as she entered the house and advanced towards a retreating Deloris.

Deloris's blood drained from her body, sending chills down her spine and soul. Dim green light made the house shadowy and dark. The hall light flickered, but only to accentuate Hecate's face. Ghostly pale images danced over the floor and walls as Hecate's silhouette filled Deloris's vision.

She backed into the house until cornered. There was no means of escape. Hecate started to grin like a cat over a captured wounded bird. Deloris felt her back against the wall. She could back up no further and with the advancing Hecate, she started to slide down it. Hecate ordered the front door shut and with a loud slam, it did. Deloris jumped causing Hecate to scream with laughter. She continued her advance until she stood over a sprawling defeated Deloris.

"So, you're his lover, are you dear?" Hecate accused Deloris. "Does he make you happy, dear?"

Deloris looked up from the floor but couldn't speak.

"Answer me." she shouted, cowering over her.

She managed to stutter. "Who are you? What do you want?"

"Answer me you whore. You're his lover? Answer me or I'll kill you."

"Who?" was the weak response.

"Phil, that's who, you little slut." Hecate said. She bent down and forced her face into Deloris'.

"Slut?" Deloris said. "You called me a Slut?" Inches from the hideous face, she found some fight triggered by the insult.

People had called Deloris a slut since she was a teenager and she had fought it all her life. Now, this disgusting creature had burst into her house, attacked her, forced her to the ground, and accused her being a slut. This caused her blood to flow for the first time since she had opened the door. She hated that word, and her blood began to boil.

"SLUT?" screamed Deloris back into Hecate's face, not knowing Hecate was a witch. She grabbed the witch's gown and threw her violently onto the floor. Deloris punched and kicked landing many flailing fists and abuse. She sat on top of the witch and pounded. For a brief moment Deloris was the witch's equal, but it was impossible to maintain such intensity. And in the split second it took for realization and doubt to enter, Hecate took command.

"Get off me you slut." The command threw Deloris against the wall. However, Deloris had lost her son that day, she needed an outlet for her pent up anger. With veins filled with adrenaline; she wasn't defeated yet. She fought to get to her feet, pawing at the ground with hands and feet and swearing louder than ever, then, standing up, she charged for the intruder. It was her last hurrah.

Hecate, losing patience, rose up off the floor without using her hands or feet. The little scrap was fun, but now it was time to dominate and dispatch this immoral woman. She locked her stare on Deloris and sailed through the air, through a torrent of fists and obscenity, and grabbed Deloris's throat in a windpipe-crushing grip. It winded Deloris and stopped her dead.

Suddenly Deloris turned from a ferocious wildcat with a fighting chance of survival, into a mouse that had sprung the trap. She wheezed for air but to no avail. Hecate retained her grip on the failing prey, and again pulled her face to face. Rank breath spewed forth as she watched her spirit and remaining strength drain.

Within seconds, Deloris succumbed to the intensity and hunger of Hecate's stare. Her legs buckled beneath her and she hung in the grasp of Hecate's hand like a child's ragdoll. The remainder of Deloris's inner strength was vanished and Hecate began to savor the offering.

"You know, your son put up a good fight, he did this." she pointed to her bruised nose.

"I can see that he got the fire from you." Hecate pointed at her, at her heart.

Deloris barely registered these words, yet she felt pride and love at the mention of her son.

"I strung him up, he's paid his dues." It was bitter news.

Her son hadn't committed suicide and probably hadn't committed the terrible crimes either. Life returned to Deloris's eyes, but in the grasp of Hecate's boney, strong hands, the fleeting light couldn't survive long. The grip tightened, it was an unrelenting, suffocating, life-terminating clasp.

"But you bore him, now it's time to pay your fee. And then after I have you, I'll kill your lover, Phil." whispered Hecate into Deloris's ear, and even from there, Deloris wanted to choke at the smell of her breath.

The final glimmer of defiance left her. She abandoned hope and accepted despair. Deloris's head fell forward but Hecate retained her hold; she didn't want another JD incident. Minutes passed until Hecate, certain this time, let Deloris go. She fell and disappeared into Hecate's grinning frame.

Hecate breathed heavily. Deloris was a big soul to absorb. It was like giving birth only backwards. Hecate could not bear the weight and she sat down cross-legged on the floor and panted like a large dog. She closed her eyes. The pleasure was intoxicating. The warmth passed through every morsel of her body, every cell tingled, and every hair stood on end. This was good. She waited; she was in no hurry. She sighed. Life had never been better.

As Hecate got up to leave, she saw something on the floor in front of the door. It was a little rectangle, a stiff white card. On it was the neatest writing she had ever seen.

A string of meaningless numbers did little for her. But a word jumped off the business card like a neon light. She smelt it and almost fainted.

It was him.

"Phil."

Life couldn't get better?

It just had.

CHAPTER 22.

BETTER START TO THE DAY.

Phil was in the dimension that lingers between sleep and denial to get up. He insisted on sleep, but his body called for action, that is, food. As he got up, he remembered yesterday and hoped for a better day today. He put the escapade at Deloris's house out of his mind and was thankful that Kelly was in the dark. Bill's phone call, even though it was rude, curt and mean, provided Phil with an ace to play.

Trying not to think about his recent failures with the two women, he got into the shower. Feeling ten times better than he did yesterday, he dressed and turned on the TV. Flipping from channel to channel, he didn't see one mention of any additional double murder, other than that of the closed case here in Hecate.

"Great. We're not too far behind." He turned off the TV, put his jacket on, and was exiting the room when the phone rang.

He rushed and snatched it off its cradle. "Deloris?"

"No, it's Kelly. Were you expecting Deloris? I can get off the line if you like?" And she hung up.

"Shit." said Phil, "I haven't even got out of the room, I haven't even met Kelly yet and already she's got me cornered. Shit. Now what do I do? Wait? Pretend I just said the wrong name."

Kelly was flat out on her bed laughing and laughing. "This made up for Bill wanting to talk to Phil and not me. But why didn't he answer when I called, but he phoned Phil instead? Thought he hated him. Sure, Phil's the reporter, but hey, not anymore. He put my name on his report. Little toady, he wouldn't have unless I made him do so. My first story, page Three, *The Investigative Reporting Team* and now we're - I'm on a second case already. Pity it's with Phil. Still, he does all the work, well the writing anyway, Bill said it was pretty good stuff too. Which meant it was really good so actually we did a damn good job.

Phil had decided the best thing to do was just nothing; as per normal. He was lying on the bed, when the phone rang again. This time he knew it was Kelly.

"Hello Kelly."

"May I speak to *a* Phil please, it's Deloris speaking." Kelly mocked. "Today will be a great day. On the long trip to Boleyn, Phil will drive, I'll sleep, and if I don't, I'll just tease and bug Phil, you know what… I think I'll stay awake." she mused.

"Yes, Kelly, what?" Phil scoffed.

"Now don't get snarky with me Phil. Just having a bit of fun. Just trying to lighten the mood for the long day ahead. Breakfast. Meet you downstairs in five."

Phil sighed and went down for breakfast, expecting Kelly to be late as always. She wasn't.

"What. You start before me? What kind of guy are you?" Speechless, he pretended he couldn't reply because his month was full.

"Anyway, never mind. We have to go to Boleyn to investigate another double murder crucifixion. Strange, eh? Another job for *The Investigative Reporting Team.* I told Bill that was my idea. To make up for you not wanting to share the story. It's a long drive, so we leave straight after breakfast" And that was that. Phil didn't have a say.

CHAPTER 23.

YOU'VE GOTTA HAVE A NEWT'S FOOT.

When Hecate coasted to her home in the belfry, she was heady with glee. She had not only acquired the bait required to lure the man *she now hated* to his death, but also a means of finding him. She had a piece of him, a fragment of his essence. Here in her hand was his card, his smell. She took the precious cargo back to the belfry and carefully stored it in a secure spot. She couldn't afford to lose this connection to a sweet slaying. She could leave Deloris and Phil together in each other's dying arms.

"Oh, how delicious."

Squeezing the card tightly into a crack in the wooden floorboards, she whipped off into the night. She had some shopping to do. The majority of her witch spells required a newt. She landed by a small stream and using her crystal ball's delicate light as a lure, she waited silently as a mouse. She went over all the ingredients that she needed. It had been a long time since she had used such a spell and she had to think hard.

She almost let out a wild cackle, but suppressed it, knowing she'd never get a newt if she did. She stayed for hours before she got one, the sun had been up for almost an hour. She kept it alive in an old kettle she found on the banks of the creek. To stop it from escaping she plugged the spout with a bit of old cloth.

"Soon." she thought, "it'll be simmering in there." After stealthily flying home to the belfry, she bedded down for the day. The coming night would entail more hunting.

The day's sleep had been good for her as it reminded her of other forgotten ingredients. At night break, she was out and about. She had a list of things to get. "Must have really been concentrating on *newt-ting*."

She sailed around the countryside gathering her groceries. Dock weed taproot, hazel bristles, stinging nettle fur, lupin seeds, and rose hips. Rabbit dropping and raccoon claw, bat teeth. "Get that back at the belfry." Virgin's breath. "Got some of that from that Chelsea girl."

By the time she had assembled all, daybreak was under way and she knew she was pushing her luck. "Better be getting back to the belfry, that's two days in a row."

Daylight didn't harm her; but a witch hunt did. Religious and self-righteous ordinary people hunt and kill them, if they can. Daylight and witches don't mix.

Only minutes passed as she swooped in through the window of the belfry like a falcon. She hoped and prayed that no one had seen her. She had got a lot fitter these last couple of days, and she needed to be. The test she would soon face was severe. She settled down, tidied herself and went to sleep.

Up at twilight, she started a little fire and put the kettle on.

"Nice addition to the home." she thought as a pot simmered over smoldering embers. The collection of ingredients sat crushed, ground or chopped on the belfry beams. They obediently waited in isolated little pyramids to fulfill their destiny. Different sized portions from each food group found their way into the simmering broth. Sometimes little chants accompanied their application.

The brew fulfilled its promise as it began to percolate nicely. She watched the scum slowly creep across the top of the liquid. The instant it completely covered the top, she touched the middle of the brew with Phil's card, and ferociously uttered his name over and over again. With every iteration of his name, Hecate's hold on the card required more effort, until she pulled on the card with both hands.

With a snap, she fell back off her feet onto the floorboards. She won the battle for the card. "Finito." Using the corner of her cloak, she pulled the kettle off the charcoals and inspected it.

The liquid was clear, no trace of scum remained, and it steamed with an evil look. Hecate let it cool down before testing it. She took the card and passed it over the top of the concoction. It was a good brew as the liquid followed the card from side to side. For the final test she held the card close to the surface: the liquid piled up upon itself, trying to reach up and grab it. It was ready.

The tiny mound of liquid collapsed as Hecate removed the card and put it in her cloak. When it was cool enough, she poured it into a cup and drank it. It didn't taste good - part of making a spell. She sat down with her back against the wall and waited for the reaction.

Starting in the pit of her stomach, a warm sickly feeling slowly spread through her body, producing a strong feeling of anxiety. She breathed and calmed herself. For the spell to work she knew she had to surrender to it; allow it to envelop her whole being. As the spell progressed through her body her feeling of anxiety intensified along and an urge to stop. If she capitulated and rejected the spell's invasion, death was a possibility.

So, Hecate let the sickly feeling transverse her torso, over her shoulders and down her arms while it simultaneously crept down her lower extremities. She fought off panic as the feeling entered her hands and feet. She feared she might lose control or even be lost, and dread gnawed her sole with the thought that once the spell engulfed her, would it release or become her? It was all part of the test. It travelled the remaining inches down her fingers and toes, and down their respective nails. Hecate struggled with the irresistible urge to retreat, to break the spell.

Her unconditional surrender cast the hex.

She was not a novice with spells.

She stood up and looked around. Night was upon her, the perfect time. She hopped onto her broomstick, soared into the dark sky and headed for the hotel where Phil lived.

But it didn't feel right. When she hovered to a standstill over the building, it resulted in a gentle tug in another direction. There was only one conclusion. He had gone.

"The Bastard." She was livid. It left her with no choice.

Like a homing pigeon, she flew in wider and wider concentric circles, higher and higher. She felt his faint trace, his signal. She controlled her panic. It meant he was a long way away.

"Damn those horseless carriages and damn this new world and all its newfangled inventions too." She followed the scent like a bloodhound.

Her progress was slow; sometimes the signal became weak, so she had to perform the concentric circle maneuver just to be certain she was going the right way. At night, that wasn't an issue, but daylight had donned. She cursed her luck and Phil alike. She should have found and laid him to waste by now. Instead, she was in the throes of a major sojourn without an end in sight, and worst still it was a bright, sunny day.

Feeding off her hatred, she forged ahead knowing that the spell wouldn't last. The weakness of the scent indicated that she was not even close to finding him.

The extra weight of Deloris also meant that she couldn't sustain a decent speed, and she required frequent stops to rest. She was beginning to think the abduction of Deloris was a mistake, as she twisted and churned inside of her even as Hecate gnawed and preyed on her soul. The energy she obtained from her was only a little more than that spent on quelling her rebellion.

Instead of easy high altitude, cloud covered cruising; her progress was exhausting, exposed and exasperating. But her persistence finally began to pay as the signal became stronger and clearer. She was starting to gain ground.

Confidence was beginning to well up in her heart. And then the signal changed direction and started to dissipate. She knew exactly what had happened.

"Shit. God damn those horseless carriages. He's in one of them. Damn it, they go so fast and so far, now I'm falling behind. Bugger, after coming so far, I could end up losing him. God, how I hate that Phil."

CHAPTER 24.

Joan's Dream House.

Zack and Joan had dreamed of this house since they got married four years ago. They were a mature couple who had met on an Internet dating service. Their high compatibility scores were evident, they did have a lot in common, especially that both loved the idea of retiring to the country. So, they began to tour quaint little villages and towns off the beaten track. One day they found an old house on a big water front lot on the outskirts of a small town. It was a farmhouse that, at one time, was the dominant structure of several concessions. The land was severed with successive generations, and now was just a large farmhouse on a large lot.

When they saw it and saw the 'For Sale' sign, they stopped the car in disbelief and excitement. With the car parked in the driveway, they walked around the building and the grounds. They looked in the windows with cupped hands and imagined where the couch and TV would go. Almost half an hour passed, musing and swooning over the place, until they couldn't find a reason not to make a phone call.

"So how much do you think it is Joan?" Zack asked his wife.

"I don't know, why don't you phone the real estate agent?"

Zack pulled out his cell and typed in the numbers then hung up on the first ring.

"What happened?" asked Joan.

Zack just pointed. The next-door neighbors, a couple of hundred feet away, had just pulled into their driveway. "Let's go. Get in."

Joan jumped into the crossover and Zack drove to the neighbors in a flash. They hit it off, and Zack, with some good inside knowledge, made the call.

Zack and Joan became proud new owners of one of the oldest properties in the state. It was in move in condition, just; but the joyful couple wasn't particularly worried. Zack was quite the handyman and Joan was no slouch either. With their respective children all grown up and out of the picture, molding the house into the dream they wanted was a good way to fill time.

Their future neighbors had told them it was a heritage building, and renovations required approval from the Heritage Foundation. Due to this certification, they could apply for grants to cover the additional costs. Being a retired civil servant, much to the foundation's gall, Joan embraced the paperwork and bureaucracy. All the professionally drawn up plans and blueprints were in place per the approval requirements and permits were granted.

The dream house however had a personality of its own. It was obstinate and temperamental. It pitched obstructions into the path of the renovations at every opportunity.

Doggedly, Zack accepted every setback and thrived on each new challenge it presented. Just as Joan had conquered bureaucratic bumbling at city hall, Zack proved he was made of stern stuff himself, just like his dad, Doug. The McKay way.

However, he couldn't face down every obstacle alone, not that Joan didn't pull her weight. She worked so hard he was worried she would hurt herself. Concerned, as some of the jobs were larger and heavier than they looked, Zack had hired a contractor, a local man called Paddy. He was a big man with a reputation for brawling, but if you ignored his checkered past, he had what it took for the job; he was cheap. Zack's neighbors, who had quickly become good friends, questioned his judgment on Paddy's employment.

"Paddy is annoying, single minded and abrasive, but a damn good worker. Skilled, willing, able and honest (and cheap)" Zack countered.

Against all odds, Zack and Paddy managed to achieve a level of understanding that baffled the neighborhood. Nevertheless, because both had 'my way or the highway' attitudes, major incidents occurred. These discussions blew over like storms. Together, they bent the house to their will, and over time, gained the upper hand.

That was until, one last remaining wall. There was just something about it, which put the two at loggerheads.

"It's a supporting wall." Zack had made up this excuse to avoid its demolition. He just didn't like its feel. Something that was impossible to explain.

The supporting wall argument prevailed, putting him at odds with Paddy, again. They had accomplished so much. As the work approached the end, the destiny of the wall was argued over and over. It wasn't long before Paddy barraged Zack with wall related jokes, taunts and barbs.

"Tear down the wall will yer Zack."

"Zack McKay couldn't make hay; the wall was in the way."

"Zack McKay, where is he? Oh, he's behind the wall."

"Zack McKay, make the call, tear down the wall."

Gritting his teeth, Zack McKay tied to ignore the childish heckling.

"Ball, wall."

"Small, wall."

"Christ Paddy. You and that wall." interrupted Zack.

"Hey, don't you take the Lord's name in vain." Paddy waded in. "Come on Zack, we've done the whole house for God's sake. We've done a great job, it's beautiful, and it's just a wall."

"Name in vain? Man, you're one to talk. Anyway, yeah, I know the place is coming together, and I know we've really done a fine job, but I don't like the feel of this wall. I think we should re-plaster it, refine it, but leave it standing." said Zack.

"Zack, we've gone over this a thousand times. The wall has to come down. Look, even Joan don't want it, it ain't holding up nothing, look, let me pick up that big old sledgehammer and..."

"Listen, Paddy no, the wall stays."

"Fuck you, it don't do nothing for the house, can't you see that you fucking idiot." His heavy Irish accent accentuated every word.

"Don't you be calling me a fucking idiot."

It was bound to happen, and the two started fighting. Paddy larger, younger and more practiced had Zack beat in seconds. With Zack in a bear hug, they swung around in a circle and smashed into the wall, destroying it completely. Slats, plaster and dust flew everywhere. When the dust settled, the two looked up from the floor.

"Told you it weren't no supporting wall."

Lied Zack laughing and Paddy joined in.

Together the two knocked out the remaining, hanging, pieces and corners with the sledgehammer. Where the wall once stood; a beautiful empty space now reigned. Zack had to admit it; the house looked better, more spacious and cleaner.

"OK, we'll shove all the debris into the corner for tonight. Tomorrow, clean up those edges; re-plaster the wall and the ceiling. That will take the whole day, then the following day we'll level out the floor ready for the slate next week."

"Sounds like a plan, see you tomorrow tough guy." Paddy slapped Zack on the back, headed for the door, and crossed himself as he left. The crucifix was the first thing Joan had put up in the house.

"Hey, aren't you going to help shovel this stuff into the skip." moaned Zack.

"Tomorrow, like you said, we'll clean up tomorrow when the job's done, don't you ever listen, even to yourself?" He left with the both of them laughing heartily. They had started to become friends.

With Paddy gone, Zack picked up the wide bristled broom and started sweeping debris into a corner of the now much larger room. As he swept, something caught the corner of his eye, and before he thought to stop and uncover it, he heard the front door open as Joan entered the house.

"Hello." she chimed.

Zack leaned on the broom as he waited for her to peer around the corner to see how things had progressed. She stepped forward excitedly into the room.

"Woah there sweetheart, the floor's really dirty."

"So, you decided to remove the wall after all, Paddy convinced you hey?"

"Not at all, we had a..." thinking about his words now, as there was no way he wanted to tell her that he got into a fight.

"No, yeah, he... No. I thought, after thinking about it... that was what you wanted, and you know, a bit of extra cash into Paddy's pocket too." scrambled Zack.

"Bullshit Zack, you got into a fight and lost. I know you." Laughing she turned around and headed up the stairs. "I'm going to take a bath, wanna join me?"

His fleeting glimpse forgotten. The broom handle clanged to the floor and bounced itself to rest.

They watched TV in their bathrobes for the rest of the evening, both happy and contented. They talked about the slate and the wall.

"I'm going to ask Paddy what made you change your mind, probably dying to tell me, he'll talk." goaded Joan.

"Not if I get there first and slip him a couple extra bucks." laughed Zack.

"He'll run you up to twenty." laughed Joan.

"Fifty." said Zack with fake shame.

Laughing and snuggling up, they finished watching TV and went to sleep happy. It was their last time.

CHAPTER 25.

OLD BOLEYN TOWN.

It was a long trip and Kelly didn't share any of the driving, which was a blessing in some respects as Phil had an excuse not to try to make small talk. The steady rumble of the road had a strange healing, hypnotic effect on the odd couple. The tension between them, that had made this trip quite an ordeal for Phil, subsided with every mile and was actually gone by the time they arrived at Boleyn.

It was late afternoon and they decided to go to the police station ASAP, as this story would not stay exclusive for long.

Kelly said, "Boy, this town sure looks a lot like Hecate."

Phil responded, "Uncanny."

As they drove towards the police station Phil and Kelly exchanged glances.

"Deja vu." said Phil,

"No kidding." said Kelly. For the first time, they were on the same page.

Was it just the look of the town or its layout? Most towns had in common: small strip malls, gas stations, places situated on a north - south, east - west, grid. It was only now that Phil and Kelly cottoned onto the fact that Hecate, and now Boleyn, didn't conform to that system.

"Pretty odd, eh Kelly, two towns, both weird." Shelving a shudder that had run up his spine, they ploughed ahead. Surprising Kelly, he asked directions from several people before pulling into the police station. They waited at the front desk for the attendant. The station looked like the Hecate police station after the double murders. Busy.

"Yes, how may I help you?" the duty officer asked them.

"We'd like to ask some questions about the double homicide." they replied.

Neither Phil nor Kelly mentioned that they had just come from Hecate. They didn't want the police to think that they thought there was a connection. They thought it'd be better to keep this information to themselves.

"How did you get this information?" asked the duty officer, unwittingly confirming the story.

Phil pondered how to answer the question, which was difficult as it was from Bill. But how did Bill find out? Should he even reveal his source? But how would the officer react if he wouldn't? While Phil struggled over these scenarios the duty officer was studying his face and weighing him up. The longer he took to answer, the more he distrusted Phil, and of course, Kelly.

Realizing what the officer was thinking, Kelly blurted out, "My boss." She sounded as if she was covering for the dithering Phil. The damage was done.

Without saying a word, the duty officer headed off towards a detective who put down his work and looked their way inquiringly.

Kelly pulled Phil's arm and said in a hushed and irritated tone, "What happened, why didn't you answer the man?"

"I was going to say Bill, when I got side tracked whether I should tell him it was Bill or not. And who told Bill? And then he let it slip that the murders did happen. And..."

"This way." interrupted another detective.

"Thank God." thought Kelly.

Phil and Kelly followed this detective down a short corridor and into a private office. Phil allowed Kelly into the room first, then entered and went to close the door behind him.

"No, leave the door open. Please sit down."

"So, what can we do for you?" he started.

This time Phil didn't hesitate. "My Boss has asked his *Investigative Report Team*, Kelly and myself, to investigate a lead on a double satanic homicide, here in Boleyn and..."

"You need a hand, Angelo?" A head peered around the corner of the open door. It was the first detective.

"Detective Connolly, I was just about to come and get you. These are reporters. Brief them on the events about... *you know.*

Nothing sensitive though: no pictures, no details, and no suspects." The detective smiled. Carte blanche to be a jerk and he winked. Phil thought, "His back was to them. Had this… Err… Angelo winked first?"

Drilling Phil and Kelly, but talking to Detective Connolly, Angelo said, "They're from out-a-town, so the story is going to break there, not here, you understand?"

Phil and Kelly nodded, but felt he was a little grimy or seedy.

It wasn't the tone of his voice, just the spirit of it, contrived, calculating, even conniving. "Over to you detective."

Phil didn't want to look indecisive again in front of the detective and Kelly. He knew he was the detective that the duty officer spoke with first, when Phil had mumbled and hesitated.

"Officer…"

"Detective Connolly." the detective said in an assertive tone.

"Detective Con…" started out Phil.

"Are you always like this?" the officer said nastily.

"Er, what?" shrugged Phil.

"Like this, trying to impress the lady, are we?" the officer continued.

"No, no, I could never impress Kelly. I mean…" stuttered Phil.

The officer didn't try to suppress his smile. Phil sank in his chair.

Kelly asked, "Phil, I think I left my purse in the car, be a darling, and go and get it for me will you please."

Phil pushed his chair back annoyed that she was so blatantly condescending towards him. His real frustration was with himself, what was it about him that caused people, especially of authority, to bully, disrespect and dismiss him. He sat down on the vinyl bench in the reception area and cursed. Detective Connolly swung his chair around so that the back of it faced forward, and sat with his legs astride the seat.

She thought, *God, another cop coming onto me, it's a fucking epidemic.* She said seductively to the detective. "Can you tell me what happened please Detective Connolly?"

"Well, Kelly, can I call you Kelly?"

"Yes, of course you may Detective Connolly"

"Call me Burt, Kelly"

"OK, Detective Connolly, I mean Burt, can you tell me what happened please."

He was a fountain of information.

"Well, I'm not supposed to tell you much, as you can see from my boss, so all I can tell you is a married couple, Mr. and Mrs. Zack and Joan McKay, were found murdered in their home yesterday."

"Thank you, Burt." Kelly had jotted this down and moved her chair back as if the interview was over. What a play.

Reaching over and placing his hand on her arm, he whispered, "There's more." She allowed him to leave his hand on her arm for longer than a casual gesture, and only moved it to take additional notes. He spilled his guts. In a hushed voice, he told her everything.

"They were crucified. The most terrible thing I ever saw. They weren't just crucified like Jesus, well yeah, crucified like that of course, but naked too… and doing it." In a panic, he said, "I didn't say that, no, strike that out."

"No problem, didn't hear it, Burt."

"So anyway, they were crucified naked and on top of each other, nailed up against a wall with the most terrifying look on their faces."

"Terrifying or terrified?" asked Kelly.

"You know, I think you're right, it was terrified. They looked terrified. Whoever did it, and we have a good lead, was strong."

"Why?"

"Because, they were about a foot off the ground and the couple weren't small people. He had to have been very strong."

"And the suspect?"

"Yes?"

"He's strong, your suspect?" she probed for the detective for a name.

"Oh, yea." said Burt, not giving the suspect's name. He didn't realize that was what Kelly was driving at.

"So, what's his name?" Trying a direct route.

"Sorry, I can't tell you that Kelly."

"Understood, Burt, not a problem."

"You know what I can do. I can give a quick look see of the crime scene, OK?"

"Great."

With that, he pulled out some photos from the folder he had been carrying to the photocopier.

"OK, Kelly, they're very graphic, I mean it." he stated somberly.

"OK." said Kelly, she became equally serious.

The pictures were face down. The detective picked up the top one, looked at it first, then showed it to Kelly, for a couple of seconds.

"Oh my god." she said shocked.

A brief silence followed. Then he showed her another one and then the last one. She was speechless for the remainder of the pictures and held her hands over her heart and her mouth.

"Who did this?"

Not trying to be macho, he said quietly, "We're looking for a guy called Paddy."

After that, there wasn't much to say. The detective escorted her back to the front desk where Phil waited obediently. Phil got up to join them.

"Still here, eh?" Detective Connolly said in a malicious manner.

"It's just something about Phil; he just gets on your nerves sometimes, somehow." Kelly deduced.

"Care to see a photo of the crime, sonny?"

"Sure." groveled Phil.

Kelly was shocked when the detective reached into the folder and he started to pull out a photo. Just when he could reveal the picture to Phil, he said. "Sorry Buddy." and stuffed the picture back into the folder meanly. Except that he missed the folder and the photo slipped down the side of the binder to the floor right next to Phil's feet. Automatically Phil stooped to pick it up. It was face down and as his hands pried it off the floor, he realized that this was a picture of the crime scene, and the detective obviously didn't want him to see it. Phil had it so ingrained to respect authority, that instead of turning the picture over and looking at it, he handed it back to the detective still face down.

The detective looked at him, took the picture and slammed it down on the counter face up. Kelly looked at Phil with utter disgust. "Is he so fucking timid that he doesn't have the balls to even look at the picture, if nothing else, out of spite for the detective who just humiliated him? God, he's fucking pathetic."

Phil just looked at the picture. It was the most innocent and innocuous picture in the file, a picture of a room under renovation, with everything scattered about the place, not the crime scene at all. Kelly looked at the picture too. When she saw it, she let out a large howl, and then the detective did the same.

Not really understanding what was happening, why the two of them had made these hoots, Phil bent down and inspected it even more closely. *Going over every corner of the picture like an eagle, he spied a shape in amongst the pile of debris, looked like the outline of a....*

The double doors of the police station burst open, as four cops crashed in, struggling to control a very large man. Phil and Kelly stood back to make room. The man was bleeding from his face and head and he was letting the cops know exactly what he thought of them. He swore at the top of his voice, police brutality, his innocence, and various comments on police officers' mothers.

Phil was the only one in the station who didn't know who had just been arrested. Cops hollered and slapped each other's backs. Hands were shaken and praise was dished out liberally.

"Who was that? OK, I get it, he's the murderer, but why has everyone gone ecstatic?" Phil knew roughly, there had been a crucifixion. Everyone else, including Kelly knew the gruesome details, the nakedness, the fornication. Not having seen the photographs of the carnage, Phil couldn't understand the relief that the police felt by having their prime, and guilty, suspect in custody.

"You don't understand Phil, how could you, you're you." yelled Kelly cruelly over the noise. She knew very well that he didn't have any way to appreciate the arrest.

"You know, Phil, sometimes you just don't seem to get it. You just seem to piss people off just by being you, sorry, it just seems that way." He was an easy target to take advantage of.

Ashamed, Phil knew that even though she was being mean, that she was also being honest. He felt defenseless and exposed, not able to keep up. Phil could have asserted that he was the one who put together the report, he was the one who invented *The Investigative Reporting Team,* but he just couldn't put it together. Every time he defended himself, he found himself cornered. He didn't think on his feet.

He was also the one who interviewed Deloris, but it would just give her another excuse to ridicule him, so he did his usual and stayed quiet. They made their way to the car and got in. Phil broke the silence saying that he wanted to visit the house and ask the neighbors some questions.

"OK." Kelly said humoring him. In her mind, they had closed the case, Phil should write the report, and then get out of *Dodge*. But she knew she had been hard on him, and maybe they could glean something else from this proposed visit.

"Good idea, Phil." managing not to sound condescending.

At the McKay's residence, Phil and Kelly stayed outside of the crime scene tape; dusk was still too light to risk ducking under it. Phil was thinking he could do all the investigative work of the property from where he stood.

Kelly stood in the front garden with her arms folded and watched Phil putter around the outside of the tape like an old man. He looked around the property, peered into the garage, and noticed some new sheets of drywall stacked up against the wall. As light faded, the next-door neighbor called out to them in a challenging tone. "Hey, you're trespassing."

Kelly shouted back. "We're the press, would you mind if we..."

"I can't hear you."

"Phil, come on, the neighbor." she shouted to Phil, as she began to walk briskly towards him.

"OK, coming." He sauntered after her like a sulking child.

They walked together and shook hands, with the late Zack and Joan's next-door neighbors, Kerry and his wife Ann. They were invited indoors as it got appreciably colder as the sun disappeared over the horizon. Kerry and Ann offered hot coffee and Phil and Kelly quickly accepted. The interview became a nice friendly chat, not work at all. Kerry and Ann just talked easily as if they knew Phil and Kelly for ages, town gossip, mainly about Paddy.

Kerry liked to talk. "He's always in trouble you know, if it wasn't some bar fight or another, then it was drunk and disorderly. Normally both." The last comment precipitated lots of laughter. "You know, Zack and Joan, being new to the town, probably didn't realize what a bad reputation he had. He was a hot head, and he always had to have it his way. You should have seen him drive. The number of times you'd read about him in the paper. But Zack, God bless his soul, we hadn't known Zack and Joan long had we love?"

"No, not long, about..." continued Kerry.

"No, not long." interrupted Ann.

"About oh." re-interrupted Kerry.

"So, I was cutting across the McKay's back garden from the river, I'd been fishing up stream and caught a couple of bass, actually not a bad brace either, anyway, as I was cutting across, I decided to drop one off with the McKay's. Well, as I was passing by the window, I heard that Paddy thug and Zack shouting really loudly, so I took a quick look through the window, and that's not me, I'm no peeping Tom, and I see them fighting. Next thing you know, Paddy throws Zack round and they smashed into a wall bringing the whole thing down. I didn't know what to do, so I hobbled home as quickly as I could, my leg you know. I decided I was going to call the police and I actually had the phone in my hand, when the next thing I know, I see Paddy leaving. So now I'm in a quandary, I put the phone down and thought what to do next, when I see Joan pull in and enter the house. Now that Joan was home, I didn't bother because she could take care of it. But, boy, it was a bit of a scrap. That Paddy you know, tough feller, too much for Zack. It's hard to believe it, they were such a nice couple"

"Nice couple" chorused Ann.

There was only enough time for Ann's comment before Kerry started up again.

"Nice couple, we met them before they bought the house, we saw them looking through the window, very much like you they were Phil, and we invited them over, very much like you there Kelly."

"Very much" chimed Ann again.

"I told the police all this you know." he concluded.

This was great stuff for the report. Phil could see the whole thing in his head and was forgetting about Kelly's insults. *Local Bully arrested for slaughter. Another exclusive from The Investigative Reporting Team.*"

"Thank you so much Kerry, Ann. We shouldn't take any more of your precious time." said Kelly as she stood up.

"Come on, Phil." who reluctantly agreed and got out of his chair as she escorted him to the front door.

"It was so nice and cozy in there, now I'm back alone with Kelly, now what's she going to berate me for?" thought the fearful Phil.

Colder and darker, they hustled back to the car parked outside the McKay's house. Just as they reached the car, Kelly said, "Come on." and dove under the police tape like a mongoose.

The shocked Phil, stood for a moment and thought, "Should I follow her? Damn it, I haven't a choice, if I don't, I'll look even stupider and she'll never let me forget it."

Kelly was at the front door. With more fear of Kelly than the police, Phil crossed the line and crept up to her.

"OK, Kelly let's get inside." They ducked under the remaining tape, went through the door, and quickly shut it behind them. It was pitch black inside.

Out from her handbag came her key ring flashlight.

"Do you carry that everywhere?" asked Phil.

"Well, where's yours?" Kelly darted back.

"Shut up Phil." said Phil in his best joking voice.

She ignored it and led them upstairs. Unlike Phil, she knew where the crime had been committed. At the top of the stairs, she paused to get her bearings and then went straight to the master bedroom. Twice - within a week, they stood in front of horrifying scenes.

The beam of light brightly shone, etching the scene into their minds. Phil saw all too clearly now why the police were happy at Paddy's arrest. The body outlines overlapped almost exactly. He was getting the picture.

"No wonder the police were happy. Probably naked and, God, copulating when they were killed. Sick bastard." Phil now had the whole picture.

"OK, let's go, enough of this gruesome scene." Phil led the way out of the bedroom and down the stairs without an ounce of hesitation.

"Wow." thought Kelly, "What happened there?" Shocked back by Phil's sudden decisiveness. "Probably scared silly and running away."

But just as they were about to leave the premises, Phil contradicted her thoughts.

"Kelly, can you shine your flashlight over there towards that heap of garbage?" he said in an uncharacteristically authoritative voice. And so she did.

Phil had remembered why he initially wanted to come here. He bent down and moved some chunks of wood and plaster around, until he found something strange. Something which he thought he saw the outline of in the cop's innocence photograph.

He picked it up and Kelly automatically shone the light on it. *A beautiful leather and suede left shoe lay cradled in his hands. It was exquisite, brogue and ancient.*

"It's just a dirty old shoe, come on. Let's go." Kelly said impatiently.

"Hang on, Kelly. Wait." said Phil, turning the shoe over continually, looking inside, outside and all over. He spat on it and polished it a bit. Phil didn't know the significance of these actions.

"What?"

"Look at it, it's ancient. I know the stitching around the toe has gone and it's dirty but..." said Phil, pushing Kelly to the edge of madness.

"Give me it." She walked over and grabbed the shoe out of Phil's tender grasp. With the shoe in her hands, she very quickly in a sham examination; looked at it.

"Yeah, look, it's a shoe." Then she threw it back down on the dirt and turned to the door.

"You're coming or not?" She spat the words at Phil as she turned the beam of light on to his face.

To her amazement and ire, he had followed the direction of the toss with his eyes and had started after it. Kelly moved the flashlight beam towards the pile of debris and then away, but he didn't stop. He had a fix on it and could locate it without the light. Seeing this, seeing that he was adamant about it, she returned the beam to the shoe so that Phil could retrieve it quicker.

"And then they could fuck off and get out of here." Kelly angrily suppressed.

"Today." said Kelly, really ticked off as he fumbled for the shoe.

"OK, OK, I've got it." Before he had finished the sentence Kelly was out the door and Phil had to rush to keep up.

Silence, again, was Phil's best company on the drive to the hotel. As he drove, he contemplated. He had a multitude of things to think about now. Though Kelly was giving him the silent treatment, for a change, it didn't bother him.

Kelly too, was also thinking a mile a minute, but on a different vein than Phil altogether.

"It's the second day since Bill phoned, what's happening? Stuck here with his stupid brother, it's been almost a whole week since we left. Does he even miss me? Even when he calls, it's not really for me. It always comes back to Phil, or it's on Phil's cell not mine. What's going on?"

The ease of Kerry and Ann with each other, their whole man, woman, relationship and general contentment, had really got to her. While Phil had jotted down keywords and listened, Kelly had watched the couple interact while wondering, "Who she was to Bill?" A tingling, niggling, feeling that she had dismissed earlier this week, had returned. She needed to vent, and she did.

"God, you can really piss me off Phil. Fuck, dithering around looking for that shoe, for what? Fuck."

Phil was so absorbed in what he was thinking that he hadn't heard Kelly at all, and she knew it. They got to the hotel and checked in. Two separate rooms, next to each other, connected with a door, so that the two rooms could become one. Kelly vowed that she would never, ever, open her door.

She was still in a huff, exasperated by Phil's non-reaction to her insults. But really, the root of her frustration was her relationship, or lack thereof, with Bill. Phil was just a convenient scapegoat and even that was losing its effectiveness. "The bugger, he's completely lost in thought and hasn't heard a word I've said all night."

"Phil." she shouted, "I'm taking tomorrow off."

It shocked Phil out of his trance. He thought, "Whatever".

"Tomorrow, I'm going to the spa, so don't call."

Phil thought, "I won't."

"Phil!" snapped Kelly.

"Yes, Sorry. You're taking tomorrow off for the spa."

Kelly was seething. "God. Both brothers are ignoring me. Don't give a shit about Phil. But that fucker Bill better phone tonight or he won't be a fucker no more." With that thought in mind, Kelly went to her room and locked herself in physically and mentally. No more hanging on every moment for a bit of attention, no more waiting for phone calls, and especially no more handoffs from Phil. The call would be for her or not at all. She was going to need that Spa tomorrow.

Once in his room Phil got down to business. It was effortless. Fifteen hundred words materialized faster than Kelly could lose her temper. Way past his limit, he wasn't particularly confident that every word would make it to print, and he was beyond caring if it did or didn't. Typical of his luck, the fax machine in the hotel was down, so he drove to the nearest internet café. As the fax rattled away, he braced himself, and phoned Bill.

"Yes." answered Bill.

"Phil."

"Hi Phil. What?" His normal response. His next words almost knocked Phil over.

"Oh, by the way, nice job on that last story." It only sounded slightly begrudging.

Taken aback, the only thing Phil could say was, "Thanks Bill, did my best, hope you like this one, sorry that it's so long but I couldn't cut anything out, not really." He always doubted himself.

"Wait. Nice job." said Bill, after reading it lightning fast.

Phil was stunned. He dismissed his work as minor. "I know it's too late for the morning edition, so…"

"No, no, it's an exclusive, yer on a roll, bro, it'll be in tomorrow's paper. Bye, wait, take a couple days off on the paper, oh and keep that Kelly girl busy, you hear me, don't want to see her in town, got it?" Without the chance to reply and plead for mercy, "But who cares now." crowed the elated Phil. "My god, he's going to stop the presses, he's going to stop the presses, for my story. Damn it. Our story, oh well, hey, it's mine and they all know it." He clapped his hands together in joy. "And he complimented me too, and he's going to stop the presses, for my story, no shit."

As bad as the last few days had been, this had made up for every belittlement, insult and snipe. This was a reporter's dream. The crowning glory of his miserable career.

Getting back into his car, he drove back to the hotel, to his hotel room, climbed into bed and fell asleep. Happy.

Mid-way through the night he woke up in a cold sweat. He sat up. He smiled. It had happened. His brother had stopped the presses for him. In a strange quirk of life, his relationship with his brother was changing for the better for the first time in memory.

CHAPTER 26.

HATE SMOLDERS IN BOLEYN.

A couple of miles upstream from the McKay's place, the river was populated by several islands, scattered randomly throughout the coursing flow. Using the islands as stepping stones, multiple little bridges created a span that crossed the river. Perfect for then, but as the horse and cart era ended many years ago, so did the usefulness of the stone bridge.

If the town council had any vision, the stone bridge, now referred to as Old Stone Bridge, should have been promoted, as a valuable heritage asset of the town. It could be a place for lovers to stroll and for children to run. However, once the new bridge, designed to handle the demands of modern-day traffic replaced it, the Old Stone Bridge quickly fell into disrepair and rapidly crumbled. The present-day council focused on liability: should someone get hurt while trespassing on its decaying arches. Consequently, a chain link fence surrounded the Old Stone Bridge with 'No Trespassing' signs.

Welcome to the 21st century Boleyn, the Witch.

Making a little pot of herbal tea for her over a small campfire, Boleyn sat under one of the condemned arches and hummed something sounding a bit like 'London Bridge is Falling Down.' She hummed her little tune and stirred her tea, as she was happier than she had been for a very long time.

The chain link fences proved no barrier for her as she just sailed in from above. It provided the kind of privacy required for a witch, being out of the way and secure from intruders and vermin.

"Just put a couple away yesterday." the chuckling Boleyn said to herself. That was the kind of sport she relished after hundreds of years in prison.

Boleyn was very small. She was born, as the only child, into a family of midgets' centuries ago. The family had been the focus of ridicule and malice their whole lives, because of their size and because they were all ugly. Her father, Arthur, a good man, brave beyond his size, spied and fell in love with his wife at first sight. Unfortunately, Beryl, his wife to be, suffered cruel imprisonment existing as an exhibit in a traveling circus.

Small nomadic circuses were common in the 17th Century, frequently boasting freak shows of nature's misfortunes. Beryl was a star attraction: less than two feet tall and with an oversized head. However, she received anything but star treatment, as beatings were common. Food was withheld and she was treated worse than an animal. Arthur had heard of the exhibit but dared not go to see her. He feared for his own capture. Two midgets? What a prize that would be.

So, he snuck onto the circus grounds under cover of night and whispered to her through the large cracks in the wagon walls. He charmed and wooed her. By the night's end they had planned an escape. The following day was the last of the circus at that site. That would be their only chance. The day came and went, the circus was over, and Arthur was going to make his move. As the dismantling of the big tent and sideshow stalls commenced, luck befriended him. A storm blew in.

A vicious wind and stair rod rain caused havoc in the darkness. Canvasses flapped, and the air was full of flying dangerous debris. Taking advantage of the confusion, he made a daring bid to free Beryl. With ease, he entered her junk filled crowded caravan. With a quick heave of a crowbar, the padlock on the cage's door broke. He secured her freedom.

Beryl's escape wasn't noticed until the circus began to setup at the following town, but then it was too late to do much about it. Wisely, Arthur and Beryl traveled far away from the circus circuit. They got married in a secret ceremony as soon as it was safe to do so. Within the year, they were loving parents of their beautiful midget daughter, Boleyn. They worked hard, becoming cobblers by trade, specializing in beautiful, intricate leather children's shoes for the wealthy. Life was not easy for the couple by any means, as a target for bullies and even ordinary people. Their existence was mired with constant insults, abuse and harassment, and names, such as witches, demons and devils. Boleyn's parents, however, endured through it all, knowing that they were building a better life for their precious daughter.

Not thriving, but surviving, they did their best to enjoy life, keeping a low profile and a friendless existence. Yet people still talked. Word got around and inevitably the circus heard of a family of midgets. This circus had a long memory and it still smarted from the betrayal of their star.

Arthur and his family stood no chance, as questions were asked and sadly, in an ever-shrinking circle, willingly answered. They were kidnapped in broad daylight at their meagre dwelling, while onlookers watched and applauded. They were beaten and bundled into small cages and paraded through the town on the back of a horse drawn cart. *The family wept bitter tears, for not one decent minded person stood up for them. Boleyn remembered that well.*

Captivity at the circus was cruel and merciless. Subjected to daily beatings, the carnies made sure they knew who was boss. Their small bodies couldn't handle the traumas waged upon them, and it wasn't uncommon for one of them to be unable to make an appearance. They performed night after night for penny paying folks, and sometimes sickness wasn't a sufficient reason for a no show.

After a couple of years, the stress of the imprisonment became life threatening and her parents had started to become habitually ill. On those occasions, Boleyn would have to do the show alone. The carnies gave them potions and herbs, but they had little effect and it was to no one's surprise when her mother passed away.

"Small bodies, small lives." said the carnies. They had not one shred of decency, choosing to deny their cruelty and confinement as the cause. They were plainly cold and callous.

Her father followed, laying on his deathbed, too weak to entertain, Boleyn was now the star. With her mother gone and father gravely ill, her spirit was weak and fragile. Boleyn was vulnerable and easy prey for anyone with malice on their mind.

Not long after her mother had passed, a nasty piece of work called Frank the Lip, himself disfigured from birth with a hair lip, raped her. Back stage, whilst she was preparing for her set he pulled her aside, pinned her in a corner, and forced himself upon her. Minutes later a laughing Frank threw her in front of the anonymous, faceless crowd, to perform her routine and dance.

Unable to cry, she had learned that lesson very quickly - she persevered. Tonight, was no different from any other. She endured jeering, gawking, and if someone thought to throw something at her, the rest of the crowd followed. Tonight, was no exception. She kept on dancing.

She had seen hundreds of people in audiences around the country, and very quickly, she had realized that all crowds were the same. They consisted of individuals wearing different coats, hats and shirts, yelling different words with different voices, and yet they were all alike. But on this particular night, a gentleman in the throng stood out.

He wasn't bigger or taller, nor was he more handsome or average. His focus on Boleyn was steady and not degrading. It was measured and pensive. With no emotion he watched as Frank came onto the stage and grasped her by the hair. Enjoying the infliction of pain, he pulled her off stage left, the final act was over. The hair pulling didn't stop there. He molested her again because he could.

Upon her return to the wagon, she ran, crying, into her father's arms. "Daddy, I'm sorry, I've been raped. Tw… Twice."

Her father teetered on the edge of death. The brave face he had been showing could no longer conceal the true depth of his ailment. His life force couldn't sustain his wracked body anymore, and he died. His beloved daughter's cries were the last words he heard.

Boleyn was distraught. She shook her dead father in her hands in a desperate attempt to retract her last, soul-crushing confession. In deepest grief, Boleyn vowed and cried out for the power to inflict vengeance and death upon the carnies, the rapist, upon 'good and decent people.'

If she had that power, she would use it…

"Give me this God, please" she wailed, but silence was her only reply.

"Then," she sobbed, "Then I ask The Devil."

"Congratulations Boleyn." resonated a voice in her head. "You see the truth indeed."

And then an audible and irresistible voice called for Boleyn from outside the wagon. "Boleyn, please come and join me. And I, I will answer your prayer."

Gently resting her father on the floor, she followed the hypnotic voice to the door of the caravan and stopped at the top of the steps. The man stood below her.

He looked at her without judgment or distain. She wore a miniature tunic, frock and leggings, stained red with blood, and a pair of shoes, that were still good, despite being old and scuffed. The rest of her clothes were no better than rags. Tears adorned her eyes.

The man on the other hand, wore expensive and stylish clothing. His coat was elegant and long, cut with perfect lines of exquisite inlays of black gold and silver. The creases on his trousers could cut paper, He wore black shoes; shoes made unmistakably by Boleyn's father. She stared at the supple kid leather and suede. Five eyelets crisscrossed with long square leather laces were tied in perfectly balanced looped bows. The heel was higher than most men would wear.

"You know, knew my father?" asked Boleyn in her high-pitched voice, immersed in pain.

"Yes, I purchased these shoes from him, as you have already observed Boleyn." he replied smoothly.

"He's dead. Just a minute ago. And mother too." She broke down and sobbed uncontrollably.

The noise and activity of the circus strangely receded to the background, as he spoke softly of comfort and hope, of revenge. The more he spoke, the more she listened. Not unlike her father, she started to trust this man's words and believe his intentions. He told her the story of her father, the bravery he showed in rescuing her mother from this life, and the betrayals played in their return to it. He spoke with nothing other than respect for them both and showed her the shoes he had commissioned from them. *However, he never mentioned the fact that he too, had betrayed them, by not paying.*

He told her that things didn't have to be the way they were, that she could exact a vengeance upon those who had wronged her and her family. Truth or not, she believed him, trusted him, and needed him. She was doomed.

That night ended for her father. But it was the beginning for Boleyn, The Witch. He used the spilled blood from between her thighs, deflowered blood, in the fountain pen. Her signature on the parchment smoldered longer than *the Devil* had seen for a very long time.

She felt power surge through her body. Virile and deadly. She convulsed as the force hurtled uncontrollably over her being as it swelled up. It had coalesced with her spirit and she was entangled. It was Entanglement. She survived the transformation.

Where there was once an innocent girl called Boleyn, now, standing before the Devil, she was the Red Witch. Boleyn's rags turned into a midnight black cape and a wide rimmed pointed hat. A crystal ball and custom sized broomstick appeared in her hands. She felt the broom's wood with her fingers. The broom was all hers, she knew it instinctively. Her mind sensed spell blueprints flooding her memory. She flexed a thought, and the broom sprung underneath her, raising her up to eye level. She couldn't restrain from smiling. Mighty and awesome, she was going to wreak havoc on mankind. Her potency would be unparalleled on Earth.

But be careful when dealing with the Devil.

She was to learn that now.

She too was incensed.

She reeled from something she'd found out. It was something she wished she hadn't learnt.

This night would be remembered by not just her.

Retribution and vengeance cruised the blank night sky. She used her broomstick savagely on fRANK the Lip. She spared his life, because he had raped her twice. The 'favor' would be returned equal fold. She let him know this. With boiling hatred, she struck fear dead into his heart.

"Your Future… your now, see Frank, will be mine.

Just when you think I've forgotten.

Just when you think you can't be found.

Just when you find happiness.

Just when you see a cloudless blue sky.

Then…"

The circus carnies cowered for years. Broadcasting her intentions with a crackling cry in the mid of night, she hunted them down, slowly and methodically, whether they stayed with the circus or not. Audiences were not exempt either. Those who pelted her during her shows suffered strange happenings, and always out of proportion with their crimes. She wielded a reign of terror.

Using the crucifix acquired from the McKay's house to stir her tea, Boleyn suddenly broke into a cold sweat. A terrible thought crossed her mind. She stopped stirring as the thought quickly consumed her. The shoe that encased her for all those years looked horrifyingly familiar. She dropped the cross in the simmering tea and summoned her broomstick. It appeared under her from out of nowhere and she tore back to the McKay's house at top speed. It was good to be back flying after so many years, but she didn't relish the flight tonight. Business was too imperative.

Following the course of the river, she left a tiny 'V' shaped wake as she skimmed over the water's surface. Less than fifteen minutes passed, from the inception of this frightening idea and the arrival at the McKay's house. She landed like a humming bird on the front door step and entered the house the mortal way. Using the default witch lighting device, the crystal ball, a shrouded blood red hue lit up the vestibule.

She remembered the room where she emerged from her imprisonment and rummaged through the dirt and dust. Tearing at the heap in the corner of the room, she started to become frantic. She ripped plaster and slats into pieces. The shoe was nowhere in sight. Turning around, she attacked another smaller pile on the other side of the room. She went back to the stack in the corner, and this time, spread the entire contents across the floor evenly so that the shoe would stand out. It didn't. Trying to remain calm, she whipped back to the other mound and did the same thing, with the same result.

She decided to look around the rest of the house, the kitchen, bathrooms, bedrooms. That still didn't change the fact. The shoe was not there. She flew dead slow and hovered over possible spots of concealment. She combed the entire house all over again. Same answer. The shoe had vanished.

She sat down on the bottom step to take a rest. It was no use; it wasn't there. Now she wanted, needed to know more than ever. Did her father make the shoe?

CHAPTER 27.

NOW TAKE A DAY OFF.

Phil woke up feeling better than he had in years. Yesterday his brother, for the first time in history, had complimented him on his work, on anything for that matter. He led in bed and wallowed in self-gratification, visioning world exclusives and interviews on talk shows, his own talk show.

After a while, the delusions of grandeur subsided as he began to mull over the nagging question that had popped up in his head. What about the similarity of the two crimes?

"Two crucifixions in one week. I mean, really? In two completely different towns, to boot, both solved so quickly. JD was such a young kid, that's quite a crime for a teenager. Then there was Paddy in Boleyn. Was he a copycat? And the hatred displayed in both crimes, it certainly was bizarre.

Also, the towns - they're so alike, old and dreary, strange names too. Their names, Hecate, a witch, and Boleyn, what is that? What about the shoes? The shoe in Hecate was just an old shoe… but the one in Boleyn, wow."

Intrigued by his thoughts, he got up and found the shoe from the Boleyn crime scene. It was a beauty. He didn't realize it, but he was polishing it with spit, *again.* He had held the shoe in Hecate, it was cheap and tacky compared with this one. But at least it wasn't broken. This one's stitches at the toe had broken and the toe had lifted off the sole.

Phil's mind raced to that moment, thinking back to the time that Kelly and he had broken into the B&B. He visualized the situation.

"That's Right! The B&B's shoe was open at the toe as well. Kelly was going to pick it up and I stopped her. Shit. I should have let her pick it up and take it. Bum. The only time I've yelled at her. I was wrong, bugger it. I could be looking at and comparing shoes, right here, right now." thought Phil.

He was completely frustrated with his apparent bad luck.

"So both shoes have their toes open now, and what did the B&B innkeeper, what was his name? Dave, that's right, say to me? *You can trap a witch in a shoe.* And that dream I had, when Deloris turned into a witch." He sat quietly, turning the questions over in his mind, until reason prevailed.

"Come on Phil you twit, it's the 21st century. They were terrible crimes yes, but the police solved them quickly and efficiently. Just a bunch of coincidences, forget about it, and get on with the day."

Forgetting his niggling thoughts, he wondered what he was going to do with his day off. He vaguely remembered Kelly saying that she was going to spend the day in the spa.

"Fine, in fact, great, I'll spend the day sightseeing." he hummed cheerfully. Phil had his shower and got dressed. The ancient shoe was still on the other unused double bed in the room. He didn't bother to put it away.

"Breakfast time." he thought continuing his off-pitch hum. Now ready to close the hotel room door, he checked numerous times that he had the door card. A thought dashed across his mind. "Why were we so scared?"

He headed down for breakfast in a semi-trance with this thought rattling about in his head.

In the hotel lobby there were pamphlets of local places of interest. Phil took a hand full of them in an unsuccessful effort to get his mind off the last question.

"When we were at the B&B in Hecate, I know that it was scary, going through the police tape and everything, but I was petrified. What was I scared of? And the drive back to the hotel, and, oh my god, that walk from the hotel car park to the hotel back door. What was going on? I was shitting bricks and Kelly was scared too, although she didn't want to admit it. Where did all that fear come from? Ah, the menu."

Half way through breakfast, another issue, his brother's problem, squeezed into his awareness. "How's he going to keep Kelly under wraps so to speak?" For a day off, his mind worked overtime. "Maybe the answer is in the pamphlets. Great idea." He went through them looking for a spa.

"Yes." he said in relief. "No." in disappointment. "It's closed for the season."

Flipping from pamphlet to pamphlet while munching on his breakfast, he managed to keep Bill and Kelly out of his brain, but all his questions returned. Phil could not turn his whirring mind off, churning over the murders, open shoes, and bad dreams. He was thankful when his phone rang.

"Hi Kelly."

"Hi Phil. Having breakfast?"

"She must have heard me chewing." he thought. "Yes." he replied, trying to swallow and not give it away.

"Can I join you?"

Phil was shocked that she asked to join him for breakfast, and it wasn't a command, like most of her requests.

"Err sure, I…"The phone call ended abruptly.

He waited for her to come down for breakfast, which she did in record time appearing only minutes after she had called.

"Hi."

"Hi, just started, I got a menu for you."

"Oh, thanks Phil."

"Was that, nicety?" thought Phil. "No doubt something is up."

Her whole demeanor and voice were subdued, and he had a strong suspicion he knew what it was, but he wasn't going to ask. He was not going to open that door, his life, up until yesterday, was miserable, but he didn't want it to end.

Kelly was silent; she had teased Phil about Deloris for the better part of the trip, but now she knew she was the vulnerable one. Bill had not phoned, and she knew it showed. She had stayed up the whole night it seemed, waiting for his call. She had heard Phil leave and come back, so he had submitted *their* report, and hence, he would have talked to Bill. So Bill would have had Kelly on his mind, but not in the way Kelly wanted. It was all too apparent to her exactly what he was thinking. The glaring absence of his attention said it all.

Phil read the situation, he was busting inside to tell Kelly that Bill had stopped the presses for *their* report, but he bit his tongue.

He wished he could rub it in, she had given him such a hard time she deserved it, but he was scared, now that he had some cards, he dared not play them. "Damn, I'm such a wuss."

They ate in silence.

"What's on the agenda today then Phil?" She spoke after she finished her breakfast in a more normal voice.

Producing a pamphlet, Phil replied, "I was thinking about paying a visit to these waterfalls and caves." He pointed to the advertisement. "It's about, well at least, about an hour and a half drive, so I don't know..."

"OK, I'll get ready. See you in ten at the car."

She was there on time.

Not asking any questions, Phil's preservation instincts were stronger than he anticipated. They were both quiet almost the whole way to the falls, not enjoying each other's company, but not getting on each other's nerves either.

"Well done Phil." he thought.

"The spa is closed for the season."

"Oh… OK. I." Phil hesitated. "Yea, I saw that."

"That's it for certain, Bill didn't call her, and she's beginning to get the picture, she never started a conversation before, unless it was to goad me." thought Phil.

To make the trip a little more cordial, Phil decided he'd try to keep the exchange going, so he ran over all the difficulties he had with the murders. It was all they had in common, other than his brother, and he wasn't going to open that door.

So he outlined the obvious similarities between the cases, which in its self was inexplicable. He discussed the other strange thing - two 17th century shoes at the scene of both crimes. Both open at the toe, *now*, although the one in Hecate *wasn't* open when he examined it before the murders. How witches could be captured in shoes, and more importantly, how they could escape.

He touched on the subject of their panic attacks, how scared they were, and the amazing coincidences, if that's what they were. He talked about the closing of the cases, it was so easy, and on and on, especially about the shoes.

She let him finish without interruption, something Phil didn't expect considering the outlandish nature of his postulations. Before Kelly replied she cogitated. There was quite a lot to take in.

After a while, she said, "I know what you're saying and I must admit, two crucifixions so close together, it certainly made me think too. It's inconceivable really, that someone could do those things. But who else could it be other than the people the police arrested? I mean you said so yourself?" She continued, expecting Phil to interrupt and defend his argument, and was surprised that there was no apparent attempt to do so.

"And I'm not discounting the shoe aspect, in terms of that they existed; just in terms of what role did they really play? They're just coincidences for me."

"Is he actually listening or just dreaming? She wondered.

But Phil was in shock and amazement. He thought that he was going to be laughed out of the car. He didn't expect to be taken even half seriously. Kelly continued, happy that Phil did appear to be listening, as he nodded in acknowledgement of her last response.

"So, I think you're placing a lot more importance than you should on those two shoes, I hear you, but just think about it? What you're saying? The shoes open, and according to the B&B proprietor, this would release a witch. Then you're saying they promptly, gruesomely, kill six people. I mean it's fantastic to believe that people have done this, but if you don't, and we take your premise, then that's just, well, unbelievable."

Kelly was shocked at Phil's following response to her tempered critique.

"Thanks Kelly, now that you've put the whole story together like that, hearing it makes it so much clearer. Thank God you're here, I could have really made a fool of myself, if I hadn't entrusted you with my thoughts first. Sorry. And Thanks."

"Wow." she thought. "That was decent."

Just then, they pull into Witchiton Falls Park. A guided tour was only a fifteen-minute wait, and so they decided to take it and relax. They had been under so much stress: having the tour with a small group would allow them to decompress, so they waited.

"It's no Niagara." they agreed, but the falls were high and beautiful and the tour was nice. At the base of the falls was an old mill, which the group entered through a timeworn, wooden door. They gathered inside a large room with whitewashed walls. Huge circular milling stones like trolls occupied the center. Closer to the main entrance stood some glass cabinets, which displayed relics of a bygone age.

The tour guide stood behind one and started his presentation in a self-important voice.

"My name is Gavin, and I'll be your tour guide for the next hour. Now the caves you will be entering are actually concealed by that door behind you." Everyone turned around and looked at another old wooden door in the cliff's wall.

"This mill occupied a prime site, because of its close proximity to abundant fast flowing water. However no one wanted to build here because a WITCH lived in the cave behind you." He spoke the word "witch" with theatrical emphasis, so almost everyone said "OO".

"Then like magic, without any warning, the WITCH disappeared. *Puff.* Millers were free to build this mill. Now, in front of you, in this show case, are some of the everyday objects used by the WITCH. Ha Ha. No, I kid you, by the family that lived in the mill. Combs, knives, an old shoe, potato peeler..."

"Kelly."

"Yes, I saw it." she whispered back.

"What are you thinking?" he inquired.

"Oops, the guide's looking at us."

The tour guide had stopped his presentation and was looking directly at Phil.

"Care to share?" He had an edge to his tone.

"Sorry." said Phil, apologizing.

"No, come on, let's all hear it." he goaded Phil, pitting him against the rest of the group. The tour guide had handled people like Phil before. Putting them on the spot always shut them up and frightened the rest of the group into silence.

"So, you are?"

"Phil. And I was only saying that I bet that witch is in the shoe. Sorry, please continue, err, Gavin."

The guide had guaranteed Phil's silence for the next hour. In the largest cavern, he turned off all the lights and in that absolute darkness, he cackled like a witch. No one was really surprised or scared, as he'd been hinting that he might do something like this throughout the tour. They exited through the same door they had entered and headed towards the souvenir kiosk.

Phil and Kelly stared at the shoe housed in the showcase, until Kelly woke them out of their stupor.

"Come on Phil, let's go, it's just a stupid shoe."

"Yer right. Superstitious nonsense, good idea Kelly. And boy, what a creepy tour guide." "Ugly." crowed Kelly.

Gavin was unattractive person, in looks and personality. He had pokey cheeks and a bony chin, with shiny-pitted tight skin from severe acne, and was nasty to boot.

"There's our witch, right there." they both laughed. They left Witchiton Falls by the same route.

With dusk settling in, a beautiful sunset greeted them as they approached Boleyn. It was yellow and red, white and gold, blue and magenta, with intermittent shafts of pure white light thrusting through the wispy clouds like stairways to heaven. They reduced the speed of the car to lavish in the warm flowing golden rays. And in kinship, the stress, anxiety and fear of the preceding days, melted away from their hearts in the evening's glory.

They sat quietly over dinner without spite for the first time. Phil chose this moment to tell Kelly that Bill had stopped the presses for their report. She congratulated him and thanked him for accrediting her in the account. There was no more talk of murders, of Bill, of work or of shoes and witches, just the pleasantries of two non-involved adults having dinner. They didn't discuss heading back to HQ, their plan for the next day. They retired to their separate rooms in a contented.

"Good night, Kelly."

"Good night, Phil."

Too early to sleep, Phil sat on one of the beds in front of the TV. The other bed was untidily covered with his clothing and whatnot. The Boleyn shoe still sat on top, out in the open. Phil looked at all the stuff and especially at the shoe.

"I'll pack all this stuff tomorrow and the shoe will be history." He slipped in and out of sleep as the TV droned on and on.

A gentle knock at the door woke him. Still in his day clothes, he climbed off the bed, approached the door and peered through the peephole.

He couldn't believe his eyes.

CHAPTER 28.

IN THE BROAD DAYLIGHT, A UFO ABROAD.

Hecate tried to follow as best she could, but it was dangerous. Flying in daylight in a cloudless sky, over a flat and sparsely treed landscape, was a perilous endeavor for any witch. There was nothing she could do; she was completely exposed. Anyone could see her from miles away. She tried to stay away from places of mortal activity, like crossing roads only when there was no traffic in both directions. She circumvented villages and towns, avoided tall strange towers of steel with humming wires, and while all these obstructions required navigation, she still had to track the signal.

The distance had grown between her and the prey and with every passing second, it increased. Sadly, that wasn't the end of her bad news. She detected a weakening in the spell. It was becoming obvious that she was going to lose him.

She desperately continued for a while before she gave up and landed in an abandoned barn. She crawled into a bunch of loose hay and closed her eyes, too exhausted for words. She didn't want to sleep, but she was so tired, that even her cursing and hatred for Phil couldn't keep her awake. She was out like a light. She had lost him.

Dreams of Phil dogged her restless sleep, when a couple of hours later, her radar picked up something, and she woke up in a start. She perked up, turned her head from side to side. She confirmed it. She was definitely receiving a signal, and it was getting stronger. She got up and smiled. Now she was back in the hunt. Slightly refreshed from the nap, she hopped back on her broomstick and darted off in his direction.

It was getting stronger, but too rapidly. He was in his horseless carriage again, driving obliquely towards her direction of travel. She adjusted her course, anticipating an intersection. She realized that she couldn't intercept him at his all too quick rate of speed. However, all she needed was the chance to follow him for a while and establish the direction of travel, and hopefully, determine where he was going to sleep tonight. That chance was possible.

The strength of the signal gradually rose to its apex and then started to fade. Chasing, Hecate flew as fast as she dared. Even with this reckless strategy, the spell's signal was fading quickly. With the spell wearing off, the signal getting desperately weak, she feared that she would lose him. In addition, the sunset didn't help, this meant that more people than ever would be looking at the sky, so she had to keep very close to the ground. Low-level flying was slow and fraught with issues, and every problem hindered her progress.

"Shit." She felt the signal stretch to breaking point and snap. She had lost him, again.

However, Hecate was no spring chicken. She had achieved her goal locating the road that Phil was traveling on and she continued to follow it. Now, if she could get close enough to his general whereabouts, maybe she could get lucky, and, if the spell had any strength left, re-establish a connection. A lot of 'ifs', but she had nothing else to try, or lose.

As the sunset ended and night descended, she gained altitude and picked up speed, flying hard and fast towards a town up ahead. Lights were flicking on and she began to see the full extent of the place. Now what? Does she assume that he's in this city? If so, how does she find him? What was her course of action? Depressed and tired, the spell had ended and she had no other ideas. He was in this city or he was lost forever.

Choosing hope over despair, she decided to fly around the town in diminishing concentric circles, and assuming that the spell had some spirit left, reconnect. At least it was completely dark, so she could cruise. Unfortunately this wasn't true. The dying spell meant that she couldn't coast; she would have to boot it and get lucky. Busting her ass, she started the first circle, the largest and the longest. Finally completed, she was back at the start puffing and panting. Resolutely, she began the second lap.

She was only a quarter of the way around when she had help from an unexpected source. Deloris. As she passed by a large four-story building, she felt Deloris twist inside.

"Bloody Hell." she exclaimed and slowed down to concentrate. She jumped for joy. The tiniest, thinnest, thread of a bond between Phil and Deloris betrayed him. It was too small for Hecate to attach to, but Deloris's feelings for Phil were enough to complete the connection.

"Oh how splendid is love, not only have you doomed yourself, but also the man you desire."

She swooped down to its roof like a bat. Not wasting a second, she pulled open the top door and entered the building. The thread had stretched to its limit and could snap at any moment. As luck would have it, it led her to the next floor, the top floor.

Then with a *ping*, the thread snapped, and the spell died. A proud Hecate stood in front of the door - the only thing standing between her and redemption. She recounted her toils and tenacity: she had remembered how to cast the location spell. Found and captured all the ingredients, brewed it to perfection and successfully ingested the lethal concoction. Then she had followed and tracked the vital cord with the skill of a vulture.

Here she stood in the body of Deloris, the switch triggered by the death of the spell. Hecate in Deloris form, lifted her arm, clenched her fist, and gently knocked on Phil's door.

CHAPTER 29.

VERY JITTERY, BUT PHIL CHARMS A GIRL.

Phil couldn't believe his eyes and without a second thought opened the door.

"Deloris, what are you doing here?" He extended his arms and gave her an awkward hug. He was so happy to see her that he didn't give her a chance to reply. He stood back against the door and invited her in.

"Hello Phil." she said and entered, a little unsteadily.

But Phil didn't care and he closed and locked the door behind them. She was the most beautiful woman he'd ever seen, even though she actually looked like hell. Her face was sallow and haggard, her hair was tangled and scrawny, and she looked like she was going to throw up. Ignoring all this, Phil continued to gawk as his imagination went wild.

She stood silently, wearing a small fitted jacket and a sexy little smile. It was the best that Hecate could put onto that face after everything Deloris had suffered.

Phil was in trouble, but he didn't know how much and what kind.

"Err, would you like a drink?" He stuttered realizing that she might think he was trying to get her drunk.

"Maybe she's already drunk, see the way she stumbled coming through the door, maybe it's me who needs a drink."

"Sure." she replied.

Phil bent down at the mini-bar and fumbled with the tiny bottles. "Drinkmore." he cracked. He felt like an ass.

He felt her move towards him. He stayed on his knees with his face buried in the bar. He could feel she was only a step away and relished the thought of turning around with her close enough to touch.

"There, she's right here, now I'll stand up." He stood up with his back to her, so that he could turn, and act as if her being so close surprised him. He turned around.

"ARGH"

Only inches away, he stared into the hideous face of Hecate. He jolted back, gasping and stumbling over his feet. He fell over between the beds.

"Too easy." she gleefully thought.

He had nowhere to turn nor could he move in any direction.

Enjoying his predicament, she menacingly advanced his way, and asked softly, "Phil, pray tell me, what year is it?"

Phil's eyes were wider than saucers. It was impossible for him to answer, his brain had frozen solid.

She waited a moment for a reply, and when none came, she hovered over the stricken man on her broomstick and shrieked, "What year is it?"

All that Phil could muster was some incoherent gurgling.

She waited another moment, thoroughly enjoying every second of this torment, and taking a large breath she roared, "WHAT YEAR IS IT?" The bellowed cry embodied Hecate's her inner essence. It was her Entanglement signature of death - Spirit and Entanglement, condensed into a force of destructive energy.

GREE.deat.
GREE.dea. GRE.de.

The strike smashed into Phil with the force of a freight train, blowing his cheeks back like a dog's jowls in a car. The air in his nostrils burned, everything in his vision turned green, and his mouth tasted blood. The bones in his face ached and his skin stung. His eyes were open and he was conscious.

Poleaxed, his mind was so debilitated and numb that he didn't have any idea what he was doing, or even thinking. Only survival instinct remained, he had a choice fight or flight. Phil was no fighter, but neither could he flee. Unconsciously, his body attempted an escape even though there wasn't an exit route. Running on automatic, he attempted to do something, feeble though it was. Each hand reached up and took hold of the bedspreads, as he attempted to lift himself off the floor. If he could think, he would have realized that it wasn't a good idea. It would have put him face to face with the witch. But instead of lifting him up, the bedspreads slid off the beds, and he fell back down to the carpet as the duvets completely covered him. With his eyes tightly shut, he lay under them and waited for death.

He waited silently for several seconds that felt like hours.

"Bang!" He jumped out of his skin at a sound of a gun.

The witch shot Phil.

He lay on the floor in the dark, dying. But after a second or two, he believed he was still alive. He couldn't feel any pain. He closed his eyes and patiently, serenely, dreamt of peace.

He waited and waited, but death didn't arrive. He still didn't feel any pain or bleeding, and he was sure that he would have felt something in the process of dying. Still with his eyes closed, he checked himself. He didn't feel any blood or even anything wet. Now he was sure he was still alive.

"So what was happening? What was she waiting for? *This thing - The Witch?* Can't be letting me off the hook. And what would *"A Witch?"* be doing with a gun anyway?"

He listened intently. He held his breath and again he awaited his imminent doom. He couldn't hear anything except his thumping heart. A crazy dare careened through his head.

"Come on, get it over with."

Still nothing happened.

He had no choice but to admit it, he was still definitely alive, his stupid thought proved it.

"For the time being."

There was nothing left to do but pluck up courage and prepare for the worst.

He imagined the evil hideous face pressed closely against his, all fire and brimstone.

He opened his eyes. "Nothing."

He experienced relief, but only for a moment.

Only the faintest dim light penetrated through the bedspreads - not even a green hue, it was essentially dark. He stayed motionless and even held his breath. He waited and strained, until he had no alternative but to breathe and he cringed as it was as loud as thunder.

But still nothing happened.

He waited. And still nothing happened.

"Now what?" Desperation choked his mind.

"Should I peek over the bedspreads? *The Witch* will surely see me and kill me then and there. What if I scream and jump up with all the blankets on top of me and scare *The Witch?*

Shock her and... Oh God, what do I do?"

Breathing now without care, deciding to stay still and wait for the end. He closed his eyes again, said the Lord's Prayer and made his peace with his maker. And waited. And waited.

Minutes had passed, and he was beginning to hope, to hope the impossible.

"*The Witch?* had died? Had left?

Was a figment of my imagination? What?"

At his wits end he decided on a bold gambit.

"Hello?" It sounded like a loud mime. "Hello? Hello?" much louder this time, but certainly not assertively.

Nothing.

"It must have been fifteen minutes, no twenty. I haven't heard a thing. I can't stay here all night. Why not? I'd still be alive. Phil come on, get up." With all these distractions going on in his head, his body started to move before his mind could stop it.

"Too late" he thought as his brain caught up with his body.

"Oh God" was his final thought, before the bedspreads fell off his head.

CHAPTER 30.

OUT OF BREATH.

Hecate hovered over Phil like an owl cornering a rat. She wasn't happy though, because Phil was still alive. Blood should have been oozing from his ears and nose. His eyes should have been pulverized into a pulp with only eye sockets left.

Somehow, he had survived her Entanglement Death assault. The energy in the shout, should have torn his soul to shreds, wrenched it from its foundation in the heart and scattered it like sand in the wind.

Should have. But it hadn't.

The reason was all too obvious. Her exhaustion. It was so profound.

The creation and survival of the location spell, coupled with the exhausting sojourn across the country, and the additional load of the rebellious Deloris had taken its toll. She was utterly drained and depleted and didn't have enough reserves to complete the formulation of her full Entanglement discharge.

GREENdeath.
GREENdeath. GREENdeath.

For Hecate to create a spell she had to use her Entanglement. The spell's power, longevity and purpose, was an extension of this dimension of her being. The stress of the chase, with its close calls of failure and its mental concentration, all taxed and sapped her Entanglement. Then the soul of Deloris had disturbed Hecate's inner balance, not easily done, but caused excessive tiredness, leaving her susceptible.

The saving grace for Phil, however, was the shoe taken from the Boleyn crime scene. She didn't know that it had also absorbed some of the attack. The combination and summation of these three things had saved his life. They all consumed energy in accordance with the rules of the universe; Witches were not exempt. Her Entanglement signatures of GREEN - her witch color; and DEATH - her moral compass, were casualties.

Grappling with the very idea that someone could survive **even** a partially composed attack, Hecate clenched her teeth and affirmed. She would have to kill him the mortal way, with physical violence. Enraged,

"I'm going to kill him this sniffling little rat, and I'm going to make him pay bad, because he's hardly worth the bloody trouble I've gone through to find him. Look at him, like a little spider. There, his little legs are trying to pull himself up. Aw. Look at him. He's pulling the bedspreads on top of him like a little baby...."

Phil, hands and legs waving comically like a fly on its back, grappled to get up and accidentally pulled the eiderdowns over himself. As the quilts tumbled, they threw something into the air which landed on the handle end of Hecate's broomstick.

It was the shoe from the Boleyn murder scene. Hecate's breath caught in her throat and she almost choked. For the first time in her re-emergence she was petrified.

The shoe rocked on the end of her broomstick, like a seesaw, balanced between the heel and toe. She had developed an unnatural aversion to shoes. So any shoe, appearing as if from nowhere, was bound to strike terror into her heart.

Hecate, however, was usually tougher than that. She could have laughed it off and seen that she was also lucky because the inside of the shoe didn't hook onto the end of her broomstick. Then she would have been captured by it, giving Phil a chance to escape. As the toe was already broken, her incarceration wouldn't have been from long, but she would have to hunt down Phil again. She still had his card and it still had enough soul for a second, albeit weaker potion.

However, the shoe staring her in the face was no ordinary one; it was special. She had seen it hundreds of years before when it one of a pair was worn by someone unforgettable.

"Oh God. Is the Phil man *he?* He can assume his form if he so desires no doubt, but why? Normally he wouldn't choose such an awkward, clumsy, classless mode of transport."

She lowered her Entanglement, making herself utterly exposed to an Entanglement attack should Phil launch one.

"Hecate!" She chastised herself.

"Of-course Phil wasn't *him;* he's lying motionless on the floor in-front of you. The Devil would never allow himself to be put in such a demeaning position. And then, to lower your Entanglement, are you crazy?"

She was fortunate Phil wasn't *him.*

Without her Entanglement to interfere, she detected a slight charge of Entanglement in Phil. She recognized the signature was hers. The man had absorbed some of her Entanglement in the survival of her attack.

"I'm so exhausted. And I thought that was impossible for a man. We'll that's at least what I'd heard, I think."

As she pondered her discovery, a flush swept over her as she realized her logic in lowering her guard was flawed. And that only luck had saved her. "Better quit while you're ahead Hecate." she wearily thought, "I've been lucky, but it can't go on. Even *he* was wary of luck, because luck was chaotic and fickle. Yes, even *he* was not immune to the whims of luck. Go."

It was time to leave. She swung her broom around, made sure the shoe fell off, and sped straight for the open sky. She smashed into the clean, clear, glass window. It had been invisible to her at first glance. It made a huge noise and left her dazed, in a crumpled black heap on the hotel floor.

Fighting to remain calm, she clambered back onto her mount, and gingerly headed to the front door knowing she'd be sporting a black eye. First her nose, now an eye. She'd been in the wars since she had escaped that buckled old shoe, but she didn't care, that was the cost of life, and she was happy to pay it.

Irritated, she fumbled with the lock. Panicky and frustrated, it lurched open. Still gripping the handle she fell backwards. Phil's card fell out from Hecate's cloak and fluttered to the floor. The momentum swung her out into the corridor and just as she glimpsed it, the door slammed shut. The card was gone.

"Shite. Blast, damn it, I need that." She stared at the closed door.

Out in the corridor, now completely exposed, she cursed, and fled towards the fire escape. She doggedly found her way to the hotel roof and the night sky in a foul, black mood.

This had been a long day and night for Hecate. She had suffered her first disappointment and enigma of her new life. Every morsel of her was dog-tired, especially her Entanglement. She had to find somewhere to sleep and fast.

Hecate was no fool and when she did her first circle of Boleyn, she noticed a secluded, derelict Old Stone Bridge, a perfect place to rest. She didn't bother circling it. It was dark, isolated and uninhabited. She made a beeline for it caring little for stealth. Once there, she found a cozy little corner and fell into a deep sleep in the fetal position.

In a tender and loving manner, an old burlap sack was gently placed over her sleeping body. Boleyn was happy. She had a baby sister.

C H A P T E R   3 1 .

REALLY, HE'S SUCH A PAIN.

Phil shrieked as the bed spreads fell off his head. To reveal, nothing. The room was empty. The witch was gone. Phil still alive, stood up before falling to his knees and sobbing his heart out. Then he thought, the door, is it closed?

A flood of terrifying visions coursed through his mind, causing him to panic and look wildly around the room for a second time. Petrified, he dashed out the door, and sought refuge in a public place - the corridor. He stood there turning his head from side to side. With dread he was looking for any sign of the witch.

"Kelly!" ploughed through his head.

He was frightened. Even in the empty corridor, although better than his room, at any time the witch could return and slay him. No, he needed to be with someone, in a room, in Kelly's room, with Kelly. He didn't just knock on Kelly's door; he pounded on it.

Kelly was enjoying a chick flick that she'd purchased, until suddenly a huge thumping noise on her door made her jump out of her skin.

"What the…" she exclaimed angrily. "Whoever it is, is going to get a piece of my mind." She stormed to the door and looked through the peephole.

"Phil." she hollered. "What the hell."

He didn't wait for an invite. As soon as the door opened, he rudely charged through the crack and slammed the door quickly behind him. He stood with his back against the door panting.

"Phil! Get out. Get out." Kelly yelled at him in her pink pajamas.

In his own world, he slid down the door to the floor and started to sob. With palms over his eyes and knees under his chin, he cried like a baby.

Immediately, Kelly realized that this was bad, even for Phil. She stopped yelling and bent down in front of him.

"Phil, what's happened?" she spoke in a soft voice. "Phil, has something happened? Are you ill? Are you OK?"

"Deloris. Witch..."

"WHAT?" and Kelly stood straight up and reeled into Phil. "You get me out of bed and break down my door, just to tell me that scrubber didn't fuck you. Her vulgarity was intentional.

"No," stammered Phil, "no you don't under..."

"What Phil? What don't I understand? That you've had the 'hots' for her ever since day one, not that I care. What don't I understand, pray tell me?"

"No, Kelly, No. Listen to..." Phil attempted to retort.

"I, listen to you? You pathetic shit, look at you crying." she screamed at him.

"Deloris came into my room and turned into a witch Kelly, A WITCH." Phil shouted at the top of his voice.

"She came into my fucking room and TURNED INTO A FUCKING WITCH, A WITCH, A WITCH, A FUCKING WITCH. WILL YOU LISTEN TO ME? A FUCKING WITCH."

And then there was silence. Followed by more of the same.

"Kelly, you have to believe me." unable to bear the silent treatment anymore.

"Don't talk to me." she answered indignantly.

"Kelly." Phil said in a submissive voice.

"You yelled at me, Phil. Yelled. You didn't have to yell."

"I couldn't stop you shouting at me. I was trying..."

"Yelled, Phil, yelled."

"Let me finish." Phil was almost shouting again.

She went super silent, looking, glaring at Phil.

"Kelly, sorry." lowering his voice.

"I was watching TV when..." and Phil portrayed the last half hour to Kelly, every detail, every nuance. Kelly listened with the attitude of a drama queen biting her tongue.

"Sorry Kelly, I didn't mean to shout, but I was, am, scared. No. I mean it. Deloris was there one moment and then Deloris was gone and this... *Witch* appeared. She hovered over me on a fucking broomstick. Christ. A broomstick."

Kelly didn't say a thing and the room fell into silence.

"Kelly, you've got to believe me."

"You know Phil, you really scared me there, screaming at me like that. How am I supposed to believe anything you say, when you can scream at a woman like that?"

"I'm sorry Kelly, I'm sorry." said Phil. "It happened. Kelly. A witch attacked me. You've got to believe me."

She categorically did not.

Kelly sat on one of the double beds. Phil didn't think she would grant him permission to enter her room any further. God forbid, sit next to her on her bed. So, he just sat on the floor, leaning against the front door. His face was red and puffy. Crumpled up tissues from wiping his tears surrounded him. He started to collect them up, and after he had them all together, he grabbed them and looked for a waste bin.

Kelly silently pointed. "Over there."

Then, in a flat voice, she asked. "So did you and Deloris do it?"

"No!"

"But you wanted too?" she persisted.

"No!" said Phil.

"You're gay?" testing his patience, knowing he wasn't.

"No. NO. no." and then continued, "You know. Oh no, that doesn't make sense, I. I. I. How did she find me?"

"Me? I don't know." retorted Kelly.

"No really, how did she find out where I am? I mean we've been here only a day, and there was no way she could have found where I was, unless she called and even then..."

"Unless she called?" Kelly pounced on Phil's speculation.

"Oops." thought Phil guiltily.

"What do you mean? 'Unless she called?' She doesn't have your number, does she?

Kelly queried Phil inquisitively, with an incredulous look on her face. Phil was cornered, how could he avoid the question? She didn't know he had gone to her house.

"Well, err, actually she does." mumbled Phil quietly.

"How, I never saw you give her your card, I know that for certain, so when did you give her your card Phil? Phil?"

Phil suddenly said in a chirpy voice, especially considering what he was about to suggest.

"Why don't we go and see my room?"

"OK." said Kelly. "OK, Phil let's go, right after you tell me how Deloris got your phone number."

Phil was cornered and outwitted. With a heavy sigh he gave in. Now he was going to have to do two things he didn't want to do. Kelly smiled as she watched his face contort, twist, and end with resignation, as he prepared to confess.

"I err."

"Yes, Phil out with it, I'm waiting." Kelly had played Phil most of the night, since she realized that he was genuinely scared out of his wits. His distress she believed - but not his story. It was after all crazy what he was saying. Probably he just had a bad nightmare.

"Well, the night before we left Hecate. Why do you care?"

"Phil, a deal's a deal. You said, we should go and see your room and I said OK, after you tell me how Deloris got your phone number. So we're going to see your room, right after you tell, so tell me, and let's get on with it, OK?"

"OK." Phil agreed reluctantly.

"Well?" prodded Kelly.

"OK, OK. The night that we left Hecate I..." again hesitating "well that night" and he finished.

"Come on, Phil, you went around her house and..." continued Kelly beginning to get a little tired of this coy act.

"Well yeah. I did but she wasn't in OK. The End." Phil said rapidly.

"No, that's not the end. How did she get your phone number Phil?"

"Well, I pushed my card under the door with my phone number on it. OK, but she never rang. I swear, she didn't call Kelly. I haven't talked to her since Hecate. I have no idea how she found us."

"Com'on Phil, you must have."

"No Kelly, I didn't, and if I didn't, how did she find us? And she's not Deloris, she's a Witch."

"OK, Phil, I believe you." she said in a patronizing voice.

They had left Kelly's room and he faced his door. Reliving his experiences was giving him cold feet.

"Hey, you, get over here."

Kelly caught Phil backing away from the door to the far side of the corridor. His eyes were wide and full of fright, but Kelly didn't care, she didn't believe, how could she? She was also beginning to lose sympathy for him with these childish antics.

Giving him one last chance she said, "Another case for *The Investigative Reporting Team,* hey Phil." trying to lighten his mood and take his mind off the impending entrance. But he didn't laugh or even crack a smile.

"Christ be a man Phil and step up." crossed her mind.

Phil, seemingly reading Kelly's thoughts, forced by Kelly's firm grip on his arm, retrieved his key card and swiped it. The door unlocked. Taking a breath, he impressed himself by opening the door wide open and stepped inside. He made sure that Kelly was committed to following him, *before* doing so himself, he thought he was so clever. In fact, Kelly knew she'd never get him in there, if she didn't lead the way by tailing him closely.

His senses on high alert, Phil scoured the room with laser like eyes, while at the same time making sure that Kelly was completely in the room. Only then did he advance any further, and then it was by a meagre single step. She had to push him physically to breach the boundary of corridor to room so that the door could close behind them.

They were crammed together in the small entranceway.

Kelly spoke. "Well, Phil, go in." She wasn't scared at all, whereas Phil was more than frightened, something Kelly just couldn't understand.

Phil moved quickly to the window and turned to observe the entire room. Kelly casually surveyed it in a demeaning manner. She looked at the heap of bedspreads on the floor between the two double beds, and watched Phil. He was wide eyed and shaking. That was it, not much, considering Phil had allegedly witnessed the transformation of a woman into a witch. She searched the bathroom, and the closet.

"Nothing." gloated Kelly.

Phil stood still contemplating, his mind a long way away. Suddenly he dove to the floor and looked under one of the double beds.

"Nothing?" inquired Kelly.

"no."

True. There wasn't a shred of evidence to support Phil's claim. Nothing to say that Deloris had been here, let alone that she had miraculously turned into a witch. Phil sat down on the bed and shifted the bedspreads.

"What's that?" Kelly bent down and picked up the elegant Boleyn shoe.

For the second time in one night, Phil's clumsiness had revealed the shoe to a woman.

"It's my shoe. The shoe from Boleyn." Phil replied.

Strangely, Kelly found herself speculating, as she turned the shoe over in her hands. She sat down on the other double bed and gazed at it. She had been in close quarters with Phil for the better part of a week, and in all that time, painful as it had been; she hadn't known him to lie.

She thought about this as she sat there. "You know, I don't believe you Phil.," said Kelly.

Phil was at a loss. He questioned his sanity. He knew it was real, he knew the difference between a dream and real life. Deloris and the witch were absolutely there. That was an hour ago, but now it seemed like an eon. Now, he wasn't even sure that it happened at all.

"You're right Kelly; it had to have been a terrible nightmare. There's no other explanation." He continued, "I'm sorry I shouted at you Kelly, truly, obviously I was upset, but my shouting at you was inexcusable. I'm sorry. You might as well go home, there's nothing to see here. I'm sorry for ruining your night. I can walk you back to your room."

Phil stood up and Kelly stood up as well. She didn't reply to Phil's apology, but she accepted it as graciously as he'd delivered it. She turned and walked to the door, and just as both of them were putting the night to rest, and everything with it, she saw something on the floor.

"What's this?" she said aloud.

"What's what?" replied Phil approaching her.

She bent down, picked up the faded card, and looked at it closer.

"I think this is yours." she said handing it to him.

"What is? Oh My God. It's the card I... I put under Deloris's front door, back in Hecate. My God." He went back into the room, sat back down on the far bed and stared at it. The implications ran crazily through his brain. If it was true - *it really did happen.*

"Shit did it really did happen? It did happen."

"Phil, hello, Phil. Earth to Phil."

Kelly walked over and sat down on the same bed right next to him. Phil turned the card over and over in his hands, just as Kelly had done with the shoe moments earlier.

"Phil, I know it's crazy, but I believe you. I mean, I do and I don't. Phil, I can't believe you. It's just too crazy."

"I know Kelly."

"I can't believe it myself; I just know it happened, but I don't believe it. That's crazy, isn't it?"

"Phil, I know we've had some issues; but you've never lied to me, have you?"

"I don't know." he said truthfully.

"Phil, why is it that every time I try to be on the same page as you, I get an answer like that?" said Kelly.

"I'm sorry Kelly, I'm trying you know..."

"You sure are Phil"

He got it. He didn't like it, but what could he do?

They sat silently.

After some time of reflection, Phil said, "Kelly. Would you mind keeping the adjoining doors open tonight?"

"In your dreams Phil." She got up and went to her room. She took the shoe with her.

Feeling scared and lonely, and just as a precaution, he got up and opened his half of the adjoining door anyway.

"She can come in and…What? Comfort me? Who are you kidding, Phil." But the door stayed open.

Phil couldn't think about anything else, not just Deloris or the witch, but also what Kelly had said. It had hit hard, again, causing Phil to wish he were a different man. It wasn't the first time he had wished this, and the worst thing was, he knew it wouldn't be the last. Defenseless, there wasn't a safe haven for his thoughts to retreat to. They whirled in his head in a demented dance, picking on every weakness and thrusting it into the foreground. Tormented by either; thoughts of his own inadequacies, or by ghosts, demons, witches and devils, and unlike most people, some were not figments of his imagination.

In the adjacent room, Kelly was reflecting over Phil, that he didn't know if he'd lied to her or not. His last answer had seemed honest.

"That stupid Phil, he's so difficult. Bill would just say outright 'No. Never, I've never lied to you Kelly.' A lie no doubt. Frigging Phil, he goes and says, I don't know." She mimicked him mockingly. "What kind of answer is that?" she cursed.

"Damn it, an honest answer I guess, and that's the frigging problem. It was an honest answer, and he has been honest, stupidly honest, with me all the time."

Kelly couldn't get to sleep. Too many things were eating at her. "It's my story. Asshole. And thinking of assholes, that brother of his, Bill, doesn't look good on that front either. Think that ended the day he sent me on this God forsaken errand. He just wanted me out of the way, him and his stupid wife. Just wanted to fool around. Should sue for sexual harassment, or blackmail him, something, anything."

She was also bothered by a tiny hint of green she had seen in Phil's eyes.

Phil tried to sleep with his clothes on. He didn't want to risk removing them in case the witch came back. The feeling of them scratched his skin, but he was too fearful and confused to take them off, so he changed into something new and fell instantly asleep.

He dreamed that he heard his name called, but he was so tired he refused to get up. The voice called again. Again he refused. But the voice persisted. He couldn't resist anymore. The voice was so smooth, so rounded and yellow. It was as if a yellow mist was lifting him up and moving his body for him. He didn't have to do anything; someone or something else controlled his being.

He got up and wandered to the door. He put his hand on the door handle. Its cold metal felt real. Real, as if he was actually holding it.

"What? What am I doing?" He turned it. Phil woke up.

CHAPTER 32.

MORE EXCUSES.

Gavin, the tour guide at Witchiton Falls Park sang to himself happily without fear of embarrassment. The park was deserted, it was the end of the day and he was closing up shop.

He was so skinny his cheek bones and squared chin protruded. He was so lean he seemed tall. He looked quite ugly and frightening. He was a weird person living mainly in his head. He didn't make friends easily and was a loner, mainly out of necessity. Girlfriends were out of the question. He took an instant dislike to Phil earlier in the day, perhaps he saw himself in twenty years' time.

He'd had a good day, performing his civic duty to educate the public. He put a couple of assholes in their place and a couple of bucks in his pocket.

"Yeah, took care of that Phil guy but good. Yeah." He continued with an impersonation. "'My name is Phil, a big idiot, oh, and I was only saying that I bet that witch is in the shoe, OK. Sorry, please continue, err, Gavin.' He called me Gavin, as if I was his fucking best friend or something."

"So what's left, everything locked up? Check. Like I care. Let's have a look at that shoe." He pulled it out from the glass cabinet and exaggeratedly scrutinized it an inch from his face. "Empty. How could a *Witch* get in a hole that size? Where's that rusty old potato peeler?" Gavin retrieved it with his tobacco-stained index finger and thumb.

"The world-famous brain surgeon examines the skull of his next patient. Ha-ha. He spies the line of attachment. Nurse, a n d… scalpel!"

He placed the shoe on the glass counter top and proceeded to hack away at the stitches with the blunt utensil. Gavin held the shoe up close to his eye and looked in through the toe. He could see light, yellowish, but light nonetheless. He was definitely all the way through.

Then he put the toe right in front of his mouth and cried, "Hello, hello there. Witchy Witchy. You-hoo." He laughed stupidly. "No answer of course." He looked again.

A tiny hand appeared from the end of the shoe.

He dropped the shoe like a red-hot poker, but it was too late. *The hand grew to normal size and grabbed Gavin's throat. The hand kept its grip and a witch was pulled out of it as the shoe obeyed gravity and continued on its downward path.*

Oblivious to the shoe bouncing about on the floor, a completely free witch rose up to eye level. Her yellow eyes, stared dreamily at her prey. "Hello." Without removing her tightly clenched fist, she spoke to herself slowly and softly, hypnotically. "What have I here, Ruebella? What have I found?"

Gavin stood still with his eyes bulging. Her grip forced his head upwards so he couldn't see her face.

"You want to see my face sweetheart? I know I'm pretty."

She slowly lowered her elbow, slanting his head forwards.

"He's trying not to look at me. That's so rude. Didn't you call out for me only a minute ago? Well, here I am." She spoke lovingly.

She bent his head towards her again, this time insistently. Gavin couldn't resist, but managed to close his eyelids over his protruding eyeballs just as his feet left the ground.

Unable to see, he felt like he was floating upwards.

She elevated on her broomstick, lifting him upwards until his head hit the roof. He opened his eyes on the impact and looked directly into her face. Her hand still gripped his neck so the scream died in his throat.

Close-up, he saw a face of moles, lumps and two massive hairy nostrils. Her large, hooked nose separated wide, jaundiced eyes. Her lips were thin, cracked and barely stretched around a mouth. A handful of sporadically protruding yellow teeth appeared lost. She was dressed as a witch, black cape and towering black hat - *she was a witch.*

Gavin's peripheral vision absorbed the hideous sight, but his focus was on her eyes. He couldn't take his off them. He was mesmerized like a snake charmer's serpent. He just stared, and would have been transported into another world if she hadn't spoken.

"Weasel!" Her voice was sharp and curt, not dreamy in the slightest, it cut like a knife.

She let him go and he let out a whelp as he dropped like a stone. Her eyes maintained their stare even as Gavin was landing in a twisted crumbled heap. His ears hurt still ringing from her last spoken word.

She lowered herself smoothly to the floor and squatted in front of him. She read his nametag. "Gavin."

Reaching out with the palm of her hand, Ruebella gently lifted Gavin's chin with her scrawny fingers. It was the first time that he had been confronted by her and not been in a stranglehold, the first time he could fight back. Even though it would have been a lost cause, at least he could have tried, but he didn't. His head rose meekly, resting in the palm of her hand. He looked into her yellow eyes and didn't move.

"So darling, what do you want? You called for me, you set me free."

"No." squeaked Gavin. He was horrified that his voice worked. He didn't mean to talk, it just popped out; it was Gavin's survival mechanism kicking in, lying. Unable to control his gut response, Gavin wanted to deny it was him, his responsibility, his action. It was nothing new; he had been doing it all his life, but maybe in this instance, it was understandable, even justifiable.

He continued only a little louder, "Sorry. No."

"It wasn't you?" queried Ruebella. "But I saw you, I saw you through the end of the toe, didn't you set me free?" Ruebella replied in a silky voice, her head to one side.

"It wasn't me." he said, with all the power he could conjure, and still, he was barely audible, causing Ruebella to bring her face closer to his.

"Keep your eyes on hers. Don't look at her face. Don't look." thought Gavin sticking to his mantra for survival. If he focused on her eyes and avoided looking at her face, maybe he would live.

He felt his soul move: the invisible beam of yellow light between their eyes was its destination. He faced a difficult choice - stare into her eyes too long and lose his soul, or stare into her face and risk death. His focus shifted to her face, it was painful, but his soul returned to his heart. Swapping his attention again to her eyes, his soul stayed in place, for the time being.

"It wasn't you, me handsome? Then who was it then? Because I want to kiss that man. The man who set me free." She tilted and moved her head to kiss him.

"It was Phil." blurted Gavin in total panic. "Phil." Gavin repeated.

"Who is Phil? I didn't see him." said Ruebella.

"He left." he instantly replied.

"When?" Her voice hardened.

"This afternoon. He made me do it, it was him. He's the one. He's the one you want. He's the one you want to kiss." said Gavin.

"Where can I find this Phil?" she said harshly.

Gavin's brain raced. He could see she was getting upset and he could only assume the worst if she did. She'd used her nasty voice on him already and he was scared she might use it again. He knew he was lucky to be alive at all. He had to think of something fast and suddenly it came to him.

"There. Over there." He pointed to the cash register.

"I don't see him."

"Please let me. Ouch." He looked into her face again.

"Let me show you." daring to be hopeful.

And in her sweet tone she said, "Yes, Gavin, love, please do show me."

Bravely, Gavin gathered himself up, lifted his head out of the palm of her hand, and stiffly untangled himself. He stood up, relieved that no bones were broken from the fall. Then he decided on another bold strategy. He was going to acclimatize himself. He alternated his gaze between her face and eyes at second intervals, and by the time he had limped across the room, he could maintain non-life-threatening eye contact.

"God, she is ugly." he thought. "Holy God, she is God, damn, bone, ugly. So ugly I could puke." Even as he was thinking these mean thoughts, he shuffled through the receipts.

"He's here." and pulled out Phil's credit card slip complete with signature.

Holding it towards her, he said, "Here, he's here. This is how you find Phil."

She took the paper in her hand and studied it. She had never seen paper this thin before, with strange fonts all blocked and numbers in every corner. This was a foreign piece of craftwork no doubt. Her yellow eyes scanned the receipt and then widened with joy. Near the bottom on a dotted line, was the mystery man called Phil. She had his mark in the palm of her hand, and with it, she could find him.

Ruebella had a goal. Now Gavin was able to look Ruebella in the face, fully immunized. He held his breath and wondered,

"Would it work? Would she want to kiss Phil instead of me? Oh My God. You lucky son of a bitch, Gavin, she's, Ouch, smiling. She can find Phil with it. See that, her yellow eyes. There, they flashed with joy, wow, that's a lot of joy... That's too much joy. OH No. OH God."

"Thank you, Gavin." She read his guide badge again. "Thank you so much. Let's go and find your friend."

"He's not..."

A cold sweat swept over him. She swooped on her broomstick to within an inch of his nose. She gazed straight into his soul with her yellow crocodilian eyes. Gavin's soul stood its ground, but was no match for Ruebella's call. It flowed through Gavin's body and into hers over the bridge of un-heavenly yellow light.

His body deflated like air out of a balloon, and when there was nothing left, it fell to the floor with a plop. Ruebella picked his body up in her hand and tucked it into her cloak like an empty wine skin.

"He was such a handsome young man; never know when I might need him." Everyone was handsome compared to her.

She turned her attention to the slip of paper and contemplated the spell she would use to locate Phil. She had just proven that her entanglement was healthy, and she was confident her spell casting would be too.

She needed a candle.

"That little glass cabinet was full of good stuff." She headed over to it.

"Damn, oh well, what's in this drawer, da da." She found a packet of little yellow, tea candles "How fitting." used to keep mosquitoes at bay.

She placed a solitary candle unlit in the middle of the floor, and then Ruebella sat cross-legged in front of it and started to hum. After a few minutes the chant developed into a pleasant chant; the location spell.

"It's been a while since I last used one." she thought to herself. She added the appropriate words to target Phil. She was ready, with the words and tune down pat.

Assuming the lotus position, she closed her yellow eyes and meditated to calm her Entanglement. Dedicating herself to the spell, she dove into a trance, chanting the song deep in her mind. Deathly still, hardly breathing. Motionless. Almost an hour.

She detected the signal she had been waiting for; her Entanglement had spun the spell. She opened her eyes, snapped her fingers just above the candle and the wick lit. Closing her eyes again, she sang the song one more time, this time aloud.

Don't even shout,
Don't even try,
Raise up your head,
And look in my eye,
It's you that I see,
No hiding from me,
Start at the mill,
Go forth, find Phil.

She opened her eyes, picked up the receipt, and continued to chant now holding the paper over the candle. The paper ignited, and the candle died. With a long fluttering yellow flame, the burning paper cast giant witch shaped shadows across the hall. The flames licked her hand in an appeal for freedom and she generously granted their desire. It headed straight for the wall and fluttered along it looking for a way through like a fly beating at a window.

"Perfect." Floating on her broomstick, she drifted up the wall and grabbed it.

Then she glided through the door, soared into the clear cool night and let the fiery receipt free. Immediately the flaming paper started in a specific direction and she flew after it. This was the first time in hundreds of years that she had flown, so with gay abandon, she cared little if she was seen or not.

She cruised and soared thoroughly enjoying the air, the sky, her liberty. There were amazing sights to see in this new world, she knew that, she felt it, but she also felt something else. Nostalgia. For the first time since her early unscheduled discharge, she took time to reflect upon her situation. She had Gavin, the flame, and the quest, all new artifacts from this new world.

But what did she have from her past? Only her memories and her broom, a great companion. But her memories were a list of all but the same. Loneliness. If it weren't for her broom, she wouldn't have anyone at all. She vowed and prayed, this time, she would not be alone.

~~~

The lights of a vast town, full of large, well-lit buildings was now rushing towards her. She gazed in awe at its size and brightness. As she approached the outskirts, she refocused on her mission. She needed sustenance and replenishment, and Phil would provide both.

"Looks like I have a place to stay for the coming day." She noted the location of an old stone bridge.

Without warning the flame flared. "He's close. Back to business." She made a toast. "To Night. To Phil. To Death."

The flickering receipt started to descend and proceed to the fourth floor of a square ugly building. The lit paper smacked against the window, its flame, burning brighter than ever. She hovered in front of the window and calculated which room it was. Then she grabbed the receipt and advanced to the roof.
~~~

Following the very steps Hecate had taken only hours earlier, she descended to the fourth floor and let the receipt free. It flew to the same hotel room door. She gently tried the shining brass door handle. It didn't budge, nor was there a key hole to look through. She looked through a little peephole in the middle but couldn't see anything.

This was proving to be a very exciting night. She had only been free for a few hours and she had assumed a quest, stolen a soul and cast a successful location spell. Now she stood to meet and kiss the man who freed her and complete her mission. With a kiss of death. Not alone at all now, she felt Death's presence.

She cleared her throat and with her most hypnotic voice she called Phil. "Phil, are you there Phil, are you there?" There wasn't a reaction.

"Phil, come to the door. Phil, come to the door." she called again. Darkness blotted out the tiny opening's light. He was right at the door.

"Phil, open the door Phil, open the door." Her silky caramel voice had lured Phil like a fish to bait. She held her breath, she listened closely. She heard a hand grasp the door handle.

She saw it turn. It was open. She felt him wake up.

It was now or never so she pushed the door with all her might, and happily it flew open as if it had been waiting for her all its life.

Knocked over backwards, Phil tumbled to the floor rolling head over heels before ending up on his back. Looking straight upwards, a face of another witch stopped his heart. The blazing credit card receipt rushed up to Phil and extinguished itself over his soul. It had fulfilled its quest. The spell was over.

Phil looked up at the witch. If the last one was ugly, this one was hideous.

The last one had green eyes. This one had yellow.

The last had a loathsome voice. This one's was gentle.

But both could easily put him to death. That he had no doubt.

"You are Phil, yes?" Just like the last witch, she hovered over him. She was profoundly ugly, and yet he had trouble avoiding her hypnotic stare. Just like her voice was in his dream, he couldn't resist it. And as the last witch, she wanted something, an answer. But Phil was unable to deliver even on his own name.

"You are Phil, yes?" This time there was a definable edge to the tone, and he didn't like it. It sounded like it could be the tip of an iceberg and not wishing to hear more, he muscled up his will and replied, barely.

"Yes." he peeped. He was still looking at her and he found the longer he looked, the more he could bear the sight and the less the connection held him.

"You are the one who set me free?" she asked.

"Err, what?" said Phil finding his voice.

"Did you set me free?" This time, it was not the smooth gentle voice, but a vicious question.

Not understanding, he failed to answer.

"Did you set me free?" The drowsy syllables should have sounded like a slowed down record player, but they didn't.

Ruebella was exercising her repertoire and thoroughly enjoying herself. But even as she did, she wondered, dumbfounded really, why she was so eager to wreak a terrible revenge upon this man. Yes, she was a witch and that's what they do, but she had cast a spell and chased him across the countryside to reach him. To meet him. She had only met him for a couple of seconds and yet she hated him. The strange thing was, she loathed him the moment she touched the paper receipt, nay, heard his name. And she had no idea why. Kissing him was out of the question, especially with those ugly green fragments in his eyes.

But he was amusing, and it had been a long time that she had had so much entertainment. A very long time judging by the shape of the world she'd seen so far. So she put all her questions behind her and concentrated on the pleasure to be.

A drop of blood trickled out of his nose. Phil felt it run over his Mount of Venus. It caused him to dither further. She didn't like to wait, as she had waited a very long time already. She didn't have any patience left. He was in trouble and he knew it, he saw it on her face, she was really going to shout at him now. On his knees, he braced for it.

In the next room, Kelly had been trying to cry herself to sleep. The emotions that Phil had stirred up, with his stupid answer, had got to her and she couldn't put them down.

"Yes, Bill would have lied, and I would have felt good, but now look at me? How do I feel now? I believed his lies. I thought we were going to be a couple, a family, but all I am is his whore. Another day and still no phone call. God, I hate myself.

Then there's Phil. He's the opposite. He doesn't go to the trouble to even think about lying. That's worrying. Maybe a witch did attack him? Shut up Kelly for God's sake.

He's drunk or something, he did say he had gone to the minibar. It's the only explanation, or he's delusional, or both.

You'd never see Bill like that. Too busy seducing me that's why. Shit, I wasn't going to think about him anymore, but I can't help it, I love him. But does he love me? Now he's had his fun he sends me away like a little boy with his idiot brother, who thinks he's seen a witch. I hate him. I hate them both."

She was positive that it was over between Bill and her now.

She despised herself for being so stupid, that she'd fallen for a married man.

So stupid for not seeing it for what it was, a big old boss screwing the secretary behind his wife's back.

So stupid that she believed him, for believing that the affair was different from the millions of other office girls, "The bastard."

You'll see, in the morning Phil will realize it was just a vivid nightmare, and the card, was just another card that had fallen out of his pocket. What an idiot. He had me believing him for a moment there too. God I'm gullible, first his brother and now him. What's happening to you Kelly? You used to have it all figured.

I've got a migraine coming on, shit. Hang on a moment. It's coming from next door. What's that noise? God Damn It Phil!"

She was already in a bad mood and hadn't had any sleep. She needed someone to take it out on.

"Luckily, the perfect target was just next door. And he's even given me the pretext. 'A witch?' He's such a scaredy-cat. I bet he's got that adjoining door open. I'll show him. I can be a real witch too. I'll beat him with his stupid darling shoe. This is going to be good." Kelly opened the adjoining door and just as she predicted, Phil's door was open. She walked straight into Phil's room, and *saved his life.*

Ruebella hovered over Phil who was cowering and crawling on his knees. Blood leaked from his nose. Phil was the condemned man. She was the executioner. She took several breaths to clear her lungs for the roar she would unleash upon him. Doomed, he accepted his fate.

She hollered. "DID YOU SET ME FREE?"

The gigantic roar channeled Ruebella's Entanglement kill signature: *Yellow* - derived from deep sorrow she experienced in a convent; and *Kill* - her mode of revenge.

YELLOWkill.
YELLOWkill. YELLOWkill.
YELLOWkill. YELLOWkill. YELLOWkill.

The windows were shaking and mirrors cracked from the explosive howl.

Just at that instant Kelly walked into the room and was hit by a shock wave that lifted her off her feet. She was thrown back through the adjoining doors. She landed in her room, spread-eagled and injured.

Phil lay motionless on the floor. His cheeks were sandblasted and bled along with his nose. The whites of his eyes were red with blood which leaked out of both corners.

"He's still alive? Damn that woman for interrupting, she absorbed some of the blow, the lucky bastard. If I wondered why I hated him, I now know the answer. I hate lucky people."

It couldn't have been further from the truth. What she also didn't know, what she didn't see, was that Kelly was carrying the Boleyn shoe. It was it, rather than her; that absorbed more than its fair share.

"And I hate good looking people. She's going to get it, whoever she is. Where did she come from? Over there, she came from that door. There she is, getting up and running away. Boy, she's going to get it good… I'll come back for him in a moment." Ruebella turned her broomstick around and menacingly steered towards the adjoining doors.

Kelly's ears rang so loud that the world was silent and distant. She got up on all fours and peered through the doorway. A witch with greedy yellow eyes was standing over and studying Phil from head to foot.

"She's going to kill him and then me." she thought.

But the witch didn't.

Instead Kelly saw Ruebella's head start to turn. She knew at that moment that the witch was coming after her. For a fight to the death. She fell forward, pushed off on her hands and scrambled to her feet. Then she dashed for the back of her room.

In front of the window, Kelly turned just in time to see the point of the witch's broomstick appear, fearsome and ominous. Moments later it revealed its terrible cargo, the witch's horrifying profile.

"Oh My God. I'm going to die."

The broom turned excruciatingly slowly. It faced the quaking Kelly who had no time to reflect that she was being chased by *a witch*. Or to shudder in disgust at the hideous creature, she threw whatever it was in her hand.

It flew in slow motion towards the witch. It should never have reached her. But it did. It traveled in a shallow arc straight for the broomstick and landed right in the saddle where Ruebella sat.

Both women watched the thing fly through the air. But neither knew what it was, until Ruebella looked down at it. THEN she knew exactly what it was.

Kelly had stopped panicking.

She watched as the witch stopped looking at her and focused on the item teetering before her. *It was the Boleyn shoe.*

Ruebella went back in time. It was a time when she was only a girl, not a woman, not a witch. At seventeen years old, and only days before her eighteenth, Ruebella's parents passed away from consumption. At least her parents had strong connections with the Church. Provisions existed for her; she would be in the charge of the Nuns of Yellow Pine Convent. Ruebella was destined to become a nun as her parents had given up finding her a suitor.

She had little choice and she didn't like it.

"No one is going to marry her, no matter how big the dowry is. She's just too ugly." said her father many times.

As a child, the name-calling was so vicious that her parents decided to buy a place in a small religious community. They moved to a remote part of the countryside where they became sponsors and major trustees of the district's convent. An agreement between her parents and the Yellow Pine Convent sealed Ruebella's fate. She would become a nun on her eighteenth birthday. The untimely death of her parents sealed the arrangement.

At the convent, things were not better for Ruebella, actually worse. So Ruebella became a recluse. Childhood teasing, taunting and ridicule became the silent torment of whispers and sniggers.

The nuns openly complained if partnered with Ruebella on chores. Her cohorts sabotaged every task and blamed her for the failures. She was included in the choir. She was blessed with a rich singing voice but a rebellion ended her participation.

"Receipts from public performances were dropping due to the lack of coordinated optical symmetry." was the rumor.

The worst thing, sadly, was Ruebella had noticed smaller audiences too.

Mother Superior disciplined her tormentors with fake anger and phony punishments. Ruebella was positive that if it was not for the hefty trust that life would have been even worse.

Even in the lengthy periods of silence, bullying in the form of eye rolling and tongue poking caused Ruebella harm and dismay. The absence of men, however, meant that physical violence against her was rare. Life outside the convent walls would provide no such guarantees. Therefore, life, miserable as it was, could have been passable, but for an event that changed Ruebella's life drastically for the worse.

In winter, Mother Superior needed a group of nuns to go into town to get supplies. The group would have to be at least six strong. It was more than a chore, it was dirty and arduous work, and dangerous. The Mother Superior had volunteered the first five, and then, pretending that she couldn't decide, picked Ruebella as the sixth.

"Yea, right." she remembered bitterly.

The five nuns now considered the chore a severe punishment, forced to be in confined quarters with *'the Ugly One.'* She was picked on the entire journey.

That there were six nuns in town was not unnoticed by a small gang of petty thieves. As the homeward bound nuns reached a wooded, isolated section of the road, they were ambushed.

They were overwhelmed in seconds and the supplies ransacked, but then the depravity of the youths was sadly revealed. For six women, alone in the woods, there was no means of escape or defense. It didn't take long for the boys to start talking about rape. All the nuns were beaten and badly hurt, except Ruebella, who fought off her aggressor. But she couldn't help the others. Although she hated them and herself for her impotence, she cried terribly as she watched them savagely molested.

Soiled and broken, the nuns returned to the convent where the five nuns received care and sympathy. Ruebella's bravery, in fending off her attacker, was scorned and by the day's end, her tale had been contorted by the five, into slander.

"Ruebella was too ugly to be raped."

Everyone believed them, and Ruebella became the pariah of the convent. She was viciously held in ridicule, the laughing stock, the object of every joke and look. This evil treatment was the last straw and Ruebella lost the will to live. She stopped eating and became indifferent to punishments. Her chores suffered. Her depression was insurmountable.

She decided to put an end to her life and left the convent in plain view to all. Unlike romantic films, not one person felt compassionate enough to swallow their pride, and dash out in full view of their peers to befriend her in her hour of need. In absolute loneliness, she headed for the river where she planned to cast herself in.

And so it was, she stood by the river's edge, and left this world. In a torrent of whitewater the river took her. Bereft of her will to live, and consumed by the desire to die, she committed herself to the churning rapids. Unfortunately the tumbling undercurrents aroused the uncontrollable survival instinct that lay deep with our sub-conscious. And although she fought against it with all her might, it is impossible to deny. When the turmoil became calm and placid, she found herself deposited on a sandy beach, alive. There she laid destitute and crying on the wet sand, for even the river had rejected her. She cried and cursed God in heaven at her betrayal with a venom of the deadliest poison. In all her years though, she pondered, she had heard many rumors hailing the miraculous doings of God, but never once had she herself witnessed one. And in the secret nooks of the convent where the bad nuns go to lust over boys and their wares, she overheard them say that God never once had answered a call, but there was one who never not. With her face in the sand and with the deepest scorn imaginable, she cried out one last time for God's mercy. Not a single sign returned, not a butterfly fluttering in front of her, not a leaf falling from a tree and rendering a deep and enlightening epiphany, only the unceasing sound of water flowing filled her sight and ears. Knowing that her command was of the foulest nature, she furtively smiled that the reputed savior failed her. For He would surely have turned her to salt to be washed away and forever forgotten for her unforgiveable contempt. With sudden reverence, she lowered her eyes and with a lump in her throat she uttered the name she had spent her life refuting. She hadn't expected an answer from God, but she knew in her heart of fear that this call would not be refused.

"I will not abandon you Ruebella." came an exquisite tenor voice. "I have seen your torments and have heard your cries for love and justice.

I have stood by and watched, but I cannot stand by anymore. Let me help you, I can and am willing, if you wish. I can give you gifts for one simple thing in return.

You know what it is that I want. I know what it is that you want. We can come to an arrangement, if you so desire. Ruebella?

Where can you get such a bargain? How can you inflict a just revenge? Where was God when you cried *her* name? In fact, where is "*She*" now? Look around. Is *she* here? And you have devoted yourself to *her* have you not?"

Ruebella had not moved. Her cheek still rested on the sand. She had not seen the man, but she knew who *he* was and didn't care. She was not afraid. She listened. She was considering.

"Yes." she replied.

They both knew the truth, that her dedication to God was a sham. It was a matter of convenience and survival. She had unconsciously wondered if this was the reason her life was so unfair? She hadn't chosen her fate to be so ugly? Why had life been so unjust? She would never allow the infinite cruelty of man to flourish against her, not if she had a choice.

"You have a choice Ruebella, make it." he commanded.

Was it coincidence or had *he* been reading her mind? Even as she spoke the words, the Devil was drawing up the contract.

"I choose."

Feet stepped onto the sand in front of her and she stared at them from ground level. Two of the most beautiful black leather and suede shoes she had ever seen, only inches from her face.

Now again, only inches from her eyes, one of the same shoes, the left shoe, rested on her broomstick in her lap. She recognized it with absolute certainty, its image and smell, indelibly etched in her memory. Even though it was hundreds of years ago, she recalled it as if it was yesterday. Cast in stone.

She had signed that deal and endured a transformation in a shroud of yellow Entanglement. However, it was a narrow escape, her soul only bonded with the Entanglement at the last possible moment. Death had knocked on her door in anticipation, and this near-death call amplified and further enhanced her powers. There was no hesitation when it came to using them on her fellow nuns. One might even say she used them liberally and jubilantly, but use them she did.

Some nuns at the convent perished in a mysterious yellow fire. Others died in the gardens. She hunted childhood bullies and killed their livestock, and livelihoods. The river was also a victim of her rejection. She periodically poisoned its once clear stream, breeding swaths of putrid decay and fouling its waters from where ever she chose. Folk maligned its once pristine wells to Rubella's delight.

The trail of death and destruction lead to a town next a high waterfall, a cave situated at the bottom. So the hamlet was named Witch Town Falls, Witchiton Falls.

Life stopped in Kelly's hotel room. Ruebella froze like a deer in the headlights, poleaxed by the shoe. Kelly was fixated on Ruebella even though her eyes ached at her sight. Without warning, the witch dipped the broomstick and shook it violently attempting to avoid *any* physical contact. She watched as it slid down the broom handle and fell to the floor. Then she turned and raced out of Kelly's room, desperate to flee.

Kelly lost sight of *the Witch* as she swiftly flew into Phil's room. She heard the front door open and slam shut. She was gone.

With a mighty gasp, Kelly breathed, clutching for her first breath after the attack. She covered her face with her hands, and fell forward onto the bed crying torrents, the tears streamed down her face like rivers. She prayed to God and thanked him eternally. She sobbed, until she remembered Phil.

"My God. Phil, is he dead?"

She jumped off the bed and dashed into his room through the adjoining door. She didn't pause for thought whether the witch was hiding and waiting for her or not, instead she ran fearlessly to his side.

He lay on the floor like a dead man. Dried blood covered his chin and red streaks marked his cheeks. His face was a pale yellow with red patches. The whites of his eyes were completely filled with blood.

"Oh My God, He's dead. Wait. Check if he's breathing?" She bent down to his face and tested if he had a breath. Nothing. Panicking, she picked up his hand and tested for a pulse. Nothing.

"My God, He's dead. Call 911." She picked up the bedside phone, dialed 91… and then hung up.

"What do I say? Oh My God. Check him again. Please God please. Let him be alive."

She frantically rushed back over to his side again, knelt down, and this time placed her fingers over his jugular.

"He's alive."

A wave of relief swept over her as he groaned.

"You're alive Phil. Thank God you're alive."

Kelly knelt on the floor and wept into her hands beside him. She no longer considered him a weakling and worse.

<div align="center">~~~</div>

Ruebella rose into the air flying on autopilot. Her mind reeled with questions that puzzled, bewildered and confused her. Ones she would never have dreamed she would be asking.

"Like what about the Devil's Shoe? How on earth did she come to acquire that? A shoe, she had… the left shoe of the Devil. That's impossible? I don't know, times have changed; maybe the Devil's dead. Now that *IS* impossible.

And he survived the *shout*. Yeah. The Devil shoe carrier took some of the heat, but even so, a direct *shout* at the loudest I can muster, that's enough to kill a horse. Strange days are these."

She flew directionless for a few minutes totally absorbed in her questions until she turned her broomstick around and headed for the Old Stone Bridge.

~~~

"Phil, Phil. Are you alright?"

Phil heard her voice, but he was in a peaceful and protected place and he wasn't sure he wanted to leave. He was warm and cozy, light and free, not responsible for anything, pure warmth and heavenly freedom. However, she persisted. He was unable to ignore her anymore and rejoined the living. He realized that the whole point was decision-making, and he made his choice. Life over death.

He groaned and Kelly's heart started in earnest.

"Phil, are you alright? Can you hear me?"

"Yes." he said.

"Thank God." she said, "Are you ok?"

He opened his eyes, his vision had a yellow tinge to it so he blinked and squinted, his normal sight returned.

"Think I am."

Kelly said to herself, "Same old Phil." She guided him to a sitting position. His chest ached, he panted with the slightest movement and the taste of blood loitered in his mouth.

"Get me onto the bed." he groaned in a husky voice.

Supporting his shoulder by his armpit, Kelly heaved him up as he gingerly staggered to his feet. He stood erect for a fleeting
~~~

moment before he fainted. A dead-weight, Kelly attempted to catch him but all she could do was guide him so he would fall onto the bed.

She left him there, and after ensuring he wouldn't fall off, went to the bathroom and soaked a facecloth in cold water. She dabbed it over Phil's forehead and face, and the fresh, cold water brought Phil round enabling her to wipe off the caked blood. The ringing in Phil's ears, and to a lesser extent in Kelly's, started to fade.

A little later, Phil sat up, and taking the flannel, patted his face gently. His cheekbones hurt, and his nose started to bleed again. He hadn't said much and neither had Kelly. Phil wanted to be strong and alert enough not to say, "I told you so."

Kelly had so many questions. It was sinking in that Phil's ludicrous flights of fantasy weren't so crazy after all. That perhaps he was keeping private counsel on many more theories, ones not so easy to dismiss in light of the recent events. Unfortunately for Kelly, Phil wasn't in any shape to discuss what had just happened.

It was obvious that Phil's first alleged encounter with *the Witch* was true. *The Witch* had indeed attacked him, twice in one night. She forgave him for just wanting to sleep and understood his reluctance to go to a hospital.

CHAPTER 33.

IN GOOD COMPANY AT THE OLD STONE BRIDGE.

Ruebella navigated under the first arch of the Old Stone Bridge and landed on a patch of bare, worn, ground that seemed like a wasteland. She felt scrutinizing eyes upon her and knew immediately she had company. *Unafraid.* Even though her last kill - attempted kill, somehow survived, she remained confident in her abilities. Aware of her awesome power she had no worries of confrontation.

Boleyn climbed out of a small crevice in the rocky bank, only a couple of feet from where Ruebella stood.

"Hello." Boleyn and Hecate said the salutation at the same time. They looked at each other and burst out laughing.

Boleyn was ecstatic, in one night; she had gone from being alone in a strange world, not afraid, just alone, to having two younger sisters. A shoe had incarcerated her and now she was free. The same for Rubella. With no end in sight, her imprisonment had abruptly ended. Her freedom was secured by the surprised tour guide's spiteful actions. For the first time, she looked forward to friendship and acceptance for who she was. Her wish had come true.

"Oh, Boleyn, dear, look what I've got." She pulled out of her internal pocket the deflated body of Gavin.

"Wow, that's incredible. You did that?"

"Yes, I did. Must say I'm pleased with myself. He's Gavin."

"Is he alive?" ask Boleyn.

"Err, sort of." replied Ruebella unsurely.

"Oh. Will he last long?" Boleyn probed.

"That's the sad thing. I've got his soul in my head, but it's not got long to go. Strange how they have to be together so that they can part." said Ruebella.

"Sorry Ruebella, I don't have that spell in my Entanglement, so I don't know what you mean."

"Wow, I have never met another witch. I don't know what you mean either." said Ruebella.

"You don't know about Entanglement, my dear? Ok, I'll explain my little one."

Boleyn started. "When the Devil transforms a female into a witch, *he* has to channel the fourth essence, Entanglement, into that being. It's a dangerous process..."

"I know." interrupted Ruebella. "I almost died when *he* turned me into a witch. That much I do know."

"Oh my poor dearest Ruebella, I'm so happy you didn't." said Boleyn hugging Ruebella endearingly. "I'm not surprised; it's a traumatic experience, the transformation. Most people don't survive. *He, he* doesn't tell you that before you sign. The bas... I better shut up. You never know whose listening."

"I know what you mean, so instead, tell me more about Entanglement." persisted Ruebella.

"Ok, sweetheart. Well, a mortal comprises three elements: the mind, body and soul. For a successful conversion from mortal - to - witch to occur, all three elements must absorb, assimilate, and alchemize the Entanglement charge. And not be overwhelmed by it. For most mortals governing and regulating the enormous breadth of the influx is impossible. It's done on an unconscious level. They can't mediate or manage the energy. It just is or isn't.

Most people exceed their capacity in seconds and are ripped to pieces. They burst like balloons. It's only special mortals who can restrain and retain Entanglement's fluidity. They are the survivors, and they become a new super mortal entity.

We are not, as you well know, immortal, just enhanced with Entanglement. Please don't ask me where Entanglement comes from Ruebella, because I don't know, but neither do I know where the soul originates. There will always be mysteries my dear.

But I know this. One's experiences and hardships are profound multipliers in the transition process. What we have endured, the loves we have lost and found, our psyche, all play a large role in forging our own individual Entanglement. By surviving the transformation, we have acquired that extra dimension. More than just mind, body and spirit, we have what mortals do not, an Entanglement. And not every mortal can get it. Only women, not men. Why, I don't know, it's a strange charm."

She whispered very secretively. "That's why *he's* so keen to offer the deal. You've got to be careful with the Devil you know. *He'll* promise to make you a witch. Odds are you'll turn out just dead. *He* doesn't know who will survive. *He* can't tell. And you know what, not just that, *he* doesn't have full control over the Entanglement current." She mouthed her next words, "Or over himself."

And Boleyn went quiet as Ruebella sat with horror etched on her hideous face. After seeing the impact of her last words, Boleyn continued to talk in a less scary tone.

"Ruebella, it's OK, we survived. We just have to remember, that *he* reports to no one, and can be capricious in *his* actions. We just have to avoid anything that antagonizes *him*, that draws attention and raises *his* awareness of our presence, not that *he* has forgotten about us, oh no, not *him*. But *he* will leave us alone, I hope, as *he* has human kind to harvest, and they're worse than we are, as you well know.

So, anyway, back to Entanglement. We are closer to the core, the elements, the fabric of the universe. You may remember the transformation, how it felt. While nature still pulses in our veins, how it feels for you is different than how it feels for me. Because of all these things, the resulting metamorphosis is a witch that has certain genres of spells that she can perform, create, and cast, due to her distinctive Entanglement. Every witch has a different color, talent and power, this is why I can't cast your spells, and you, mine.

We're all special, individual, unique, but we are all sisters, my love. By the way, I've never heard of a man ever becoming Entangled, strange, eh?"

The recovering Ruebella was fascinated and impressed. Now it was her turn to share her knowledge, and she was happy to do so. She already loved her older sister, who was giving her more love and acceptance than she had ever had in her old life. Even from her parents, whose love seemed out of guilt and obligation.

She told her that she could cast a spell of absorption on a mortal, and its result was the separation and collection of the mortal's body and soul. Once done, the energy of the two entities quickly drained at unequal rates according to their constitution. When one piece approached its expiration, they merged again for one last time, and established the image and identity for the afterlife, enabling judgment. It had to be.

"Wow." said Boleyn, "I wonder if that goes for us too?"

"That I don't know and I don't want to try." laughed Ruebella.

Their banter and laughter were natural and unencumbered as if they had known each other all their lives.

"Come." said Boleyn, I have one last surprise for you. She led Ruebella to a sandy bunker, where some old potato sacks covered something. She pulled back one end of a sack to reveal another witch.

"Ssh, this is your little sister." said Boleyn proudly. They cried tears of happiness.

"She arrived earlier this night, so exhausted that she fell asleep as soon as she landed. She looked terrible, so I gave her something to recuperate. It takes a full day's rest. Should be right as rain for the evening. Let's join her." Ruebella and Boleyn snuggled up to their youngest sister, name unknown, for the happiest moment of their lives.

Hecate had walked barefoot on broken glass. The pain was terrible and her feet bled. A bright sun beat down on her relentlessly, and no shade was in sight. She kept on walking but didn't know why. Something compelled her so she endured the pain. A yellow cloud appeared in the sky that provided shelter from the sun's piercing rays.

Then the glass parted revealing a path with someone walking on it. Beckoning Hecate to join her, it was her older sister. Beautiful yellow eyes shone and gleamed. They hugged and kissed. They looked so good together, green and yellow. They left the fields of glass behind and entered a cool dark cave, where a small bigheaded woman with bright red eyes awaited. Boleyn knelt down at her bleeding feet and kissed them better.

"She's our oldest sister." said the other, "She's going to look after us. We are family."

In one night Boleyn had gone from being alone in a strange world, to being the proud oldest sister of two beautiful younger girls.

CHAPTER 34.

THE VIGIL.

Kelly decided to sleep in the same room as Phil. She wouldn't admit it, if Phil had been conscious enough to ask, but she had been really shaken up and was petrified to be alone. She understood what Phil was feeling when he forced himself into her room earlier that night, when she had meanly played on his emotions.

"Sucks to be him." she thought. "Kelly! You can be callous sometimes." Then she reversed her position again.

"Oh my God, I'm turning into Phil."

She quickly put that thought away too. She had to because she was wasting time and needed to get down to business. She needed to go back to her room to get some things, and she wasn't looking forward to it, not one little bit. Kelly had little choice. Either stay in Phil's room dressed as she was or take the plunge and get the necessities a good-looking woman needs to sleep at night.

She wasn't as sure of herself as she used to be. She felt nervous and uncertain in there all alone. Suddenly, a chill of fear ran down her spine. She panicked, grabbed some stuff and ran back to Phil's room, where she slammed the door behind her, locked it. Then she pushed the nearest bedside cabinet against the locked adjoining door.

"Safe." she sighed.

"The front door." She scampered to the bathroom, grabbed the doorstopper and jammed it under it. Now she breathed more easily. She approached the unused bed next to the window. Seconds after settling down, she jumped up.

"The door chain." Kelly raced back to the door, panicking, and fumbled the door chain into its slot.

She stood back a couple of steps and looked at the door. It hadn't moved, it wasn't pulsating. Nothing was seeping under it, yet. Dashing back into the bathroom, she rolled up a couple of towels, and stuffed one of them at the bottom of the front door. Then she faced the adjoining door. To stuff the other rolled up towel there, she'd have to push aside the bedside cabinet that she had moved in front of it moments earlier. She considered her options, move it and complete the job, or not do it, and risk something evil coming under it. She had seen too many horror films - the evil thing always came under the door.

"How else did the Witch get into Phil's room?" With that thought, she heaved the bedside cabinet out of its position and stuffed the towel along the crack. "Good job I did that, that crack was huge." She pushed the bedside cabinet onto the towel anchoring it there.

She had a respite. "Safe."

Slowly regaining control of her breathing, Kelly stood over the precariously balanced body of Phil. He didn't look good, yellow and shabby, but at least his breathing was steady and strong, so she let him rest.

"Anyhow, I couldn't get him to the hospital on my own and I don't want to get an ambulance here. Look at the place. It's a mess, and see, a cracked mirror, seven years of bad luck. There's a fucking *witch* after us, how much bad luck do you want? Surprised nobody called the police. There'd been so much noise in here, doesn't say much for the area of town we're in, and it's the best district in the city. It's the best hotel, approved by that asshole brother of Phil's."

She sat down on the bed, beginning to wind down.

"Screw you, Bill." she said softly.

She could hear Phil's breathing, and it reminded her of Bill, of how she needed a man in her life.

"Need one to fend off witches, won't have a shoe to... the Shoe. It's what stopped the Witch. Where is it? Oh No. It's in my room."

It was now impossible for Kelly to sleep. The key to thwarting the witch laid in her room, barricaded behind a bedside cabinet and towel.

"What was in that room now? It has been almost an hour since I left. The Witch could be in there waiting, for me to go back in. And the only thing stopping the Witch from entering this room was that towel." Frantic thoughts rushed through her mind.

"But if the shoe was in the room, then the Witch would be scared of it, so, the Witch can't be in my room. So should I do it? Fuck it, here goes nothing. I won't be able to sleep if I don't have it."

She got out of bed and went over to the adjoining door and took a big breath.

She moved the bedside cabinet.

Moved the towel.

Unlocked the door.

Opened the door.

Located the shoe.

Locked her eyes upon it.

She did not see a Witch lurking in a corner, ready to spring a trap on her.

Her tunneled vision did not wander.

She ran into the room.

Reached for the shoe.

And missed it.

She fell backwards and almost over.

She regained her balance, and reached forward for it again,

And Missed It Again.

"FUCK IT." and reaching out again, she finally grabbed it.

She dove back into Phil's room slammed the adjoining door and locked it behind her. Feeling safe finally, she collapsed on the floor, panting as if she had just run a marathon to save her life, not far from the truth. She got up and returned the towel to the crack, the bedside cabinet to the door, and herself to her bed. She slept, clutching the shoe close to her breast, safe and sound.

Almost at the same time, a band of witches clutched one another in dreamless, cozy slumber.

Hours later, Kelly woke up to the sound of Phil groaning. She opened her eyes and quickly headed for the crack of light beaming into the room. She grabbed the curtains with each hand and flung them apart.

She was happy, for the first time on this trip to see his smile.

"Hi Kelly. You're alive." he said quietly.

"Yes, Phil, and so are you. But it was close, I thought you were dead back there."

"So did I." He squinted from the blazing sunlight.

"Room service?" she asked.

"Biggest breakfast they've got. Screw the cholesterol." When the breakfast arrived, they cautiously spoke through the door and then only opened it with the shoe at the ready.

They sat around the small round table in the corner and ate. There was no shortage of conversation now and they were finally becoming less than enemies.

"I'm sorry I didn't believe you Phil. How could I? *A Witch?* If I hadn't have seen it myself, I wouldn't have, couldn't have believed it."

"*Witches*, Kelly. *Witches*."

"What do you mean *Witches*?"

"*The Witch* you saw was not *the Witch* that attacked me the first time. There are two different *Witches*, Kelly, *Two*."

"Are you serious?" she said incredulously.

"I know it's crazy, doubly crazy, but the first *Witch* was smaller, had green eyes and wasn't half as ugly." They shivered in response to the memory of that face.

"God, yes, oh my God, yes, she was ugly." Kelly agreed.

"Yes, she was. And those eyes though, I couldn't tear myself away from them, even though it hurt to look."

Phil continued to tell Kelly about the dream, or sleep walk, or trance, and about the questions she asked, and the way she asked them. In the daylight and safety of Phil's room they laughed about their stories. Understandably, they were so unbelievable they had trouble accepting them.

If it had been a person who attacked them, it would have been simple. Call the police. Write the story and get the exclusive. But here, they could do neither. They didn't believe their own eyes, or ears, so how could the police? And say, by some miracle, that they did believe them, then what? Police would canvass the neighborhood with descriptions of two witches? They would be the laughing stock.

"And we would be working for the tabloids." they chuckled.

They laughed a lot, but they also had periods of comfortable silence, they had truly bonded.

"How are you feeling now Phil?" asked Kelly after a quiet moment. "You look pretty tired again."

The whites of his eyes were bloodied red. But she could also see that his irises had changed color slightly. She couldn't recall what color they had been yesterday; just a plain boring color she supposed. But now they had miniscule dashes of green and a spattering of yellow. They were not nice at all.

"Kelly, I need a shower and then I'm going to have to take a nap, I'm knackered." said Phil in a lack luster voice.

"Ok, Phil, you go ahead, but first would you mind escorting me through my room, so that I can have the same. Not that I'm scared that there's a witch in there, but you know…"

They rolled up the towel and pulled the cabinet away from the adjoining door, and after Kelly had Phil move the bedside cabinets against both of their front doors, he showered.

In the daylight, Kelly had felt confident she was safe. She had told Phil to go ahead with his as he looked like he was on his last legs. Then Kelly also showered, and when she eventually peeked into Phil's room, she saw that he was in bed fast asleep.

"The bugger. Just 'cause I said he didn't have to stay didn't mean that he didn't have to stay. He should have been watching out for me."

Kelly's mind had never worked so much. The stress of the attack, discovering that there were two witches, and then of course the failure of Bill to call, was overwhelming. Fatigue flooded over her and she realized that she was exhausted too.

However, she still had things to do. She brought all her belongings into Phil's room, and as a precautionary measure of course, closed and locked the adjoining doors. After checking them again, she checked the front door and chain, before she poured herself into the second bed and fell asleep, not before thinking, "We may be friends now, but that's as far as it'll ever go."

CHAPTER 35.

COVEN SISTERS.

Hecate woke up to find herself cuddled up between two other witches. Instead of being scared or alarmed, she just hunkered down with them again, and snoozed. She was with family now, and she was safe. It wasn't long though before they had all woken up and were happily getting to know one another. It was automatic, Boleyn, the shortest by a long chalk, was the oldest sister. Ruebella, the middle, and Hecate the youngest, quite how this was, no one was sure, but it was, and that was it. They sat around Hecate's kettle with a brew merrily bubbling and exchanged their sad stories of childhood. The similarities were amazing. Nevertheless, Hecate and Boleyn cried and felt the worst for Ruebella.

When they became Witches, their black capes, pointed black witch's hats, broomsticks and crystal balls, all came automatically with the transformation. Now clustered around the kettle; the closest thing to a cauldron in these modern times, the picture was almost complete. Several black cats joined the clan, now it was.

The witches were stronger as a unit than as individuals, the critical mass attained at the number *three*, and the three were most happy. The trouble with three was that it is harder to keep secret, and being secret was part of a witch's power. So stealth was rule number one, stipulated by Boleyn.

The end of twilight was the perfect time for when witches come out to play: when the smells are crisp and rich, where colors fade to gray, where sounds echo and scare. Hecate had brought her older sisters up to speed on the modern world. Both in awe, they were excited to try one of the best new things this advanced world had to offer; toilets.

"Sisters, it's time to get to work." said Boleyn the oldest.

"Get the man called Phil?" the other two asked in unison.

"Yes, and to see this shoe?" they are intertwined.

"When I escaped, I didn't even give that damn shoe a second glance. You know it will be a very twisted twist of fate if what I think is true. As I've said, the Devil owned the shoe that served as my cage. Not an earth-shattering coincidence as you both appreciate, but I suspect that the shoe may be one of a pair, made by my father no less."

The other two witches let out a little gasp.

They became dedicated to any plan that would return the shoe to its 'rightful owner.' No one cared that the Shoe actually legally belonged to the Devil. However, as the Devil never paid Boleyn's father for them, they may have been right after all.

Life was doubly agreeable; two quests, both equally delicious, both involving the slaying of Phil. Could it get any better than this?

"Hecate, Ruebella you both know where Phil lives, can you find him again without a spell?"

"Yes."

"Night has fallen. What are we waiting for?" the smiling Boleyn proclaimed.

CHAPTER 36.

HARDLY RECOVERED.

Phil woke up, yawned, and then screamed. Kelly woke up, frightened at the sound.

"What." and she then screamed as well.

The open curtains revealed the source of their fear. Twilight was a memory; it was approaching night. They both vaulted out of their beds and rushed to stuff their clothes, toiletries and anything else they thought was theirs into their suitcases. The priority was the shoe.

Grabbing their wallets, handbags and car keys, they left the room without regard to the mess. At the end of the corridor, they pressed the elevator button and waited. Eons passed, they poked and prodded the button until the shiny, sliding doors finally slid open. Then, just as they could make good their escape, they turned for a weird reason. Maybe they both unconsciously heard the stairwell door crack open. As they stared, the door opened further. A broomstick handle came into view. The couple stampeded into the lift. The elevator doors all too slowly closed, they seemed to take forever. As they shut, they watched, and froze, stricken. The broomstick came into full view, followed by the janitor who was carrying it.

Laughing feverishly, they entered the lobby and sat down in the open, cheap, sunken rest area in full view of the reception desk. Privacy was not a high priority. In fact, the opposite was true; they wanted to be around people, safety in numbers. Nevertheless, they needed some degree of isolation to talk freely without eavesdroppers overhearing. The 'Pit' afforded both. Here they were in public and yet secluded.

The hotel staff, that is, the men, all took note. Good-looking woman with older nerd, "Must be rich", and one even had the audacity to approach them. Being spurned by Kelly hurts, and he cowered like a dog with his tail between his legs.

Phil and Kelly wondered what they were going to do. Or more importantly, stay that night, because they couldn't stay here. The full enormity of the previous night was now coming home to roost, the janitor's broomstick, although funny, made them come back from reality to fantasy. They had discussed the situation sporadically throughout the early morning but hadn't fully grasped that Phil was the target of two separate murder attempts. What else could they be called? Attempted by two super natural entities. That worsened their predicament.

They couldn't seek assistance from the police as they couldn't report it.

They didn't know the extent of the Witches' powers. Or why they were after Phil.

Could this go on forever?

No more laughing.

They continued to discuss their quandary, that they were screwed.

Phil noticed that the line at the reception desk had shrunk and told Kelly that he was going up to pay the bill. As he walked to the desk, Kelly realized that she was on her own, and raced up to Phil's side. The concierge made a comment along the lines of "Separate rooms but not separate beds." Kelly needed an outlet for her pent-up anxiety and loudly responded by hurling insults and threats at him. He attempted to placate her with two free meal coupons at the best restaurant in town.

"Like we need those asshole." but she took them anyway and gave them to a passing couple. He didn't know who was more frightening, the yelling woman, or the quiet guy with completely blood shot eyes who insisted on getting the receipt.

They sat back down in the lobby and continued where they left off.

"Seriously Kelly, we're in trouble here. I don't know if it's me they're after, I believe it is, as they came into my room twice, and not yours. I'm not saying this to make me out as someone special, but they both knew my name. How? We're only co-workers forced together, because Bill wanted to get you, I mean us, out of town."

"What do you mean, Phil? Bill wanted me out of town?"

"Kelly, I'm sorry, it's not my place to say anything, so…"

"I know Phil." Kelly said, with tears welling up in her eyes. "I know. I get the picture. Hardly any calls, sending me away on this crazy reporting trip, but I, I love him, loved him. I don't know."

For the first time on this trip, Phil saw the tender side of Kelly, who now failed to hold back the cascading tears. She had held them back for days living on false hope and spite but couldn't pretend anymore. Bill was avoiding her. And now she couldn't take it out on Phil any longer. He had crossed the line. He wasn't the enemy.

Phil was on the spot. He'd never been good with women; that was Bill, and he didn't have any idea what to do if a woman cried, not a clue. Consequently, he said nothing. Phil's MO.

Kelly yakked and cried about her relationship with the (ex) lover. How it all started and matured. Sneaking into hotels during the day and watching him go home at night. Breaking her heart, and then making it up to her time after time. She spoke of the office gossip, the alienation in the work place, her loneliness.

Phil listened, but was getting a little fed up. There he was with not one, but two, *witches* trying to kill him, and she was worried about a little heartache.

"Christ, she's been riding me all this time without worrying about my feelings whatsoever. God we could be back at HQ by now."

"But lately, he's been aloof and distant, I don't know why, did I do something wrong? He was going to take me places, he was going to leave her, but look who he's with now, he's with her and I'm with you." Her eyes were almost as red as Phil's.

"Well this is flipping great, my life's been threatened by fucking *witches* and she's still sticking it to me, thanks a lot. Bitch." he thought.

"Sorry Phil. Didn't mean it like that." Kelly apologetically wept.

"Thank God I didn't say that out loud. She's apologized, a first." thought Phil.

While Kelly had been baring her heart, Phil was tuning into his own issue. He'd been thinking about *the witches*, that they were after him, and about doing the right thing.

"Listen Kelly, it appears to be my fight with the Witches. Go home, go back to HQ and have it out with Bill. That's your fight, this one here, this is mine." he said. "I'm not trying to be brave or noble, Kelly, but this is real, if they attack again, I could die, and if you're around, you could be hurt or worse, killed too. I think we should split up and go our separate..."

A police car siren blared through the lobby which caught everyone's attention. Then the officer parked his cruiser on the sidewalk right in front of the sliding front doors. He strutted into the lobby and headed straight to the reception desk. The concierge readily dropped everything.

"There's a domestic disturbance on the fourth floor, I need you to give me access. Bring your key to room..." the officer said loud and clear.

Phil and Kelly were stunned - it was their room. Phil's room. They looked at each other dumbfounded and then back at the officer who was heading for the elevator. They had to move quickly if they were going to find out what was going on.

Moreover, they had a problem, the shoe was in Phil's case, and there was no way they were going anywhere without it. Phil quickly unzipped his bag. Kelly grabbed it (successfully this time) and stuffed it into her purse. By now, the lone hotel elevator had gone. It seemed an eternity before it returned and the doors slid apart. They jumped in, jabbed the fourth-floor button, and the elevator slowly ascended to the top floor. The doors opened just as the police officer slid the card key into the lock and opened the door.

"Stand back." he shouted at the concierge. He grabbed his radio and called in. "We have a homicide, double homicide at..."

"What?" said Phil and Kelly to each other, only steps from the elevator. "Who's dead?"

They were half way down the corridor before the officer, who had closed the door and was busy giving instructions over the radio, noticed them.

"You guys stop right there, turn around and leave." he stated authoritatively.

"What's happened? That was our room." Kelly replied loudly, "The one you're looking in." She raised her voice as the officer had already shouted over her to "Vacate the vicinity."

"This is your room?" He boomed.

"Was. Mine, actually Officer." said Phil mildly, and thinking how incredibly quick and stubborn Kelly was, just to say the truth, not to be frightened off by the voice of authority.

"It was my room officer, is there a problem?"

The officer advanced menacingly towards Phil, but as soon as he saw Phil's eyes, he pulled his gun out of his holster, and bawled at them both.

"On the ground. On the ground. Face down on the ground. Put your hands over your heads. HANDS BEHIND YOUR HEADS."

At first, Phil was so shocked, that he stood there wondering who he was yelling at. "Me?" he innocently thought. He looked at the gun pointed at him but couldn't figure it out.

Kelly moved first. She started to lower herself to the floor and as she got on her knees, she tugged on Phil's arm and pulled him down with her. Phil's hesitation actually made the officer even more suspicious and threatening.

"Ouch." said Phil, as the officer roughly knelt on his back and handcuffed him. Initially gentler with Kelly, he became progressively rougher, as she moved and twisted and laced him with the back of her tongue.

Phil was quiet as a mouse. Kelly spat and hissed like a cat.

Kelly eventually stopped complaining. It was obviously a lost cause, no matter what she said, they would remain arrested. The officer radioed in that he had two suspects in custody and the radio chatter became very excited.

Momentarily they heard sirens in the distance followed by footsteps sprinting up the stairwell. Still on the ground, hordes of police turned up. Their pockets, wallets, handbags were stripped from them and searched.

"Get your hands off me. Hey. How many times do you have to pat me down eh? Eh?"

Kelly shrieked every time a pat down befell her, which occurred whenever a new pack of police arrived. They called it *securing the suspect*. Kelly called it *any excuse to grope*. She noted every man.

Hefted to their feet, they faced a barrage of questions and accusations. The Police were especially interested in why they were leaving with no idea of where they were going.

Phil's bloody red eyes were a huge alert. Unable to come up with a passable reason at first, he said he had burst blood vessels in both eyes in a fit of sneezing, and then stuck to the explanation. Not answering immediately was one thing, explainable as nerves. Changing a story? That would be another.

The police interrogated the occupants of the other rooms, taking their names and addresses, asking what they heard and when. Police in white coveralls appeared sporadically. To a man, they said it was the worst they had ever seen in all their years of service. Cuffed, waiting for the elevator, they overheard a voice on the radio ordering that the suspects be detained in the lobby. Both recognized its familiar and irritated owner.

The coroner, skillful as she was, surpassed herself. She knew to the minute the time of death. A broken watch and bedside clock. Three 911 calls from the adjacent rooms, reporting domestic violence, collaborated the truthful timepieces. It was exactly the same time that Phil and Kelly, well Kelly, was chewing out the concierge.

Unfortunately for the police, additional supporting evidence of the pair's innocence kept being uncovered. There was the credit card receipt. The couple who happily accepted the two free coupons, the one's Kelly had just moments earlier acquired from the concierge.

Worst still for the police was the video footage.

It encompassed the pit and captured Kelly and Phil gossiping in the crucial hours before and after the 'incident'. They even accidently apprehended a guy in the lobby. It was the same one who'd made the failed pass at Kelly. He gave them both the finger and unwittingly provided another alibi.

The police had no choice, the evidence was overwhelming and they obviously, no matter how much they wanted them to be otherwise, were innocent.

Nevertheless, the handcuffs stayed on.

"Hello Phil and Kelly." uttered a pseudo-friendly but stern voice, and they turned round to see the officer that gave them the exclusive on the McKay's double crucifixion murder, detective Angelo D.

"So you had just vacated the room, Phil?"

"Yes, the receipt is in my wallet, and you've got the witnesses over there. Ask them?"

"I have, alibi confirmed." but then the detective continued.

"I see that the room was in your name, and Kelly, the adjacent room was yours, yes? And the adjoining door was open because, you left through Phil's room, because the bed side cabinet was against the front door, correct, yes?"

"Yes." replied Kelly not appreciating that Angelo seemed to be filling in the gaps with innuendo. With every omission in his interpretation her dislike found another foothold. She was also mad at him too for his lack of command of his men. HIS officers had more than vigorously 'searched' her, and she wanted retribution, now. Kelly's demeanor changed from passive to anger in a second when she thought this.

"You know, your men. The groping I had from your people, five times. I have all their badge numbers. You want me to cause a stink, because I can. I'm a reporter, remember? I consider it assault, sexual assault." and she showed him unashamedly several smudged hand prints in places where they certainly didn't belong.

It wasn't something Angelo relished, a police sexual scandal on two, obviously innocent members of the press. The papers were something he didn't want his name in (anymore). His 'voluntary transfer' could be scrutinized (more thoroughly).

"Sorry, Kelly, please accept my apology. So I guess, considering the treatment that my possibly overzealous officers have given you that an exclusive is in order?" Finally the handcuffs came off, and taking both their arms, Angelo escorted them to the pit and sat down in the 'L' of the cheap, red clothed sectional. They were back in the 'pit.' He showed them, both of them this time, selected pictures of the crime scene.

"Oh My God" another crime scene of blood, and then

"Oh My God, it's Deloris and that ass… tour guide from Witchiton Falls, Gavin." they said in tandem.

"You know these people?" Angelo inquired, in his pressed and clean white shirt, black tie, trousers and shoes. You could spot this cop a mile away.

"Yes." they both said unconvincingly, as Kelly was expecting Phil to reply first and he didn't, not quite, just like their first encounter with the duty sergeant. Just like then, it gave the appearance of having something to hide.

Lightning *can* strike twice.

"Detective." said Phil, taking the lead in another, and this time seemingly successful attempt to redeem himself, "Kelly and I investigated a double homicide in Hecate a few days ago. Deloris was the mother of the murderer. We interviewed her along with several other people, what's she doing here?"

Kelly was flabbergasted. Phil was answering the detective's questions (and veiled accusations) so naturally, smoothly and effortlessly that he couldn't possibly be anything but innocent.

"Wow, Phil, nice." Kelly thought, it was now her chance, and she picked up the torch and spoke.

"Then, after filing the exclusive that you, thank you Angelo, presented us here in Boleyn, Bill, the chief editor, gave us a couple of days off, and we went for a trip to Witchiton Falls. Phil, show the detective the receipt." Phil rummaged around in his wallet, found the receipt, and handed it to Angelo D. He looked at it, date and time, and he thought that it smelt burnt.

"Well anyway, Phil had a little argument with Gav…"

"He was an asshole." interjected Phil with no remorse "Gavin, our tour guide. That's him. That's Gavin." continued Kelly as she pointed to a picture.

"Well," said Angelo "thank you for being so amazingly frank with me Phil, Kelly. Any idea why he should be in your room Phil, with Deloris, I mean you got to admit it, it's more than strange?" Phil honestly didn't know the answer to this one, so his reply was as pure as the driven snow,

"Detective. I have absolutely no idea." and a millisecond later, he did.

Phil got to work as quickly as possible. The Investigative Reporting Team had another exclusive. Indeed, this one was the definition of 'Breaking News.' Angelo, on the other hand, sat in his car tapping the top of his pen on his chin in deep thought. Despite everything, (not being the straightest arrow), he was a good judge of character. He could tell if people were lying (because he'd told a few himself), he was good at his job. So this was his problem. Both Phil and Kelly were telling the truth he had no doubt. They volunteered information without prompting,

"I mean, he had no reason to tell me this poor woman was Deloris Drinkmore. Her body was so mangled, for the want of a better word; that it would have taken weeks to identify her, if at all, as she was from way out of town. Yet he told me who she was, where she was from, her connection in a prior murder, without hesitation or questioning. In fact, he incriminated himself in some respects, although his, theirs, alibi is unfortunately rock solid.

The frigging 'M.E.'s' time of death, right in the middle of the video footage. And I can spot a killer, (takes one to know one), and he ain't one.

But I sure get the feeling that there's something else to the story, like some elaborate con job or something? Nevertheless, even if there was one, how does Kelly fit in? True, their relationship has changed since I met them a couple of days ago.

She despised him then, there wasn't even an attempt to hide it, but now, they're a team, and I don't mean *The Investigative Reporting Team*, but a real team. You don't go from disgust and revulsion to admiration, which is what I see now. She's not sleeping with him that's obvious, but to gain the respect that she has for him now, that takes a lot.

A life-threatening lot.

Something has changed.

Something big.

Then there are their eyes. When I first met Phil, he had blue eyes, now they're blue, with green and yellow smudges, can't blame a sneezing fit for that. Kelly's got a bit of a yellow stain in hers too. What the hell?

OK, The Gavin enigma - how do you explain that? They went to Witchiton Falls, why did Kelly remember Phil had the receipt in his wallet? What a small detail to remember, like proving they were there, when if they were guilty, they would do everything to prove they weren't. In addition, why did it smell burnt, but it wasn't? I mean again, it would have taken us ages to find out whom this corpse was, and Phil didn't hide his dislike for the guy whatsoever, even in death, he called him an asshole.

A killer could have said the same, if he was really clever and tried to hide it with honesty, but I would have seen glee, I didn't see glee, I just saw dislike. It doesn't add up. How did he get here? No car, and that goes for Deloris, it's a long way. Did Phil and Kelly abduct these people?

Their car, I should search it. People always forget the car, if Deloris' and Gavin's prints are in there, then I have a chance. Need a warrant. I'll ask them, if they refuse a non-warrant search, then they're hiding something."

Angelo got out of his car and walked over to the hotel door, watching Phil and Kelly working feverishly on their exclusive. Like a seasoned hunter, he was careful not to spook them as he entered the hotel, "Damn those noisy sliding doors. Oh, hey, they didn't look up, good. Easy now. Gently."

"Hey, Phil." he casually called him, as if he was his friend.

"Yeah. Sorry, let me just finish this sentence." Phil didn't even look up. "Nearly, nearly, OK. How can I help you detective?" but now he did, it was more of a glance really.

"Sorry to have to ask you this Phil, but can I search your car? I mean take finger prints etc. Forensically like. Actually, impound it."

"This is it, now I'll see some sweat if they have anything to do with it." Angelo thought.

"Knock yourself out." Phil reached into his jacket pocket and threw the keys onto the glass tabletop hardly even looking up.

"Shit." said Angelo D, not even close.

"Oh wait a moment." said Phil, now looking up anxiously.

"Hallelujah, touchdown." Angelo smiled as Phil reached back down for the keys and picked them up.

"I need my home keys." he started to pull the house key off the key ring.

"Damn, but it's not over yet." thought the disappointed detective.

"Leave the house key on there buddy, we may want to search that too." Detective Angelo D. said in a snappy voice.

"OK." and Phil threw them back down onto the table and refocused on the report, ignoring the spite in the detective's last request.

"Oh, OK, thanks. I have your full permission, Phil?" He was irritated now more than ever.

"Sorry, Detective." Phil stopped writing, looked straight into the detective's eyes, and said mildly, "I am sorry Angelo."

Angelo's heart jumped. "Finally, this is it, the retraction."

"I'm sorry detective. I didn't mean to be rude and upset you." Phil dipped his eyes towards his papers. "Of course you have my permission." Then he retrieved the keys off the table, causing Angelo's heart to skip a beat in anticipation, and stand then stood up and politely handed them over to Angelo as if was his last dying gesture. Unknown to Angelo, this is exactly what Phil believed it was.

Phil had resigned himself to the fact that *the Witches* were indeed after him. Deloris and Gavin were additional proof of that. They were in his room, not Kelly's, they were after Phil, he could come to no other conclusion.

He knew why Deloris and Gavin were in his room, they both had a connection to Phil, the card and the receipt, love and hate. Now he realized how Gavin got there, he was marginally wrong on the fine details but he had the general idea, and he also saw the reason for their deaths tonight, they were already doomed by association.

So who cared what this Angelo detective wanted or was going to do? Phil was a dead man walking.

Kelly piped up "Detective. I trust you will return Phil's car back to his residence when you're finished with it. Detective? Yes? I mean he's not stopping you, but it's going to cost us, we're from out of town as you well know. We need a car." and for Kelly, she was being extremely diplomatic.

"Well that's your problem, get the newspaper to pay for it, I've just handed you two exclusives, we're not about to start subsidizing potential suspects." he said belligerently and without provocation.

Standing up, Kelly, with a raised voice, attacked the detective, "Well, there's no need to be so mean about it, Phil has not even…" She looked down at Phil and suddenly realized what he was doing, he was writing his own obituary.

"Not even… You don't have to be so mean." and sat down in a huff.

"Finally, a reaction, only not from Phil, and we're clearly not going to get anything out of the car or the house. Shit, I'm going to have to go to all the trouble of filling out all the paper work etc. etc. for nothing. God, I hate murders."

"Another murder suicide, violence against women seems to know no bounds, another exclusive from *The Investigative Reporting Team*, Phil and Kelly."

Phil read out aloud the last line of the testimony for Kelly and the Detective to hear.

"So that's what you think it is Phil?" said Angelo, attempting to be agreeable.

"Angelo, tell me, in all honesty, what else can it be?" said Phil continuing. "Try me? I'll write it down, right here, right now, Lead Detective Angelo D. of the Boleyn police force believes that …"

"Phil. That's enough. I know that you and Kelly aren't telling me everything…" Angelo D. retorted angrily.

"Come on Phil." said Kelly, "We've got a story to post." and she stood up and led the way towards the reception desk. Phil dutifully followed, he so desperately wanted to tell Angelo everything, but he knew it was impossible.

The report was two thousand words long and their best yet. He asked the hotel bursa if the fax machine was working and to cap the night, it actually was.

Phil got off the phone with Bill who thought it was just 'so so.' *However, he was going to stop the presses; that's how "ordinary" it was.* And so, for the second time in a week, Bill stopped the presses, for his brother no less. Although he would claim later, it was for *The Investigative Reporting Team*, which was gaining a minor reputation for itself, he had cause to point out: begrudgingly.

"The bastard." said Kelly, refusing to talk to him when he asked to speak with her.

No sooner had they left the little fax machine office, they became "Persons of Interest". Several police officers escorted the two to separate police vehicles, and drove off to the Boleyn police station in a flashing red and blue lit motorcade. Meanwhile, the night shift tore through his car checking every fingerprint against those of Deloris' and Gavin's.

The officer's pummeled Phil continually; and always the same thing. "Why did you kill them?" They had the good cop, Angelo D, the bad cop, Detective Connolly act straight out of a TV show. Connolly thoroughly enjoyed bullying Phil, causing tears to leak out of the corner of his eyes. Kelly bore the brunt of the police's mind games, she was an accessory to murder, "Phil had already confessed, he's blaming it all on you Kelly; you've got to save yourself."

Neither of them broke, and nobody knew why.

Ironically, Phil felt safe in the police station, with his police bodyguards who he wanted, needed, to get him through the night. As for the interrogations, he'd faced *Two Witches* in less than a day, and lived; this was not even close.

Next room over, Kelly knew that Phil could not tell the truth, so she just stayed polite, cool, smiling; driving them insane. She was especially happy; to overhear Detective Connolly and Angelo have a brief exchange outside of her interview room,

"Have you considered the idea that they could be completely innocent?"

"Very often." replied Angelo, but there was just something that irritated him about Phil. An evil thought crossed his mind; but it was too late to plant a hair in the car now. Anyway, he had come far too close to being caught the last time he 'assisted' an investigation.

"Shit." and he knew there was more bad news to come. The results of the car were a foregone conclusion, no matches, fingerprints, DNA, nada, and as night turned to light, Phil and Kelly, requested their release, and there was nothing to be done, except to set them free.

~~~
~~~

Angelo was completely obsessed with the case. He hated ignoring his gut, but there was no evidence that linked Phil and Kelly to the murders.

His gut was telling him, "That these two were in it up to their eyeballs, and yet were too scared to tell me what it was. It was a strange kind of nervousness too, when I threatened them by linking them with Eastern European Mobs, the Drug Cartels or whatever, he, they would shrug and almost dare him to implicate them. It wasn't the normal behavior of innocent people; innocent people quake in dread at the sound of those names. They plead their innocence desperately, normally clutching and pawing him. And the guilty ones, well they really go nuts, they'll get out of their chairs, and pace around swearing to God their innocence, and then seconds later will beg for a deal. But these two, not a concern or a performance, just a shrug and a whatever. I don't get it. It was like they were relieved to be in custody for the night, but soon as daylight came, bam, they were out of here. They weren't scared at all."

"What? Sorry love; what?"

"Dad, haven't you been listening, it's this weekend."

"What is?"

"The Witches Fair in Salem, it's this weekend. Remember; you're taking us; Madison? Remember, Dad?"

"It's this weekend? Already? God, Natalie, I've been so busy with work."

"DAD! She's sleeping over tonight, and we're leaving early tomorrow morning. DAD, I can't believe this."

The doorbell rang, and Madison's parents holding her carry on were at the doorstep.

CHAPTER 37.

ENEMY NUMBER ONE.

Hecate, Boleyn and Ruebella soared and sang, they laughed and cackled, flew in circles held hands and danced. The Old Stone Bridge wasn't feeling so old anymore. The jet-black sky rejoiced too. Ages had passed since it had seen such a sight, such a long time that the clouds jostled for a ringside seat with eager anticipation.

At Boleyn's insistence, their frolicking had to stop, but not before Hecate and Ruebella completed several more loop-d-loops around each other. Boleyn was impatient for answers, so with sisters corralled in, they flew towards their target.

As they approached the hotel, the youngsters became more and more excited and bold. Not caring for cover and stealth even when they were in full view of the building.

Though Phil had developed resistance to Hecate and Ruebella, Boleyn had no fear of the shoe. A pensive and serious Boleyn was determined to find out who this man was. Then she'd kill him. There were so many coincidences. Was there something special about him? Hecate and Ruebella couldn't remember anything even remotely setting him apart. He was a real puzzle. Why, for instance, did they all hate him so much? What was his connection with them? They had been three separate and distinct trapped witches, unknown to each other prior to this day.

How had he brought them together? United in hatred and love. Was there a why?

They landed on the shingle roof and snuck into the hotel by the familiar route of the younger two witches. Hecate and Ruebella rushed ahead to stand in front of Phil's door. They moved aside to let their eldest sister see the entrance, and watched as Boleyn pulled a small shammy leather out from under her hat, and place it on the door handle. She whispered.

Lock of Ages,
Turn the Pages,
And let this be the Key.
Do it out of spite,
For people you don't like,
But especially for me.

Boleyn retrieved her cloth as the lock quietly surrendered and a soundless entry procured. Hecate and Ruebella were duly impressed. A gentle click signaled the closing of the door behind them. With hunger in their eyes, they looked around the room. To their bitter disappointment it was empty. The beds were unmade and were even still warm, the curtains were open. Did someone see them? The witches were silent. Still, they were in the room and maybe Phil had left the shoe behind. A long shot. But as they had nothing else to do, they searched the place anyway. Unfortunately, for Hecate and Ruebella, no matter how hard they prayed, it wasn't there.

It was the second time that Boleyn had searched for the shoe to no avail. Boleyn was going to blow. She had tried to persuade the others to take a more surreptitious route to the hotel. One that wouldn't have revealed their presence, one not visible from the window. However, to her reticence, she allowed the sisters to convince her, to throw caution to the wind. Eagerness for revenge blinded them.

"This Phil is dangerous, girls, I tell you this, there is something about this man I can't detect, but he's making me so GOD DAMN ANGRY." screamed Boleyn.

Not more than two feet tall, and half of that head, she constantly hovered on her broomstick to make up some height. The angry gaze of her red eyes penetrated their bones and they quivered under the weight of her accusing gaze.

Cowering together the younger sisters realized that Boleyn blamed them for their prey's escape, and they knew she was right, big sister did know best.

To survive the wrath of Boleyn, their hearts drew all their remaining energy to their souls. And then it happened. From the titanic pressure, both Hecate and Ruebella ejected their dying captives.

The weak willed and uglier Gavin inflated his body and groaned as he lifted himself to his hands and knees from his crumpled posture on the floor. He looked up and surveyed the room. One, two, three ugly witches. Yes, he recognized the ugliest standing directly above him.

By the feet of a green-eyed witch, there was another woman. "Pretty."

A bone chilling shadow of the once sexy Deloris materialized on the floor at Hecate's feet. Her last breaths of life saw her look at the faces of the three hideous witches, and she smiled, for she knew she was still prettier than they, because the gawky guy desired her. Ruebella saw the look on Gavin's ugly mug and the look of superiority on Deloris's face. In a desperate bid to inflict pain before she died, Ruebella flew across the floor like a javelin and impaled her heart with the tip of her broomstick. It was too late. Deloris had laughed a laugh to outdo all the witches combined. Mirrors smashed, watches stopped and light bulbs shattered. Deloris' died at peace.

Sobbing as the thoughts of her life flooded back, she picked up the body of Deloris, and threw her at Gavin. "Fuck her now you bastard."

Ruebella was having a bad day as it was also too late for Gavin. His life played back in his mind like a crappy cheap movie. He closed his eyes in disgust with himself. His life had been a series of petty thieving and malicious acts. Unable to endure the shame, he struggled to his feet, and stood up straight. Then he raised his hand to chest level, gave them the finger, and died.

"What was that?" The witches were silent, and a stillness filled the room. The witches had no idea of its relevance or imparting insult. Gavin's only brave, if not noble action of his life fell flat on its face. However the witches forgot their issues. Hecate and Ruebella came back to the fold, and Boleyn's leadership solidified.

They'd made enough noise to wake the dead, yet, in a futile and vain attempt to maintain some semblance of secrecy, the three left the hotel room as quietly as possible. In a final act of failure, it was as if the door remembered its coerced opening as it snapped shut with a corridor shaking wallop. Deflated, shamed and exhausted, they headed back to The Old Stone Bridge in silence.

They sat around in a circle and watched a cup of char brew. Whoever Phil was, they despised him now more than ever. Hecate and Ruebella were solemn, they weren't sure if they had any means of finding him now, and they needed too, for the sake of Boleyn. As a last resort, they considered serious spell making, but that was risky, dark, and even Black. It was something one might not survive but done when one was fervent about retribution.

Boleyn, having punished her sisters long enough, revealed that they still had another method of finding him. Boleyn's shoe. As long as Phil kept it, she could find him. The two sisters sighed in relief; they would never piss off Boleyn again.

CHAPTER 38.

LACKING EVIDENCE.

Without the slightest evidence of any involvement, just a string of bizarre coincidences, and his gut feeling that Phil and Kelly hadn't told him the whole story, Angelo D. the Detective, had released them. All bluffs called.

The first thing they did, after checking that the police hadn't removed the shoe from Kelly's handbag, was to get out of Boleyn as quickly as possible. Away from the police, and maybe even the witches. Not particularly hopeful that they had achieved either, they headed in the general direction of home and double-checked the Shoe again out of paranoia. As long as they had it with them, then they were safe. It had saved Phil twice. They surmised the shoe frightened away the Green-Eyed Witch. It had saved Phil and Kelly from the Yellow Eyed Witch, so now it never left their side, with it, they were safe.

They didn't know.

Not wanting to stop until they had a couple of hours between themselves and Boleyn, they drove until hunger couldn't be denied. So, stopping in a small town, they found a cheap old diner, one of the originals, a silver caravan with double wheels in the middle. Hungrily they ordered breakfast which produced portions that were huge.

"Not many people finish that order, but you two put it away good." the waitress commented, after recoiling at Phil's blood shot eyes.

They let the food go down a bit and then started to talk in earnest. There were some tricky decisions to make, but the first decision wasn't up for discussion.

"We're in this together Phil, I know the witches are after you, but now *The Yellow Eyed Witch*, knows about me, thus, I might be a target too. It'll be better if we stick together."

If the opportunity to leave Phil's company had presented itself a few days ago she'd have gone in a second. But now things had changed. She had written off Bill and had a growing respect for Phil's pedestrian ways. He never tried to compete with his brother, even now, that he, they, had stopped the presses twice in one week. Furthermore, since they had the argument about the ownership of the reports, and he had relinquished sole ownership of them, he hadn't held it against her. She had teased and tormented him in general, especially over Deloris, and he hadn't lost it with her. Not until the first witch had attacked him did, he raise his voice. It was understandable after she had doubted his word, but how could she not? The plausibility of his accusation? Wearing a jacket with patches at the elbows and old worn shoes, he looked anonymous and expendable, and up until this point, he had been.

Kelly considered her present situation. "Right now, he's the only man that would believe me if I said there was a *witch* outside, that is, believe me without thinking of it as a means to get into my pants. So here I am, now with Bill's brother, scratch that, here I am, with Phil, in a fight to the death with two evil super natural witches. I should write a book."

They got back into the car and drove away, still unclear on where they were going, after about an hour, Kelly spoke up.

"Phil, you know they searched the car, right?"

"Yeah?"

"They didn't find something, because I'd taken it out of your glove compartment ..."

"The envelope from the B&B, I'd completely forgotten about that, where is it?" said Phil excitedly.

"As I was saying Phil." Kelly chided happily, "I put it into my handbag a couple days ago, I needed the space to put my…"

"So, open it and read it." he didn't care about the reason.

There were a couple of pieces of paper, most of it about the B&B, but there was one article, photocopied from an old piece of paper.

"It's about how *the Devil was captured in a Shoe*."

Here's a pamphlet, "A fete of witches is being held at Salem to commemorate the unjust execution of alleged witches. Old witches' stuff, maybe a guest appearance of the John Abbott Shoe, memorabilia of old witches, blah blah blah. This weekend. Hey, it's tomorrow. Phil we should go, there might be something to help us fight our witches."

"You know that's a great idea, but I heard, that they were all actually innocent so..."

"There you go again Phil, you're frigging analyzing everything, you…" She stopped herself. "Sorry Phil, I get it, if they weren't really witches, then what weapons they had, won't work against our witches, real witches."

"But they might." said Phil not missing a beat for a change. "OK, let's go."

At the next junction they began zigzagging across the country in Salem's direction. They were getting along well and when that happens, time flies. Before they knew it, the sun was below the horizon and they were miles from civilization.

"Next stop?"

"Yeah, anywhere."

But it was a long time coming… and it was night by the time they found something in the black, cloudy evening. Perfect weather for *Witches* they thought, and correctly so. They were, now after all, the world's experts.

In a dingy looking strip mall motel, with a flickering "NO" vacancy sign, they stopped just in case there was one, and luckily, there was. The grimy clerk took the only key off the wall and walked them over to the last end unit in the "H" shaped motel complex. Neither of them had a good feeling about it. There were no lights, it was close to the woods, and the car couldn't get within thirty feet of its shaky door. They were stuck here.

"Shit, we're really screwed." thought Kelly.

Then it went from bad to worst. The clerk opened the creaky screen and then pushed the front door in with the palm of his outstretched hand; inside, they saw there was only one bed.

"No, No." said Phil and Kelly together, "Separate beds, we need separate beds."

"Whatever. Come with me, there's a cot you can have in the office." the grubby clerk said with a slimy look at Kelly.

~~~

Hecate, Boleyn and Ruebella slept the night's disappointment away, and kept warm with a haram of black cats snuggled in amongst them. In the evening, they got up, and had a boiled pot of something meaty, they all knew what it was. Luckily, cats can't count. After the snack, Boleyn kept the water for the spell she was about to cast. The spell to find the shoe that was in Phil's possession.

She took out a little, circular, ornate pewter tin from her cloak, that wasn't more than half an inch in diameter and carefully prized it open. The tin had two thin strips of metal crisscrossing the inside, making four separate compartments, each packed with herbs and the like.

She added a tiny pinch from one section; her minute fingers were like tweezers, the only fingers in the world small enough to get into those tiny little compartments. She was so small, that everything she possessed was miniscule.

She happily sang a little song, and when she forgot the words, she hummed. Then she retrieved from the inside of her hat, the same small well-worn stained piece of Shammy cloth she had used to unlock the hotel door. It was a piece cut from the finest Shammy ever made, honed by the tiny hands of Boleyn's Father. Its softness was seductive, its toughness impressive. Because her spells had gradually grown in potency for no apparent reason, she suspected that it concealed an Entanglement. But she had no way of telling. She hoped it was true.

It would be a secret slight against the Devil if it were. She could construe it as partial repayment for his betrayal. It seemed that something special had been bestowed upon the Shammy, its relation with the Shoes seemed the likely reason.

With unrivaled suppleness and patina, the Shammy was one of a kind, reserved for the lining of her father's most expensive
~~~

shoes, made for an exclusive client, who turned out to be none other than the Devil. With every spell, the Entanglement of the Shammy deepened and augmented, it was old and worn, stained and blotched, with residual, homeopathic, spell making Entanglement.

"Was it possible? No." She put that thought aside.

She suspected the lining of the shoe she sought, was cut from the same cloth. If the minute 'ciseau dentelle' edge from the shoe matched the edge on the cloth, it would confirm it.

"Damn, I wish I had looked at that shoe when I escaped. It would have saved me all this trouble. And I had the nerve to blame my two younger sisters for being impatient. Look who's calling the kettle black." she thought.

She brought it over to the substitute cauldron, held onto one of the corners carefully, dipped it into the 'Cat Broth' for a couple of seconds and then she slowly pulled it out. She held it by the corner for some time while the Cat Broth drained from it until only drops remained.

"Ruebella, could you bring your broomstick over here please, sis? Thanks." Still holding the corner, she carefully placed the Shammy onto the exact spot the shoe had landed during her attack on Phil.

Black as night,
Dark as might,
Shoe like night.
Go find,
Take flight.
Take the scent,
And my intent,
What to do?
Find that Shoe.

"Ladies, please, join in, but softly, and Ruebella, would you lead?"

The soft ghostly chant echoed under the Old Stone Arches. They repeated it until they had achieved three consecutive chants in harmony. Then Boleyn held up her hand and called for silence, signaling the end.

The trees, the stones, the river all obeyed, as they all waited with baited breath.

And waited.

And more time passed.

Nothing happened. Hecate and Ruebella by now thought the spell had failed. It had been more than a couple of minutes. And how could it not? There were hardly any ingredients. No time to steep, and the chant was too small for any enchantment to procreate.

Just as the two were about to commiserate on the failure, the cloth slowly rose into the air and started in a certain direction. Just like the spell of Ruebella's.

"Shammy. Wait." called Boleyn. Unlike Ruebella's location spell, the leather Shammy obeyed. The younger sisters were exceptionally impressed. Indeed she was an awesome witch.

It was plain to see that Entanglement was clear and strong in Boleyn the oldest sister, of whom they were proud and perhaps a little scared too. Hecate put many ingredients and risked her life to cast a spell. Ruebella meditates for hours. Boleyn just snapped her fingers.

"Shammy. Resume."

The cloth went back to its original direction.

The three flew into the comfortable low-level layer of clouds as they chased the leather.

"He's a long way away. We need to make time. Shammy. Wait. Come."

Like a well-trained dog, the cloth obediently returned to Boleyn.

As the Shammy returned Boleyn said, "Oops. Can't use it without breaking the current spell." She set the cloth back to its task.

Hecate and Ruebella looked at each with the words on their lips. "What was that all about?"

Boleyn maneuvered herself between Hecate's and Ruebella's broomsticks. She took her hat off and placed it on the brush part of Hecate's broomstick and chanted.

Brooms apart,
for a lark.
Brooms together,
hell for leather.

She asked Ruebella to fly close behind Hecate's broomstick until it touched. Both locked into position. She retrieved her hat and placed it on her own broom. Then she repeated the chant. She maneuvered her tiny baton sized broomstick in front of the conjoined pair and gently reduced her speed, until Hecate's broomstick's point touched her broom's brush. When the brooms touched, they linked. All three broomsticks were one. Boleyn at the front, put her hat on the point of her own stick, and completed the spell.

Three aligned,
Hearts entwined,
No longer apart,
Now we start,
Complete the deed,
Go at speed.

The hat blew off the front of her stick at the sudden acceleration and landed on her head. She turned to her younger, but bigger sisters and smiled like a huge Cheshire cat; her red eyes blazed like fire. She was alive. Boleyn loved her younger sisters. The family she always wanted, she had. Her life was complete.

The cloth maintained its lead and the trio sped across the night sky like black lightening. Relishing the night, Hecate and Rubella felt safe, secure, and invincible, under the protection of their oldest sister.

Brooms bowed,
hearts glowed,
love flowed.

"Now let's get that bloody shoe."

They made amazing progress, as the cloud cover afforded them the luxury of speed with stealth. Before too long the cloth slowed down – and they stopped.

"Wait here."

Boleyn disengaged from the broomstick caravan and descended towards a lonely light in the middle of nowhere. Hecate and Ruebella had no doubt that Boleyn could handle it alone.

CHAPTER 39.

LAST RESORT MOTEL.

Were they going to go back to the front office to get a cot just so they could stay in this dilapidated dump? Kelly didn't like it. Not at all. Staying here wasn't the right thing. The feeling kept prodding her, it was insistent.

"Ooo, it's pretty scary here." she said to the slimy clerk. Dressed simply in black turtleneck and matching slacks, she easily turned heads. Her hair was sleek, straight, blond and her face symmetrical, smooth and clean; her deep liquid hazel eyes, with a touch of yellow, were big and bright.

Then a meter soared off the charts, alarm bells rang - called intuition. It had been trying to warn her, that something was about to envelop them, to descend from the sky. Apprehension and fear were approaching fast.

"No." said Kelly, "No, we're not staying."

"What." said the flabbergasted clerk.

"We're not staying, Phil, Phil!" Kelly shouted at Phil.

Unlike most men, Phil acknowledged, his spider sense was tripping too. Even now, the Phil who had survived onslaughts from two different witches could have frozen if it had not been for Kelly grabbing his arm as she raced for the car. It was only twenty feet but it could have been a mile.

Waking up he connected to himself. "Ok, get in the car. Let's Get Out of Here." The fear was becoming tangible.

They dove into the car and raced away as the wheels sprayed loose gravel towards the dumfounded clerk.

"One moment they were going to stay, the next they're running for the car. Look at them, they're rushing like crazy. Wow, those woods are close, pretty scary. Think I'll get back to the office. Think I'll run." And the clerk ran as hard as he could back to safety. He swung the glass door open and slammed it shut, not worrying whether the glass would break. He locked the door in total panic, scared witless.

He was in such a state that he thought he saw something whip by the motel in pursuit of the visitors' car, "What the hell was that?" It was suddenly over, his fear passed, and he went back to being the rake he was.

"Weird couple? Scared of the dark. Chickens. Nice ass." and turned the volume up on the twelve-inch tube TV.

Phil had felt a creeping irrational worry at the same time as Kelly, making the hair on the back of his neck stand up. They had experienced this fear several times now. Things were now different. They had talked about the panic attacks, and surmised they were caused by witches. They dearly wished that they hadn't been but were now convinced they were. It sent shivers down their spines just thinking about it. Had they been stalked? Maybe missing death by pure chance, was this the truth?

However, whatever the cause was, the plan was the same, run, and they did. Once they were both in the car, Phil drove off as fast as he could. Phil was the kind of man who never sped, but his foot was made of lead this night much to the relief of Kelly.

"Well done Phil." the relieved Kelly breathed to herself.

Their warning siren started to ebb. They were gaining ground on whatever it was. *Witch* ever it was. They both believed it to be a witch, both witches. How could Phil and Kelly possibly know?

"Put your seat belt on Kelly. What the…?" cried Phil in panic.

A piece of cloth slapped against the windshield right in the middle of Phil's line of sight.

"Wind shield wipers!" screamed Kelly.

"Yes, great idea." shouted Phil. "My God, she is so quick, I'd have never thought of that. Thank God she's here."

The wipers went on, but the cloth would not budge. At least Phil could see the road if he skewed his neck over towards the rear-view mirror. It was awkward, but not a reason to slow down. With the lights on high beam and the way clear and straight, their initial reaction of panic decreased and now all they needed to do was get that damn cloth off the windshield. However, just as they were hoping that escape seemed possible, the cloth on the window started to grow.

At first, it was only a couple of inches bigger on all sides, but it kept on expanding. It quickly doubled its original size and kept going. The wipers just glided over as if it wasn't there. It was becoming a real hindrance, hampering visibility, and reducing it further by the second.

"Phil, do something." shrieked Kelly.

He tried the windshield washers, nothing.

"PHIL!" it was double again.

Without thinking, Phil wound his window down and reached out for the cloth with his hand.

"God, are you crazy?" Kelly barked, and then. "Any luck?"

The glass was the only thing between them and the trailing witch, and they both knew it.

The driver side windshield was now completely covered while the passenger side remained unobstructed. Unconsciously, Phil had let off the gas and as the car slowed, their terror returned.

"What else can I do?" shouted Phil.

"Let me steer." shouted Kelly, "Put your foot down. TRUST ME."

Kelly reached across Phil as he stomped on the accelerator and let Kelly steer, and immediately their fear started to fade giving them a little confidence.

Phil had wound the window completely down and was using both hands in a last-ditch effort, to pry the leather Shammy off the windshield. But his foot couldn't reach the accelerator anymore and it slipped off the pedal again. As they started to slow down, Phil decided to use both his legs to get additional leverage in tackling the Shammy, since he couldn't reach the accelerator, nothing to lose. It was a desperate moment as Kelly's luck had run out too. She couldn't see either because the leather covered the entire windshield, they were coasting blind. Still holding onto the steering wheel with both her hands, she thought about winding her window down and sticking her head out. Phil on the other hand, was half out of the window trying to pull the cloth off. Neither had their eyes on the road.

Just as Kelly took one hand off the steering wheel, the car left the road. The road turned a severe right, but luckily, a track continued straight. The car rumbled down the track losing speed as Kelly tried to hold onto the steering wheel with one hand and locate the window opener catch with the other. Their anxiety grew with every passing second as the car slowed, bounced and lurched to a crawl.

Phil let loose a cry of triumph as he had finally pried a corner of the Shammy off the glass, and now the leather Shammy peeled off the windshield easily. He pulled with all his might and almost fell out the window. The windshield was now free and clear, and they could drive away.

They felt, saw and heard it. The engine cut out; the headlights went out. All hope went out. They sat in the dead car, panting, waiting and dreading. With every passing moment, the intensity heightened. It was silent. They couldn't talk, say a prayer, or hardly think.

The fear was stupefying, especially for Kelly, whose immunity to witches was limited to a single onslaught, and she had another reason. Kelly was focusing in the rear-view mirror on an approaching un-natural aberration. Kelly's window was half down, but she didn't know it.

In a little cloud of red mist, Boleyn's tiny frame softly descended to earth, leaving Hecate and Ruebella hovering in the clouds on their broomsticks. Before she disappeared from view, they both reached into their cloaks and pulled out their crystal balls. They were going to watch from the bleachers.

"Ruebella, she's incredible." said Hecate after a little while. "Have you ever seen such spell casting, she does it so effortlessly. I mean, my God, they're beautiful. She uses so few ingredients, none, sometimes. Then a little chant, and voilà, done. When I cast my search spell, I have to risk my life. I have to gather all kinds of stuff, make a potion, drink it, and then survive."

"And I have to meditate for want seems like hours, chanting over and over again without a lapse in concentration. The stronger the spell, the longer the meditation has to be, and it's all or nothing, if I lose concentration and daydream, then I lose the whole spell. You know how hard that is, not to lose concentration?" replied Ruebella.

"God, I hate that Phil." they both said together.

"Have you noticed, Ruebella, that all her chants are mild, no shrieking or yelling, no prima donna crap, always in a gentle tone. She must have been really pissed off at us." Hecate whispered.

"God, I know, Christ, when she yelled at us in Phil's room, I almost passed out I was so scared. She really wants that shoe bad. Wouldn't like to be Phil right now." said Ruebella in an equally quiet whisper.

"God no." agreed Hecate.

Boleyn dropped to earth like a feather as she followed the Shammy. It was working well, and she felt she was closing in. In the distance a horseless carriage, "I've been told it's called a car." violently pulled out onto the road, outside of a disgusting dirty white building.

"I bet that's them, but I'll let my Shammy confirm that, I'll follow for a while. Wow, these cars go fast. Yeah, the shoe and Phil are in that car. Really fast. I better sprint after it or I'll lose it." The tiny broomstick sped up, but the car had just got started. Now it was really motoring and leaving Boleyn in its dust.

"My God, I better get cracking; I need to slow it down. I need to... blind the car."

Cars that drive,
Don't arrive.
If Eyes that see,
Don't agree.
Shammy,
Run ahead,
and let it be.

The Shammy accelerated ahead towards the car and Boleyn slowed down. She was getting a little tired having cast several spells and flying a long way. She needed to conserve her energy, especially her Entanglement, just in case there really was trouble. Boleyn was smart. Why waste herself? Let the spell do its work and get prepared for whatever the night would bring.

"Look, the car has left the road." She watched the car bounce around on the dirt track and as it slowed down, she started to gain ground. "It's still alive. I need to kill that car, with all that noise and lights, it could call attention to it and it's quite a distraction too. And who knows what else it's capable of."

Car so proud that ran away,
Listen to what I have to say,
You've worked so hard in every way,
Save it for another day.

"There, peace and quiet, but only for a little while if I have my choice." Boleyn slowly and silently advanced. She dispelled her shroud no longer needing its cover and she wanted them to see her in all her glory. She wanted to strike terror into the heart of Phil and his companion before she killed them. It was her way. She came upon the car, its engine silent and its lights, off.

"It is time."

Her red eyes were so bright that they could have lit up the sky, but she saved her energy and let her crystal ball earn its keep. Gliding up to the car, she bumped into the trunk on purpose, just to scare the occupants. Her tiny broomstick made a little tap.

"Ting."

"Arg." came two voices, a man's and a woman.

Boleyn took stock of the quarry. "The girl is on the right; she's watching me in that inside mirror. He's on the left looking ready for the taking. I can see his dumb face in the outside one."

Kelly watched the tiny cloud of red mist advance upon them. Three points of piercing red light emitted from its center. She was too terrified to consider opening the door and attempt an escape. The cloud started to evaporate before her eyes, and revealed a tiny two-foot-tall witch, with red-eyes.

"Phil" she whispered, "I thought you said the other *Witch was Green.*"

He replied in a hushed shout, "I did, and it was. This is a different *Witch, another Witch, a Red Eyed Witch.*" He watched, less fearful than Kelly,

In defiance, she gritted her teeth and said, "What are we going to do, Phil?" in the bravest voice she had ever used.

"Phil?" Prompting him again.

He wasn't day dreaming, but was concocting a strategy, most un-Phil like. "Get the shoe ready Kelly." he said with authority, and although he was afraid, it didn't show in his voice.

"The *Witch*, I can't see it." quavered Kelly.

"Neither can I." croaked Phil.

Boleyn had ducked under the rear window level of the car and was floating inches off the ground behind the trunk. She was determined to kill these two no matter what, but first she needed answers, and instilling the fear of God into them was her way of getting them.

"So they're captives in their car, let's keep it that way." Boleyn pulled her hat off, placed it on the car's fender, and quietly chanted.

> Doors unlocked,
> May free my prey,
> So lock them up,
> And they will stay.

Phil jumped a mile and Kelly shrieked as the locks next to their shoulders popped shut with a crack. That's when Kelly noticed her window was half-open.

"Phil, my... my window's open." she cried unable to keep her voice from trembling.

"Just keep the shoe ready." Phil replied sternly.

She looked down at the shoe and looked back at the window.

"Argh."

Boleyn was right there.

At the window.

Clad in her black cape.

Peering into the car.

A foot long ugly face and tiny body hovered on a broomstick only inches from Kelly.

Kelly's scream was so loud that Phil nearly hit the car ceiling he jumped so high.

"Give me the shoe dear, and you may live." in a voice like a fingernail down a blackboard, that made the hair on the back of one's necks stand up like a soldier at attention. Boleyn put her tiny hands on the half-open window and easily pushed it down.

"Tell her Phil, tell her to give me the shoe." The voice spoke loudly of bad things to come if he didn't.

But Kelly was poleaxed. Phil couldn't pump enough air into his lungs to tell her to do anything. Kelly wanted to give the witch what she wanted. She just couldn't move her muscles to make them do it.

"Give Me the Shoe!" shouted the Red Eyed Witch, seething with hatred.

Kelly forced her arms into action, although they felt heavier than was possible. With blood now dripping from her nose and her ears, she lifted the shoe, which lay flat in the palm of her hands.

Boleyn reached out for it with eyes greedily gleaming.

"No." Phil yelled. Faster than he had ever moved in his life, he grabbed the shoe.

"*No, it's mine.*" Phil shouted as he snatched it away from her and yanked it over to his side of the car like a football player protecting a fumble. It shifted in his grasp so he unconsciously wrapped it in the expanded Shammy leather cloth.

The suddenness of his defiance took Boleyn by total surprise. She couldn't remember any instance of someone having enough willpower to stand up to her like this. Now she saw the reason - the slightest spattering of green and yellow populated his eyes. Thinking quickly she had seen some yellow in Kelly's too, although much less. They had acquired Entanglement, unique amongst the human race, and unheard of in a man.

Astonished, she looked again just to be sure. He had a double dosage.

"Why they hated him, became clear. He was indeed special. Only at the intersection of exceptional conditions, combined with the rare trait to ingest Entanglement safely, could this be true. FOR A WOMAN.

For a man? *Only one. Him – The Darkest Lord. And none other.*

Phil was worthy of their loathing.

The woman too, to a lesser extent. This explained why they were paired - Entanglement attracts."

With Entanglement, he was dangerous. It was time to end it. "DIE." she bellowed at Phil.

Boleyn's Entanglement was RED; and Die was always her intent, and everyone she had ever wished it upon did. The Entanglement signature of

REDdie.
REDdie. REDdie.
REDdie. REDdie. REDdie.
REDdie. REDdie. REDdie. REDdie.

It swamped the car. The back windows shattered. The car horn blew. But Phil didn't die.

CHAPTER 40.

CONCEPTION.

In the course of grabbing the shoe, Phil had wrapped it in the Shammy - the shoe's lining and the Shammy were one of the same, *cut from the same cloth*.

The zigzag scissor cuts made by the master cobblers, Boleyn's parents, matched perfectly, and the match occurred at exactly the same instant Boleyn's Entanglement discharged.

The world shifted at that moment. It took no time and encompassed, not just the world, but also the universe. From across the ocean, a shock wave traveled faster than light, and was blacker than black and whiter than white. The world appeared to sleep, silent and peaceful, but it was not so. The unseen storm from another land touched the world. Only a handful, the very special, truly psychic and perceptive felt the shudder, and questioned it in their unconsciousness; but like a fleeting glimpse or a vague impulse they dismissed it instantly and completely.

If there is a place between being dead and the living, if there is a place where nothing and something exists, then the world was a brand-new place the next instance. For a very few the world and the space-time continuum were conceived anew. Akin to portal been briefly opened, it penetrated those able to detect it and passed through the rest. Not life force, not even an elemental particle - it was invisible and undetectable, but it touched the Entanglement of anything that was in the process of birth, which was already alive, but had never lived.

The shoe was incarnate. The shoe had been worn by the Devil. It had been the host for Boleyn for hundreds of years. Shards of their beings had been absorbed in its leather heart. It had brewed and steeped, fermented and emulsified, but had never been able to cross the line between death and life, until now.

The latent spells inherent in the Shammy, the blotches and stains were islands of Entanglement waiting for a conception. The joining of the two, *Shammy and shoe, parent and child*, gave birth. Now it had a will.

Not just a new life form, not just a new dimension, it was something new. The collisions of coincidences had forged this new kind of spirit.

RhomSong

The shoe sowed itself together at the toe, re-stitched the lining, patched and bolstered the heel, and polished itself until it shone. Its black leather restored, the black suede flexed, its black gold and silver threads pulsed. It had become now. It absorbed the shout; stored it, converted it, re-energized it.

It protected the one who had brought the four halves together and given it new life, the one who joined the Shammy and the Shoe. It remembered the man who had pulled it out of the graveyard of debris, had given it water and polished and cherished it. He had loved it even though it could not reciprocate and had ignored the insults of his company. Phil was his name. He was the Father and the Mother, Brother and Sister, Son and Daughter, Rhom.

Boleyn, hovered in disbelief, even though she was not quite at full power, she couldn't believe her eyes. Phil was bleeding from his nose and breathing heavily. But breathing wasn't in the plan. The blow she had delivered was enough to kill a dozen men. His face should have been wiped out and his head bouncing in the back seat. He should be dead; the attack's moderated Entanglement couldn't account for it. And even with his green and yellow immunity, her *shout* should have done him in.

As her mind raced, she thought, "Where's my Shammy?"

She looked at Phil's lap, where she had seen Phil wrap it around the Shoe.

"Oh My God. The Shoe. The Shammy must have matched the lining, and it's restored it. Look at it, it is beautiful, and my dad made it. There is no doubt. By rights it's mine."

She dashed to the back of the car and put her hat on.

"That should do it." Boleyn continued her forward direction round to Phil's door and open window.

Phil looked at the shoe in his lap, *it was incredible*. It wasn't possible for leather to be that shiny without being patent. It was still black, but radiant, the black suede was deep and rich, intricate veins traced throughout the shoe, melding the essence of the shoe into one. He ran his fingers over the lace holes and the pristine laces, which tingled to the touch. Man and Shoe.

He turned and looked at Kelly. Was she dead? Her eyes were glassy; her whole body was slumped in the chair and her breath, no more. He was just about to cry out, when he heard her gasp.

"Kelly, you're not dead. Thank God." Phil said in utter relief.

"*She's* not here." said Boleyn hovering at Phil's window.

"But I am, and if she's not dead yet, she will be soon. And so will you."

CHAPTER 41.

HATE.

They studied each other. Phil terrified, knew this was the end. Boleyn, confident she would be the architect of his death, knew too she faced a man of incredible resilience.

On a whim, in an inspired moment, Phil bargained for his life. "If I give you the shoe, will you let us live?" Then he thought, "Did I just say that?"

Boleyn stopped. She saw a flick of red in his eye, her Entanglement, which explained why he was so calm.

"Ok, deal."

The shoe was so beautiful and hard to give up: he felt he was losing a part of himself. But it was also a no brainer. So Phil handed the shoe over to Boleyn.

"A deal's a deal."

As Boleyn looked at the shoe, she saw her father, her mother, herself. She remembered the terrible treatment they all endured at the hands of everyone: betrayals, starvation, torture, humiliation and finally, rape. She held back her emotions for she had to attend to business.

"Did you know Phil, I was trapped in this shoe for several hundred years?" she declared confidently. She prepared to tell Phil some of her story. "Boleyn. Phil, that's my name, I want you to know this. Do you know what irony is, Phil?"

"Yes." said Phil, surprised by his steadiness.

"You know Phil," said Boleyn calmly, in a secretive, but chatty voice, "this shoe, one of a pair, was made by my father, did you know that?"

"No, I didn't." replied Phil, hardly believing he was conversing with a witch.

"That is irony, is it not Phil?"

"It is."

"Hundreds of years ago, my mother and father sweated and toiled making them. They poured their heart and soul into that pair, for a rich powerful client. You have any idea who, Phil?"

"No." he said quietly.

She drew in her own breath. She had trouble saying these next words, but she was determined. She drew in closer to Phil's ear, and barely whispered.

"It was... it was… the Devil."

"Yes Phil, the Devil." she repeated the name in the same whisper to emphasize its true magnitude.

"My mom and dad worked their fingers to the bone making that pair of shoes, Phil, THE BONE, and you know what? He didn't pay. He did not pay them. You know how I know Phil? Do you?" Her voice was a little louder now.

"No." he said again.

"He told me." she started to raise her voice.

"*He TOLD ME.*" She was shouting now.

"After he made me a witch. The BASTARD. He laughed when he told me. He betrayed them.

He did it to them.

I'M DOING IT TO YOU.

DIE. PHIL. DIE."

Her Entanglement was like a rapier, its signature sharp, crisp and pointed at Phil's heart.

REDdie.

REDdie. REDdie.

REDdie. REDdie. REDdie.

REDdie. REDdie. REDdie. REDdie.

REDdie. REDdie. REDdie. REDdie. ……......

CHAPTER 42.

EVEN, ODD AND CUBED.

John Abbott the XXVIIth was packing his suitcase. After putting a couple of shirts and an extra pair of pants into it, he zipped it up. Tipping it up onto its wheels, he pulled it into the middle of his bachelor apartment living room. He picked up his jacket from the dreary ordinary sofa, grabbed his keys from the plain console at the door, and left.

For the first time in his life, his lame family was pulling through for him and he was excited. His dad, John Abbott the XXVIth, had received an invitation to present the John Abbott Shoe at a witch convention in Salem. However John Abbott the XXVIIth had just turned twenty-one and as the last in line, he was now the heir, the one chosen and obligated to perform the honors.

John Abbott the XXVIIth had been force-fed his heritage from his childhood, and his family's traditions had almost driven him insane. His father was the culprit. He popped in to see his dad before leaving for Salem. He was going to meet the curator and sort out what his role was going to be in a show, a modicum of justice that XXVII would reap the benefits now, small as they were.

"Hi John." said XXVI, the dad. They were look a-likes, small and skinny, with mouse like features and squeaky shrill voices. The greeting only enforced XXVII's opinion,

"Fuck, I'm not ugly or anything, just thin faced, and… frail, weak, stupid, poor, unpopular, clumsy, mousy, nerdy, small and short."

They were freaks. He felt it was a curse to look exactly like his father.

XXVI showed his son the invitation from the museum and his contact in Salem.

"Yeah, yeah." said XXVII.

"John, please have some respect and reverence for what you're doing. You're carrying the family name now John, the family heirloom. The deeds that resulted in the capture of the Devil are a precious heritage and it's our family secret. It's dear to us." whined number XXVI.

"To you, not me." replied XXVII sharply.

The only reason XXVII kept the family secret, was because he knew he would be looked upon as even stupider by the kids at school, and the bullying he was experiencing would only get worse.

"Look, here's the descendant of the Devil catcher. He could beat up the Devil, but he can't beat us up." were thoughts that played in his head and haunted him. The outcome was always the same, and sadly, he knew he was right.

"John." implored Dad, "Please John, it was an incredible feat, people traveled days to be at his funeral.

"Dad, I've heard it a thousand times. OK. I want to do this, but I don't have to believe all this crap."

"JOHN." shouted dad.

"No Dad, its crap. He captured the Devil in a shoe? Yeah. Right." shouted XXVII.

"If you think it's all crap, why are you even going John?"

"Cos with all them girl witches there, I might get laid." Then he grabbed the invitation out of his dad's hands and left.

From the window, John Abbott the XXVIth watched his son drive away. He understood his son very well although he didn't dare admit it to him. Actually, he had been feeling it for twelve years at least, ever since his wife had left. He too had been the smallest at school and had been the victim of bullying, just as his son. He never talked about the black eyes. Just like his son, he too, had struggled to find a girlfriend. The issues were the same, there were so small.

The woman that he married was of course taller than he, and it was more of a partnership than a marriage. They both wanted children. John knew what was in the cards, but he had decided not to tell her, because she would never have agreed had she known. A dirty trick and the root cause of all that followed. He had justified his actions with the knowledge that he had an obligation to have a child, which was the truth.

The turning point, that ended the sham marriage, was when he told her in one of their arguments that he was under tremendous pressure from his parents to have an heir, which was why he needed her. There was no love from that point on. It became just a matter of time before the inevitable happened and she left him for another man.

The toll on John the XXVIIth had been terrible. She gave him up for nothing. He had heard his mother say, "You wanted him, you have him. You and your stupid heirloom."

John the XXVIIth acted out for a long time after that, and continued to this day. John the XXVIth, also damaged, had become a secret alcoholic and suffered sporadic bouts of depression. He hated himself. He would swing from apathy to tyranny on his son's obligation to the heritage. As a result, confusion and bewilderment added further pressure to his adolescent son.

So he watched his son drive away. In his possession was the reason for John Abbott the XXVIth's last farewell. XXVIIth's had snatched something from his father's hand besides the invitation, something he didn't want his son to know that he knew.

Fate had conspired against him again. He finished the last bottle in the house, tied a hangman's noose in some white twine, and said goodbye to the world.

CHAPTER 43.

LEGACY.

Ross Hughes was the current curator from of the dynasty of the Hughes Curators. The museum was proud of this tradition and boasted of it to others, and even the British Museum in London, England recognized its significance.

This weekend, he was busily supervising the preparations for the transportation of the John Abbott exhibit showcase, destined for Salem. He ordered the transport truck to arrive a day early for specific modifications, an honor reserved for elaborate and valuable exhibits. His word was law and as such, he was unquestioned.

Ross was fully aware of the significance of this piece. This was stressed and ingrained in him by his father and grandfather. It was exciting to be part of history. Whilst people did their genealogy and then raved about their great, great whoever, Ross calmly claimed his lineage back to an adoption over twenty-five generations ago. In addition, their work was responsible for an accumulation of wealth and prestige to the community that brought acclaim to the family.

However, the secret job was that his line was custodian and keepers of a terrible treasure. He took his hat off to his ancestor Allan Hughes and to John Abbott the First for their foresight and guile, and he was going to match them. "Just you wait and see." he gleefully anticipated.

Of course he had read all the publicized literature, the fading narratives in the exhibit case, and especially the secret literatures documented by generations of intelligent, curious and dedicated Hughes.

Later generations had mounted a multitude of expeditions to different village graveyards, in a clandestine quest to locate the original gravesite of John Abbott the First. *They found it.* The family had made a pact that the resting place would remain unpublicized and concealed, notably *in original plain sight.*

Skullduggery on behalf of the present Ross Hughes entailed secret night visits, and ground-imaging technology confirmed the story of the burial of shoes. Fascinating and true, what else was? Another tale also turned out to be accurate. Because of a flick in the granite, John Abbott the First, it seemed did not perish - as the grainy granite obscured his date of death.

He believed. He believed everything.

His granddad had sought out and re-connected with the Abbott family, and had confirmed another myth, that they were clones of the original. Of course there were no photographs going back to the First to prove this. Nevertheless, upon seeing the last Grandfather and Father: how identically small and mouse-like they looked; it was clear and absolute. He considered it a reasonable and certain assumption, that this had been the case for every generation. No one could discount the hard fact that there had only been one child, and always a son, per generation.

He believed. He believed everything.

The Hughes's had never let the museum down. Their relationship had lasted for hundreds of years and was symbiotic and successful. There was no sign of it ending.

With the exhibit in waiting, the truck sat in the loading dock bay with security cameras running and doors locked and armed. What could go wrong? Still Ross had the night shift doubled, as he was smart enough to trust his intuition.

"Nothing will go wrong if you're sure that it will. Everything will go wrong if you're sure that it won't."

Nothing went wrong. The night was uneventful - at the museum. The exhibit, as far as he knew, was safe.

The next day he arrived at the museum at seven sharp. All personnel were in position. The John Abbott exhibit was loaded up, the convoy set forth for Salem, and Ross Hughes brought up the rear in his own car.

CHAPTER 44.

LIFE FOR THE EMANCIPATED JOHN.

John Abbott the XXVIIth arrived in Salem much later than he thought. The drive was hellishly long and winding single lane roads had frustrated his progress. The hotel was just adequate but luckily it was only a block from downtown Salem.

As he lay in bed, he thought about his heritage and his destiny. He had always detested who he was; his dad had drummed it into him that he was the twenty-seventh.

He hoped he kept a secret from him – but it wasn't likely as he'd ripped something out of his father's hands just earlier this morning. It should never have been in his dad's hands in the first place - these mix-ups with their names happened all the time at the post office.

"Hope he's alright?" XXVII thought. "These numbers: XXVI or twenty-six; and XXVII or twenty-seven; have been the source of multiple foul-ups in the past. Still, I'd rather be XXVII than XXVI. *Three cubed*, not so bad I guess."

He was sure it was what got him through high school. "Please Three cubed, just slip though the school bathroom window and get tomorrow's test." Then the good-looking girls would peck his cheek. Being the smallest kid in his year was not a recipe for popularity. Number XXVII, at least it stopped him from being the school punching bag; some of the time.

"Hope he's alright?" he thought again. "Hope he didn't take it personally? Fuck. How could he not? The whole tradition and father son thing. Shit. I better call; hope he's not drinking again."

He called, but there wasn't an answer. "Oh well, he's a big boy, and it's not cast in stone by any means either. I'll call tomorrow."

With his eyes closed, his mind wandered to the Abbott Exhibit and Legacy.

An Allan Hughes of old accepted the shoe as a donation to the state museum. Then he organized the funeral of John Abbott the First, which turned into a shoe ceremony. Each Abbott generation would bare only one boy, always called John. The shoe remained in the museum, the museum that paid for this hotel.

"Maybe it was true, forking out good money for me to have a holiday, OK. I'll be John Abbott the XXVIIth. Life was so strange. Bring on the witches."

He fell asleep for the first time contented with who he was. He would accept the mantle of the Abbott's in the morning and make his father and twenty-five generations before him, proud.

He woke up refreshed and immediately called his father to tell him how he felt. Again, his father failed to pick up. Still concerned, XXVII decided to call Ross Hughes on his cell. He wanted to inform him, if his dad hadn't already done so, that he, John Abbott the XXVIIth, was to be expected, and not his father. Ross Hughes' cell number was on the invitation and so was something else - the acceptance speech of John Abbott the First and more.

"Holy Shit actually appear on stage in front of hundreds of people and act out the speech. Typical. He didn't even tell me. And now I am expected to do this. Better learn it quick."

The speech was almost word for word the same as a bedtime story his father had read to him in his younger, happier years.

"Phew, that was close, now I'll call Ross."

He called Ross on his cell, updated him and told him his concern.

"Maybe you could give him a call please. I'm worried that I may have done something that I now regret."

It wasn't the best choice of words.

John Abbott the XXVIIth spent the rest of the morning strolling around town. He went to the town square where the reenactment would take place that night. Construction of a deep, high and broad stage dominated the proceedings. A hoard of roadies, yelling at each other, were having a great time impressing the haggle of fake, pretty witches, swooning over their big tattooed arms.

XXVII looked at his arms, he had ear marked his right forearm for a tattoo of a skull. Here in Salem, there were scores of parlors to choose from and the prices were cheap. With all the time in the world, he strolled around the temporary tattooing tents, his mind intent on choosing his fancy. The place was full of witches wearing tall witch hats, vampires with strange colored contact lens and black cloaks, and other assorted supernatural entities. Young girls and boys, couples and middle-aged oddities were plentiful. He had wanted a skull tattoo for ages. Now was the perfect opportunity.

John Abbott looked at the tattoo mass production line churning out Chinese lettering and his beloved and changed his mind.

"I don't need a tattoo to define me, I'm number twenty-seven. No. I'm John Abbott the XXVIIth. And the work those roadies were doing, I'm the one appearing on stage tonight, not them, they're doing all this work for me."

Ross had called John several times and he hadn't picked up, so he asked the police to go round to John Abbott the XXVIth's residence. But there were things to do rather than worry. He focused on inspecting the backstage, with the organizer and coordinator of tonight's event, Harry Adams, modern historian. He had served an internment under Ross in his early days as Curator. The position was his to refuse as they had become good friends at law school and Ross needed an assistant. Now, successful in his own right, Harry taught at the university and consulted at the museum part-time. The friendship was strong enough for him to be the only non-Hughes on the ground-imaging mission of the John Abbott the First's grave.

"I spoke with John the XXVIIth this morning, Harry." started Ross. "John the XXVIth has conceded the mantle to him. It would have been nice if he'd called and told us as much."

"But then XXVIIth said he was concerned about his father. I must admit, I am too after his call. He said that he regretted his actions, and that has me worried. XXVII hasn't been the most accepting of the legac… John!"

He was easy to recognize - if you knew the father, then you knew John the XXVII[th.]

"Mr. Hughes?" queried XXVII. He wasn't too sure it was him, even though he recognized Ross from the inset picture on the invitation.

"John, this is my good friend Harry Adams." said Ross always good at introductions.

The three started to discuss the night's arrangements. The two towered over John, but they directed their conversation around him, ignoring their differences in stature and gave XXVII a great deal of respect.

John was amazed that for the first time in his life his opinions mattered. He couldn't believe who he had become and could hardly recognize himself. Yesterday he had been a rebellious disbeliever, antifamily. Now acceptance, belief and passion stirred in his veins.

CHAPTER 45.

LIMP LIFE.

The shout from Boleyn was like a thunderbolt. Phil's eyebrows almost blew off his face. His cheeks flew back, and blood spurted from his eyes, ears, nose and mouth. Yet he was still alive.

Boleyn just stared at the breathing Phil. Now this really was impossible. Her attack was a narrow spectrum foil, tailored for the being of Phil - the worst kind of attack, personalized, customized, and delivered at almost full power. Her Entanglement was high, not complete, but high enough to stop a cannonball. She should be scraping Phil off the car ceiling.

"Even with the tiny red immunization he had received from my first attack, it shouldn't have saved him. How on earth has this man acquired Entanglement? Not that it was that much of a factor then... of course, now it is.

He's survived two attacks. Now he's severely immunized. In fact, I could deliver another designer shout, of greater magnitude and even then, it probably wouldn't kill him. I can see his eyes changing in front of me." Completely lost, she went over the attack again in her head.

"I had my hat on, my father's Shoe in my han..., wait, WHERE'S MY SHOE?"

She stopped dead. She had the shoe in her hands, and now it was gone. She looked down to the ground. It wasn't there. Panicked, she twisted her head from side to side. Nowhere.

"Shit, I'll find it in a moment; in any case, it shouldn't have made any difference. Phil should be dead."

Shock engulfed Boleyn as her prediction came true, she found the shoe.

It was on PHIL's left foot.

It chose to protect him.

Its RhomSong had done just that, invisible to all detection, only summation.

DEFLECT.Rhombus.
ABSORB.Rhombus. ABSORB.Rhombus.
DEFLECT.Rhombus.

Too shocked even to hate him, she stared at the unconscious Phil, still defying the odds by breathing. She cheated Phil and now the shoe cheated her. She was double crossed by what she believed to be her own flesh and blood. The shoe, which he had traded for their lives, had saved him. It was now his, this was obvious and there was nothing she could do about it. She turned and slowly flew into the disappointed night, defeated and humiliated.

"Why is it, when I renege on a deal, it never works out for me. Not like the Dark One. It always works out for *him*. *He* did it to my parents and *he* boasted what *he'd* done, twisting the knife with that evil laugh. The suffering *he* caused us, and worst of all, it was the reason we had to go out in public, exposing ourselves to the masses. *His* default revealed us, and publicized us, and the circus found us because of it. The bastard.

What a shitty night. And another thing, even that woman, what had he called her, 'Kelly', that's right, even she lived. Ruebella's yellow Entanglement saved her. Fuck. It couldn't have gone worse."

She flew up to her sisters, only they were spared her loathing.

They met her in silence, having watched everything in their crystal balls and knowing there was nothing they could say. They just held her and let her cry. They rocked her, consoled her and supported her, and swore allegiance and revenge.

"Phil. Phil. Phil." said Kelly shaking him. She turned his head towards her and jumped back in fear and horror.

The white of his eyes were crimson, no white showing, none at all. Before the attack, his irises were pale blue flicked with green and yellow, yet now they were entirely porcelain white. His pupils were diamond shaped. They only served to highlight the white irises more - or the other way around, it didn't matter. It looked pure evil.

Kelly backed away from him. She wasn't sure if he was Phil, or a demon or even *a Witch*. She didn't know who or what he was. She was as scared of Phil as she had been of the witch. She didn't think to ask Phil anything and she wasn't going to hang around. She reached for the door handle.

"Best run now. Phil's turned into a demon. I don't know, it can't be, can it? Oh God, what do I do?"

Phil spoke for the first time, "Ouch, Oh No, err, I think I've peed myself."

Kelly stopped her escape plan, or more accurately, put it on hold.

"Oh Thank God. It's Phil. I think. I hope…"

"Oh, and I think I've, err, shitted myself too." shifting his torso very gingerly.

"No demon would ever say that. In fact no one would ever say that." She was sure. He was still Phil. "Thank God."

"Oh My God Phil. Are you alright? Talk to me. Awe, I think you're right, I can smell it."

"Is it safe?" Phil asked Kelly shakily, and he shifted in his seat uncomfortably once more.

"I don't know Phil, I think so. I don't feel afraid anymore." she replied.

"I don't care anymore. I'm getting out, I stink." Phil climbed out of the car and stood up.

He shook himself. His pants were soaking wet and worse. Kelly already thinking ahead of him, as always, threw a pair of his trousers and underwear out of the car that she had retrieved from his suitcase.

"Thanks. Kelly." It took him a second to remember her name.

"She's so quick." he thought.

"Yep, it's Phil, he's so slow."

Kelly had also thrown bundles of tissues and a bottle of drinking water outside and he changed in the open.

"He'd never think of these things if I hadn't of done them for him. Still, he's amazingly healthy after surviving that." She herself wiped blood away from her own face, and then put a ton of tissues on his seat to soak up the mess. After some considerable time, fussing and dropping things, Phil threw the tissues out of the car and clambered back in. As they sat there quietly together for a moment, they both understood one thing. They were alive.

"Man that was close." said Phil "Why'd she leave? Her voice exploded inside my head. Then my head imploded. So why didn't she kill me? Us? What happened? Kelly?"

"Phil. Have you looked at yourself?" she quietly asked after a little pause.

"No, why? Have I still got blood on my face?" Phil turned the rear-view mirror towards himself and shrieked.

"No doubt about it. *It's Still Phil.* Thank God. Again."

"What's happened? I can still see. But I'm a..." he was going to say albino, but he knew he wasn't that. "*A Witch?* My God, what's happened?" Gaping at himself in the mirror, he pulled his eyes from side to side and up and down.

"Phil, stop. You'll hurt yourself. Look. You. You've started the bleeding again." She took a tissue, wet it from the water bottle, and dabbed Phil's eyes.

"Like cleaning a little boy." she thought.

He finished looking at his eyes and checked the rest of himself. He had a couple of grazes from leaning out the window and now they were beginning to hurt. His left foot felt different too.

"Oh My God Kelly. The SHOE."

"IT'S ON MY FOOT."

"Didn't you notice when you took your trousers and underwear off just a minute ago?" Kelly asked searchingly.

"No?"

"Phil! How can you not notice? Didn't you take it off to put your clothes on?"

"No. I don't know?"

"Phil! God you're hopeless." she said in desperation.

"Kelly, look at it, its gleaming." He reached down and ran his fingers and palms over the suede and leather.

"Did you hear that? Sounded like..." said Phil

"Purring?" replied Kelly.

"It can't be. It's just in our heads." said Phil, wanting it to be true

"It's not possible." Kelly said also agreeing, worried and confused that Phil could be wearing a shoe that purred?

"Look Kelly, its toe is fixed. Look at the Black Gold threads, they are incredible." he exclaimed. His foot was now in Kelly's face.

"Phil you idiot, you almost kicked me." She pushed his leg away roughly.

"It growled?" said Kelly, shocked.

"Phil, I think it growled at me." As his foot was near her face, she heard it.

"I didn't hear it." said Phil.

"PHIL, your fucking shoe growled at me; take it off. TAKE IT OFF."

"Kelly, I didn't hear it, OK, I believe you. OK. But I don't want to take it off. Besides, where is my other shoe?"

"Who cares, you've got a SHOE on your foot. And you don't know what it can do to you?"

"Well?" hesitated Phil, "it can save our lives, has saved our lives, three times."

They were both silent.

"Phil, I'm sorry, but I'm scared. I believe it saved us, you, tonight. But who knows what it can do to you. You said you saw *the Green Witch* capture 'your girlfriend' Deloris, well maybe the Shoe can do it to you." Kelly could barely hold back her anger and sarcasm, and a hint of something else.

"Bloody' El. What great thinking. I'd have never thought of that."

"I know Phil, but I have. Please Phil..." she didn't have to continue; Phil had already bent down and was pulling at the shoe crazily. But it wouldn't come off. He pulled, and twisted, and clawed at it, until he gave up. It was on to stay. Kelly looked worried.

"Kelly, it won't come off."

"You think?" in a pissed off tone, but also full of trepidation.

"But you know when I took my 'wet' pants off and put the clean ones on, the Shoe was definitely not on my foot. It couldn't have been, otherwise I could never have got them on, could I? Yet I have no memory of taking it off or putting it on. So maybe it does come off if I'm not trying to take it off, I don't know, I'm just saying."

"Phil, are you trying to convince me or yourself?"

"I don't know." said Phil tiredly and yawned.

They hadn't slept for ages. They were exhausted, worn-out and they wondered where they could get some sleep as it was obviously too late to find a place now.

"Kelly, sleep in the back, I'll sleep under the car."

"No." said Kelly quickly, "We'll both sleep under the car." Understandably, she didn't want to be alone in the car for the rest of the night. It stank.

So they both slept under the car, leaving its doors open to air it out, and being so tired, they slept like babies.

CHAPTER 46.

LIGHTS ANGELO.

The morning came quickly for Detective Angelo, who had been tormented the whole night over the murders of Deloris and Gavin. He climbed out of bed in a haze. He felt he had been on an all-night bender as his head pounded from thinking, instead of sleeping. He struggled to keep up with his daughter Natalie and friend, Madison.

They had made breakfast for Angelo, pancakes. Now they were jumping around the house making a racket, which didn't help until his brain cut him a break. Never under estimate the power of food.

Madison packed the cooler with the sandwiches they had made the previous night, and placed it next to the luggage and witches' costumes. Barely containing their excitement, they pushed Angelo into the driver seat and, laughing, ordered their chauffeur to drive. This was going to be a great trip, at least for the girls.

"Drive, Dad, let's go."

The two teenagers sat in the back seat and talked their ears off. As he sat alone up front, he contemplated Phil and Kelly. He had plenty of time because it was a long drive, so he turned the enigma over and over in his head as it were some Chinese puzzle.

CHAPTER 47.

A BRAVE MAN.

The sound of a truck's brakes negotiating the sharp bend woke Phil and Kelly. They had slept the whole night uninterrupted and had woken up surprisingly refreshed.

"Wow, Kelly, it's late, it's almost noon." said Phil, looking at his watch.

"And we're still alive Phil." chirped Kelly happily.

All the anxiety of the previous night lost in the day's light, until she looked at Phil and winced. She had forgotten about his eyes. She was OK with them now, but on the first glance, she couldn't control her reflexes. She was sorry, as she could see that she had struck a chord.

"I know." smiled Phil softly.

"I'm sorry I flinched Phil, I'd forgotten all about them, sorry." said Kelly apologetically.

"Sorry Kelly, I didn't mean to scare you. They feel exactly the same, and I feel exactly the same too. Unfortunately, it's as if you're hit by lightning, but you don't get any super powers. Bummer. Not to mention another attack. But, yes, we're alive." said Phil, trying to brighten his sagging mood.

Kelly recognized his attempt and joined in, and together they managed to salvage the morning's glory.

"Let's get breakfast." they both decided.

Luckily the car started. As the broken windows were at the back, it didn't look like the car had been 'in an accident', and so they drove at their normal pace to the first roadside diner. They had completely forgotten about their eyes. Kelly's once beautiful smooth Hazel irises were blood shot and looked infected with speckled yellow and red flecks, but they were inoffensive. Phil's eyes, however, stood out like a lighthouse beacon. But the couple only remembered their disfigurements after everyone in the diner turned and stared.

Phil and Kelly froze as the patrons' gaze went straight to their eyes. "Oh God." they thought, "We're going to be lynched." Incredibly, they all went back to their business. Astonished and relieved, Phil and Kelly found a booth as secluded as possible near the back door, and seconds later, a waitress appeared at their table with the menus.

"On your way to Salem then?" she asked as she took their orders.

"Yes." they replied. "How did you know?"

"Oh, we've had a couple of vampires in today already. What you having?"

It was a free pass, and Phil and Kelly talked about the previous night without regard.

"How many *Witches* are there Phil? According to you, Oh and I do totally believe you about the first one by the way, there's three, right? A Green, Yellow and now a Red One." queried Kelly speaking quickly.

"Yeah." replied Phil, enjoying Kelly's company as if they were old friends. "And each one seems to be worse than the last. But what I don't understand, are my eyes. Besides everything else that is. Like, everything."

"I know Phil, and I have to say, they all seem to be after you. This Red One came to my window, but she didn't know my name, but she knew yours, and I think if it hadn't been for the Shoe, she'd...."

"Yeah, why was that, the Green and Yellow Witches, I think, ran away from the shoe, but this one wanted...." he fearlessly interrupted, which affirmed how much their relationship had changed.

"*In Fact*, now I remember. Oh My God."

Phil leaned forward, and Kelly did the same, getting ready to tell and listen to a terrible secret. Whispering, he continued...

"She told me.

Kelly.

That the Shoes were made.

By her father.

Hundreds of years ago.

He made them for a special powerful client.

She whispered it to me.

Kelly.
She told me who the client was.
It was.
The Devil."

Phil was barely audible by now; Kelly had moved closer to be inches from his mouth just to hear. Unfortunately, what she did hear almost choked her. She knew he wasn't joking. They never joked about this stuff. This was real.

Before it was temporal, super beings, yes, the *Witches* were all that, but not Biblical.

But *the Devil.* That was everything. If someone mentioned God, then *the Devil* was not far behind. That's how far up *The Devil* was.

God.
Devil.

Good.
Evil.

Heaven.
Hell.

Salvation.
DAMNATION.

"GET THAT FUCKING SHOE OFF RIGHT NOW PHIL, OR SO HELP ME GOD, I'LL CUT YOUR FUCKING LEG OFF." screamed Kelly at a stupefied Phil. The whole place looked round, but Kelly didn't care or even notice.

Realization of the implications crashed down on Phil and he sprung out the back door of the diner. Dashing from pillar to post in the grimy backyard, Kelly grabbed the panic-stricken Phil, and sat him down roughly on a barrel. With all etiquette cast to the wind, she started frantically pulling on the Shoe. It wouldn't budge. She pulled and tugged, but it didn't even shift, and they both thought they heard it cursing. She went back inside the diner and appeared moments later with a dishcloth soaking with grease. She slapped it on his ankle and massaged the grease into his sock. But the Shoe pressed tighter and the grease wouldn't seep down into the shoe.

Desperate, she reached into her bag, pulled out her little manicure scissors and cut the leg of the sock completely away. Then she tried to pull the rest of the sock out.

"You're doing it Kelly, the sock's coming away."

She pulled and pulled, and piece after piece of the sock came out. But the shoe just seamlessly closed in behind it.

"Don't move." and Kelly disappeared and, again in an instant, reappeared with a hacksaw.

"Sit down there and put your foot up here." she commanded Phil. He obeyed without question, desperate to have the shoe off too. She placed the hacksaw blade in the seam between the upper and sole and moved it a fraction of an inch.

The scream Phil let out could have stopped the world.

"STOP, Stop, Kelly, it's killing me." tears pouring down his face. She dropped the saw. The shoe was on to stay.

She waited for Phil to stop crying. "What a big baby, his brother wouldn't have cried. Stop it, Kelly. You don't know." she talked to herself. "And I thought you were never going to mention his name again."

"The pain, it went right up my leg, through my body, my eyes and into my brain. It was like being jabbed by red hot needles with barbs on them." blurted out Phil in between breaths and sobs.

"Sorry Phil, it was...," said Kelly.

"A good idea." completed Phil for her.

"You tried so hard and thought so fast, I'd be useless without you."

"Thanks Phil, I try." she said sitting on the adjacent beer barrel in resignation.

They sat, thought, and kept their peace.

"I don't want to go to Hell." thought Kelly, "If I don't watch out, I'd get there quicker than I thought - sleeping with a married man, and now, guilty by association with Phil."

Phil was thinking, and it wasn't nice what he was thinking about, but he couldn't see any other way. He had to say it. "If *the Devil* comes after us ..."

"There's nothing we can do." They both said at exactly the same time, but instead of bursting into joyful laughter, depression swamped them.

Phil broke the long silence that followed in a monotone voice. "*The Witch* also told me her name was Boleyn, same as the town. Bet the town was named after *the Witch*. Bet the same goes for the Green Witch, bet her name is Hecate. The third witch, the Yellow Witch, I don't know, from Witchiton Falls I don't doubt.

As I said, Boleyn's father made the shoes for the Devil. For some reason, she didn't say, *the Devil* made Boleyn a Witch. When that happened, he told her that he never paid for the shoes and that's why she wants them back.

I gave her the shoe Kelly, the shoe for our lives. That was the deal. Then I guess she decided, or had already decided, by the way she acted, to break the deal and kill me. Us. All that stuff she told me, she didn't think that I was going to live to tell anyone, not that we can tell anyone anyway. That's why she wanted me to know her name - she wanted me to know who my executioner was."

"You, Phil, it was you. She tried to kill you. Nevertheless, she probably would have killed me afterward. I was almost done anyway. I felt dead you know, and I know you know. My brain felt like it was a Ping-Pong ball bouncing from wall to wall inside my skull. I wasn't sure if I was going to hang on. I wanted to die, I didn't want to live, I wanted the pain to end."

"Yes," said Phil, "I know what you were feeling, and I thought you were dead too, until I heard your breathing and that's when she appeared at my window."

"Phil, I didn't hear her talk to you at all, none of what you just told me. I know I was out of it, but even so, obviously she only wanted you to hear her. And even when she tried to kill you, I just saw your head whip back and I barely heard what she said."

Feeling his neck, Phil said, "Ouch, yeah. Man. It was like a bomb going off. I think when she tried to kill me was when the Shoe appeared on my foot. It was in her hands when she attacked,

I know it for sure because I had just given it to her. I know it sounds crazy, but I'm sure that's why I'm still alive. The Shoe protected me from her. I don't know why, and I could be totally wrong. What do you think?"

"I don't know, sounds as plausible. Last week I was a normal person Phil, now you're asking me if I think a Devil's Shoe protected you from a Red Witch, and I think it's as good as anything I can think of. What happened to my life?" her tears rolled down her cheeks.

"I can't go on. I wanna go back to my old life, except for no Bill. Find a decent guy, get married and have children. I don't want *Witches* chasing me. I don't want *the Devil* to have a legitimate reason to want me. I'm truly scared of *the Devil* and for good reason. I wanna go home."

More silence.

They had been outside for quite a while, when the back door opened and the waitress, looking pretty upset and trying to hide her annoyance, said,

"My shift's over, can you pay the bill please."

They got up and Kelly went to the Washroom.

Phil paid the bill.

And drove away alone.

CHAPTER 48.

THE LONG DRIVE.

Angelo tuned out the two teenagers in the back, they were watching a teenage movie about Witches and alternate worlds, and squealed and laughed all at the same time. It made him happy, they were sharing time together, no matter that she was absorbed with her friend; they were in the same car and enjoying the trip.

He was making good time on the narrow lanes. It was unusual for him to be on these country roads, normally the freeways took him to his business rendezvous'. But Salem wasn't near any freeway, the only way there was by these twisting byways. He didn't mind, he'd budgeted for it and was enjoying the whole thing.

As for the case, he had worked it to death. He couldn't think of any other angle, they were innocent. He forgot about it and instead smiled in contentment in this beautiful moment he was sharing with his daughter and her friend.

Up ahead was a hitchhiker, a woman.

"God, will they ever learn?" The shit he'd seen in his life, women ending up dead just by getting into a stranger's car, and not always women, but mainly.

"Girls. Never, ever, do this, promise me." drawing raised eyeballs, as he passed the woman. He was also going to say, 'and never pick anyone up either' when he reacted before he realized it, as he braked a little too violently to a halt.

"Dad, what are you doing?" cried out Natalie with attitude in overdrive.

"I'm picking up this hitchhiker." thank God he didn't say 'woman' otherwise he would have been in for a world of hurt from his daughter, and his divorced wife, and Madison. This was going to be bad enough as it was.

"She's a suspe... suspici... a person that I know from work. Let me handle this." He assumed work mode.

He got out of the car as the woman approached,

"Hello Kelly."

CHAPTER 49.

FEELING BAD, ARE WE?

Phil left Kelly behind. He had thought about doing this since this morning. The witches were after him, not Kelly. They had been lucky up until now, but now the stakes had been raised. Now not just their lives were at stake, but maybe their souls were too. If he cost Kelly her life and he lived, he could never forgive himself, but if he cost Kelly her soul, could God ever forgive him? He should have left her back at Boleyn; thank God she survived the night.

"That was irresponsible of me, God I can be so slow and weak."

It was the most unselfish thing he had ever done. He didn't know if he was doing the right thing or not, after all, she was an adult, and it wasn't up to him to make her decisions. She was responsible for her own life, and soul; but back there, just before the waitress interrupted them, she was crying. That was when he knew that she had given him permission to leave her behind. She had said,

"'I wish I had my own life back,' that's what she said. Now she has a chance to get it back. Get a taxi, a train, a bus, whatever; and get back to civilization, alive. My path is different. I have a bad feeling. I believe this is a road that will take me to the bitter end."

He knew the witches wanted him dead, but he had a suspicion that they couldn't do it. His white irises were evidence of this. Somehow, the green, yellow and double red had combined into White. Maybe *the Witches* colors worked differently than regular prime colors.

"Maybe it was green, yellow and red and red that made white. Just a Guess." He didn't know how close he was to the truth.

But not just the eyes, there was the Shoe. This threw a completely new curve ball into the equation. Undoubtedly, this Shoe had saved his life: but why? Obviously, it had chosen him above *The Witch*.

"What a betrayal, I mean, who was he?

Her parents made it.

Shouldn't it be hers?

They sold it to *The Devil*.

He didn't pay, so you'd think it would be loyal to the family and go to her; she's like the Shoe's next of kin.

Stop Phil.

Think.

The Devil wore it.

Think about it Phil.

You are wearing a SHOE THAT THE DEVIL WORE.

It's not a dream, is it?" He pinched himself stupidly.

"Idiot: and before you start doubting yourself anymore Phil, look at your foot, physical evidence. Look in the mirror, its right in front of your face, more evidence. You have no reason to disbelieve Boleyn, she confessed her secrets to you on the premise that you would be dead so there was no reason for her to lie. This is real life Phil, not a dream, not a movie. You are alive. This is real. Three *Witches* attacked you and you lived. One of The Devil's Shoes has chosen you. This is not the end, this can't be. But whatever it is, I'm in trouble and way over my head, and there's nothing I can do about it."

He drove alone for the first time in a week. It was so quiet.

Road resistance noise came through the broken back windows, but the rumble of passing cars was no substitute for the absent Kelly, that presence was irreplaceable. Even when she was in a snot and in super silent mode, there was still the noise of nothing, now there was just nothing. He arrived in Salem, and took the first hotel that had a vacancy, he didn't worry what it was like, he wasn't sure if he'd survive the night to care. He led down, took a nap, and conserved his strength for the night ahead. Tonight was The John Abbott Show, and after that, all bets were off.

There weren't any witches in the show but he wasn't concerned with witches much anymore. He felt it in his heart that he had enough 'Witch Stuff in Him' and with The Devil's Shoe as a shield, he didn't care what color witch attacked him tonight, he could handle it. The problem was, Kelly was the only one in the world who understood what he was going through, and he had decided that he didn't want to endanger her anymore. So he was going to have to deal with this alone, and he didn't like the idea. He hoped that the John Abbott show would give him some answers, because he needed all the answers he could get.

CHAPTER 50.

GIVE IN?

"Detective Angelo D.. It is you? Yes, well hello. Are you arresting me or giving me a lift?"

"That depends, have you done anything wrong?"

"Slept with a married man."

"Sorry can't arrest you for that."

Neither had smiled yet to this point.

"What happened to your eyes?" It was unavoidable to see her blood shot eyes. And did he see, a tad of yellow: and a splash of red in the iris too. Yes, he did.

"I'm going to Salem; you're giving me a lift there or should I wait for another car?"

"You think I'm going to Salem?"

She tilted her head and Angelo looked in that direction, his passengers were playing with witches' hats.

"Quite the detective Kelly."

"Not like you."

"Ouch, maybe I won't give you a lift?"

She reached out, and placed her hand on the door handle, opened the passenger side door and started to get in.

"Yes, you will, you can't resist the chance to question me some more." and got in.

Finally smiles, tense, but smiles nevertheless across the board.

"So, Kelly." Angelo asked. She had noticed he had several voices, the nice cop voice, the nasty cop voice, and this one, the subtle pressure 'I'm not interrogating you' interrogation voice. She didn't like any of them now.

"God, I'm so hopeless when it comes to guys, I liked this cop when I first met him, now I despise him."

"So?" Kelly replied.

"What happened? To your eyes?"

"I had a sneezing fit." Kelly's guard was on high alert.

"Like Phil?"

"Yep, just like him. Your children?"

"Natalie, say hello to Kelly"

"Hi."

"And her friend; Madison."

"Hi." and they both turned back to their own devices, but not before Kelly caught a dirty look.

"Where's Phil?" he continued.

"He dumped me." she said in a flat tone.

"Oh, when?"

"About a hundred cars ago." same flat tone.

"Why?" Angelo persisted.

"Why does anyone dump anyone?" she answered the question with a question. This caused the questioner to falter. Feeling a crack in his armor, she took the initiative.

"Where's the mother of your daughter?" she had been questioned for a whole night by this man and his team two nights ago, now it was her turn.

"OK, OK, I'll stop asking." he said with a little laugh, but it was too late.

"So where is she?" Two witches had attacked Kelly. She wasn't afraid of this bully in sheep's clothing. He wanted to call a truce as soon as he started taking casualties.

"(I don't think so.) Well?"

"My daughters back there, it's not for discussion."

"Ok, Angelo D." she said with every ounce of viciousness she had. A tense silence commenced for about fifteen seconds, before he pulled the car over and stopped.

"You can get out here Kelly." he said.

She opened the door and got out without even the slightest reticence. As she shut the door, she said.

"Last known person of contact, Detective Angelo D." and walked to the back of the car and stuck her thumb out.

The car didn't drive away.

Moments later, he got out of his door, closed it, and walked up to her.

"My wife and I had some..."

"I don't want to hear your petty little soap opera. Are you going to be an asshole the rest of the trip, or am I going to be the second woman you've left out in the cold?"

"Sorry, Kelly. It won't happen again." Angelo had gone back to his nice cop voice.

"Ok. Let's go." she said, and walked back to the door and got in.

"No wonder Phil dumped her." thought Angelo, his white shirt's armpit's betrayed all.

CHAPTER 51.

HUNTED OR HUNTING?

The three witches rested the whole day in a derelict barn, all tucked together in a bed of old hay. Hecate and Ruebella had nestled Boleyn in between them and had snuggled up, cuddling and consoling her, until she had fallen into fitful sleep. As night rose, they all felt better especially Boleyn who had revenge and death clearly on her mind.

Unfortunately, she knew - they all knew that Phil was invincible to them. So what? They decided to hunt him down and see what transpired. They had time. What else are they going to do? *Witches?*

They sat in a circle with Boleyn's hat in the middle. Their left hands were placed on each other's right shoulder, and their right hands held her hat. Boleyn cast the spell.

Car.
Star.
Ever so Far.

Find.
Bind.
Hat entwine.

Go.
Slow.
Let us know.

Fly,
Sky,
Low, High.

Seek,
Peek,
Phil at our feet.

Kill.
Phil.
That's our Will.

The hat climbed into the clouds, followed by the three. Boleyn cast her spells to combine the three broomsticks and they sped after the hat, arriving in Salem in double quick time. The spell actually tracked Phil's car as the hat had rested on the car's trunk, but they rightly presumed, that where Phil's car was, Phil was not going to be too far away.

When they got there, they were shocked to find the town was alive with people dressed as witches. But witches they were not. Ordinary people dressed in the most traditional witches clothing that any witch could imagine. They were dressed almost identically to them; they wore those tall tapered witch's hats, the midnight blue black capes and brandished plastic brooms. There were other humans wearing thin glass like lens on top of their eyes, giving their irises different colors and cat shaped pupils. The only problem the three witches had from completely fitting in was, the aura of loathing that they exuded, they couldn't conceal their contempt for these imposters. So they chose a perch on a building surrounding the main square, it was safer for their countenance, it stopped them from randomly killing multitudes of pretenders out of malevolence.

It was also fitting; it was an Old Stone Church with a small steeple. It reminded them of the Old Stone Bridge, and it purchased a perfect view of the whole square and the distant stage. They sat back and waited in plain sight of the charlatans as the excitement grew for the people below, as for those above. A show had started on the large stage at the far end of the square. An amazing array of lights coordinated with knife edged music ripped through the night, as a beautifully choreographed show filled the evening. It portrayed a terrible story of a village that endured the savagery of The Devil for no reason other than they were good looking, the witches were torn on who's side to take. Disregarding their conflicting loyalties, the witches watched the stage intensely, were they about to find out the whereabouts of him? They had all secretly wondered where he was, but never brought the subject up, it was best not to think about him, if you did, *he* might find you.

You didn't want that.

The witches lost focus of their goal as they watched the amazing show, forgotten was the search for Phil, but like him, they hoped the show would reveal answers to their questions.

"You never know, it might even reveal answers to who this enigma Phil is." Their instincts were so good. The show continued until the stage went dark and a lone figure advanced to front and center, and started to speak. He told of how he captured *The Devil* in a shoe. The witches all looked at each other, there was no need to say anything; their faces said it all.

"*Him* too?"

At the end of his speech, he revealed *The Shoe*; cold shivers ran down the witches' spines.

It was the right-footed Boleyn Shoe.

CHAPTER 52.

WRONG AND WRONG AGAIN?

The police, in the form of two street cops, finally got round to visiting the house.

"We've been requested to come to this house because John Abbott the XXVIth wasn't answering his cell. His son had told someone that he was sorry and regretted his actions. Well, that was the gist of it anyway." one of them said.

They knocked on the door but no one answered, all was quiet at the Abbott residence, too quiet.

"Hey, have you got the guys cell number? Call him."

"Call him what, John number thirty-four, come in please your time is up" He joked over his name, and on purposely erred in a conversion from roman to imperial.

"Get on with it." laughed the other officer.

The officer dialed the number while the other listened at the door. He could hear it ringing inside of the house.

"His cell's in there, when was the last time anyone went out without their cell, never."

"Go look through the window." and he did.

"Call it in, we've got a body."

The police broke the door down. They waited for the coroner and the crime scene investigators. All the appropriate personnel had performed their jobs, but no one was certain if it was a suicide or not.

There wasn't a suicide note. They sensed and experienced the same genuine and grave concern of Ross Hughes, the person who requested the call.

The police called Ross Hughes and conveyed the news, that John Abbott the XXVIth was dead. John Abbott the XXVIIth was the next of kin, and even if he was a person of interest in his father's death, they couldn't negate his right to know. They didn't waste any time either, as they divulged that John Abbott the XXVIIth was a wanted man.

CHAPTER 53.

ROSS THE CUNNING.

Ross watched the show from his vantage point backstage; all eyes were glued to the performance. He was pleased about this, because what he was about to do was not for prying eyes. He casually looked around his friend Harry was particularly engrossed in the show, understandably as this was his baby too. This was Ross's chance.

Without drawing attention to himself, without any hint of deceit or tension, he bent down next to the John Abbott Cabinet. Only two other people knew the sequence of knobs and levers built into the design by Allan Hughes no less, hundreds of years ago. Unlocking it was secret kept to this day.

In plain sight, he picked up the Shoe.

The Shoe numbered 614.

Then he moved the shoe, item 666 to 614 to complete the deception. "HAH."

There was no way he was going to risk the real Devil's Shoe out in the open. The stakes were excessively high. He was a firm believer in the legend and didn't want all hell, literally, to break out on his watch.

He examined the Shoe, wow, as forgeries went; this one surpassed the original in beauty, style and grace in every dimension. People would understand if you mistook this shoe for The Devil's Shoe, little did he know that it was. He had no way of knowing that Allan Hughes had performed the same switch hundreds of years earlier.

Maintaining the ruse, he had a large bouncer, and all bouncers are large, so this person was huge, escort him the twenty or so yards to Harry, and loudly decreed the terms of the required security to protect the Shoe from harm. With sincere reverence and fake trepidation: he completed the exchange into Harry's hands without suspicion.

Harry gave it to John, John Abbott the XXVIIth.

Five minutes later, Ross pronounced himself a genius. He had just received word from the John Abbott the XXVIth residence, the Police were more than interested in questioning John Abbott the XXVIIth in connection with the murder of his father.

He breathed a huge sigh of relief for NOT handing a potential weapon of mass destruction into the hands of the son, who'd allegedly killed his father just so he could be front and center. He watched as John Abbott the XXVIIth in his period loose tunic and pants approach the microphone, with the substitute, beautiful, shoe in his hands.

"God I'm smart. We'll deal with John after the show."

Hardly able to contain his smugness, he stood next to Harry in the dark shadows back stage and watched John Abbott the XXVIIth give his speech. The Shoe tucked in front of his stomach. Ross was smiling until it hurt, he couldn't contain himself any longer; he had to make some kind of comment to Harry. He wasn't going to tell him about the switch, no, but he required an outlet for his glee, he needed some idle chatter on the subject.

"That old Allan Hughes was pretty smart eh, Harry, had the shoe in the catalog as number 666. The Devil's number."

"Ah." said Harry, "You know; there's new evidence that The Devil has played a tricked on us. His number may not actually be 666. It quite possibly isn't The Devil's number at all. Did you know that, Ross?"

"No." said Ross, his interest rocketed. "So, err, what is the number, The Devil's Number? 667?" he said trying to keep worry out of his voice.

Not knowing the gravity of his next words, Harry answered,

"There are 613 Jewish Laws. The Devil was an outsider. Outside of God's Laws. An Outlaw. His number is…

"614" said Ross in a ghostly whisper.

Suddenly, Ross felt not quite so clever.

CHAPTER 54.

NOT WRONG AGAIN SURELY.

Angelo D. pulled into the hotel car park, it was an outdoor concrete yard at the back of the town square, and you could hear the music from even there. They all got out of the car and entered the hotel. Angelo went to the front desk with the kids, they were going crazy, they wanted to go and see what Salem had to offer. Angelo gave in,

"Hey that's why they were here." and told the Kids "Remember the hotel name and where it is. Be back in an hour." He turned round and the kids were gone, just like that, and so was Kelly.

She went out into the square through the front door of the hotel and looked back. The hotel was five stories high, one of the biggest buildings in the square; it had a white front and that, along with its size, made it the most prominent. Other buildings snuggled up to it, smaller hotels, register office, town hall, stone and brick; the whole square had that European look and feel. In the furthest corner was an old stone church, its tower ended with a short spire, even so, it made it the tallest building in the plaza. At the other end stood a stage, and a new age band played Celtic music in front of a crowd of toned-down hippies.

She went back into the hotel, sat down in a comfortable chair and closed her eyes. Here she could relax and go over in her head what she was doing here, because she wasn't that sure.

She hated Phil.

She was now trying to find Phil.

She was miles from nowhere.

Oh, two witches had attacked her.

Oh, and just in case she forgot.

And this is bad.

Phil was wearing a shoe worn by no less than the Devil.

It would not come off.

She was now trying to find Phil.

Still.

Was she crazy?

Phil drove off without her back at the diner.

He probably saved her life as the witches are after him.

Or worst.

And he may be a witch himself.

She was now trying to find Phil.

She hated Phil.

A burst of loud music woke her up; it was night. As luck would have it, she just saw Detective Angelo D. and the kids, dressed like witches, disappear through the front door. She decided to tail Angelo into the town square, even though she disliked the man intensely, it would still be handy to be within earshot of a cop if something went down.

"Yeah, like if he could put up a fight against The Three."

Nevertheless, she did just that. Unaware of his tail, he wound his way through the crowd until he was satisfied he could get a good view. The show went on, the actors told a story of The Devil inflicting torture and degradation upon a village until a man, (and whose direct descendant was just about to address the audience), stopped it somehow. The music stopped and the lights dimmed, and then Angelo saw something right in front of his eyes. Amidst this whole crowd, free flowing and standing wherever they wanted, he had chosen to stand directly behind...

"Hello Phil.," said the detective. The production had enthralled Phil. He was so absorbed, that the Detective's voice made him jump.

"What a baby, to think that I thought this man was capable of murder. That was nothing, to pull Kelly. I must have been delusional." thought the superior Angelo. Phil turned to face Angelo and this time it was Angelo's turn to jump as Phil's eyes met his. It quickly changed Angelo's mind, on everything. Red whites, white irises and diamond shaped black pupils, Phil looked the part of some 'Goth' super dude, unfortunately; he didn't act it.

"Detective Angelo D. you scared me, what are you doing here?" said Phil in a hushed voice.

"Cool eyes dude." his daughter and friend cooed.

"The show." said Angelo regaining his composure, inside though, his mind raced. "What the hell is wrong with his eyes? His whites are red, and his, blue eyes were it, yeah blue, are pure white. It has to be contacts to have square pupils, but his eyes were red back at the station, and they were real. And Kelly's eyes? Both said it was a sneezing fit; but white irises; that is scary. He never struck me as a guy who would get into that kind of thing but, well, you never know. That's the streets for you."

"You still looking for that murderer of yours Angelo?" said Phil as he took a step backward to be side by side with the detective.

And Kelly took a step forward to be side by side with Phil.

"You bastard, Phil." she said.

"Kelly! What Are You Doing Here?" said Phil in astonishment.

"Making sure you don't die without me?" she replied.

Angelo heard this, but he didn't like what he heard: now he wanted to hear what Phil had to say even more. Perhaps, finally, he would get the whole story.

Careful what you wish for.

"Sure, Phil. Enlighten me." he said with sarcasm.

"They up there, on the church steeple, look behind you." said Phil without turning, and he took hold of Kelly's arm at the same time to stop her looking too. Angelo turned round, and after a moment spied three witches standing on the tower base that supported the steeple.

"You asshole Phil. They're just kids. You expect me to believe that, you're in trouble Phil." said Angelo venomously. "Big trouble."

"Not as much as you Angelo, if I were you, I'd take my kids now and leave, before something bad happens, if these witches..."

"You're under arrest asshole." and Phil felt handcuffs clasp over his right wrist and heard them clink onto Angelo's left arm.

"Are you crazy detective?" said Kelly attempting to keep her voice lower than the address John Abbott the XXVIIth was wrapping up on the dimly lit stage.

Ignoring Kelly "Threatening a police officer and his kids, you're heading for the big house Phil." said Angelo in a wicked voice with unconcealed hatred.

On the stage in front of them, mirroring the events in the audience, the show was coming to its climax.

"I present to you. The Shoe!" John Abbott the XXVIIth cried, and he held the Shoe high in the air like a soccer trophy.

CHAPTER 55.

XXVII.

The Devil's shoe on Phil's left foot took off towards the stage like a greyhound out of the gate. Phil's left foot whipped straight out in front of him in a half goose step, and he wasn't strong enough to pull it back down to the ground. Instead, all he could do was hop on his right foot to keep up with the shoe's charge for the stage. Phil's right hand was handcuffed to the detective, who was pulling him in the opposite direction; it was all Phil could do to stay on his feet. He looked like a clown and a mime at the same time, stretched in diagonally opposite directions.

The desire of the shoe was much more than the two mortals' wishes and combined strength. Against their will, and as if no obstacle opposed it, the shoe relentlessly advanced upon the stage.

"FREEZE." shouted Angelo, his arm projected straight out in front and Phil's arm trailed behind, with the handcuffs taut between them. The shoe kept on going, deafly ignoring the detective's command.

The first few unlucky people closest to the pair fell victims to the clumsy, unannounced charge towards the stage. However, as the commotion grew, the people in Phil's path turned around and scurried out of the way; it was like the parting of the red sea. Kelly and the two girls followed, as the group headed noisily and inexorably forward.

By now the performance had stopped, all eyes were on the interruption, as the shouting Angelo drew attention to them. Bouncers stood in their way, but only slowed their progress as Phil's body bowled them over. He hopped frantically up the stage stairs, stretched out with his foot in front, and his arm and hand chained to the screaming detective, behind.

He hopped across the stage until he stood in front of John Abbott the XXVIIth who, unknown to everyone, was fighting a battle of his own. Frozen in the trophy celebration position like a statue, John Abbott the XXVIIth hung on to The Devil's Right Footed Shoe: his hands, clasped tightly around it in mortal combat. He looked strange, his image was blurred, there seemed to be multiple *images* of him all in the same body, all occupying the same time and space, and *all desperately hanging onto the shoe.*

The stage flood lights came on, bathing the whole unscripted scene in business like white light. On stage was John Abbott the XXVIIth, Phil handcuffed to Detective Angelo D, Kelly and the two teenage girls, Natalie and Madison, Ross Hughes and Harry Adams, and a host of roadies.

The show was about to begin.

CHAPTER 56.

THE STAGE.

John Abbott the XXVIIth was standing, like a porcelain statue, with the shoe raised high in front of his face. He hadn't moved since the moment he hoisted the shoe in acclaim, and his eyes had paranoia written all over them. He stared, fixated on the shoe, but despite his confusion and racing anxiety, he was still aware. His peripheral vision was telling him of another story unfolding right in front of him in the crowd, and it started the instant he raised the shoe.

A raucous had erupted in the crowd below him in that moment, and in that same instance, he his hands involuntarily locked. He had no idea why, but now he wasn't going to let go of it, for some reason, he had the profound feeling that his life depended upon it.

The instant he raised The Devil's Shoe into the air, life surged through the Shoe like a dormant volcano, the two shoes connected, their bond was not unlike that shared by Siamese twins. The two shoes were one; the three were one. They strove to be together, only immense forces would keep them apart, and that force was definitely not Phil, his summoning from the town square was witness to that.

He had seen Phil dragged across the square, desperately trying to stay upright as his left leg stuck out comically in front of him. The Shoe's desire was stronger than Phil's strength to keep his left foot on the ground, and stronger than the weight of Angelo pulling Phil back. Its desire would allow it to take only one path, the shortest, and that path led to the shoe now in John Abbott's grip, the shoe that contained The Devil.

Phil stood in front of the blurred image of John Abbott the XXVIIth, and as he panted, he wondered whom, or better still, what, he was looking at. To look at John Abbott the XXVIIth, was to look at someone trapped in-between two mirrors opposite each other, you could see a mirror image trail of John Abbott's, twenty-seven of them, all hanging onto the Shoe. From the most distant faintest image, that of John Abbott the First, to John Abbott the XXVIIth the closest and sharpest image: the real and tangible person. Their faces all-identical, only slight differences in size, and they were dedicated to a common purpose, to stop the reunification of The Devil's Pair of Shoes.

He was a shimmering blur of identical images existing in the same space and time, and their combined strength was the only force able to stop the Shoe from becoming whole. As long as he held on to it, a hand on the toe and a hand on the heel, he might avoid a consummating union. John Abbott the XXVIIth and all, stood unified in their purpose, foiling the reunification.

Focusing on one thing and one thing only, Detective Angelo was blind to this aberration of nature, he was intent upon arresting this threat to the free world, to arrest Phil. Angelo was a strong physical man, a man of authority, and he wasn't in any way shy about using either. He wasn't even a man who didn't look for trouble. He wasn't stupid though, if he was out gunned, then he wasn't above looking away, that was certain, and what else was certain, was he'd get them back. One way or another, and it'd be for keeps this time. Another god damn Scorpio.

In the performance of his duties, circumstances had occasionally forced Angelo to use his physical prowess in the subduing of suspects, and he secretly enjoyed it. He never lost; he was always the better man. He didn't plan to arrest Phil in the town square, not to say that it wasn't something he didn't want to do, but now he had a clear mandate. Nobody threatens his family.

"Nobody."

Even with those eyes, (and really, why should scary eyes make someone any tougher) Angelo would be more than a match for Phil. Nevertheless, Angelo along with his entire prowess could not have anticipated the strength that Phil exhibited in his attempt to get away. "And the stupid antics he pulled, running, hopping, in his escape attempt like that, the idiot. Although I have no idea how he did it, and I don't really care right now. I've got him."

"On your knees asshole!" screamed Angelo, he dearly wished he had a gun to point at him instead of a threatening fist, and he lowered his handcuffed hand so that Phil could comply. Angelo wasn't the only one shouting, Kelly was yelling at him, and the girls were screaming too, crying, asking Dad to stop. Angelo, however, wasn't going to, he was more than pissed that he had to do all this in front of his girls. Natalie that is. Madison? Maybe not.

It was all Phil's fault.

"Thank you, Phil.," sped through this mind.

"And that bitch Kelly." he thought, as she was pulling his arm in a vain attempt to turn him around so that she could yell right into his face.

"Stop screaming at me Kelly or I'll arrest you too. Natalie; Madison, get off the stage before you hurt yourselves."

"Do as your dad says." said Phil.

"Shut your trap Phil" Angelo yelled, putting his face an inch from Phil's. He was so mad that Phil's eyes didn't put him off one little bit.

"Ok. I was just trying to... save their lives." said Phil. He couldn't help himself; he couldn't think quickly enough to get the right words out. He had just seen The Witches launch into the night sky and they were heading for the stage, flying high above the unseeing stirring throng below. The audience was intent on the new, real-life drama unfolding in front of them. It was much better than the show - it was formidable and intense.

Angelo said nothing, but looked quickly from side to side, and then made full body contact with Phil as he concealed a heavy punch into Phil's stomach. He buckled over in pain and shock. To his chagrin, the girls saw it and screamed, never having witnessed violence in men first hand, especially at the beset of Natalie's father, a cop. Kelly saw it too, she never missed a thing, and she ducked around Angelo and slid on the stage floorboards to be in front of Phil.

"Are you alright?" she asked, but Phil only looked into her face and directed his eyes to the sky behind her.

She looked up.

The Witches were on their way.

The John Abbotts was still in a dead lock with the Right Footed Shoe, it was stalemate.

The Shoe was the mirror image of the one on Phil's left foot. Beautiful, dark and alive, but inside that Shoe, life, a terrible life waited.

And waited.

Their heavy gasps from the initial onslaught were now gone, replaced with even but sustainable breathing. John Abbott the XXVIIth (and descending numbers down to the First) had established equilibrium, and as long as this fine balance endured, the struggle with the shoe looked like it could go on forever. As his initial panic subsided, calm came over John XXVIIth and he was able to look within him and see his father, John XXVIth inside him, behind him. Then he looked back further, and saw his grandfather, and a host of other people all identical to himself.

The penny dropped and he knew they were all his ancestors, and in the far distance, the faintest image, was the grand patriarch, John Abbott the First.

His father was right behind him crying, and John XXVIIth started to cry with him, for he understood that his father was no longer amongst the living. He knew what he had done and why, the piece of paper in his wallet.

"I'm sorry Dad. I was so tired of hearing it. I didn't want any part of it, and so I looked into it Dad. However, when I got here to Salem, I understood how special the legacy is, how privileged I am to be part of it. I want to be part of it, I am part of it, I'm here Dad, here and now, I'm proud Dad, I'm proud to be John Abbott the XXVIIth.

Your Son."

The heartfelt apology and obvious pride moved the whole ancestry, muted and muffled praise rippled through the exclusive club. But none more so that John Abbott the XXVIth, who sobbed, laughed and proclaimed, overflowing with pride, that number XXVII was his. So with John Abbott the XXVIIth leading the way, they all felt united in their struggle and quest, and no matter what doom laid ahead, they knew they would be facing it together. This thought, however, raised a question, and each successive generation began to look back upon the preceding, until they were all looking at the faintest image in the distant past, John Abbott the First, the source.

John Abbott the First heard and felt their need to know, and knew that he was the only one who could answer them.

"Why were they here and what were they doing?"

They needed answers.

Sympathetic to their bewilderment, John the First sent a message through the throng, explaining what he intended to do, and after all had agreed: he initiated his plan. He swapped positions with the image, his son, number 2, in front of him, he intended to advance through the images one at a time. He went from the 27th position to the 26th and then proceeded from the 26th to the 25th, and so on. When he did this, his son, number II in the 26th position followed him and likewise for his son, number III in the 25th position. Every time he advanced, the images would tag on behind the next lowest number, until he had only John XXVIIth to pass. He stopped behind his most distant heir and told him how proud he was of him and his father; and that it was his honor to be their ancestor. Then, as tears welled up in both their eyes, he slipped his hands onto the shoe, and watched his youngest heir cascade to the back of the line. The whole lineage had inverted, he was now again John Abbott the First, in pole position.

Ross Hughes and Harry Adams walked towards Angelo at the front of the stage. They shooed away the roadies and bouncers that were accumulating on the stage wondering what to do, wondering if there was any way they could inflict a bit of ultra-violence themselves. Ross approached Angelo as he stood over the kneeling Phil and when he reached the detective, he whispered something into his ear. The audience was enthralled,

"What did he say?" and all the time, unnoticed, The Witches were getting closer.

Angelo was talking back and then he gave John Abbott a sharp look, a look of hatred and he started towards John like a man on a mission. John had seen this look before when the detective had punched Phil moments earlier and he feared the worst. The delicate balance between the Shoe and them was in jeopardy, the equation must remain unchanged, but it looked that it was going to in a very short while. He had to warn the crowd that they were in grave danger, because if they stayed, they could become caught up in the cataclysmic events that would surely follow. He needed to tell them to leave, to save themselves.

The crowd had focused on the exchange between Ross and Angelo, and they were intrigued on what was happening, what did they say to each other? The muted silence was unexpectedly broken when out of the blue, John Abbott *the First* leaned forward to the microphone, and said, as if he used a microphone all his life.

"Leave. Everyone leave, or you're all going to die."

The captivated crowd stirred and an occasional shout echoed around the square, but no one left. Certainly, if you want a crowd to go, you shouldn't warn them of impending death. To a person, they stayed.

However, Detective Angelo construed the warning in the only manner a detective in the middle of an arrest, with adrenaline running, could, as a threat.

Detective Angelo D. was elated, he already had his prize, Phil, and now he had another suspected murderer, John Abbott the XXVIIth in his sights, he saw his old job back, all controversies forgotten. It couldn't get any better, but it did, he finally put it all together, it was obvious.

"Phil and John have a BOMB. My God, I've been so blind. It all fit, the random killings, the eyes, their confidence under questioning and the threats. They must be taking drugs; I bet that's what caused their eyes to change color.

My God, RADIATION, that's what had caused the eyes.

IT'S AN ATOMIC BOMB."

"YOU'RE UNDER ARREST ASSHOLE." Angelo's favorite phrase, but he especially relished this capture and he said it with unrestrained gusto. The handcuff that joined Phil to Angelo came off Angelo's wrist and was moved on to the left wrist(s) of John Abbott(s) in a split second. Angelo was relieved and ecstatic when he heard the snap of the handcuffs click into place,

"It's done, I've done it. Now to get them to a police station ASAP, and 'persuade' them to reveal the bomb's location."

John Abbott was so short that Phil was still on his knees, Angelo hauled Phil to his feet and turned him around, Phil and John stood facing a jeering crowd, locked together by the handcuffs and fate. They could have been Jesus and Barabbas. The focus of everyone's attention was on the arrest, they all forgot about the Shoe, no one saw what happened to it. Except one person, Phil.

Before Detective Angelo D, "Soon to be Head of the CIA Detective Angelo" dreaming of his reward, could whisk them into the hands of the authorities, the nights events overtook him, and became a nightmare.

A hush crept over the crowd like a gentle ripple on a still pond, as people pointed towards the sky, and then sporadic clapping broke out as the flight of The Witches finally caught their attention.

"It's incredible the special effects they can do now-a-days." murmured the assembly.

It was a short-lived belief.

The Witches floated closer to the stage, and the bright lights flickered and crackled as a hush imposed its will over the once joyous assembly. A cold and hard spear of fear penetrated their very hearts and The Witches relished their might as they continued their descent. When they approached the stage, they swooped from side to side in front of it, and all the time getting lower and lower, closer and closer, subduing all in sight.

All thought of special effects had vanished, as white-hot fear filled the crowd's minds, The Witches were real. Their green, yellow and red eyes shot arrows of ice into hearts and souls.

The crowd now completely quiet, as only the occasional sob from the closest to The Witches broke the stillness, as they watched and cowered.

And stayed.

Ross and Harry gradually backed away with every flyby. Angelo and the girls looked on in horrified realization; this was no special effect. He was dumbfounded. He couldn't believe it, the truth, could it be this?

Almost everyone on the stage was finding it hard to breathe, frozen where they stood, consumed with foreboding and apprehension.

All except, Phil, who stood calmly, unafraid, right hand cuffed to John Abbotts's left.

Kelly, who stood and watched, was scared, but could still think. She had cleverly moved closer to Phil, whose presence and aura was causing the Witches to give a wide berth.

John Abbott(s) stood and watched, scared to death - for an entirely different reason.

The words "You're all going to die." echoed in Angelo's head. The sight before him whirred in his mind as he slowly he started to fear the worst.

"He was wrong?

Is there a Bomb?

Was Phil really a terrorist?

What had caused his eyes to go like that?"

He looked at Phil who had turned his head towards Angelo, his face a picture of sorrow, pity and compassion. Angelo still didn't get it. But he was getting there slowly.

A Witch with terrifying red eyes closed in on Angelo, which caused him to topple back, just missing his crying girls. Had he found his terrorists, his murderers? He had scoffed when Phil had told him, "It was these three." But now when he looked at Phil's eyes, they were more painful than the witches as his carried truth.

He couldn't retain his gaze but he couldn't be wrong, could he? Did his EGO have the better of him? He wanted to arrest Phil, confirm a bomb, and earn his place in the CIA. He wanted adulation but instead was on course for infamy.

The Witches landed on the stage like airplanes on an aircraft carrier landing deck, one after another, first Hecate, then Ruebella and then their rock, the tiny Boleyn. They were a terrifying but awesome sight. Impossible to look away, but impossible to bear, people's eyes would rotate between the hideous Hecate, the giant head and tiny torso of Boleyn and the Medusa Ruebella.

Hecate, Ruebella and Boleyn, floating on her broomstick, dominated the stage. They glared with evil intent at the masses. Their green, yellow and red eyes penetrated hearts, with their deafening, blinding gazes. The fear was oppressive, and anyone who resisted and dared eye contact, received burning eyes and soul in retribution. No one dared challenge twice.

The Witches ceased their intimidating rounds, congregated on the front of the stage, stood in a tight circle with joined hands, and began a chant. The audience clasped their hands to their ears as they heard their voices for the first time, but still no one left, possibly missing the last chance for escape. The chant escalated. At first, the mantra's words were inaudible, only the rhythm of chant, but by the sixth iteration, the words were clear and sharp and bore into everyone's heads.

They ended on a very unpleasant high note.

Everyone here,
Those who are dear,
Men and Women both,
And children that loath,
Hear what we say,
Hear it today,
Those Standing Tall
Fall to the Floor.
If you please.
FALL TO YOUR KNEES.

The witches dropped to their knees.
The crowd followed suit.

The stage lights also obeyed and dimmed in unison, and a hush muffled every breath. With eyes of fire, the Witches proudly relished their potency under the pale ghostly lights.

For the time being, this was their show.

The three stood up and scanned the stage. They saw only Phil and John, and for a moment, they didn't know what to do. All they knew was that this night was a special night and like two opposing gangs in close quarters; it wouldn't be too long before something would happen.

Phil and John concurred.

The Witches didn't have long to wait. The impossible happened. Phil, of all people, took the initiative. He walked over towards them, handcuffed with John Abbott who followed dutifully - neither displayed a hint of nervousness. To the amazement of everyone in the crowd, the witches backed up a step in apprehension.

He looked at Hecate first, her eyes green and filled with malice, then at Ruebella, and finally at Boleyn. Loathing oozed from their beings. They stood confronting one another, for the first time as equals and opposites - and an uneasy truce maintained the quiet balance.

Only Phil could look them in the eyes. "Why," Phil asked with all sincerity, "do you hate me?"

Their silence seemed eternal.

Hecate recalled the reason for pursuing Phil across the country and realized her incarceration in the shoe wasn't his fault. Nor was it his fault that he was the instrument in revealing the present date to her. She stayed silent.

Ruebella reviewed her scant reasons for hunting Phil. She could only think of one reason. If that disgusting creature GaVIN hated Phil, then he must be worthy of hatred. Besides, she was a Witch and didn't need an excuse to hate anyone. She withheld her counsel too.

Finally, Boleyn broke the silence. "You took my Shoe."

"But Boleyn."

The people, Angelo, and the others on the stage gave a gasp. He called her by name, and in a non-fearful, non-confrontational, non-defensive manner. He was conversing.

"I gave it back to you and then you tried to kill me."

"I am a Witch and can kill anyone I want." she shouted back and the other two nodded in agreement.

Angelo was slowly coming round to the truth, and he bowed his head in shame and stupidity. Now he understood what Kelly meant when she retorted 'Not like you.' when he had picked her up.

"But Why Me?" begged Phil.

And the answer came from behind.

"Because you're you, Phil." Kelly had come over to the group despite her fear, her tinge of yellow and a dash of red shielded and enabled her. She placed her hand on Phil's shoulder, and turned him to face her.

"Because you're just you. There's something about you Phil, which just makes people hate you."

The Witches nodded, and Angelo too. It did not go unnoticed.

"I don't know what it is. Your temperament, your dithering, your slowness, your personality. Whatever it is, you drive us crazy." Kelly continued, trying her best not to be harsh.

Even though his eyes were terrifying, even though he could stand in front of Witches, he was still Phil. Kelly's words sank deeper into his soul than the witches' attacks. He recalled his torments from his childhood at the hands of his brother. He recalled the mean words of school bullies, co-workers and the occasional short-lived relationship, the dismissals, the back stabbing and teasing. More recently, he endured the unjust jabs and hostility, directed at him at the hands of the police, the Witches, and Kelly.

It was just him, innocent him, not just his actions - but who he was, a broken man.

He stood in front of the Witches and fought back tears.

There was nothing to be done, it was in his DNA - he was Phil, the loser.

It couldn't get any worse. But it did.

His right foot.

"Run!" shouted John Abbott the First.

People didn't listen, including Angelo, Ross, and Harry. They were sadistically enjoying themselves at Phil's expense. Secretly smirking. Here was this man - powerful with eyes of dread, almost weeping. "Like a little girl, because nobody liked him." The hatred directed at him by the crowd was more than towards the murderous witches who had just ordered them to kneel.

The Witches were right to hate him, the sniveling weakling.

"RUN." cried John Abbott the First again. He pointed to Phil's right foot. Attention finally shifted away from Phil's eyes, to his feet, to his right shoe.

For the first time, everyone realized that they had lost sight of the Devil's Shoe. With all the drama of the arrest and then *the Witches*, everyone, even Ross, had temporarily forgotten about it. But now, Ross was all too aware of the possible apocalyptic implications, if what he was observing was the result of what he feared the most.

"RUUNNN" screamed John Abbott the First for a third time.

And this time people listened, however, they didn't obey. Who was he, chained to Phil to ordering them to leave? They hated him too.

Phil's right ankle was swelling. "Oow." cried Phil.

"Here was the crybaby Phil, trying to draw attention to him and get some sympathy, what a wimp." muttered the crowd.

However, they gasped when they saw Phil's right leg expand. Then the trouser tore and revealed a severely swollen and evilly *black* ankle and lower leg. The *blackness* looked alive under Phil's skin - *the black moved and squirmed like a serpent, and always in an upward direction.*

"OWW." yelped Phil.

The onlookers were less callous.

The trouser leg continued to rip as the *black* infection ballooned and continued to slowly advance.

"OOWWW." screamed Phil. Tears were streaming down his face, as he bent down and tried to stop the advancement of the disease.

Kelly and the Witches started to back away, their eyes glued to Phil's spreading ailment, leaving Phil and the adjoined John Abbott alone in the middle of the stage.

The Witches spell broke. The lights flashed back to full strength, John Abbott was screaming '*RUN*' constantly now, but no one turned and fled, and the people on the stage just backed away, but stayed. With the Witches' spell annulled, everyone stood up and people at the back of the crowd actually pressed forward to get a better view.

Phil's leg continued to balloon. His trouser leg ripped up to the top of his thigh. His screaming was deafening. The *blackness* visible through the shirt, had steadily progressed up the right-hand side of his body, and was so massive that it pulled his shirt out of his trousers. As the swelling marched towards his head and his shirt started to split down the right-hand seam, it ripped apart revealing Phil's bulging *black* chest muscles. The large *black* infestation concentrated around his right shoulder before disclosing its intension.

The *black* began a march down Phil's arm.

John Abbott froze in horror as the *black* confirmed his worst fears. He started to scream in total panic.

"Get me out of these." frantically waving the handcuffs in the air that locked his left and Phil's right wrists together.

However, the owner of the key, Angelo didn't dare get any closer than he already was, let alone unlock the cuffs. He could see the *black* pulsating under Phil's skin. A brief pause at his elbow only highlighted the surge down his forearm, at the handcuffs it stalled and pooled.

John Abbott was going crazy and would have sawn his own arm off if there was any way of doing it. The bright red blood spilling from Phil's wrists, caused by the abrasive handcuffs, turned black.

Kelly screamed in horror. Finally, the people on the stage, especially Ross, were beginning to get the true picture.

All eyes were on the handcuffs, as the *black* was bottling up at the point where the cuffs clasped Phil's wrist. His wrist grew and inflated, swelled and stretched, and was approaching the width of his thigh. Phil was going insane with pain and threw his head back and let out a howl that would put wolves to shame.

Kelly couldn't bear to see the torture anymore. (On the man who was unknowingly stealing her heart.) The sight of Phil in such pain left her paralyzed, and without a clear course of action, she was close to collapsing in despair and hysteria.

In an explosive spurt, the handcuff around Phil's wrist started to turn black. It started to ooze slowly across the bridge of iron. More than anyone, John Abbott didn't want to see this. He wrenched, tugged, and pulled himself as far away as possible from the chain. Unfortunately, the chain resisted John's tugging and wrenching and held steadfast. The *black* pus kept creeping across the chain until it reached the junction of handcuff to John Abbott, where it too started to bottle up again, just as it had at the junction of Phil to chain.

Kelly was first to notice that the *black* had ceased to plague Phil's leg, and as the *black* receded up his body, like a miracle, the affected areas returned to their normal color and size. However, his arm had swollen beyond recognition as almost all the *black* was now contained in it. The handcuffs started to glow and sweat *black*, as the metal stretched, squeaked and steamed. With the *black* draining from Phil's body and down his arm, the pressure inside the handcuffs started to reach bursting point. Phil was unintelligible as he writhed and wailed, and Kelly cried wildly and begged any of the men to intervene. But no one knew what to do, except stare.

The handcuff dam burst, and scolding hot *black* injected itself into the most distant image of John Abbott under immense pressure. It was John Abbott the XXVIIth. Minutes earlier, his great ancestor had relegated him to that position. His distant haunting screams echoed through the John Abbott lineage and sent a chill of things to come rippling through them.

Black was surging through the spot where handcuffs attached John Abbott the XXVIIth to Phil. The pressure that had built up at Phil's handcuff junction had stabilized at the expense of John Abbott the XXVIIth, who was quickly filling up with *black*. The *black* flowed easier down Phil's arm now and his screams started to peter out in correlation with the growing cries echoing from the John Abbott's clan.

XXVII was filling up fast, already his left side was full and the rest of his body was destined to follow. But before that happened, the *black* spilled over into John Abbot the XXVIth's wrist, and he wailed as the *black* acid forged up his left arm. The *black* had appeared in the same spot as his son's and was flooding, as it did to his son before him, into his body unabated.

As for John Abbott XXVIIth, the end was nigh. His whole body had filled up with the vile *blackness*, only his eyes remained their natural blue color. Their blue held out for a second. His last sight on earth was the hideous Ruebella, her yellow eyes, tear filled. His whole body changed back to its natural color, as his eyes swapped to *black*. Black, horizontal, rectangular pupils. It was over. The only redeeming thing for XXVII was that his death was swift.

As the last drop of *black* left Phil and entered John, the handcuffs fell off their wrists, and shattered into hundreds of brittle shards on the stage floor.

The only one not completely hypnotized by John Abbott's abduction was Kelly, and she raced forward to Phil's side catching him as he collapsed. She jumped back and cursed herself, still not used to Phil's changing eyes. She saw her reflection - small and distant in the metallic convex mirrors that used to be Phil's red and whites.

"Phil let's get out of here." Kelly hauled him to his feet and pushed him along towards the back of the stage. Phil thought to himself, as he stumbled and fell, how amazing she was not to get up and run and leave him.

"Come on Phil." As light as a feather, she picked him up off the floor.

Only a couple of moments passed before John Abbott the XXVIth's body filled up with the *black*. He waited for death again, twice in two days. He had stopped yelling early on in the onslaught, one of the few noble gestures he had done in his life. He wanted to send a message of grace under pressure to his ancestors.

He could see the *black* flooding into the arm of John Abbott the XXVth, his dad, in front of him. Behind him, he could feel the penetrating gaze of the black, rectangular eyes of what used to be his son.

With a tangible pressure, their focus bore down as they patiently waited for his inescapable transformation. A *black* tsunami roared through his mind as his eyes swapped from blue to black as alternately, his body returned back from black to his natural color. The *black* had consumed his whole body and any lingering remnant of John Abbott was gone. The black rectangular eyes of John Abbott the XXVIIth and XXVIth connected and the body that used to be John Abbott the XXVIIth took a step forward. The two John's, XXVIIth and XXVIth, became one. Their faint images merged into one sharper and clearer, and those in front looked back with alarm and terror.

The progression moved steadily forward down the descending numbers; the initiating screams made the announcements. The faint image of the black-eyed John grew darker and clearer as the screams grew louder and shriller. The engrossed crowd, which still hadn't attempted an exit, now performed a contemptible act. As the John Abbott's of single digits were consumed, the obviously demented crowd had started a countdown.

Black finally started to empty into the only remaining image left, John Abbott the First; he attempted to cry. "The Sh…" but he couldn't finish the word. The pain was just too great.

He was the First in line, and the *black* that had invaded his descendants, was consolidating the lineage, into a, soon to be, single entity. Out of spite and sheer malice, the *black* crept slower and more painfully through John Abbott the First's body, than the other twenty-six combined. He writhed, squirmed and tore at himself, but the black-eyed beast behind him held him fast, and there was no escape.

Revenge had been in waiting for a very long time. Mercifully, the end came, but not before some elements in the crowd booed, not because of the terrible torture endured by John Abbott, but because they had become bored.

The dark, black, horizontal, rectangular eyed image of what was once John Abbott the Second walked into the being of John Abbott the First, and John Abbott of any number, was no more. Unbelievably, the crowd cheered.

C H A P T E R   5 7 .

THE HUMAN CONSTANT.

Angelo watched the demise of the John Abbott images and like the rest of the audience, he should have taken his kids and run while the focus was elsewhere. Any spell the witches had cast had long gone. People were here now because of their morbid sense of excitement, and he felt ashamed because he was one of them. He had spent his life serving and protecting people, and had always thought of himself as superior to those who couldn't control their primeval desires and emotions. How recent events had proven him wrong.

"SHIT."

Although no one knew it but him, he'd been a fool, falling for the compliments and flirtations that a young, pretty girl had given him, a much older man. It was only natural for her to look up to him, a cop, and she was young, inexperienced, and impressionable. He should have told her directly, that there were limits. But he was swept up in the attention. Showing her his gun. Letting her hold his gun. He slept with her. He should have known better. It never happened again, but it cost Angelo his marriage. His wife found the evidence in their bed - there was no denying it. He never revealed who she was, because he was trying to save his ass. She was a minor.

The hush on the crowd was so intoxicating that it pulled Angelo out of his self-pitying daydream, to the small man at the front of the stage. This man with *jet black rectangular eyes* was growing to the size of an average person. He radiated peace and strength, order and justice, tenderness and elegance. He was back.

"Welcome." The tenor voice was beguiling, charming and comforting, impossibly smooth. The word filled the town square, no nook or cranny skirted. The crowd bathed in its milky currents and drowned in its depths.

He began. "There shouldn't be any need for introductions, but I have always considered myself to be a polite and proper man. As I want to ensure that there is no doubt about who is addressing you tonight, I'll ask Ross Hughes, back there." He turned round, and beckoned Ross to the front of the stage. "Be a good old chap and be the MC for the remainder of the night. Please perform the introductions, Ross, my good man." he requested in a cordial voice.

The Devil waved his arm again in a friendly summoning fashion. Looking from side to side, knowing there was no escape from the task, Ross walked towards the microphone. As he walked across the stage, the lights dimmed, and a spotlight illuminated his passage.

Ross leaned down to the short microphone, at John Abbott height, and spoke in a clear strong voice, that even surprised him considering his nervousness.

"I present to you his eminence, the Devil."

As presentations go, it was one of the finest - short, completely accurate, and saved his life. Any hint of disrespect or flippancy would have cost him it.

As Ross finished enunciating the last syllable, lights blazed from behind him. Epic film music erupted as the lights illuminated a black gargoyle creature of dinosaur proportions, with outstretched bat like wings. The crowd let out a massive collective gasp and involuntarily screams echoed. The music pumped and reverberated as their eyes feasted on the creature.

The Devil performed a full three sixty. His thick scaly legs and clawed feet didn't move, he just rotated on thin air. His wingspan stretched across the entire stage, and he folded and flexed them around the various obstacles they encountered. The black leathery wings had ribs that connected claws at the top with evil looking hooks at the bottom. Lines of black scales with large ornate patterns covered the underside.

The demon like face had two piercing white, rectangular eyes. They were inset above a large wide mouth brimming with many rows of thin sword length teeth. Its shoulders seamlessly emerged from the neck and thick burly arms bulged with muscle. Claws as large as tables with six fingers hung from the forearms. Its tree trunk sized legs flexed and stretched. It's long crocodile tail wrapped around appendages underscoring its size and weight. The armor on the tail ran in parallel rows up the middle of the broad back between the wings. With this creature stalking the earth, Tyrannosaurs would no longer be Rex.

The lights flickered out. And in that moment of darkness, the behemoth vanished, and the Devil reappeared in person.

Something was very different in the persona of the man who had returned to the stage. He looked the same as the man Ross Hughes had introduced but his aura was different. It frightened the crowd.

The Devil turned around to look at the people on the stage - Ross Hughes, Harry Adams, Angelo and the two girls. "Where have Phil, Kelly and the Witches gone?" His tone was one of displeasure. He spoke in a quiet voice that hinted of malevolent intent.

Everyone looked at one another. The atmosphere took on an unearthly chill and grew tense in seconds, across the stage and the square, over the audience. Some people, at the back of the crowd, turned and started for the exit. They had seen all they wanted to see, and now it was time to 'get out of Dodge.' They had seen and obeyed Witches, witnessed the terrifying infection of Phil, and the torturous consumption of John Abbott. Now it was time to go, they'd got their money's worth.

"Where do you think you're going?" Although he faced away from the crowd his voice thrust daggers into the hearts of those that had turned to leave.

They froze. Some turned around. Some pretended that they hadn't heard and attempted to forge ahead. They could see freedom only blocks away down the narrow streets. However, the time to escape had passed. They remembered the opportunities they had to leave and hadn't. The ones that didn't turn were the first to feel the Devil's ire.

"You turn your back. On Me? Please turn and face me.

Have I done anything to offend you? You did not answer my question, civil as it was. Have you not the decency to answer me?

Where Did the Witches Go?"

With every spoken word, skin ripped and peeled off the individuals' faces, until only red facial muscle and exposed eyeballs remained. They clutched their faces in agony, and bloody cries spilled between their fingers.

They fell to their knees with pain-filled souls and shock-filled minds. "We were just innocent bystanders just trying to go home after the show." they remonstrated.

The rest of the crowd watched the punishment. The victims were no different from themselves; ordinary people who tried to flee had been hurt. Not just the people on stage were in jeopardy, everyone was fair game.

Smiling, the Devil turned his attention back to the people on the stage, who understood how fragile and defenseless they were. They had just witnessed the Devil kill about twenty people without a hint of reticence, and they anxiously worried whether they were next. Furthermore, the Devil had made his intentions clear, they were here to stay, leaving wasn't an option.

"Anyone?" He asked again.

"They escaped." said Detective Angelo D. deciding that the best defense was a good offense. "Fuck." he thought.

"Sorry, they left, out the back of the stage just here." Angelo pointed to an opening at the back of the stage, and dearly hoped that he had deflected attention away from his gaff.

"Escaped? What do you mean escaped?" pressed the Devil, who walked swiftly to confront Angelo. Having spent centuries in solitary confinement, the Devil was sharp, eager for blood and powerful.

"They looked like they were escaping. They flew away really in a rush." trembled Angelo.

"What are you, a rat?

You squeal to your superiors?

Want me to thank you, for telling me that they left?

You want me to chase after the witches, and reward you with your life?

You think I didn't know when and where they left?"

Angelo had answered the Devil's question, in a sly attempt to deflect attention away from him and get the Devil to chase after the witches, thinking he was smarter. He was used to having the power and authority and had never been made to squirm like he had done to others. Now he didn't know what to say or do.

"Err, err, they... You wanted to know…" he whimpered.

"You think you know what I want, do you? You think you're my friend?" stabbed the Devil. "What's your name?"

"An, Ang. Angelo" stuttered Angelo, who never stuttered. The Devil's question was precisely what he had hoped to avoid

"Angelo WHAT?" shouted the Devil.

"Angelo Diablo." he replied shakily.

"HA HA HA." roared the Devil.

"That's rich. You have the same name as me? Are we related?

Are we... brothers?" teased the Devil in vile torment with his face inches from Angelo's.

"Oh, hang on, *The* Angelo Diablo?" queried the Devil.

"I. Err. Err." said Angelo with this strange weird look on his face.

"Why did he look like he knew what the Devil was talking about? He should be totally lost and confused, but instead he looked like he was hiding something, like he was guilty of something." thought Natalie.

"I'm detective Angelo Diablo, Homicide, if that's what you mean?" said Angelo.

"Yes, thank you, Angelo. Now why don't you tell Natalie who you *really* are?" said the Devil calmly.

"What...," said Angelo.

However, Natalie knew something was up. She had noticed a couple of side way glances from her father in her direction and could see, as could everyone else, that his consternation was not that of the Devil, but of what he wasn't telling her.

"Me?" said Angelo, "She knows who I…."

"Dad?" spoke up Natalie not able to contain herself.

"Yes, *Dad*. Why *don't* you tell your daughter? Come on now

Detective Angelo Diablo; tell her. You'll feel so much better, this is *your* chance to make things right." The Devil gave an exact impersonation of Angelo's interrogation voice.

"Dad. What is it? Dad?"

"TELL HER." commanded the Devil. Angelo unwillingly walked towards his daughter who was looking at him pleadingly.

"Dad, what is it, what?"

"Natalie, you know I love you and always will, but sometimes men are weak and succumb to... Err. Well, the reason that your mother and I split up was because..."

"Natalie. *Your father slept with me.*" said Madison bluntly.

"Natalie, it just happened." pleaded Angelo, bending down and using both hands to turn Natalie back in his direction.

"No it didn't, you seduced me. You're my best friend's father and you…" retorted Madison angrily pulling one of his arms off Natalie and turning her back around.

"I did no such thing." snapped Angelo.

"Dad, did you? You slept with Madison?" Cried Natalie.

"Yes, He Did." interrupted the Devil, whose voice resounded across the stage and crowd. "Yes, he did." he said, softer and meaner.

"You Bitch." shouted Natalie, as she launched herself at Madison, and they started to fight. Police training or not, Angelo tried to stop them by getting in-between them, but it just wasn't his day. They scratched and tore at his hair and eyes, and all three were shouting and screaming. The Devil was clearly enjoying the spectacle.

Until, from the brawling ball, someone screamed, "I'll kill you."

"Who said that?" the power of the Devil's voice stopped the fight in a second.

"Was that you Madison?"

"No." she replied adamantly.

"Was that you Angelo?"

Angelo paused, weighing the possible ramifications of his response, who did he wish to protect, said "Yes."

"Liar." laughed the Devil. "And you who dare to lie to the Devil; you'll pay for that soon enough. He turned round and addressed the crowd. "That includes you. But don't fret. It's too late.

E n j o y."
Their blood turned to ice.

"Who did you want to kill, Natalie my dear?" he said with feigned charm.

"Dad!" She shouted back with all her might.

"Then your wish is granted." A dagger appeared in her right hand out of nowhere. She looked down at her hand, shrieked, and tried to drop the knife. Even though her hand was wide open, the dagger wouldn't leave her palm. Her fingers were now curling up to make a fist as if to hold it.

"NO, no, I. I didn't mean it." Her grip now firm and strong. Her arm lifted high into the air. She took a fateful step towards her father.

Angelo tried to speak, but he couldn't move his jaw, so like a ventriloquist, he spoke through his teeth. "Nooo."

Unable to obey his request, she took another step. Her hand, shaking under the force of The Devil's will, was descending closer and closer to Angelo's neck.

Angelo forced out between his teeth, "STOP IT."

The knife, with its thin and needle-sharp point, stopped, but Angelo's relief was short-lived. Reversing its direction and orientation, it charted a new course, for herself. Only inches from her stomach, it pressed her clothing tight. A pinprick of blood stained her dress.

With every ounce of strength and willpower, Angelo broke free of the spell. He jolted forward. He fell onto her arm that he saw for a fleeting moment was springing back. It dawned on him, that the Devil had stopped the spell on them both.

However, Angelo's momentum was too strong and he inadvertently lurched forward and drove the knife into her heart with his own body weight. He killed her.

Only the Devil knew what he had done. To the horrified throng, it looked that Angelo had killed her on purpose to save his own skin. To boos and hissing, Angelo cradled her in his arms and rocked her dead body as the crowd wept for the dead girl.

"Poor girl, I guess she didn't get her wish after all." said the Devil dismissively.

Behind his back, Angelo was still rocking his daughter's empty body with one thing on his mind. Then Angelo pulled the dagger out of Natalie's body, and getting a good grip on the bloody handle, he turned and threw himself with all he had at the Devil's back.

Faster than lightening, the Devil turned and caught Angelo by the throat in midair with an outstretched hand. He held him there, his arm not waiving an inch with the weight of this grown man hanging from the end of it.

Oh how I hate you Angelo." said the Devil, who turned and addressed the crowd. "You know, hundreds of years ago, John Abbott the First tricked and captured me in my own shoe. He showed bravery no man has ever shown before or since. He was cunning. He understood me and catered to that end. (I even bear a scar).

Of-course, I hated him from the deepest recesses of my heart. I corrupted his line and seed. It was all I could do. Tonight, I took pleasure and delight in his death. I punished him, excessively, and now I possess his body, their bodies: all *twenty-seven* of them.

As for you Angelo if you were one twenty seventh as good as he; you would be a great man. However, you are not. He was one to be admired and respected, not like you the cockroach I now have in my hand. You think I didn't notice you nod when Phil sought solace? You think I don't know about the false evidence, the forced confessions, and the bodies?"

"Go to hell." whispered Angelo through his teeth.

The Devil groaned, "What are you going to say next, see you in Hell? You're corrupt, the kickbacks forced them to send you to a country post, and still you abused your authority, Madison. Just one instance of many. You had a choice. It was bestowed upon you with your name, Angel, Devil. Your daughter could not decide, but I can. That stupid song in your head "I'll walk through Hell with my head held high." We'll see how you feel in a couple of *SECONDS*" The last word ripped his face, eyeballs, tongue and lips with a hundred paper cuts. I will go to Hell, *ANGELO.*"

The Devil opened his hand and Angelo dropped to the floor.

"And I WILL see you THERE." Lacerations from head to foot, tore, gouged and cut him, and his body went into spasm. The Devil didn't let his soul leave however, evilly holding off DEATH with his other outstretched hand. He lifted Angelo's body off the floor. Levitating the broken man to eye level, he looked into his eyes and saw he couldn't hold his head up high.

"Just like the rest of them." the Devil said to himself. "See you in Hell." and dispatched his name's sake to Hell in a ball of black fire.

He had seen and dispatched thousands of people like Angelo.

"They all think the same; they think they can take pain, that they're special, that their will is somehow stronger than everyone else's. That they can face me, but they can't, of course. I have just slain the only one that could, John Abbott the First. *Now he was a man.*

And I needed a man to escape, but not just any man. I needed the John Abbott lineage to contain my being. Three-times-three-times-three.

Three Cubed.

A Good Square.

He stopped and looked around.

There was not a movement or a sound from the stage or the audience. Not a cough or even a scratch of the nose broke the crowd's hush. Everyone was trying to be invisible. The Devil could see it. They were all getting away with it way too easily. That he was doing their bidding. Their lust for blood and pain, as long as it was not theirs.

"Soon, but I almost forgot about the temptress Madison."

"Madison, if you please, come and join me."

Reluctantly, she began her tortuous slog, unable to do anything else.

"What's your pleasure?"

"Sorry? Mr. Devil." stuttered Madison. "I don't understand."

"You're dressed as a Witch. Yes? You want to be like the Witches we have all seen?"

"Yes, but it's just a costume. I don't really want to..." she quavered.

"But I heard you say it be great to be able to cast spells, to turn people into toads and rats, make them hurt or ugly. Cast your spell darling, make them all ugly."

"But I don't want to make anyone ugly." said Madison.

"Sure you do."

"No I don't." squealed Madison.

"Oh, but you do. I know why you encouraged Angelo. Why you went round to Natalie's house that night, when you knew Natalie and her mother were out of town at her sick grandmother's." the Devil insisted. "Because, Natalie was prettier than you and you envied her looks. So you trumped her. The one she would never have, her father. You savored it every time, a look passed you by. Every time Natalie *complained* about boys looking at her in her annoying *whiny*, "like," voice. They should be looking at you. You wished she was ugly.

"OK. Everyone. Get Bone Ugly." shouted Madison.

The truth was that the Devil didn't know, as he was only guessing.

"Unlike God of course, *she* knew everything."

That thought always gnawed at the back of his mind.

"Yeah, called that one pretty well, nice bit of deduction, been awhile. Like to have seen God call that one."

The Devil had pondered about things in that Jail Cell for the last few hundred years.

The stakes were enormous, the calculations, extreme.

Every division had a remainder, and every circle had its Pi.

"It would be so much easier if I were *her.*" *he* thought, which took him back to the question, the ultimate question, which had plagued *him* forever.

"Us. She. Pi. Me."

She was a circle, the freak of all the ellipses. Slice a cylinder perpendicular or *square* as an engineer would say, results in a circle. You need a *square* cut to make a circle.

He was rectangle. The opposite - the square rod cut on an angle. Only if he could be perfect, could he be *square.* However it was impossible. You need a *square* to cut a *square*, he could never be square to cut and create himself perfect. *He Is the Devil.* Hence, *he* is rectangle.

"So who cut *circle? She* should not exist. But *she* does. And how did *he* exist? And this was the worst, because the angle of cut was *Pi.*" He had mused for centuries.

The moment there was *square*, there was *circle*.

The moment there was *circle*, there was *Pi*.

The moment there was *Pi*; there was *rectangle*.

But there had never been *square*: impossible to make.

Therefore, there could never have been *circle*.

Therefore, there could never have been *Pi*.

Therefore, there could never have been *rectangle*.

Tied in a knot as always, wondering which came first the chicken or the egg?

He liked order, accountability and process, and was always so close to achieving it. *Close*, but close wasn't good enough. *His* rectangles would never completely cover the tapestry - either they overlapped, or they left empty squares in the oddest places.

Vacant space, *a perfect negative square could exist.*

It utterly irked him.

That was just the beginning.

Where *she* pissed him off, was just as *he* started to fill in a negative square with multiple rectangles, *she* put circles into them. As *he* refashioned acres of space to try to cover these unsightly curves, the process generated more negative squares. Again, *she* bunged them up with circles. Then, *he'd* have to figure out how to cover them before being left with a mess of circles, rectangles, fleeting negative squares and raw tapestry. Today's physicists now know this as vacuum fluctuations, a phenomenon of quantum mechanics.

It drove the Devil insane, and one day they argued and fought. He recalled it bitterly, "And of-course *Pi*, Lady Luck, took *her* side, like as if *she* needed it, and wham.

The Big Bang."

Instead of cubed sensible atoms, the universe became full of meaningless, minute spheres, randomly bashing into each other without consequence. It took *him* millions of years to sort out that mess, get some rules in place, and bring some sense to it all. By that time, however, the only thing that he could do was to work with the circles and spheres he had, his precious rectangles were amiss.

"'Course, there were fucking millions of negative squares: and every time he focused on one to fill it up with rectangles, *she*, as if she was psychic, would stick a circle in there, and fuck it up."

Consequently, the universe was expanding out of control with no end in sight. The only consolation was, at least the rules to govern some of the now universal circles, were squared and cubed. Everyone looked at the awesome product of his rules, the Galaxies, Suns and Planets, but nobody saw *HIS* contribution.

He detested the statement, 'There's no straight lines in nature.' *He* reasoned that no one considered the process, planes and dimensions. For processes and formulas to be uncovered, people had to exist, and there had been an obstacle. *He* thought that the time when *he* decided to get round the obstacle - was when *she* schemed against *him*. *He* justified that *he* had to do it. It was *he* who re-directed the asteroid towards Earth.

For millions of years, *he* watched God's magnificence strut the earth, as his rules, squares, processes and rectangles; that made all of her round shit work, went unnoticed. It was a sad day when *he* doomed those majestic dinosaurs with the asteroid. And *he* was so happy when the fossils in the Bad Lands were unearthed, the ancestors of the buffalo, thank God. She did have mercy.

"Yes. She did have mercy.

But mercy isn't justice.

No wonder Hell had so many vacancies, and yet the world had never been in a worst state. People were so evil that even to this day I still have to struggle to keep up." the Devil vented.

"How the hell could *she* grant pardons to some of these guys? It never made any sense. No accountability for your actions as long as you repented.

Yes. Mercy is sweet, but is it *fair?*"

It took a long time, but finally Mankind made its appearance. *He* remembered that day well. Finally, the discovery of *his* rules and processes was on the horizon. Someone would peel the onion. A thinking man would discover his secrets and *he* would finally be acclaimed. But when man got going, thinking, exploring, *she* got involved again and screwed it all up for *him.* Again. And they started to worship *her.*

"How did they even know about *her?*" Every time *he* tried to stop them, it backfired, and *HE* got the blame.

"How did they know about *him?*" *Her* influence. *He* was sure of it.

"*Her*, that's how." *he* cursed.

He was sure that *She* was the root cause of *His* near insanity.

He had to get truly creative to get things back on track. Deception was the only way it seemed. And this is where all kinds of things went terribly wrong. *He'd* convinced the world that God was male. As people abused the beauty of *her* natural world, with pollution, over population, over fishing and deforestation, it didn't matter, *he* was the root cause. The lie *he* spun, twisted every resulting action.

"Oh my God, I am so, so sorry." the Devil cried. "But unlike *her* precious humans, (who were *mine* to start with,)" *he* whined, "there was no redemption for *me.*"

None.

"Yes. God did have mercy.

But where was *Her* mercy now. For *Me?*"

God had justified her actions, "You want consequences so much; you killed the dinosaurs. You made them think I'm a "*He*" instead of a "*She*". You go and live with the humans. You're grounded." And she had the circles to keep him there on Earth. *She* believed that *Her* response was prudent, required and not mean.

Indeed… Fair.

Her circles, simpler and easier to draw always out maneuvered *his* squares on all fronts: size, volume, multitude and strength. Every time *he* tried to blitz a path of rectangles through the swarming circles, *he* failed. By these means, God imprisoned *Him.* Here, on Earth, with the Entanglement War.

In a Devil's Jail.
He'd answered every mortal's cry, but for his own?
He had none.
And there was worst to come.

It wasn't until *he* had tried many times that *he* realized; *he* was losing *his* potency.

And as *he* cogitated, *He* made a terrible discovery.

"Where is all my non-Black Entanglement?" (*He'd* never admit *he'd* stolen it from *Pi*). *His* Black was all present and correct. But the colors? Somehow, *he'd* forfeited all *his* (illicit) colored Entanglement's spectrum.

All Gone.

"Easy now Devil, don't lose it." *He* refrained, *He* was left with BLACK, *his* dominant, primary, defining color. Grounded, *he* only had *his* conscience for company. *He* riled and twisted against *his* imprisonment.

He knew it was *his* fault.

He should have waited.

The accidental universe was an infant. There was plenty of time, which could have revealed squares and cubes in harmony with circles for all *he* knew. But *he* couldn't wait. *The considerate, thinking being of the future, would have treasured the Earth and animals upon it, conserved it, not plundered it, or one another.*

He needed gratification now, and billions of years were exactly that. Sixty-five million years was only a fraction, and so *he* had done it. But what *he* didn't predict was the terrible side effects of *his* action.

It wasn't the massive collision that had ingrained an ungodly seed into the psyche of man. It was the act of its re-direction. *His Desire. The Yearning. The Need* to change the great rock's direction. And not by a parsec, not even close, by only a single inch.

An inch.

That was enough.

It was the equivalent of a billion numbers into Pi. And it was there that he'd pilfered swathes of Pi's Green, Yellow, Red and Silver Entanglement. The original sin. The smaller the action, the further down into the depth of *Pi*, the greater the consequence. The redirection meant the massive rock unswervingly sought its target. An inch became a mile, a mile became a million, *he* had directed the boulder into Earth's path. The minute became massive.

Its voyage tainted, corrupted, untrue:

Desire to lust.
Want to obsession.
Leadership to tyranny.
Food to famine.
Governance to totalitarianism.
Confinement to imprisonment.
Pain to torture
to
Suffering.

"All *I* wanted was someone to see my involvement, the squares the cubes." cried the Devil in dismay. At first, *he* couldn't forgive himself. But after considering *his* lost entanglement - *his* loathing was turned against *her*, *his* warden.

God, on the other hand, was relieved that she had *him* confined. The asteroid had opened *her* eyes, and everything *she* had seen of *him* on Earth confirmed *her* worst fears. But *she* knew Earth was no place to get help for him, but what choice was there?

"They're all crazy down there." *she* had said more than once. "Their terrifying ability to descend into the most debasing acts at the slightest provocation was ample proof of that. They could easily push *him* over the edge." Already, *she* had seen way too many human traits in *him*.

But where else could she hold *him*? *He* had chosen Earth for his own purposes, and once there, *he* was cornered. She also had hope. Maybe man *would* uncover the rectangles. It was a long shot, but no one else in the universe had come close. If man could become civilized in actions, and not just words, maybe together, with the Devil they could evolve and achieve an enlightened state. Maybe *he* would be cured. "(Maybe even Man, talk about long shots.)"

Her decision to impound *him* had left *her* with few options. Any help *she* had secretly inserted, the Devil exposed. The Gurus, Prophets and Messiahs were all found out, and *he* dealt with them without mercy or understanding. *His* mental state worsened. *His* calculating thwarted any help or comfort *she* could give him. *He* always exposed *he*r plans and resented *her* more because of them.

Meanwhile, his cruelties escalated. Sometimes even in excess of man. But *she* had to let it be. Let things work their course.

It was the only hope.

Hope, however, took time, and as *she* listened. *She* heard him rile, rant and rave. *She* knew what it would mean. *She* couldn't watch. *She* was going to have to look away. The Devil seethed,

"Easy now, Easy.
Stay composed.
But, how can I?
Why should I?
Continually scorned, ignored and treated like a child.
Restrained, imprisoned, confined.
Where's My Entanglements?
FUCK YOU ALL, NOW YOU'RE RIPPING ME OFF."
He was the Devil and would live up to the name.

Madison cast her spell.
Who could blame her lack of foresight?
So callous is hindsight it's wicked.
The spell entertained the Devil's pleasure.

Her bones creaked and scrunched. She felt her facial frame move under her skin. She cried out in pain begging the spell to stop, but it kept on going until it had run its full course. With blood oozing from every pore, she fell to her knees hiding her face in her hands. She cried her heart out before dying.

"You Bitch." some idiot shouted who obviously didn't understand that *the Devil* didn't need any further reason to despise the crowd.

"Thank You Sir." said the Devil with heavy emphasis. "I was beginning to forget what disgusting and loathsome people you

all are. You stayed when Phil warned you and when John Abbott warned you too. You stayed when I escaped the shoe and scoffed at Phil's pain. (*How he survived is something I'll have to explore, it's beyond comprehension.*)

You counted down the end of a great lineage of descendants, as if it were fun. In addition, you enjoyed their pain and suffering, even though he still tried to warn you to get out and leave. And now you're going to wish you had."

The Devil saw their thoughts, threw *his* head back, and broke out into a laugh, the laugh of pure evil. It echoed around the square and off the buildings, causing their walls to shatter and crumble, and penetrated the patron's bodies and chilled their souls.

It was now or never, and paralysis turned into panic. Everyone made a mad dash for the exits.

Black fire erupted. The ground tore apart and revealed a glowing red and yellow fiery Hell below, blocking their passage from the square. Screaming and attempting to back away from the edge of the clefts, the people closest were pushed in by the momentum of the crowd behind. No one cared about anything other than saving their own hides.

With *his* laughter still resonating in their heads, they looked at the roaring, towering flames and despaired. Any prospect of escape was over. They were still alive, but it was a short-lived reprieve.

A rumor had spread, like fire itself, that there was another way out, at the stage. As the frantic crowd rushed the raised platform, the Devil opened his arms and another fissure opened up that swallowed tens of people before they knew what had happened. Trapped like rats in a cage, the remaining people, hundreds in number, backed up upon each other.

It took them a while, as they jostled, screamed and fought, as multiple fights had broken out, before they realized that the soles of their shoes were hot. The conflicts ended as their feet turned from uncomfortable, to painful, to agony. The floor was so hot that their shoes caught fire.

Horrific screams wrenched the sky as people realized they were slowly starting to sink into the pavement, which was turning into molten lava. They sank deeper into the black hot stew of boiling tar. It wrapped around their ankles and then it flowed over their knees until it was waist deep. The Devil stood and watched. *He* didn't allow them to sink any further than waist deep. The crowd shrieked in anguish as they waited for their agonizing and miserable deaths.

"Not you two. I need you." The only ones spared were Ross and Harry. They didn't know for what. Ross and Harry stared at the scene in disbelief. What they were witnessing now, was truly blood thirsty, vile and excessive. He could have ended their lives quickly without all the unwarranted pain. He had that power. He didn't need to torture them.

The Devil grabbed Ross and Harry by their chins brutally hard.

"Fuck you. I learned everything from you guys. Yeah, the human race taught me everything I know. This *is* a quick and merciful death by human standards. You look at me like that again and I'll give you a taste of your own medicine. Think about the torture that's going on right now at this moment in time, across the world of your making. You want that?"

They didn't.

They couldn't answer him without shame, so they shook their heads.

"Anyway, time to get back to business, enough of this fooling around. There's work to be done." said the Devil cheerfully to the two lawyers as the last of the crowd died.

Could he keep that smile off his face? It was good to be out and about again. Life was frigging sweet.

CHAPTER 58.

THE FLIGHT AT NIGHT.

Kelly lost her footing. She had expected the heavy weight of Phil's bulk to act as a counterbalance when she tried to support him. Instead of falling down, the ground fell away from her. She was flying, with Phil in her arms.

"What's happening Kelly?" Phil asked.

"Why? Is he an idiot? Wasn't it obvious?" she couldn't help thinking. "The Witches have saved us. The Witches are flying us away from the stage, Phil."

"The Witches?" repeated Phil in shock.

"Yes, The Witches, *are you blind?*" She said full of vitriol, before she thought… and that maybe he was…

"Phil, can you see?" she inquired compassionately atoning for her previous impatience.

Without emotion, he just said "No."

This explained why he fell over a couple of times in the escape.

"So what's happening Kelly?" he asked again.

"They are flying us as fast as they can. They're all lined up in a row, the Red One."

"Boleyn." said Phil.

"Yes Boleyn, chanted some spells and we're really zipping along. They're in a panic. The Devil traveled through your body Phil. *He* came out of the shoe that appeared on your right foot. He's occupied John Abbott, The Devil Catcher. It was horrible."

Phil knew all this. He had felt the magnitude of the Devil. Unimaginably big, the whole galaxy condensed. An ice-cold condensate squared and squared again. It was too much volume for Phil's body to handle, yet it had. The years of imprisonment in the Shoe had caused the Devil to become dense and lethargic, like the molten tar of Salem's Square.

The Devil's Entanglement wasn't fluid enough to flow evenly and smoothly. It sought the only being capable of containing the Eternal Mortal's transformation to freedom, the Souls of Twenty-Seven John Abbotts. A square's square, a cube.

If the Devil had chosen to convert into Phil's mortal coil, Phil would have exploded. As it was, he was almost ripped in two even as a conduit.

Phil had suffered un-survivable pain in the Devil's escape. He wondered how he ever endured it, but even while the Devil was traversing his body, a sensation of soothing and healing was replacing the agony and harm. It was soft and gentle, loving and tender, and it came from his feet.

Now he realized that the only reason he was able to withstand the pain and remain not just alive but sane, was because his shoes had coursed RhomSong anesthetic into him. They never once encroached on the Devil's Black path, wisely avoiding contact and discovery. Because of their action, Phil's life was preserved and even enhanced. Only through their deft action was Phil able to survive.

No one else could have; no one.
The Shoes kept their secret.
And so did he.
They were three.

Kelly, with yellow and red Entanglement, continued. "So we're sitting on a broomstick between Hecate and the yellow eyed witch. They're not talking much. Too busy flying. It's really neat, like a flying motor bike."

"Shit." said Phil, "Wish I could see."
"I'm sorry Phil." she said.
"Why? Why are they doing this?"
"I don't know Phil.," said Kelly.
"Do you know where we're going?"
"Sorry, don't know that either."

They kept on. The distance they were putting behind them was enormous. It was a clear cool starlit night, but the witches didn't care. Distance was more important than stealth.

After several hours the Witches spied their destination, and started to descend towards a desolate and deserted village nestled between rolling hills. Old derelict stone buildings and a tumbled down church formed a town square, and a small weedy trickling stream meandered between the cracked roads and broken bridges.

The three landed as one in the middle of ClearStream, where it all began. The Shoes that once adorned the Devil's feet, magnificent as they were then, were a shadow of what they were now.

Awareness and perceptiveness existed in their souls.

The two shoes knew where they were.

Dread and foreboding filled their RhomSong.

And Phil's too.

CHAPTER 59.

THE DEVIL AT HIS BEST.

Lit only by starlight, it was just bright enough to see gray sickly weeds prying through the uneven cobblestoned ground. Tumble-downed buildings surrounded them and only the church had a roof of any kind. A decent thunderstorm would see it off in a second.

Aided by Kelly, the blind Phil dismounted. The rest all stood around looking at one another without any idea of what to do next. Phil wasn't looking in any direction at all and was still trying to figure out how to manage.

The real problem was they all knew that they weren't masters of their own destiny. It was now up to the Devil. If *he* decided to find them, *he* would. Their flight to ClearStream was only a delaying tactic, as if they could stall him.

"Then maybe *he* would just forget about us?" A desperate hope.

The Witches had just escaped centuries of solitary confinement in their respective shoes. So had *he*.

"Go!" said Phil breaking the silence.

The Witches looked at him, but his mirrored eyes told them nothing.

"Go and take Kelly with you please. It's me that he's after."

"Shut up Phil. Just shut up, you're not helping. It's not always all about you, you know." said Kelly sharply,

"Could she really be jealous that the Devil was after me and not her? Because that would be really dumb." thought Phil. "Why else would she want to stay?" How could he know? A beautiful woman seeking his company? Never happened.

"We have to figure out what to do. We can't just keep on running." Kelly continued. Her fear of the Witches was long past. With her yellow and red Entanglement, they considered her more one of them, than mortal.

Phil's response, however, carried considerable weight. "I have his shoes, and I think that *he'll* be able to find me, and if you're with me Kelly and you Boleyn, Hecate and…

"Ruebella." spoke the yellow-eyed witch, the first time Phil and Kelly heard her natural, non-assaultive voice.

"Ruebella, from Witchiton falls I presume, then *he'll* get you too." finished Phil.

For the first time they had to decide to collaborate as a group. On the stage in Salem, Phil had initiated a truce of a kind. Before that, each witch had attempted to kill him. It was a strange turn around. The Witches had rescued the man they once hated.

Witches of a sort, Phil and Kelly were more akin to the three, than mortals. They stood awkwardly in a circle, all looking at each other, waiting, pondering on what lay ahead.

Hecate reached out and held Kelly's hand - something had certainly changed. Hecate too was different. She had absorbed Deloris and had experienced her longing for Phil. Now, here with Kelly, she felt something familiar.

Everyone was confused, on how they felt, and on what to do. On the surface, they appeared so different, the three witches, dressed in medieval black capes, pointed hats and broomsticks and Phil and Kelly, dressed in modern everyday clothes.

However, they had things in common. One was Entanglement of varying degrees. The other was a common enemy, an invincible foe. It could bind them together, or as Phil suggested, separate them. Whatever the decision, the result would last a lifetime. In their hearts, they all knew this to be true. They were at the crossroads of fate. They were either friends or ships passing in the night.

"He's after…" Phil tried again.

"He's after us too." said Hecate.

"We all have contracts with him." And she, followed by the other witches, pulled scrolls out of their cloaks to show Phil as proof, before remembering he was blind.

"Well I'm glad to see that you remember your obligations Ladies." A smooth silky and terrifying voice resonated around the square. They all looked around in the direction that it came from, including Phil. The Devil stood in front of the church looking like John Abbott the First, with the mass of the First and Second combined, to make himself average size, except John Abbott the First *had never looked this mean.* To his left were Ross and Harry, looking very pale.

"Witches, please come and let us have a look at what they say. Phil, Kelly, you're invited too."

There was nothing to do but obey. There was no conceivable route of escape so they all reluctantly walked over to the church, like kids returning from break.

Phil's arm was in Kelly's as she attempted to lead the way, but as they started to walk, Hecate grabbed Kelly and hugged her. It was her last chance to make amends, Kelly guessed, but for what she didn't know? Hecate was the only witch who hadn't attempted to kill her.

"Boleyn, Ruebella, Hecate good to see you again."

They curtsied. It was never a bad idea to show respect to the Devil.

"And Phil and Kelly: nice to meet you." Kelly froze and stared at his outstretched hand.

"See." thought Boleyn, "These two have never met him before. They must be petrified and rightfully so."

"Don't be scared, I won't hurt you." said the Devil endearingly.

Earlier that night, Phil had endured insufferable pain in the Devil's escape.

"Phil, so sorry that I caused you so much suffering this evening. Unfortunately it was unavoidable if I was to escape my Jail. And that I was determined to do. And I must say, I am surprised, impressed, one might even say astonished, that you survived, so, please, accept my apology." He twitched his hand, inviting Phil, again, to shake it.

And after Kelly placed his hand in his, he did.

"Kelly?" Extending his hand again.

She also shook it.

Sadly, they all knew the genial Devil wouldn't last long. It was only a matter of time before his demeanor would take a turn for the worse. That was his modus operandi.

"Now then," *he* could be so charming, "let's have a look at those contracts, but before I do, may I suggest we take shelter in the church where it's a little warmer." The Devil stood to the side and invited them in.

"Incredible." thought the perplexed Phil "The Devil wants to get into the church because it's warmer? Stepping on top of the broken-down door, they walked into the church through the open arched Gothic doorway. With a generous wave of his hand, *he* restored the roof, the door and lit its interior with beautiful candlelight.

"Saw these frescoes in a little church in Rome, beautiful, don't you think?" With another showman like gesture, magnificent art and statues adorned the chapel.

"This is really bad. *He's* showing us his power." Kelly thought to herself, deciding to say her last prayers now.

"So, let me have a look." said the Devil. He retrieved his own copies of the witches' contracts from inside his silk shirt, and laid them on an overturned pew that acted like a table.

"Ross and Harry, lawyers, correct?"

"Yes." Although they knew he knew.

"Ross, would you be so kind and be the counsel for Boleyn, Ruebella and Hecate? And Harry, you're mine."

Both lawyers sat next to each other and did what lawyers do. The witches, Phil and Kelly sat down on the remaining benches.

While this was going on, the Devil gave Phil a complete once over, not missed by Kelly. Their eyes locked.

The Devil's black, horizontal, rectangular pupils drilled into Kelly's hazel, yellow and red eyes. She held his gaze, sweating, not breathing.

"What's happening?" asked the ever-repeating Phil.

The wait seemed like hours as they were meticulous museum curators, historians and lawyers.

The contracts were written on supple kid leather and inked in the blood of the parties. The black ink of the Devil burned Harry's fingers. Beasts' horns and hoofs filled the corners of the scrolls and their eyes were embossed inside the Devil's coat of arms. Beautiful calligraphy highlighted the flowing cursive. The capitals were pictures in various poses - a witch on a broom, the Devil endowing Entanglement, and mortals cowering in fear. Murals in gold and silver adorned the parchment edges.

Under the names of the parties were hundreds of lines of fine print, and then at the bottom, dates and signatures.

"The contracts are valid." announced Ross and Harry together.

There was hardly a stir from the witches. They had willingly entered into the agreements and they knew the price. The witches stood up, lined up in a row in front of the Devil, and awaited their fate.

The Devil had changed his form, now the mass of John Abbott the I, II, III and IV - a very large sized person. He moved to address them. Everyone was silent. The Devil was closest to the entrance as if guarding it from any (crazy) would be escapees. The Witches, and Phil and Kelly (who was still explaining everything to Phil) stood together. Ross and Harry sat in the pews, and then stood up.

"Thank you." said the Devil.

"Boleyn, Ruebella and Hecate, tonight I have escaped from centuries of imprisonment. I was happy to see that my three favorite Witches were there to welcome me back to the land of the living. I was very pleased and willing to forgo the payment for the contract - but then all three of you RAN." His amiable voice turned to visceral hatred.

"That's right; I was going to set you free. But you ran and now I'm going to make you pay, by sending you to HEL..."

"You Bastard." shouted Kelly, pushing between the Witches and the Devil to confront him face to face. "They were trying to save ours, Phil's life, and now you've got the..."

"Quiet." yelled the Devil. His voice knocked everyone over.

But Kelly didn't quit. Like Phil and the witches, she had some resistance and she got back up to her feet and attempted to resume her tirade.

"All they…"

A backhanded slap from the four-hundred-pound Devil, sent her to the floor in a heap, and blood dribbled from her split lip. She looked up and her eyes blazed at him.

He pounced on her like a panther, his right hand on her throat and his face in hers. His face was no longer that of John Abbott, it was that of the Gargoyle, inches from her face, and *he* spewed black rank breath into her mouth. She tried to control her gag reflex but couldn't. Burning black bile erupted in her throat. The Devil wrapped his evil tentacle demon tongue around her neck and over her face. She was drowning in her own vomit. She tried to evacuate the disgusting foul matter from her gullet, but she couldn't. She could feel it burning and choking, she heaved and sweated. She had no choice but to swallow the poison or choke to death. It was an incredible feat of discipline. The Witches and mortals watched as she forced the black boiling pus down her throat in a display of herculean willpower.

The Devil retracted his tongue from Kelly's face. No matter what she thought, the Devil deeded it. This was just an appetizer of worse things to come. The craving in his eyes said it all. *He* was going to rape her.

"There's nothing left to be said. The witches go to Hell." the Devil proclaimed.

The Witches looked at Kelly and with sorrow. They were sorry that they tried to kill her. They were impressed and grateful for her attempt to save them.

From his evilness.

John Abbott's face had appeared back on his body, which had increased in size; his mass had attained the volume and size of nine John Abbott's.

He looked down upon them and spoke.

"IX.

Nine.

Yes, that is appropriate, one for each level of Hell. All rise."

"Witches, you are condemned to an eternity in H…"

"Excuse me Mr. Devil." interjected Phil's voice from behind the Witches.

"What now?" said the Devil in a very frustrated, but human tone.

"The Witches' contracts are invalid." said Phil, looking in the general direction of the Devil.

"WHAT? NO. No, no, no, no the lawyers have said that the contracts are valid. What are you, a lawyer too?" said the Devil, getting perturbed with the delays.

"No, but they are invalid." Phil said.

"They ARE valid." shouted the Devil. Everyone was thrown to the floor, except Phil.

"Twenty one." said Phil.

"What?" responded the Devil.

Phil, cowering, but also insisting, continued albeit in a whisper, but not a whimper

"Twenty one.

Not Eighteen.

Twenty one.

Not Eighteen like it is now, in this century.

But… but… twenty one.

Eighteen is… is… a very recent reduction from… from twenty one.

So, in their century, the age of majority must have been, and was… was…

TWENTY ONE."

It was probably the loudest whisper the Devil had ever heard.

"They *weren't* twenty one. To enter into a binding contract, both parties must be of the age of majority, I think. When the Witches signed your contract, they were minors, weren't they?" said Phil with his usual, uncertain voice.

"WHAT? Lawyers. Is this true?"

"Yes." The lawyers had trouble looking into the eyes of the Witches, which was nothing compared to looking into the Devil's. Their only hope for redemption was to lie. But they couldn't, they weren't like that.

"WHAT?"The ground shook.

"WHAT?" screamed the Devil.

The Witches' contracts burst into flames corresponding to their colors.

They were free.

Hecate's and Boleyn's eyes changed to that before they were transformed.

Witches no more.

Boleyn fell to the floor.

Her tiny broomstick no longer functioned.

However, Ruebella inexplicably remained a witch, and ugly.

Emancipated from their contractual obligations, the *Witches* however, still did not feel free to leave.

Phil's fate, on the other hand was certain.

He would never be free from the Devil from this moment on.

The Devil marched towards Phil with murder on his mind. Phil felt the vibrations through his feet as the floor reverberated with every thunderous step. He retreated down the middle of the narrow aisle, feeling his way from pew to pew as if swimming the back stroke.

The Devil had a score to settle, *he* boomed. "You cheat me out of my rightful souls?"

Phil was busily trying to keep his feet and didn't catch what the Devil said and so he didn't answer.

"Now you Dis me" thundered the Dark Lord.

Still Phil continued to stumble blindly backwards, and not answer.

Enraging the Devil to unbelievable heights.

Finally he reached the front row of pews that faced the Altar. He could feel something was happening through the quaking floor. As with every step the Devil took towards him, *he* increased in size, a John Abbott size.

X

XI

XII

XIII

XIV

XV

XVI

XVII

XVIII

XIX

XX

XXI

XXII

XXIII

XXIV

XXV

XXVI

Finally, the mass of XXVII poured into him. *He* stood as a giant in front of everyone. *He* was half naked as most of his clothes had shred to pieces. *He* dominated the Church and ruled the world. *He* was the Devil and now *he* would prove it.

Pausing to take stock, the *he* reviewed Phil's paltry dossier. "Just as I thought, Phil's done nothing in his life, but be a victim. Always with an excuse.

'I didn't have a chance.

My brother stopped me.

It wasn't my fault.'

Who cares if he had never had a chance? Tons of people never have had a chance in their lives, and still somehow, they manage to get by. That is, do something bad, something that could send them to Hell. However, this man probably couldn't get into Heaven either he's so boring. Ah, just as I suspected, he blamed his stepbrother, Bill, for everything. Yeah, and who I'll be dealing with later, that's for sure… Shit, who cares? I've got Phil right here."

The Devil squeezed the trigger. "DIE." he commanded.

The Entanglement signature of the attack was colossal. His essence dwarfed that of the witches. Death was its default.

It was clean. It was clear. It was concise. But it had its one flaw.
A negative square.

> BLACK. BLACK. BLACK. BLACK.
> BLACK. BLACK. BLACK. BLACK.
> BLACK. BLACK. BLACK. BLACK.
> BLACK. BLACK. BLACK. BLACK.
> BLACK.   BLACK.
> BLACK.   BLACK.
> BLACK. BLACK. BLACK. BLACK.
> BLACK. BLACK. BLACK. BLACK.

It hit Phil like an explosion in a quarry. The air pulsated causing slates to fall from the roof. The marble tiles on the floor buckled and jumped. The group scrambled for cover from the teal stones pelting them.

After the last slate shattered, they peered over the bleachers. Through the settling dust, they rubbed their eyes in disbelief. The Devil was lying on a floor, smashed wood all around him.

And Phil, Phil, stood over him.

CHAPTER 60.

THE RIVER CHORUS.

Phil's silver-mirrored eyes reflected the Devil's attack. And the Devil was in its line of sight. The convex shape dispersed the original focal point, diluting 'BLACK' into 'Black'. His shoes bolstered the returning echo with their own unique property. Their RhomSong filled the negative square with a perfect *rhombus*. Unknown to everyone, RhomSong had distorted the attack's essence and inserted the shield that saved Phil's life.

And its rebound slammed back into the unsuspecting Devil.

It floored *him* with an Entanglement reflection of *his* own making.

Black.
Black. Black.
Black. Black.
Black. REPEL.Rhombus. Black.
Black. REPEL.Rhombus. Black.
Black. Black.

Phil stood unharmed. His repelling RhomSong blew the giant Devil into the air before *he* crashed to the church floor. Pews were shattered into matchsticks, and everyone had scrambled to hide.

The reflection had taken the Devil completely off guard. *He* wasn't physically hurt, but his pride was as he momentarily flushed a bright shade of red. Embarrassed about being seen embarrassed, his already bubbling up anger intensified. Humbled and angry, *he* got up and lashed out at the witnesses to his shame. They ducked as a wave of Entanglement

BLACK

thundered into them. The attack was ordinarily lethal and not one person didn't shudder in under its suffocating weight. But as two of them had Entanglement, the blast wasn't strong enough to dispatch any single soul. Luckily, the Devil didn't care about them living or dying, as he suddenly became pre-occupied with something troubling that demanded his immediate attention. So while the group was checking one another to see how they were, the Devil was brooding on this latest and disturbing issue.

He had felt a negative square in his launched assault upon Phil, in bigger attacks it was clearly visible and he vividly recalled its image in this one. Logically then, he should have detected it in the rebounded reflection, albeit smaller and warped like the rest of the dissipated echo. Just as mirrored light from the convex back of a shiny spoon, it should have been there, but it wasn't.

Not even an outline of it.

Something had filled it.

Perfectly.

Doubly worryingly, it was something un-Godly.

Not in the normal sense, but something not originally from God.

Because it wasn't circular.

God had the circles and *he* had the rectangles, and a circle would have either left gaps in the corners, or overlapping edges on the sides.

There was neither.

Neither could he fathom the contents, it was filled, but he couldn't tell with what.

This was new, and the unknown, even for super mortals, was scary.

He went to Red Alert.

With his senses heightened, it was at that moment that *he* detected Phil's Entanglement - something only the Devil and females were capable of receiving, accepting, acquiring.

This was impossible.

Although this elevated Phil into a league of his own (that was exclusively the Devil's a moment ago), it still didn't account for the missing negative square.

The Devil was completely unprepared and stunned with these developments.

Phil was certainly not going to Hell, no surprise there. Up until recently, many would have said he was already there he was so dull.

And even with all his Entanglement, he still didn't seem to have any powers, other than resistance to an eternal mortal attack.

HIS!

It took less than a second for all these thoughts to race through the Devil's mind. But for now *he* deemed them incidental because above all, *he* required revenge. *He'd* been bested by a mortal so this was no time for introspection or philosophy, it was time for retribution.

"Sure he's wearing my old shoes. Who cares? It's the 21ˢᵗ century and shit is way better now. I'll get an exclusive pair from New York, of-course they'll be imported from 'I ta li a'… As it goes for Kelly, yes, there is something special about her alright. *What's she doing falling for the village idiot?* Such a fool is Phil that he has shamed and humiliated *ME* in front of HER. Yes, for that and that alone he is an idiot and a dope. *Me? The Devil? Then the Contracts? Count two. BEYOND STUPID.*"

The Devil wasn't about to let that pass.

Not in a million years.

Looking his way and then hers, "Let's deal with Phil and then I can freely move on to better things."

He prepared himself, calculated the wave-length, the trajectory, deduced the required amplitude, and doubled it.

"Die Phil. The Entanglement of the attack was earthshattering.

BLACK. BLACK. BLACK. BLACK. BLACK. BLACK.
BLACK. BLACK. BLACK. BLACK. BLACK. BLACK.
BLACK. BLACK. BLACK. BLACK. BLACK. BLACK.
BLACK. BLACK. BLACK. BLACK. BLACK. BLACK.
BLACK. BLACK. BLACK. BLACK. BLACK. BLACK.
BLACK. BLACK. BLACK. BLACK. BLACK. BLACK.
BLACK. BLACK. BLACK. BLACK. BLACK. BLACK.
BLACK. BLACK. BLACK. BLACK. BLACK. BLACK.
BLACK. BLACK. BLACK. BLACK. BLACK. BLACK.
BLACK. BLACK. BLACK. BLACK. BLACK. BLACK.
BLACK.   BLACK.
BLACK.   BLACK.
BLACK.   BLACK.
BLACK.   BLACK.
BLACK. BLACK. BLACK. BLACK. BLACK. BLACK.
BLACK. BLACK. BLACK. BLACK. BLACK. BLACK.
BLACK. BLACK. BLACK. BLACK. BLACK. BLACK.
BLACK. BLACK. BLACK. BLACK. BLACK. BLACK.
BLACK. BLACK. BLACK. BLACK. BLACK. BLACK.

Phil's Entanglement and his shoe's RhomSong bounced back at the Devil. However, this time the Devil was braced for it.

Black.
Black. Black.
Black. Black. Black.
Black. REFLECT.Rhombus. REPEL.Rhombus. Black.
Black. REPEL.Rhombus. REFELCT.Rhombus. Black.
Black. REFLECT.Rhombus. REPEL.Rhombus. Black.
Black. Black.
Black.

Both the Devil and Phil were blown into the air and crashed to the church floor. Out of the two casualties, the Devil recovered much quicker as *he* got back to his feet smartly.

A prostrate Phil lay on the marble, hurting badly from his clumsy landing. His whole body throbbed as if his blood was too thick for his veins. His protective silver reflective eyes were shattered and his irises had reverted back to white.

Phil was able to see for the first time since Salem.

His vision was filled with the image of the giant John Abbot, nonchalantly brushing himself off, and savoring his imminent and rightful role of domination. A most un-welcome sight it was.

Almost wishing he was still blind; Phil knew the aberration was preparing for a final assault. Not unlike having his life past before him, he thought of the birth of *The Investigative Reporting Team.* The first significant meaning he'd brought to his life. Then the terrible physical pain of the Devil's escape from the shoe, and apparently, a correlation. To live, you risk pain.

Then a fleeting tingling sensation swept over him, its source was the shoes. The unknown casualty. They were exhausted beyond empty and lay close to de-RhomSong. They could not repel a further attack. Wounded, but not dead, they called.

An internal whisper,
"Phillip"
It was barely perceptible.
But he heard it nonetheless.
He heard a Diamond.

The Devil looked down upon Phil. "Hello Phil, pleased to make your acquaintance, again. This time, however, I do not extend my hand in friendship." He laughed mildly.

The Devil had not yet broken Phil's resistance to an eternal mortal attack, but *he* was certain *he* could. *He* had gambled with a massive second strike and was relieved that *he* had won, though *he'd* never admit that there was any doubt.

He had noticed that Phil had acquired Black dots on his silver mirrored eyes as a result of his first assault. The Devil had studiously noted Phil's ability to absorb Entanglement, and although the Black dots gave Phil an additional degree of immunity, they may have also revealed a potential vulnerability.

The Devil had hypothesized the Black dots on Phil's silver-mirrored eyes would bear a deficiency. When using a magnifying glass to set a piece of paper on fire, one focuses the beam on dark botches. The Devil had done the same.

He'd targeted his foray on the spots in Phil's eyes, thus avoiding the reflective property of his silver eyeballs.

Accordingly, *he* circumvented their immunity with an intense, targeted and laser like thrust. And like that soiled piece of paper, *he* surmised that they would be overloaded if *his* attack was prolonged, massive and above all, precise.

His calculations had been accurate, and his theory, verified.

He was proud to be right.

Because, he hadn't used just plain brute force, he'd been surgical.

Only the edges of the attack reflected anything at all, and consequently it was smaller and weaker.

Being prepared for it too, it'd inflicted only minor injury.

And he was also puzzled.

His failed first attack had actually worked to his advantage. If he had used the mass of the second attack initially; its reflection would have blown him into the sky and it would have given Phil almost unlimited immunity.

"What was this, a change of heart in Lady Luck? Had *Pi* quarreled with God while I was imprisoned? No, that was just how Lady Luck worked. Even God wasn't safe from her whims."

The Devil was rightfully wary of *Pi,* there was much *he* didn't know about *her*. *His* transgression into *her* depths that day when he re-directed the Great Meteorite pained *her*. *He'd* syphoned off some of *her* Entanglement. In light of its disappearance, had she wreaked revenge?"

The Devil looked at Phil with his defenses more than weakened, "Let's tidy up here and move onto better things." He glanced Kelly's way.

He attacked again with Entanglement that was calculated and exact, heeding his lessons learned.

"Die Phil. Bye."

BLACK. BLACK. BLACK.
BLACK. BLACK. BLACK.
BLACK.   BLACK.
BLACK. BLACK. BLACK.

Phil's remaining Entanglement evaporated. All the double red, yellow and green in his eyes disappeared. He was left naked and exposed.

The Devil towered over him and looked into his blue eyes. *He* could see that Phil was not terrified and was ready to accept his fate.

"No more mercy." said the bitter and resentful Devil; he'd had enough of this man's company.

"Phil, I L..." Kelly cried.

The Devil turned to look at her and stopped her in her tracks. *He* lusted after her openly and evilly. *His* mind was filled with sex and violence.

Groveling on the floor, Phil no longer posed a threat as there wasn't any retaliatory reflection in the Devil's last attack.

"HAH" snorted the Devil assuredly.

He did rue, however, that *he'd* spurned any last opportunity to detect the absence of a negative square. ("That's what imprisonment in The Devil's Jail, the Ninth Level of Hell, is for. *Answers*.")

"I wonder. Could it have been the silver-mirrored eyes?" *He* didn't think so, but eternal mortal or not, *he* still made mistakes. (*The Shoe*) The Devil's long and lonely confinement in that shoe was finally catching up with him. Reason and logic would have to take a back seat soon as lust was demanding its turn at the helm. It was all Kelly's fault. Still, it'll have to wait, impatiently.

"Let's just get this stupid Phil out of the way and get down to real business." He didn't mean to glance her way, but he did as *his* subconscious wasn't to be denied. Refocusing on the matter at hand,

"Look at him, like a little insect, groping around down there." *He* wasn't in the least concerned with the bested Phil.

"Oh Lookie here.

What's that he's got in his hands?

It's John Abbot's wallet.

Must have fallen out of my pants as I was growing to my present (and rightful) stature.

What?

He's going to pay me off, is that it?

This puny little insect.

I'm going to step on him."

Slow and fumbling in true Phil fashion, Kelly watched him open the wallet and take out a piece of paper. She peeked up at the Devil's face and smiled to herself. Even the Devil was getting pissed off with his infuriating ministrations.

"Good old Phil, he's hurt the Devil more today than anyone could ever imagine, physically and now mentally. Look at him tormenting him with his ineptitude. The longer he takes, the longer the Devil doesn't rape me. Way to go Phil."

Indeed, the Devil was getting agitated, and he badly wanted to kill him. Though *he* had Kelly on his mind, this fumbling clown kept demanding his attention.

"What? What? What the hell is it, Phil? WHAT?" said the Devil angrily as he watched Phil slowly unfold an official looking piece of paper.

"Oh God, he's dropped it" smirked Kelly, daring to think.

Phil picked it up, and like a fish, it slipped out of his grasp again. His hands waved but he missed. It might have even been funny, but it wasn't. The magnitude of the moment saw to that.

After what seemed like an eternity, after wasting more of the Devil's precious time, after sparing Kelly's rape for longer than was humanly possible. He finally got hold of the paper and started to read.

Slowly.

It was killing the Devil.

The paper was central. It had driven John Abbott the XXVIth to suicide, was Phil hoping the same for the Devil? Not knowing that it would signal his father's final act, John Abbott the XXVIIth had snatched this paper from his hands and stuffed it in his wallet before driving off to Salem. That was only a day ago, now it seemed forever.

"WHAT?" shouted the Devil, "Was Phil that clever, that he had planned this? Get me so wound up that I'd lose my temper and smite them. God always told me to be patient. Clever? NO. He's just God damn slow."

"WHAAAT?" shouted the Devil.

When Phil spoke, his voice was weak at first, but it grew stronger and clearer. "You, you, were stuck in a shoe for hundreds of years, right? Mr. Devil. Right? You can't escape shoes, right?"

"Yes." responded the Devil unbelievably answering Phil's question, that's how pent-up the Devil was.

"Well." said Phil.

"Well, what?" said the Devil shaking with rage, *he* really might obliterate the village.

"Well, look." and Phil held the piece of paper up for the Devil to look at.

The Devil was so tall that *he* couldn't see from that height, so *he* bent down, albeit awkwardly.

"Let me read it for you." said Phil, and before the Devil could reply, Phil whipped it away from the Devil's nose and started.

"Dear John Abbott, the XXVIIth.
Blah blah blah.
Blah blah blah.
Blah blah blah.
Blah blah blah.
Blah blah blah."

"Oh My God, it won't be the Devil that kills us, it'll be Phil" thought Kelly.

"Blah blah blah.
Blah blah blah.
Blah blah blah.
Blah blah blah."

"WHAT?" screamed the Devil.
"Here it is." said Phil casually.
"America is a free country, God have mercy on her, and if you wish to be known as Mr. Shoe, then we have no law to stop you being known by that name."
Phil looked up from the paper and into the Devil's face.

"You spent centuries in a shoe.
You escaped a shoe, through my body, over the handcuff bridge and into the first John Abbott image.
That image was John Abbott the XXVIIth, who had just changed his name.
From John Abbott the XXVIIth to... to Mr. Shoe" he said softly.
"You escaped from a shoe and went straight back into one. Mr. Shoe.
Sorry Mr. Devil.
No, I was right the first time, Mr. Shoe.
Look."

And he held the paper up again so the Devil could see the letterhead. It read.

"The American Department
of Name Change."
"Notice. Name Change"

There was silence and then more. The entire group looked on, numb. Kelly looked blank in astonishment. Phil looked apologetic. His initial hint of a smile had disappeared.

Maybe because he was saying his prayers but no prayer was going to save him. Tears trickled down the side of his face.

He just stared at the Devil.

He didn't turn away.

And the Devil looked straight back.

Blankly.

Time passed.

Then without a sound, The Devil started to move. His arms and legs shifted, but they couldn't leave his sides. He tried again, this time with more effort. But not a finger moved out of place.

He shuffled and shifted. He twisted and turned.

But an invisible strait jacket held him tight.

He tried again, and this time with all his might.

It wasn't just a twitch or a mannerism. It was a punch.

The Devil's fist didn't leave his side. He couldn't budge.

He was stuck. He was stunned. He shrieked.

Every stained-glass window in the church exploded as the church blew apart. Shards of jagged glass rained down on everyone there, causing them to take cover under the dark wooden benches. They peered back over the tops of the pews and ducked again rapidly, putting their hands over their ears and heads.

He screamed and roared, and failed.

It did not free him.

His face turned black and his arms were bulging as he flayed and lashed. He tried to change shape but was only partially successful. Parts of him were now gargoyle and other, human, but no matter what his manifestation was; he couldn't escape the invisible border.

He shrank down to only one John Abbott size, and then expanded rapidly into the giant John Abbott in an attempt to break through the imperceptible frontier. The barrier stretched as it was forced in every direction, but then it shrank back to its original size, causing the Devil to wobble like a jelly. He futilely tried the complete shrinkage and expansion routine again. Again, his prison confined him. He tried again, and again, and like charging a spinning top by pushing the center pump up and down, he started to rotate. Just as everyone was realizing this, they heard a voice.

"Come to me, Ruebella." said John Abbott the XXVIIth.

And a gentler image of John XXVIIth appeared (blue eyes and a tiny physique) over the top of the trapped image of the raging Devil. All eyes veered towards Ruebella, the only remaining witch and she looked to her sisters with excited and scared yellow eyes. It was her dream to have a man want her.

But before she had a chance to respond, the Devil's face reappeared. After the first rotation, the round kind eyes of John Abbott the XXVIIth had been replaced with the malignant white rectangles of the Beast.

Ruebella decided there was no time to lose. She had lived her life in fear and shame, the burden of letting her parents make her choices. She was going to make her own from now on, even if it killed her.

"Thank you, Phil, for bringing the three of us together. Thank you, for saving me from Hell. I'm sorry I tried to kill you, and you too Kelly." she said turning to them.

"Hecate and Boleyn, I love you, you know I always will, but now, I must... I must..."

She looked at the spinning image of the Devil, who was rapidly accelerating with every passing second. He had expanded in size and continued to whirl, blur and spin faster than ever. The ground was starting to shake underneath him. At the base where his feet touched the marble floor, a red-hot glow was appearing. It ignited the spinning column with an explosive woof. With the surge of heat singeing their faces, everyone leapt back. An explosion was a real possibility.

Ruebella speedily mounted her broomstick, picked up Kelly and her sisters and flew past the town square to a clear pool in the river. With her tears streaming down her face, she dropped them into it. She recalled how the river once rejected her, and she prayed it wouldn't do the same for her friends.

Like a yellow javelin, she headed straight back to the church. Phil, Ross and Harry were hustling to join the women.

The Devil had turned into a roaring tornado of red, yellow and black fire, making it more obvious than ever that his swirling mass was going to blow.

Ruebella had made her choice, to call on John Abbott the XXVIIth or die. She owed it to herself and to Phil. The blazing roar from the Devil was deafening. How could she call him? Her only gift was her voice. She started to sing, to serenade her love.

> "There shall not be mighty dread,
> I… am not frightened to my bed.
> Shall I hear thee one more time?
> I will be your Valentine.
> There's nothing that can dismay,
> Nooo matter what they say.
> I… will join you here today,
> Just show me the way.

From the tornado, John Abbott the XXVIIth's ghostly voice echoed.

> Trust your God to help you by,
> O p e n your heart it's not a lie.
> You will see the time is nigh,
> Yellow, gold, low and high.
> Come Ruebella, let it be,
> Time will come, you will see.
> Like an arrow to a tree,
> Come Ruebella, come to me.

The black night was lit red, black and gold by the fiery giant dust devil. And then the organ miraculously started to play. Rich organic music of power and worship surged through its pipes, and together Ruebella and John Abbott the XXVIIth joined in the last verse.

Phil, Ross and Harry had submerged themselves next to the women in the pool and were feeling a lot safer. As confidence emboldened them, they bravely, one by one, peered over the bank and looked at the tiny Ruebella. She was facing down the deadly force with nothing other than her beautiful smooth golden voice.

They were all integral partners in *The John Abbott Story* and were destined to play an active role to its end. They climbed out of the stream together, dripping wet, to view the hellish scene. Strong and tall, with solidarity, they filled their chests.

Somehow, they knew the words would come. As the organ's royal green music bellowed in its build for the final chorus.

They started to sing.

Into Hell you can die,
Ascend to Heaven you can fly.
Together, we can be,
For life's eternity.
We… are both clean and true,
You for me and me for you.
Fly through fire and through pain,
Together we'll reign.

The organ music, rich and voluminous, reverberated across the square and they sang with heart and tears.

The song united heaven and earth, mortal and all.

Tears poured like torrents from everyone's eyes.

As Ruebella reared up and flew into the fire, a black demon's face appeared. Its wide-open mouth, filled with thousands of gleaming, rapier like teeth - swallowed her.

The Tornado exploded.

A black flash tore the sky above like a huge sheet of lightening. The church surroundings were levelled to rubble. Everyone dove back into the pool, except for Phil, who was too slow.

The massive boom that followed the shock wave would have deafened everyone if their heads hadn't been underwater.

They popped their heads out, bursting for air, and they gasped.

They had survived.

It took a few moments to realize that Phil hadn't joined them and was actually in desperate trouble. Blown off his feet he'd landed in the water, and that's where he was discovered, floating face down.

"Quick, everyone, get Phil." Kelly cried out frantically, as she waded towards him.

The men were there first and they turned him over before heaving him out.

He wasn't breathing.

Trying to stop Kelly from hindering them too much with her yelling and screaming, Ross held her back as Harry attempted CPR. He persisted even though beads of sweat started to sting his eyes, but there was no sign of recovery. After several of minutes of hard work, he sat back on his heels and looked up at everyone with a resigned stare.

"NO." shouted Kelly and she broke free of Ross's loose grip and she threw herself to Phil's side, beating him furiously with her fists.

And Phil coughed back to life.

Brought back by Kelly's touch.

His eyes opened.

"Blue." she thought. "Blue, glazed and lost, typical Phil. Thank God."

The remnants of the witches' entanglement were still in her, yellow of Ruebella, red of Boleyn. Unknown to her, the Entanglement charge of her being wasn't unlike that of a defibrillator, she had resuscitated Phil, she should have shouted 'clear'. Phil was alive. As she cradled and rocked him in her arms, she thought to say that she loved him. But she wasn't ready.

Everyone cheered, shouted and hugged one another. They even bent down to hug Boleyn, who was looking a little sour, maybe it was the thought of being grounded and doomed to a mortal life. Or maybe that she'd just seen her entanglement spent on the saving of Phil's life. The man that had her shoes.

Kelly turned to Hecate, who had been very quiet since the initial Devil's summoning. As she embraced Hecate, she felt the same shiver she experienced when they first hugged prior to their audience with the Devil. Hecate sprang into life as the light in her green eyes returned. Her broomstick jumped to her side, hovering and ready for action.

Hecate had used her ability to absorb people and their souls in reverse. When she held Kelly's hand then clasped her in her arms prior to the audience with the Devil. She had stored her soul in Kelly in case if the Devil went looking for it as was his wont, he wouldn't find it. It was a long shot, but it worked. She had tricked the Devil. The last entanglement in Kelly, Green, flashed back into its rightful owner and Kelly, was mortal again.

The Witches' Entanglements that had saved Phil was gone.

"Phil, Phil, speak to me, are you OK?"

He wasn't.

Kelly grabbed him into her arms and shouted at the others to do something, but they couldn't do anything.

Witches and lawyers aren't well known for saving lives.

Daylight was breaking on the horizon and darkness started to lift on the group. Where the church once stood, a deep chasm was all that remained. The small river drained into the gorge and the sunlight shone on its beautiful thin waterfall, reminding Kelly of her trip with Phil to Witchiton Falls.

"We've got to get him to a hospital." cried Kelly.

"I'll go and get help." said Hecate, the only one who could travel far and fast. Realizing she might not be able to enlist the help of a stranger, she said, "I could take Kelly." She looked at Kelly and received daggers in return.

"Or Ross or Harry." she added quickly.

CHAPTER 61.

DEAD AND BURIED.

Ross and Harry drove up to the gates of the graveyard. They parked the car on the gravel and got out, ready to pay their last respects to John Abbot the First, just as their predecessors did hundreds of years earlier. Ross and Harry were among the few alive who knew the true story in full.

They ruminated over the disastrous exhibition in Salem. Hundreds were killed and mutilated at that fair, yet the inquest would eventually determine, after years and millions were spent; that the cause of the disaster was a terrible gas leak.

It was the only feasible explanation.

The museum had also invested heavily in the exhibition, not just money, but also its reputation and it had lost on both counts. The ongoing investigation reflected badly on it.

Someone had to pay, and that was Ross. It cost him his job. He didn't seem to care about being fired and had pleasantly shaken his bosses' hands thanking them for the opportunity of a lifetime.

They thought he meant the job of course.

Soon after Ross's dismissal, his good friend, Harry, resigned his post, and Ross and Harry formed *'The Investigative Archeological Team.'* They had the most strange and diverse staff.

A beautiful long-legged woman, a midget woman, and a woman who looked like a witch. There were rumors that a man in a coma was on the payroll, and that the good-looking woman had hardly left his side at the hospital.

However, the creation of *The Investigative Archeological Team* had the museum board worried, as these two men were premier in their fields, and could represent a fearsome challenge in the world of Archeology. The two turned down their offers of re-employment.

~~~
~~~

The two men opened the back doors of the car for their associates, Hecate and Boleyn. Both of them had been invited to join the new company because of their talents. They could provide incredible insights into the authenticity of archeological artifacts, and in the discovery of new finds. They had big plans for their team.

Yes, Ross and Harry were a different kettle of fish now, but before they embarked on their first assignment, homage was demanded.

They entered the small, anonymous graveyard. They slowly and quietly approached the grave, in reverence for the deceased.

Ross and Harry had been here before on an Archeology expedition, to determine if this really was *The Devil Catcher's Grave.* They had confirmed it by the radar image of hundreds of shoes.

As they approached John Abbott's resting place, horror engulfed them. Someone had vandalized the headstone. They stood before the gravestone and stared in disbelief. Who would do such a thing? The top part of the stone had been broken off, and the rest was split in half along a fault line in the granite. Once it read:

John
Abbott.

The Devil Catcher.

The group recalled the last time they saw the body of John Abbot alive, and his consumption and transformation into the Devil. Was it possible that coincidence was the only reason for the remaining inscription?

Because now the person whose date of death was obscured by an imperfection in the granite, who could not die, who was lying in the grave, had his name engraved in stone above him.

The Devil

Ross was the only one to speak. "With all those shoes in there, he'll never get out."

CHAPTER 62.

HOSPITAL.

"Typical. The moment I leave the hospital, he comes out of his coma." Kelly had just answered her phone. The nurses called from the hospital with the good news. It had been awkward at first since she wasn't actually Phil's girlfriend, but she had been by Phil's side day and night, and they had come to know her very well.

She hurried back, through the hospital emergency entrance, took the conveniently waiting elevator up to the third floor and ran down the corridor. Phil was sitting up in bed and conscious. They were all alone. For the first time since she had met Phil, she was nervous, and strangely enough, he didn't seem to be.

"What's going on?" she asked herself. "I don't remember feeling this way, or him, being that way. Check his eyes - whew - blue."

She sat in the chair next to his bed and the old Phil returned, as he chatted in that awkward manner of his.

"Yeah, it's Phil. I was just a little, cautious, nervous, I don't know, paranoid?"

Kelly relaxed. The Phil she knew (and loved) was stumbling, but talking, just like the Phil of old. It was small talk to start with, but yes, he was feeling alright, and he wanted to know what happened, and Kelly obliged.

"Hecate had taken Ross to the nearest sign of civilization, and apparently it was quite a ride. Ross isn't small by any means, and Hecate's broomstick could hardly bare his weight. It was slow, of-course. Oh, Hecate, sorry Phil, in case you didn't know, she's still a witch."

"Yeah, I know." acknowledged Phil rather curiously.

"Wow, thought Kelly, how he caught that when he came round the first time I donno. I'm impressed."

"So, anyway, obviously she couldn't go on her own and get help, and nor could Hecate take Boleyn. She doesn't know the modern world. So it had to be Ross or Harry - I wasn't going to leave you. So, Ross went with her.

They followed an overgrown old trail until they got to a road. They followed it until they reached a chip wagon in a gas station lot. Ross asked Hecate to drop him off, and he stole a car that had stopped for refreshments."

"Why?" asked Phil.

"Yeah, that's Phil, who didn't understand why?" Kelly continued. "Because he had to come and pick us up. No one was ever going to drive down that old trail, through those fields to come and get us. I mean, would you let a stranger, a big guy like Ross, get in the car and tell you to drive down some lonely, deserted dirt track? To pick up a bunch of people and some guy who just killed the Devil?

We were in the middle of nowhere and he didn't know how bad you were. We needed to get you to a hospital as quickly as possible. No questions asked. To call the police or an ambulance, he would have had a huge amount of explaining to do. And they would never have believed him either."

"Why didn't he just ask if he could borrow it?" asked Phil.

"My God, another stupid question." she thought again. "Why can't he just accept the story as is?"

"I don't know. Who cares. That's why." she said. She had forgotten how frustrating Phil could be. But he had just come out of a coma, she could forgive him. She had never experienced feelings like this before, forged in the most binding of connections. Life threatening experiences. They ran deep.

"He stole the car and brought us back to civilization and you, straight to this hospital in Evelyn Mills. Then he dumped the car. Said the police would just say it was a couple of kids taking it for a joy ride. Phil, you've been in a coma for five days, thought you weren't going to make it for a while."

"Well I'm feeling better now Kelly; thanks to you." replied Phil, in a very assuring and comforting voice, and he looked it too.

His skin was healthy looking and his eyes clear and *blue* - she couldn't help but check them again.

"I know he can be dithering and frustrating, but at least he's nothing like his older brother. That's in the past. Maybe an ordinary man is just what I need. Stop, this man faced down three witches and the Devil. There's nothing ordinary about him. And now he's looking stronger, more masculine." She was beginning to open herself up and accept the feelings that had been brewing in her for some time.

"Phil, you know, you were... amazing back there." Her comment broke the silence.

Phil said nothing.

Kelly knew he was just being modest, that was Phil. "Nothing like his brother."

She carried on after a little while. "You know, the witches were very, very thankful, you understand that, Phil? Hecate and Boleyn are employed by Ross and Harry. They've left their jobs and have formed *The Investigative Archeological Team*. And we're part of it too, I mean if you want to be."

Kelly could have gone a little red after her last remark, so she quickly continued. "Phil, Harry and Ross talk about you all the time. As lawyers, they were thoroughly impressed that you caught that legal thing about the witches being minors, and then having the guts to tell the Devil himself. I mean, my God. Phil you were incredible."

"I'm glad, I'm happy for them.

"Pretty smart and insanely brave," said Phil.

Kelly laughed; it sounded like a joke the way he replied. His dithering was now charming her. He had come a long way in the last couple of weeks.

So she continued. "Then at the end there, when you picked up John Abbott the XXVIIth's wallet and read to the Devil, that John Abbott the XXVIIth had changed his name to "Mr. Shoe", that was...

"I lied." Phil said.

"Huh?" said the puzzled Kelly.

"I lied Kelly. He hadn't changed his name." Phil said a little wickedly, unable to suppress a very unlike Phil smile.

"No." said Kelly. "You showed him the piece of paper, from the 'The American Department of Name Change. Notice. Name Change.'

"Yeah." Phil said idly.

"So he changed his name." repeated Kelly.

"No, he hadn't" insisted Phil gently. "I showed him the paper, Kelly, but I used my finger to cover up part of the letterhead. It wasn't a confirmation. It was an application.

'The American Department
of Name Change.'

'Notice. Name Change *Application.*'

He showed Kelly the piece of paper that he showed the Devil. There it was.

'Notice. Name Change *Application.*'

"Application." Kelly echoed back in a whisper. A long moment passed as Kelly wrestled with the enormity of what she had just heard.

She broke the silence. "You mean, the Devil was trapped in the body of John Abbott the XXVIIth, but he only thought he was trapped in a Shoe again - in the body of Mr. Shoe. You tricked him. He exploded trying to get out of that body, that prison, when in fact, he wasn't trapped at all?"

Phil said nothing, smiling smugly.

"Phil." she said warmly. She leaned forward and clasped his two hands in hers intimately and looked right into his eyes.

He had done it, not beat the Devil, but charmed the girl he loved. She had fallen for him, and she was going to tell him now. Tell him that she loved him and that she wanted to have adventures with him. Join *The Investigative Archeological Team* and tour the world. Discover and uncover amazing artifacts and treasures.

Tell him this had been the best two weeks of her life.

CHAPTER 63.

KELLY HAS TO KNOW.

Kelly looked deeper into his eyes than she had ever dared.

"That's the most incredible thing anyone has ever done. I don't know what to say."

They were bluer than she could ever remember. Not a trace of green, yellow or red, just pristine, crystal clear, and masculine.

He looked at her. His smile was warm and inviting and they said to her, that he knew things, that he knew what she was going to say next.

"My God, Phil. You lied." said Kelly.

She continued, "My God Phil, what got into you?"

"THE DEVIL."

Blue eyes turned into horizontal, rectangular, jet-black vaults and his smile turned into a smirk of evilness.

His eyes bore into hers and a black laugh materialized inside her head without the aid of hearing. It echoed and reverberated back and forth through her mind, like a stone dropped in a birdbath, and each time it collided with its own resonance, it left an imprint; a shadow of letters.

At first, the characters were just faint silhouettes, but slowly their outlines coagulated and solidified to form words.

The inscription continued to sharpen and hone, until they became unbearable and impossibly black. The phrase devoured all thought but one, heralded in Steel and Mercury.

I am The Devil.
First and Last.
Alpha, Omega.

The End.

The story continues with "Don't Make an Emeny of God"

Fate has not done with him; our protagonist has gone from the frying pan into the fire. Try as he may, he is unable to reclaim his old life and regrettably has raised the ire of the supreme deity. Lovelorn, alone, shunned and belittled, he thought it impossible it could get any worst. He is wrong.